AUSTRALIAN NIGHTMARES

AUSTRALIAN NIGHTMARES

MORE AUSTRALIAN TALES OF TERROR AND THE SUPERNATURAL

EDITED BY
JAMES DOIG

WILDSIDE PRESS

Contents

INTRODUCTION

James Doig

This is the third in a series of Wildside Press anthologies whose aim is to resurrect forgotten tales of terror and the supernatural by Australian authors. Australian supernatural and horror fiction is still very much an uncharted territory, especially for the pre-World War II period. One reason for this is that early Australian fantasy and horror stories have not, over the years, attracted serious attention.

In Britain, the early 1970s saw the appearance of several important anthologists—in 1971, collector and book-dealer Richard Dalby published, *The Sorceress in Stained Glass*, an anthology of sixteen rare ghost stories. The following year saw the publication of Peter Haining's *Gothic Tales of Terror, Volume 1: Great Britain* (though the prolific Haining had produced several earlier anthologies). In the same year, Hugh Lamb's *A Tide of Terror* (1972) appeared. For me, Hugh Lamb set a benchmark in finding quality rare stories; he has published about twenty anthologies, and it can be said that he rediscovered some of the masters of the genre such as Bernard Capes, Eleanor Scott, L.A. Lewis, R. Murray Gilchrist, Frederick Cowles, Dick Donovan, Richard Marsh, the French writing partners Erkmann-Chartrian, and many more. In the United States, anthologists such as Sam Moskowitz and Alden Norton, and Doug Menville and Robert Reginald were undertaking similar work.

In Australia, the only similar work to appear was Gordon Neil Stewart's *Australian Stories of Horror and Suspense from the Early Days* (1978). This is a fine anthology that collected stories from well-known authors such as Marcus Clarke, Henry Lawson, Barbara Baynton, and Tom Collins, along-side lesser-known writers such as Ernest Favenc, Lewis Becke, J.A. Barry and Morley Roberts. However, Stewart focussed on realistic, 'grim' stories, not supernatural horror tales or ghost stories that were the focus of the British and American researchers. For a long time, early Australian supernatural fiction appeared only in overseas anthologies. For example, Hugh Lamb published stories by Guy Boothby ("Remorseless Vengeance," "The Black Lady of Brin Tor," "A Strange Goldfields"), Hume Nisbet ("The Haunted Station"), and J.A. Barry ("A Derelict").

It was not until the publication of Ken Gelder's *The Oxford Book of Australian Ghost Stories* in 1994 that early Australian supernatural fiction was the subject of serious research. In 2007, Ken Gelder and Rachael Weaver published *The Anthology of Australian Gothic Fiction*, which included seventeen stories, seven of them reprinted from Gelder's earlier collection. This anthology was an attempt to collect the "best" Australian gothic fiction; in other words, to establish a canon of Australian supernatural stories. This was an ambitious undertaking—to produce an anthology of the same quality as Fraser and Wise's *Great Tales of Terror and the Supernatural* or David Hartwell's *The Dark Descent*—but I would argue that research into this field is still too young to be definitive about the best Australian gothic tales.

In many ways, the anthologies I have compiled are extensions of the work already undertaken by the likes of Lamb and Dalby. I have tried to find stories either by Australians or authors who spent some time in Australia, which those anthologists reprinted in their books, for example Nisbet, Barry, Boothby, and Dick Donovan. In this I might not have found stories of the quality they published, but I hope I have selected stories that deserve to be reprinted and enjoyed. But I also hope I have found stories by writers that they didn't know about and who should be better known—for example, Mary Fortune, Ernest Favenc, and Lionel Sparrow. None of these authors has been represented in the many guides, encyclopedias, and biographical dictionaries of horror fiction that have appeared in the past fifty years.

Over the past two decades, an enormous amount of work digitising Australian books, newspapers, and journals has meant researchers do not need to leave the comfort of their own homes to follow new lines of inquiry. Two online initiatives are undertaking fiction indexing projects on magazines and journals. AUSTLIT is an Australian academic initiative, which unfortunately is subscription-based and so closed to most people. AUSTLIT has already indexed many of the most important Australian magazines, such as *The Bulletin* and *Lone Hand*; however, there are some important lacunae, such as the *Australian Journal* after 1900 and the popular men's magazine of the 1950s such as *Man*. Fictionmags is an international initiative that that has the lofty ambition of indexing all fiction magazines; it is an open, free undertaking with no restrictions on membership.

What are other sources of rare Australian supernatural fiction? There are any number of important bibliographical and reference books. Perhaps the most important are the checklists of E.F. Bleiler. The first of these, *The Checklist of Fantastic Literature*, was published in 1948 and lists about 5,000 titles. The book was updated in 1978 as *The Checklist of Science-Fiction and Supernatural Fiction*; this version adds titles missing in the 1948 edition but inexplicably removes others, so that the earlier book is not completely redundant. Also important is Bleiler's legendary *The Guide to Supernatural Fiction* (1983), which describes 1,775 books from 1750-1960. Another valuable reference is the series of three volumes called *A Spectrum of Fantasy*, by the book collector and dealer George Locke. These books describe his remarkable collection of science fiction and fantasy literature, including many fabulously rare titles. He has a particular interest in vintage antipodean fantasy and science fiction, and his lists are important sources of information about Australian fantastic literature. Of Australian references, the most important is Graham Stone's self-published *Australian Science Fiction Bibliography* (2004), which is the result of a lifetime's work in the field, and it included fantasy and supernatural fiction.

Although it has long since been superseded, another interesting early checklist, modelled on Bleiler, is S.L. Lanarch's *Materials Towards a Checklist of Australian Fantasy* (to 1937) published by the Futurian Society in 1950. A standard reference book of lasting value is the *Oxford Companion to Australian Literature* (1st ed: 1985; 2nd ed: 1994); both editions are useful, as the second, as well as adding entries, removes others, for example the entry on James Skipp Borlase. There are many more reference books that are useful source tools, including Tasmanian Donald Tuck's three volume *Encyclopedia of Science Fiction and Fantasy* (1974, 1978, 1983); John Clute and John Grant's *Encyclopedia of Fantasy* (1997); David Pringle's *St James Guide to Horror, Ghost and Gothic Writers* (1998), and S.T. Joshi and Stefan Dziemianowicz's *Supernatural Literature of the World* (3 vols., 2005).

Of course, nothing can replace research into primary sources, and most of the stories in this book were found by reading long out-of-print books and journals at the National Library of Australia or the State Libraries, or through the help and advice of friends and researchers in the field. Certainly, it is much more satisfying working with physical objects than scrolling through digitised material online. In either case, there is the thrill of the chase and the pleasure of finding a long-forgotten tales that deserves to be reprinted.

ACKNOWLEDGEMENTS

I am grateful to Mike Ashley for sending me a scan of Ernest Favenc's "What the Rats Brought"; Douglas A. Anderson, for pointing me to Helen Simpson's collection, *The Baseless Fabric*; Dr Gregory More, for sending me photocopies of "The Silent Sepulchre" and "The Odic Touch"; and Milan Smiljkovic, for sending me a copy of "The Undying One."

THE BLIGHTED MEADOW

Mary Fortune

Mary Fortune (1833-1911) has the distinction of being one of the earliest women detective writers in the world and enjoyed an extraordinarily long career. Her police procedural series, "The Detective's Album" appeared in the *Australian Journal* between 1868 and 1908. She was born in Belfast, Ireland, and raised in Montreal, Canada; in 1851 she married Joseph Fortune, a surveyor, and they had one son. Mary followed her father to the Victorian goldfields in 1855, evidently leaving her husband in Canada. She had a second son, of uncertain parentage, in 1856. She remarried in 1858, but this marriage also failed. Mary's eldest son died in 1858, while the surviving son became a habitual criminal. Her first published work appeared in 1855, but it wasn't until 1865 that she began writing as 'Waif Wander' for the *Australian Journal*. Her early ghost story, "Murder and Madness" was published in the *Australian Journal* in 1866, and reprinted by James Skipp Borlase under his own name in his collection, *The Night Fossickers and Other Tales of Peril and Adventure* (1867). "The Blighted Meadow" is from the January 1888 issue of the *Australian Journal* and is a fine ghost story that has not been reprinted. The author and researcher, Lucy Sussex, has done an enormous amount of work over the years uncovering Mary Fortune's story and bringing her tales to a wider audience.

Farmer Greyson had been looking after some rail splitting, and he was returning homeward in the afternoon just when the richest glow—a September sun—was upon the far-famed Jansen's meadow. I do not think that anyone could have resisted pausing to look with admiration at that broad expanse of rich verdure; at all events, Andrew Greyson couldn't, and he did more than pause, for he struck along the fence that separated his own ground from Jansen's, and, stooping at last under it, walked across the field itself till he came to a man who was working where a little creek made an outlet for the drainage he was attending to.

"Well, neighbour, I don't think I ever saw the paddock looking grander than 'tis this year," said the old man; "there's promise of a many tons to the acre this time."

"Aye, please God," said Jansen, as he straightened himself and looked smilingly at either side of him where the green acres lay, of which he was so proud.

"And it puzzles me as well as everyone else in the neighbourhood how this land has prospered in your hands, Gregory; I remember it in your father's time a dead failure."

"It was undrained until I got it; that's all the difference, Andrew."

"There's a vast difference somewhere, Jansen. It is true your father spent neither money nor labour on the farm, but if he had he would never have made such a grand job of it as this. Your father would never have sacrificed the fences, and risked all on one sort of crop."

"I suppose not; father was a bit timorsome."

Gregory Jansen was a tall, angularly-built man of about thirty-five, with a weather-stained face, full of repressed power, but without any pretensions to good looks. It is true that there was intelligence as well as strength in the broad brow and deep-set grey eyes, but neither the face nor the ungainly figure, with the slightly-rounded shoulders, was such as would be likely to attract a woman's regards, nor had any living being ever seen the tenderness of which those calm eyes were capable, save the dog, Faithful, that lay on the grass at his master's feet.

There was an awkward pause when so much had passed between the neighbours, and Greyson, aroused by an inquiring look in Jansen's eyes, was hastily turning to make his escape.

"Stop, Andrew; I want to say a word to you."

"If it is about that, Gregory, it will be as well to say no more about it."

A look of pain came into the eyes that fell to the dog's face, and Faithful rose from the grass and licked his master's brown, hard hand.

"You have no good news for me, then, neighbour?"

"Not in the way you mean, my lad; no. I am sorry to say no, for I would be glad of it, Gregory. You will believe that, won't you?"

"I have no reason to disbelieve you, Andrew. Why should I? You have spoken to—her again?"

"I have, indeed, Jansen, and so has her mother."

"And there is no hope, you think?"

Gregory Jansen raised his eyes as he asked this question and looked into Farmer Greyson's face with such piteous appeal that the old man was fain to turn his face away, so that he might not see the effect of the pain he was unwillingly inflicting.

"There is none, my friend; indeed, there is none."

"But she is so young. Perhaps in time—"

"Jansen, I will not be cruel enough to give you any hope of a change, for it is better for yourself that you should know the truth. My girl is young, truly; but she is old enough to know that she has a heart, and she has set it on another young man, Gregory."

The words carried to Jansen the heaviest blow a man could meet, and he could not speak a word in reply for a little. A great lump seemed to rise up in his throat and choke him. With a friendly anxiety his friend and neighbour tried to cheer him, but the words had no meaning to the faithful and unchangeable nature of Gregory.

"I am very sorry, Gregory, as you know, but you are too much of a man to let such a trifle wear you down. Minnie is a good girl, but I doubt if she is such a girl as would be the best wife for you. She is as innocent and light-hearted as the child she was so little a while ago and would be but a poor companion for a steady, sensible man like you. You will soon find a better wife, Jansen."

Gregory shook his head and turned again to his work as Greyson bade him a kindly "Good afternoon" and went homeward. It was only when quite certain that there were no longer even sympathising eyes upon him that the man so little understood lifted his white face, and, with his hand on his dog's rough head, walked slowly up to his home through the green expanse of the wide-stretching paddock, the possession of which so many envied him.

As he reached the threshold of the brown, stone building that was his, and had been his father's home, Gregory turned and looked down and across the soft, gently-sloping, verdant acres. It is true that most of the gladness had faded out of his life since he had learned his doom from Farmer Greyson, but there was yet some consolation mingled with the bitterness at his heart as he swept with his eyes the green slopes whose value had been so enhanced by the hard labour of his own hands. No one knew it; but it was not the less true that for years, as he laboured, he had pictured to himself a prize that should reward him for all, and that prize had been the growing light of a young girl's eyes, who should one day look from that threshold with pride and love as the mistress of it all. It was beautiful, and it had been hardly wrought for, but the labour had been in vain. Another man had won the prize; and Gregory turned with bitterness into what now seemed to him his doubly desolate home.

He crossed the large and old-fashioned, but comfortable-looking, living room, and sat down by the broad hearth in the chair that had been his father's. The dog, Faithful, followed close and nestled fondly against his master's knee, with his eyes full of that true love and sympathy that no other animals can express or copy, and uplifted to the hard, gloomy face of the master he loved. As Gregory's hand was placed among the dog's rough, tangled hair, Faithful whined in a low, fond tone, as one should say, "Don't despair, dear master; you have one friend that will be true till death, and after it;" and Jansen understood the language and answered it as he caressed the animal.

"Yes, you are right, old fellow; we are no worse than we were, after all, eh? I have good old Faithful, that loves me, always loves me, eh, my lad?" and the hard face brightened a little while Jansen's eyes were resting on the dog's honest face. But when he looked up again the wound was as deep as ever. There, opposite to him, was his mother's chair a great, heavy thing of old oak, that had come from England fifty years ago, and was the fellow to the one he was himself sitting in at that moment. This old chair was cushioned in a homely fashion with patchwork, worked by the mother's own hands; and how often Gregory Jansen had pictured to himself a pretty form seated there, when the day's work was done, with her blue eyes and happy smile, making heaven of the old home! But all was over now, and when Gregory turned his eyes towards the open door he saw his broad, grand, green acres through tears that burned the unwonted channels as if they had been of liquid fire.

* * * *

"I saw Gregory Jansen to-day," said Farmer Greyson to his wife that same evening when they were alone.

"Yes," returned Mrs. Greyson, rather anxiously; "what passed? Did he say anything?"

"Oh, yes, and I felt so sorry for the poor fellow; but he asked, and I had to tell him the truth."

"*All* of it?"

"Oh, no; I daren't. We musn't hurry matters, wife. It would never do to tell him that the favoured man is his own brother, until he gets over his disappointment a bit. Minnie's but a child yet, as I may say; and, indeed, they're both too young, for the matter of that."

"I don't see it. You and I were just about of the same age as them; you seem to have forgotten that."

"No, I haven't; but you have forgot that there is as great a difference between you and Minnie as there is between the style of young man I was and what young Walter is now."

"What difference?"

"Well, my dear, when you and I were wed there wasn't your equal as a manager—aye, and worker—among the young girls of Essex."

The wife smiled a little well-pleased smile, yet her tongue resented the implication on her daughter.

"It was different with me, Andrew. I was always full of health and spirits. It was only play to me to work, and our Minnie has never been strong and rough, as I was. But what difference do you talk of between you and Walter?"

"I was independent, Nell; and he has his brother to look to."

"I don't know what has put that notion in your head, Andrew, though you're always harping on it. Why should there be any difference between the two? They are brothers."

"I don't know how the idea has come about, but it's a very general one that Walter is depending on Gregory. You see, we were not here when the old folk died, and Gregory is a man that you couldn't make free with to ask any questions."

"No; and he's too gloomy and old for our girl, in spite of your good opinion of him, and I'm sure a finer young fellow than Walter never stepped."

"He is fine-looking in a woman's eye, I daresay, but I am very much mistaken if he has not a dangerous temper of his own. I saw him in a passion once, and he grew white as death."

"I wouldn't give sixpence for a man that hadn't a bit of temper in him!" cried Mrs. Greyson. "But he'd never show it to our girl. You can see he worships the very ground she steps on."

"If it was ground like that paddock of his brother's I shouldn't wonder," said the farmer, with a laugh, "but we have none like it. It would be worth your while to step over and see the heart it's in. You have never seen the land since the dividing fence was down."

"It's unbroken now, right up to the house?"

"Yes; and laid down in meadow. It's a splendid sight—nigh a hundred acres of English grass without a stick or a stone in it. I don't wonder that Jansen is proud of it."

"Let him keep it, then," Mrs. Greyson said, shortly. "As far as I'm concerned, I would like this side of the farm best. If he shares with Walter, Minnie would be nearer me."

"Wife," said Greyson more seriously than he had yet spoken, "I am afraid you and Minnie are jumping too fast in this business, for until Walter speaks to his brother, and Gregory and I have some understanding about the affairs of the farm, there can be no certainty. I hope that, if there should be a disappointment, you will talk to Minnie, so that she may be a little prepared, and not quite break her heart about it."

"What disappointment could there be, Andrew, when the two are agreed, and neither you nor I are against it? It is not as if Gregory were his father. He must share the property in some way. As for a disappointment, if one was to come to our child it would kill her."

"Nonsense! Minnie is young. Young hearts don't break so easily, my dear."

"Hers would break. I am her mother and know. Minnie idolises the lad, and I am sure that her thoughts are full of him from morning till night."

The mother in this but truly judged the girl. Just about the same time when Gregory sat by his silent hearth with all his hopes in life shattered, and only the sympathy of his dog to help him, Minnie Greyson was on her way through the sunlit bush to meet her lover, Walter Jansen.

She was a slender girl of eighteen, with a face full of prettiness and hope, and that look of trustful innocence, or, perhaps, ignorance, that is so childlike in her large blue eyes. She had sunny brown hair and a graceful figure, but it was only in the eyes of those who loved her that Minnie Greyson had more than the fading prettiness of youth. Perhaps Walter Jansen would not have cared for her so if she had been cleverer or more intelligent, for his was an overbearing and self-dominant nature that would have borne no rivalry of opinion from even the woman he loved. But he was not likely to meet it in his chosen one, who believed him the wisest and most worthy of all men who had ever lived before or were likely to live after him.

Not that she ever thought of an 'after,' poor girl, for there could be no time to her without Walter's living presence. As she neared the spot now where he was wont to join her for a few precious minutes when his employment would permit it, and she looked upon the stalwart young figure approaching, she found herself wondering how she had lived before she knew Walter and learned that he loved her.

And at a casual glance anyone might conclude that Walter Jansen had nature's own right to the love and admiration of the opposite sex. He was not so tall as Gregory, nor was he like him in build or feature; yet there was, at a distance, a resemblance in the set of his head upon his shoulders, and also in his step and movements, to those of his elder brother. But when he came nearer, and Minnie saw his eyes light up with happiness, and his sinewy, lithe, young form grow more elastic as he hastened his pace, no one could have denied his claim to be as handsome a young fellow as eye would wish to light upon.

"I was afraid you would not be able to come, Walter," she said, shyly, as she was caught and pressed to the young man's breast.

"It would be a queer thing that would keep me away when I knew you were waiting, my darling."

"But, your brother—?"

A sudden cloud came on the flushed face.

"Oh, he was down in his pet paddock. Look here, Minnie, I'm not going to wait any longer. I must have an understanding with Gregory at once, before I speak to your father. We have your mother entirely with us, you know."

"Yes, Walter; but even she says we are too young," the girl said, shyly, as she laid her soft cheek against her lover's shoulder; "and—and I am afraid of—of Gregory."

"And *I* am afraid of him, too, dear. It is a shame to have to say it, but the shame is not mine. Ever since I can remember he has had a queer, stand-off way with me, as if he was better than me, as well as older. I sometimes think he hates me."

If there had been anyone to see the dark, fierce expression that came into Walter's eyes as he uttered that suspicion of his brother's feelings towards him, they might reasonably have doubted if the hate was not mutual.

"I have always been afraid of Gregory," murmured the girl. "I do not often see him, but when I do, he is so silent and gruff that I am afraid to speak to him."

"He's a hard, selfish chap," said Walter, with proud decision; "and cares for nobody or nothing but his pet paddock. But he will find out that he has a man now to deal with, and not a boy. I am twenty-one to-day, dear Minnie."

"Are you? I'm so glad! It's something for a man to be of age, isn't it, Walter? According to law, I mean."

"Yes, I suppose so. At all events, it's time for me to know how our father left things, and I mean to know this very night."

"You will tell him about *me*, Walter?" she asked, timidly.

"Yes, darling; that I shall. None of his sulks or grumps will prevent me from making a home for my Minnie. If he chooses to vegetate alone in the middle of the paddock he dreams of, let him. I will have my wife, and there shall be a home for her on my father's land."

The young girl looked with pride in the handsome, animated face of the speaker; and when, after many exchanges of lover's nonsense, they parted with a lingering embrace, Minnie stood to watch her promised husband's figure until it was hidden in the bend of his homeward path.

Perhaps the poor young thing felt a little disappointed that Walter had not once looked back to her ere he turned the bend; but he was thinking of the explanation he had determined on having that night from his brother, and was, in spite of his assertion to the contrary, a little afraid of it. He was quite ignorant of Gregory's secret, for Gregory had never said one word to Minnie of the deep love his heart had conceived for her—awaiting humbly and fearful for one word of hope from her parents. Nor was even Minnie aware that the grim elder brother had one thought of her.

Thus it was that the brothers met in total ignorance that the heart of each was engrossed in one object. There was little help at Jansen's farm save in ploughing and harvest time, and the third at the supper table on this eventful night was the hired man, Chris Daly.

Chris Daly had been engaged at Jansen's for nearly two years, and he was a powerfully-built fellow, about thirty, with a stolid face and a fist like a prize-fighter. He had a queer look about his seldom seen eyes, however— a sort of leer, a suspicion of a cast in both eyes, as it were—that made them unpleasant to look upon, but he was more depended upon and consulted by Gregory than his brother. It might have been because he was nearer his own age.

They were always a quiet trio at meals, Walter, more especially almost refusing to join in conversation at any time. And he had by manner that he considered the company beneath him, a contemptuous way of his own; almost as if he wished to express by manner that he considered the company beneath him.

"I'm going to open the big drain again to-morrow, Chris," said Gregory, quietly, as he dropped a big bone to his dog who was always as close to him as he could get.

"Aye!" mumbled Chris, with his mouth full; "what's wrong with it now?"

"I think it's foul by that clump of wattles; the ground's low there, and it looks a bit mildewy. You'll go down with me first thing in the morning, both of you."

"Confound the drains!" cried Walter, hotly. "From the day when you first took that big paddock fad in your head there hasn't been a bit of comfort in the work! No sooner is a man set to one job than he's carted to the drains again! It's about time there was and end of this."

"What do you mean?" asked Gregory, looking up at Walter in quiet wonder.

"What I say. Are you getting deaf?"

He had finished his supper and risen while he spoke, and Gregory saw that the young face was flushed and angry enough to match his words.

"Have you been drinking, Walter?"

"No, I haven't; but if I had it's none of your business. You're not my master!"

"No?"

"No!"

The elderly widow, who was the only woman about the place, came in to clear away just then, and no more was said at the time. Chris left the room with a twinkle in his eyes, and Gregory sat down in his father's chair and began to fill his pipe. As for Walter, he stood at a window, and waited, with his heart throbbing so loudly that he fancied his apparently unimpressible brother must hear the beats. Gregory had filled his pipe, but he did not light it. When the door had closed behind the woman he turned, with the pipe in his clenched fingers, and spoke to his brother.

"Now, Walter, we will have this out, if you please."

"Just what I have been waiting for," the youth cried, hotly, as he flung himself from the window and faced Gregory, "and I think it is high time that something was out. And I mean to have it out, for I won't be kept in the dark a day longer!"

"In the dark about what?"

"About my father's will! Oh, don't believe I'm a boy whom you can push on one side and order about any longer. I'm a man, and I'll let you know it!"

A look of pity softened the eyes that so rarely softened to anything but his dog's affectionate caresses, and it was in a low, gentle tone that he asked: "What has put these ideas in your head to-day, Walter? Better let them sleep."

"No, I won't let them sleep. Why should I? What has put ideas in my head, eh? Well, I answer you that the ideas have been in my head long enough, but this is the first day that I have had a right—a *lawful* right—to let them out."

"A right?"

"Yes; a lawful right. This is my twenty-first birthday."

"Twenty-one. Is it so?" the elder man murmured thoughtfully.

He was going back in his memory to an old man's deathbed and an old man's dying words.

"Yes; did you want to forget it? Well, I didn't; and I want to know what is my share of my father's property?"

Gregory did not answer. His head drooped so that his brother could not see his face, and he fumbled his pipe in his trembling, weather-browned fingers.

"Did you hear me?" the youth persisted; "or must I ask you again?"

"Will you tell me your reasons for wanting to know, Walter? You have had a good home, and your share of all the comforts I have enjoyed myself. Are you dissatisfied? Do you want to go away?"

"Go away!" roared Walter, furiously. "Why should I want to go away?"

"Young men are often unsettled and want to see the world."

"Are they? Well, I'm not one of them kind of young men. I don't want to see any world off my father's property, and I'm going to marry and settle down on my share of it."

"To marry!"

"Yes. One would think it was an unnatural thing. Is there anything awful in a young chap bringing home a wife?"

"Who is the girl?"

"The girl is one that even you can have nothing to say against, and her present name is Minnie Greyson."

The pipe fell from Gregory's hand and was broken on the floor. The name his brother had just repeated was formed on his lips, but his voice failed him to utter it. As he stared into Walter's face his own grew white as death, and the lips that could not speak were blue beneath his rough beard. Walter saw his great agitation but totally misunderstood its cause.

"Ah!" said he, tauntingly, "that doesn't suit your plans, eh? You'd rather spend my father's loose cash in making a big meadow than bring a brother's wife into his home with it; but I'll have my rights!"

"You have no rights!" gasped Gregory, hoarsely, as he rose to his feet.

"I'll let you see whether I have or not. What share did my father leave me?"

"None."

There is no doubt, whatever, that poor Gregory had felt the deepest pity for his brother until he heard the name of Minnie Greyson; but then it was only natural that his jealous despair should overcome him. Could it be true that this lad, who only now insisted on knowing how little claim he had to either his name or home, had crept into the heart of the girl he loved, and shut out from him all the hopes of happiness he had built the future? It was with the voice and look of a fierce and angry man that Gregory Jansen stood before Walter and repeated his reply.

"Rights! You have none! The very name you bear is not yours, though it is mine."

In that moment of Walter's awful, yet incredulous, surprise, Gregory had entered his own room, and after a few moments' absence returned with a paper in his hand, which he dashed violently on the table.

"There is my father's will. You can read it."

Walter strode to the table, seized the folded paper, and opened it. His hands shook so that the paper rustled, but he had no need to strain his eyes, for every word before them burned into his brain. The document was short, and devoid of legal superfluity of words, and it bequeathed everything the old man had died possessed of, without lieu or charge of any kind, 'to my only lawful son, Gregory Jansen.'

Walter dropped the paper that rustled to the table and lifted his eyes to the stern face before him. The young man was too thunderstruck to speak, and his meaner nature cowered for a while beneath the position in which he found himself; but only for a while, however, for the devil that was within him grow strong and helped his own.

"Well, are you satisfied now?"

"No, I'm not!" was the bitter reply to the taunting question. "If the words in that will are true, who am I?"

"You are the illegitimate son of my father by a faithless servant of my mother."

"And he left me a hanger-on for charity, like a dog?"

"He left you to be dealt with as I thought you deserved, and I have dealt faithfully with you, as I promised. But I am master here and will be while I live. If you want to marry, you must seek employment in another home. Better content yourself, Walter. I shall never marry, and when I am dead you shall take my place for my father's sake."

There were curses in Walter's heart, but no words on his lips, as he went out into the dusk of evening. He went out by the front door, and the great sweep of meadowland that his brother loved lay between him and the western sky, where the red and gold of sunset yet faintly lingered. All the landscape, even the belt of bush where he had met Minnie but a few hours ago, looked dark and gloomy to him, for the sunlight was blotted from his heart, and the clouds of disappointment lay heavy on his soul.

But it was not all disappointment, nor was Minnie's the only face he saw between him and the blood red streaks of the darkening clouds. There was the hate of hell within him, and curses were murmured against the memory of him who had begotten him, and against the brother who had repulsed him. He could have struck the dead man in the face had he stood by his open coffin. He could have stabbed the living one to the heart had the weapon and the breast been near.

He had turned from the dismal scene, scarce knowing where to go or what to do, when near the end of the house he stumbled against the feet of Chris, who was sitting on a log smoking in the twilight. There was just enough of light for Walter to see in the pose of the head and twinkle of the eyes lifted up to him that the man was aware of his discomposure, and a livid light broke upon him, with a possibility of revenge suggested of the devil.

"Come back into your hut, Chris, I want to talk to you," he said; and the man raised his huge figure silently and followed him.

The men's hut at Jansen's was behind the homestead, and at some little distance from it. During the busy seasons on the farm it accommodated many hands, but now its slab walls were bare, and its bunks empty, for Chris was its only tenant. It was quite dark inside, and as the man struck a match and lit the candle standing on the rough table his first glance was into Walter's face, and he saw in its pale lines a story that he already guessed.

"This has been a bad job for you, Walter," he said, as he sat down on his bunk.

"You know, then."

"I heard every word of it. I was passing the window, and—well, my curiosity was natural."

"I'm glad you heard it; it saves me the telling, for that's what I was going to do."

"Aye, it's one o' them heavy blows that makes a man feel the want of a friend."

"And you *could* be a friend to me, Chris?" Walter asked, as he gazed anxiously at the face with the queer, downcast eyes before him.

"Plain talking is best. I could be a friend to any man as will pay me well. But I feel for you, boy; you've been cruelly treated. I call it the very height of cruelty to let a young fellow grow up without a hint, and then crush him down to the ground just when he had nearly got the girl he wanted.'"

"But I won't be crushed. If I die for it, I'll have my revenge, Chris."

"Just so; that's how a man talks and acts, and I daresay now you'll lose that girl if you don't mind what you're about."

"Chris, speak out. What would you advise me to do?"

"Hum. There be some things that it is scarcely safe to speak out about. All I can say is that if you make it worth my while I'll do my best to help you."

"How can I make it worth your while? I? You know now what right I have to a pound of my father's gold."

"It's very hard," Chris murmured, with his queer eyes fixed on the table where the candle only illumined a small circle of the greasy surface. Suddenly he lifted those queer eyes and met the eager gaze of the youth.

"If Gregory would go away now and leave you in possession, it would be all right, wouldn't it?"

"Go away?"

"Aye, go away for good." The eyes of the two men met, and in the moment of silence that ensued a terrible tale was told without words. When Walter's eyes fell his face was as pale as a sheet of paper.

"You are afraid!" whispered the other, with a sneer of contempt; "and perhaps you are right, so we'll drop the subject."

"No, we won't! I'm not afraid—that is to say, if I could see—a—a way."

"There's plenty of ways.'"

"Tell me one of them?"

"See here now, let us understand one another, so that there may be no dispute or nonsense after. Do you quite understand what I am driving at?"

"About Gregory? Yes, I do."

The words were uttered in a whisper, so low that it was more by the motion of the lips than their sound that Chris comprehended them.

"You are sure?"

"I think so. You mean to make him go away for ever."

"To put him out of the way, just so; now, are you man enough to strike a blow for yourself—one that will give you all with the girl you have set your heart on? I say nothing of your revenge for the shameful treatment you've had at his hands, though that would be what *I'd* do it for."

"And it's what I'll do it for, too! Now, Chris, for the way. My heart is strong enough to strike two blows if one will not do!"

The queer eyes flashed a triumphant glare for a second on Walter's white face, and then were hidden when he spoke.

"It's the strangest thing," he said, in a low tone," that the very last time that big drain was opened, and you, me, and Gregory were at work there, I thought to myself how easy it would be for two of us to knock the other into the drain, so that he would never get out again."

"Go on," said Walter, eagerly, as the other paused.

"Jansen's farm is a lonely spot at any time, and in the middle of that fifty-acre paddock, with the clump of wattles all round the drain, anything could be done."

"Go on!"

"The drain is opened, we will say, and one of us three men is stooping down to see about lifting the pipe, when another of the men gives him a knock on the back of the head with the shovel or pick, or whatever may happen to be handiest. Well, the first man falls dead or stunned, head foremost into the drain, and the third man shovels the soil back into the drain so quick that the dead man is covered before the living one could wink twice. What do you think of that, now?"

What did he think of it, unhappy young man? What, indeed, did he think of it? His face was white to the very lips, and his tongue clung to the roof of his mouth as he spoke thickly.

"Who—who is the man?"

"To strike the blow, eh? Why, the one that gains most by it, of course. You are that man. My share in the business will be so much hard cash as will take me out of the country, while yours is the finest property in this neighbourhood and—Minnie Greyson. You said you were not afraid. You said you could strike a blow that wasn't a coward's."

The sneer at the end was enough.

"And so I can, and so I will! But there are many difficulties—a blow would not finish it."

"I see only one difficulty, and that is the dog. He never leaves his side, so he must be put out of the way this night—that is, if you decide on the job."

"You shall not harm the dog!" cried Walter, with such energy that Chris raised his hand in sudden warning. "I will not have him touched!"

"By gar, that's queer! You set a higher value on a dog than—well, well, every man has his weakness, I suppose. We'll say no more about that. Is the job to be done?"

"Yes."

"That is enough. Now, I am going to take a turn round to see that all's quiet, and then we'll sit down here and settle it all straight ahead. The candle is near gone, and I haven't another; but it's no matter—we don't want light to talk; darkness will suit us best."

Yes! For ever and ever after that night darkness would suit them best, and yet they would dread its approach as a thing of horror that brought no sleep, and only the remembrance of a deed that cost two souls. As the candle flickered and went out, the shadow of evil that hung round Walter Jansen that night knew that his temptation had been successful, and his prize won.

The housekeeper had long been in bed ere Gregory rose from his seat near the empty hearth. For hours, while those wretched beings outside were planning his death, he had sat there with his face bowed and a heart full of bitter thoughts. The poor, silent being had neither love nor hatred for his half-brother, but had treated him as well as it was in his nature to treat any young man for whose youth and conceit, he had all of a man's contempt, though he gave no utterance to it. Now, however, when he knew that it was this Walter—whose birth had brought sorrow and shame to Gregory's mother—who had been preferred to him, Gregory, for the first time in his life, hated the good looks and lissom youth that had been successful in his rival.

But against this feeling his better nature fought, and before he went to his bed, he had tutored himself into something of a brother's pity for Walter. He slept but little, and when he arose his first movement was, as it always had been of late, to the front of the house, from whence he could see the green and gently undulating acres that had been coaxed into wealth and beauty by his labour.

The sun lay on it, and the morning breeze swept the wide meadow into the soft waves of a summer sea. creek glittered in the warm light, and nearer was the cluster of wattles, feathery foliaged, and with the perfumed yellow balls of blossom hanging on them and swaying in the breeze. It was as lovely as it had been before, but, somehow, Jansen's heart was no longer in it.

"What's the good of anything?" he thought, bitterly. "There's an end of a man some day, and what does anything matter?"

Just as this thought was upon him, he saw Walter doing something to a pick near the grindstone, and he walked hurriedly towards him, full of those feelings that had beat down the evil in his breast during his long, weary struggle of the past night.

"Walter," he said, "you are my father's son, after all, and I am sorry there have been hard words between us. There is no one by now to hear me tell the reason, but I think it is due to myself and you that should know. It was because Minnie Greyson chose you instead of me that last night's hard words passed my lips. I have loved the girl so long that it was a cruel blow to me to know—"

"*You!*" shouted Walter, as he straightened his tall figure and turned a furious face towards his brother— "you loved Minnie?"

"Aye did I. Well, it is all over now. She would have none of me, and she has chosen you, my brother. Forget all I said last night and, believe me, I will not prevent you from making the child happy. There is my hand on it, Walter."

"I will not take your hand," cried the youth, dashing it aside as it was held out to him.

"You will not prevent me from making Minnie happy! No, by heavens, you won't! Stand out of my way, Gregory Jansen;" and he went away with a face that might have been that of a fiend, such evil passions were stamped in it.

"It only wanted that," he said to himself— "only that to make the blow easy! Loves Minnie, indeed! Confound him!"

The three men were at work at the drain before the sun was above the horizon, and soon a great heap of soil at either side of the excavation told that the pipes could not be far off. Once or twice the wretched youth, Walter, had raised himself, and, while wiping the sweat from his face, tried to meet the eyes of Chris, but that cooler villain refused to be consulted. Feigning to be absorbed in his work, he never lifted his head until the last shovelful was thrown out and the pipes were bare. Then he stood up and looked questioningly at his accomplice.

Gregory as well as Walter had stepped to the surface, and all at once, as a man awakening out of a dream, Gregory looked around him, missing his dog.

"I wonder what's become of Faithful," he said. "I don't think I've seen him this morning."

"I saw him trotting up towards Greyson's boundary," said Chris; "he's got a friend there, you know."

"Aye; Jack, the shepherd's dog."

Still Gregory did not turn to his work again. He was looking through a break in the wattles at the green landscape and the shimmering water, little thinking he was looking his last.

"I believe," he half whispered, almost unconsciously, "that if I were dead, I should come back to see all this again;" and then he turned to the drain.

"Which pipe is it, do you think, Chris?"

"This one, boss," and the man stooped to point—never, however, letting his eyes leave the figure that, with a grip of iron on the pick he had been using, stood, white-faced and terrible, behind the unconscious victim. Gregory stooped, and in a second the pick was uplifted in two straining hands, and with a thud fell on the crashing skull of the unsuspecting man. He fell forward, rolled heavily against the opposite side of the drain, fell over on his back, and lay with his awful, accusing eyes gazing up into the face of the fratricide.

Was it to gratify the in-bred cruelty of the wretch's nature that Chris drew back, instead of shutting that terrible sight from the murderer's eyes? It was evident that he had got his death blow, but as the dreadful shades of death stole down over his face, Gregory's lips opened once to curse the unhappy, lost Walter.

"Fratricide!" he gasped; "may the just God of heaven curse you and the ground you stand on for—for ever!"

The last words were bubbled amid a stream of blood, as it gushed from between his lips; and, with a convulsion that drew the great limbs almost up to his chin, Gregory Jansen was dead.

Even then, ere he dashed the first shovelful of earth on the dead face, Chris paused, with a sneer, to gaze on the horrified visage of Walter, as he stared at the terrible spectacle, and it was only the very desperation of his fear of discovery that gave the wretched being at last strength to help in the work of hiding his deed from the light. There was not a word spoken between them until the soil was filled in, and Gregory Jansen was lying hidden in the grave he had helped to dig for himself. Then Chris went a little distance off and returned with a bottle and glass he had ready for the occasion.

"That's what I call as neat a job of the kind as was ever done," he said, when he had watched Walter swallowing the drink he handed him; "and I defy any man to find a trace of it now, unless it's on your pick, Walter."

Already had the murderer dropped the tool with which he had done the deed, and now, as Chris stooped to lift it, he staggered back against the butt of an old wattle tree and covered his face with his hands. All in vain, unhappy lad, for never again—by night or day, in darkness or in light—will the brother's dying look fail to meet your sight, and his dying curse to sound in your ears.

"He never even suspected that we had tied up the dog," Chris went on, as he rubbed the head of the pick with a wisp of grass; "and now it's all plain sailing. What are you groaning there for? Are you of a mind to accuse yourself, or give me a chance of doing it? If you are not a man, try to look like one, anyhow."

The quick change in his accomplice's tone roused Walter, and he tried to recover himself.

"I wish I was like you," he moaned; "and able to take it so coolly. But—oh God! I can see his face and hear his voice yet."

"I don't doubt that; for, to tell you the honest truth, I shouldn't like to have such a memory as yours to carry about with me. But then, you see, I had not so much to gain by it. Come now, shake yourself together, for you must go over at once with your news to the Greysons."

* * * *

The sudden departure of Gregory Jansen from the farm created no surprise at Farmer Greyson's, and the forged letter that was handed to Andrew made matters so clear that no objection was made by the old people to the almost immediate marriage of Walter and Minnie. The letter told Andrew how deep was Gregory's disappointment that Minnie could not care for him, and how impossible it was for him to stay and witness his brother's happiness; and added that Walter was left in full possession of the farm, where he hoped soon to hear that Minnie was settled as Walter's wife.

And so the simple wedding was solemnised, and Walter took Minnie home to his brother's house as its mistress. Chris yet hung about the place, and did his usual work, for he had changed his mind about leaving—at least, no word of such an intention had been spoken since Gregory was buried in the big drain.

For a time, it was a pretty sight to see Minnie, in her new role of mistress and wife, flitting happily about the grey old homestead of the Jansens; but the cloud on the young husband's face grew daily heavier with the terrible fear of discovery that was eating his very life away—a fear that was intensified by the presence of his dead brother's favourite dog.

That Faithful missed his master and mourned for him was patent to anyone who looked in his honest eyes or watched his restless movements. Day by day he tracked every wonted step of his lost master, whining now and then, and refusing to be comforted, and night after night he lay by the empty bed, or wandered to the door, listening for Gregory's return. But at last, he almost lived among the wattles where the big drain had been opened.

More than once, Chris had whispered a proposal to Walter that Faithful should be shot, but with the horrible moroseness that seemed a new feature in the youth's disposition, he had declared against the deed.

"He will forget by and by," he would say, "for he is getting fond of Minnie."

And it was true. The dog took greatly to the light-hearted, childish wife, and would follow her home when, from a hint given by Walter, she would go to the meadow wattles to see if he were there. And he was almost always there, lying at the edge of the covered drain, with his nose on his outstretched paws, and that look of pitiful wistfulness in his eyes that we see nowhere but in the eyes of a dog pining for the return of a master he loves.

On that spot Walter Jansen had never set foot since he struck the fatal blow; and even Chris, the hardened, had avoided it until one day he took a shovel in his hand and went down there to see if the drain that was a grave had fallen in at all and wanted filling up a bit. Something he saw there made him seek out Walter and tell him a queer story.

"Have you been down at the wattles lately?" Chris asked.

"No; it's not likely to be a favourite walk of mine," was the bitter answer, as the young man's pale face grew whiter.

"Well, you'd better come down with me now, at all events; for there's something wants looking after, I guess."

"You don't mean? There's nothing turned up—"

"Not what you fear. No, but there's something for all that, Walter. I needn't ask you if you remember the—the words—the curse he said?"

"Oh God, if I could only forget them! May the just God of heaven curse you and the ground you stand on for ever!"

"Yes, that's it. Well, that curse is working double, I fear; the glory of Jansen's paddock is over."

"What do you mean, Chris? For mercy's sake, speak out!"

"Well, the grass where you stood is withered as though a hot blast had passed over it, and from the drain where he lies a yellow blight is eating into the meadow on both sides. Come on down."

Walter followed, walking down the narrow path among the luxurious green meadow-grass, with the sweet smell of English memories in it, and the dew among its blades sparkling in the morning sun. He had never trod that path since he had followed his brother with murder in his heart; and now worse than the bitterest bitterness of death was upon him.

The two men reached the spot, and there before them was the blighted patch, and the spreading curse of the murdered man that was creeping out from the unknown and unhallowed grave. And now that Chris examined it more closely, he saw that withered lines, as yet but faintly defined, were shooting from the grave all around into the meadow, as it might be like rays from a central light.

"This is a bad job, Walter; it may draw attention to the ground. I'm afraid we'll have to shift him out of this."

"I wouldn't look upon his face again if the rope was waiting for me!" said Walter, desperately.

"Bah! If I had believed you such a coward, I wouldn't have lifted my hand to help you! There's one thing certain, at all events—the meadow has been the talk of the country, and when this failure gets wind, you'll have plenty of visitors and advice."

The man's words were confirmed almost on the instant, for they were joined by Farmer Greyson, who had taken a short cut from his own land on seeing the men coming down from the homestead.

"Aye, lads, that's a bad look-out, eh? I noticed it yesterday evening as I was going home and was coming to tell you of it. The drain's at fault,

Walter; you'll have to open it up."

"It isn't a month since we *did* open it," Walter said, almost fiercely.

"If it was only opened yesterday, my boy, it'll have to be done again. The drain's evidently foul again. You know how hard Gregory worked at his drains, and that's what made the meadow what it is. If you like, I'll give you a hand to open it to-day."

The look of awful fear in Walter's face made Chris, for his own sake, hasten to the rescue.

"If you take notice, Mr. Greyson, you'll maybe think with me that the fault don't lie just here. I should say, them streaks of dying grass makes me think that the leakage is up in yon cross drain, and only settling here like."

"At all events, we'll look after the cross-drain first," Walter said.

"It's an easier job, and we won't trouble you to-day, father." Greyson turned abruptly as he was about to leave.

"By the way, I was going up to see Minnie. The mother tells me she's not at all well—pining like. What do you think, lad?"

"She's not as bright as she used to be, father. I've noticed it myself; but I hope 'tis nothing of any consequence."

"I'll try and coax her over to her mother for the day," said the sturdy farmer, as he stamped away, leaving the two men looking in each other's faces with an uneasy expression depicted on both.

"*Now* don't you see that it must be done?" said Chris, doggedly. "It's very likely that it is the drain that's at fault, and it must be opened sooner or later; it's not safe to leave him here. What do you say? Will we do it to-night?"

"No; I have told you already that if it was to save even my already damned soul I couldn't do it," cried the wretched being. "Couldn't you manage it yourself, if it must be done?"

"Manage it myself! Thank ye, Walter Jansen, for nothing. There is no reason that I should lift my finger to help you. I committed no murder, thank God. What I got from you was for holding my tongue; and now, as I see your cowardice won't let me do that much longer, I'll be off. It was for your sake entirely I offered to help again. What do I care if the whole meadow was blasted by to-morrow morning? It's not *my* plant that lies there."

Having pointed to the spot from whence the murdered man's eyes seemed at the moment to be staring into the awful face of Walter, Chris turned on his heel and made for the house, leaving Walter stupefied with his terror and remorse, but with one awful idea growing within him—an idea of escape at the sacrifice of all he had sinned for; aye, and more!

* * * *

Greyson trudged sturdily up to the house and entered the open door.

Minnie was sitting just inside it, with the dog Faithful lying beside her. The poor child was doing literally nothing; her hands being crossed on her lap—her eyes fixed on the far-stretching meadow outside. Her father actually started when he recognised the change a few days had made in her. All the charming gaiety of manner, all the pretty colour had disappeared; she was as pale as a white rose, and the picture of a hidden grief. When she started at her father's unexpected entrance, however, a flush covered all the pretty face, but only to die away almost as quickly as it had appeared.

"Why, Minnie, my dear, whatever is the matter?" he cried, anxiously. "Have you and Walter been quarrelling."

"No, father; oh, no. I do not feel very well; but it is nothing. I shall be all right to-morrow."

"That's what you told mother yesterday, and I am sure if you had looked as you do to-day she would have been here long ago. My child, tell your old father what is the matter?"

He had taken her in his arms; and now, as she laid her hot forehead against the fond breast, the girl burst into tears.

"Oh, father, I don't know what to do. I don't think I ought to tell you; but, indeed, I'm frightened. I don't know what to do."

"If it is anything that frightens you, Minnie, I am sure you ought to tell me of it."

"Dear father," sobbed poor Minnie, kissing him, "I will tell you; but you must promise me to say nothing to Walter—at least, not yet."

"Well, my dear, I promise."

"Father, Gregory Jansen is hiding somewhere about the farm. I have seen him twice."

"Gregory Jansen!" almost shouted Greyson.

"Hush! you will be heard. Yes, father, I have seen him twice—down at the wattles. Poor Faithful has taken greatly to lying down there, near the big drain, and I have been trying to get him home. I went down at dusk yesterday and the evening before, and both times I saw Gregory standing looking at me from the other side of the drain."

"Did he speak?" the father asked, hoarsely.

"No; it was so nearly dark that he seemed to fade away as soon as I saw him. But, oh! he must be unhappy, for he looked so white and sad. Father, I have been fretting since you and mother told me that Gregory cared for me. I have been thinking that it was for me the brothers quarrelled."

"Quarrelled? I never heard they quarrelled."

"I know they did," whispered Minnie; "for Walter talks of it in his sleep. And it must have been something terrible, for he wakens panting, and with the sweat standing on his white face in great drops. Oh, father, what shall we do?"

Greyson put his daughter gently back into her seat; and as she looked anxiously into his rugged face, over which a great seriousness had spread, he answered her:

"My darling, leave it to me, and say no word till I see you again. If Gregory is in the neighbourhood I will see and speak to him. Don't be afraid; we'll set things straight, never fear."

But though the old man spoke cheeringly, and left his child partly reassured, he went away with a growing, terrible dread in his heart. Now that Minnie's words had suddenly recalled the strangeness of Gregory's disappearance, he began to think it over and find peculiarities that he had not considered before. At the time, indeed, he fancied he had seen Gregory the very morning he was said to have left, going down to the big drain with Walter and Chris, but he had concluded himself mistaken. Now, however, he remembered a dozen circumstances that corroborated and increased his dread.

When he got down as far as the wattles on his way home, he met Walter just turning, as it were, from the drain, which he had, indeed, been hanging round now for nearly an hour. When the young man saw his father-in-law he avoided him by going at the other side of the bushes, but Greyson saw enough of the fear in that awful white face to make his suspicions almost a certainty, and to almost break his heart with thoughts of the future misery of his beloved child.

At dusk, again, that same day, Farmer Greyson crept through the rails that divided his own ground from Jansen's meadow. There was no movement of living thing over its broad expanse, nor around the homestead, that Greyson could see. Satisfied that no one would observe him, he crossed the meadow and gained the clump of bushes, where was that drain and the spot from which was proceeding that rapidly spreading blight. Here the good man paused and looked down upon the *grave*.

He little guessed that the man he had so truly respected, and for whose disappointment he had been so truly sorry, was lying with his dead face within a few feet of the clods he was gazing at; yet he had some strange idea that there was a hidden connection between this spot and the disappearance of Gregory Jansen. If he were alive, why did he hang round this part of the meadow? If he were dead—. Greyson raised his eyes and saw within two yards of him the shadowy figure of Gregory Jansen!

At the first glance he knew it was no living man that stood there, for no man ever lived with a face of such pallor, and such glassy, dead, staring eyes. He tried to speak, but the tongue clove to the roof of his mouth; he tried to lift his arm, but it was glued to his side. It was but an instant that he saw the shadow of his old friend, but it seemed minutes ere he had desperately controlled himself to speak.

"In the name of God, tell me, Gregory—" but ere he could say another word the finger seemed to point with its hand to the ground at its feet, and its place was vacant.

For another moment Greyson stood there, staring at the quickly darkening space. He heard the breeze sighing and rustling among the flowering wattles, and softly moving across the soft surface of the broad meadow, as a man hears such things in a dream. He was facing what he had before him with the desperate determination of a true man, and, above all, a father; and when he was strong he turned and went for the second time that day up to Jansen's homestead.

The door was not open now, but Greyson lifted the latch and pushed it in. The supper was on the table, and the young wife was seated at the head of it making tea for Walter and Chris, who sat at either side of her. She was facing the door, and when it opened and her father appeared at it the teapot dropped from her hand, for there was a terrible something in that father's face that she had never seen there before.

Walter saw it, too, and rose to his feet; but before he could speak Greyson's hand was on his child's shoulder, and his words had reached her ears.

"Minnie, my child, you will come home with me at once."

"What is it, father, dear? Oh! is mother ill?"

"Don't waste time, child, but get your shawl. You need not wait for anything else."

The shawl happened to be over the back of the chair she had been seated on, and in a moment, it was around the girl's form. Walter, full of a terrible fear, dared not speak; and the farmer had, as it were, ignored his presence.

"You will come, too, Walter," the poor young wife said, as she approached him; but her father's hand was on her ere she could touch her husband, and he drew her away to the door.

"No, my dear, he will not come."

There was no time for the wretched youth to even exchange a look with the young wife of his bosom. His eyes met those of his father-in-law for an instant, and Walter knew his fate as if it had been told to him in words. As the door closed between them, he fell back to his seat, helpless.

"By jingo!" cried Chris, rising, "the business is blown. You'll never see your wife under this roof again; and if you take my last advice you'll do as I do—make tracks and save yourself."

Save himself! He laid his arms on the table, and his face fell upon them. The serving woman came in to remove the supper things, but he took no notice of her. The candle burnt down to the socket of the candlestick, flared up two or three times, and then went out; but his state was too hopeless and despairing for him to either know or care that the darkness he had hitherto feared had gathered closely about him. No man will ever know more of his thoughts during those terrible hours than that they were full of despair; and when at last he rose, the moonlight was creeping in the windows before which lay the meadow that had been the pride of Gregory Jansen, and which now held his grave.

As he passed the window, and the moonlight for a moment lay on his face, no one would have recognised in it the handsome lineaments of the youth Minnie Greyson had loved. It was ghastly and stamped with a despair beyond all words. He went to Gregory's room and took from the wall his brother's gun; there was some comfort in the thought that justice should, at all events, be done with his weapon.

He opened the door and went out. In the holy calm of night, the meadow lay broad in the moonlight, with not a shadow upon it, save what was thrown by the wattles down yonder in the dread hollow. But there was no dread in Walter's heart. He was past that now, and he walked steadily to the fated spot, with his quick feet brushing the dew off the sparkling grass, and his brother's gun in his drooped hand.

A ray of moonlight lay across the clods that covered the dead breast of Gregory, and in that ray. Walter Jansen knelt. He did not raise his face to heaven; he bent it to the earth. He did not plead for mercy—he offered sacrifice.

"If I had twenty lives they would be forfeited, Gregory," he murmured. "I have only one, and it is just that I should die where I have sinned."

Then there was a heavy report in the lonely night, and a dead man's blood was soaking through the soil to the breast of his brother.

It was Greyson who found the body. After a sleepless night, in which he had to hide his terrible fears from his wife and child, he went out in the fresh morning with the cool air on his hot face. What was he to do? Must he leave his murdered friend unavenged to save the man who had been his child's husband from a felon's doom? His child's heart was broken either way—it needed no prophet to tell him that.

Almost unconsciously his steps were turned to the spot where he had seen the shadow of Gregory, and there the question was solved. Walter had confessed his sin by the suicide that laid him dead on his brother's grave.

For a while the unhappy parents succeeded in hiding the truth from poor Minnie, but the day came when she knew all; and thereafter she faded like one of the blighted blades of grass in Jansen's meadow. Of all she knew in the home that had been hers so short a time. The dog Faithful alone was left; and when the Greysons were childless, poor Faithful deserted his old home altogether, and saw many a silent tear on the wrinkled faces that always looked kindly on the dog for Minnie's sake.

The brothers were laid in the same cemetery, but with many silent tenants between them. The farm went to Gregory's heirs; Walter having no legal title to leave to Minnie.

But Jansen's meadow is blighted to this day, and no green thing ever flourishes for many yards around the spot where the murder and suicide were committed. And often in the twilight the new dwellers in the homestead whisper and point down to the wattles round the big drain, where the shadows seem to them like the haunting forms of Gregory Jansen and his unhappy brother.

THE SILENT SEPULCHRE

Charles Junor

Charles Junor (1864-1901) published only a single collection of short stories, *Dead Men's Tales*, published in 1898 by George Robertson. A British edition was published by Swan Sonnenschein & Co. in the same year. Junor wrote in the introduction, '[t]he tales and sketches contained in this volume consist chiefly of republished magazine stories illustrative of Melbourne life, though several others dealing with external localities are included. To some critics, certain yarns related herein may appear too grotesquely weird or extravagant for serious consideration.' "The Silent Sepulchre" is a fine macabre story that features catalepsy, premature burial, romance, madness, and a man-eating dog. Junor tragically drowned in Sydney Harbour in a ferry accident.

1. THE SOLEMN CHARGE

The gloomiest mansion in Rockwood—one of Sydney's most respectable suburbs—was undoubtedly that owned by young Victor Russell. Three years prior to the present narrative, when Russell was twenty five years of age, he had settled in Australia, with the view of checking certain tendencies towards consumption, which anticipated in time, might become easily eradicable. His father had just died, and left him the bulk of his large fortune. Being of an intensely studious and retiring disposition, the seclusion afforded by an establishment like "The Grove" at once took his fancy, especially as its price was remarkably cheap; but whether this was on account of its back premises adjoining the local cemetery, or its old-fashioned style of architecture, and comparative remoteness from the city, the agent did not explain. All he volunteered was that the last proprietor had built it for his personal pleasure and convenience, and that after residing therein for nearly fifty years, when he died, the trustees received instructions to realize for whatever it would at once fetch. The legatee allegedly was in need of immediate cash to invest in West Australian gold-mines, and so Mr. Russell's first offer was promptly closed with.

Standing back some eighty feet from the road, the house was completely hidden from wayfarers by the tall cypress and beech trees which intervened, and its neglected shrubberies and unkempt grass gave the place an unmistakable air of desolation. As Russell had no relations in Australia, and rarely interested himself in the doings of his neighbours, few visitors ever troubled the gloomy quiet of his *entourage;* and as time progressed, it became a recognized thing among the small boys, hawkers, and general idlers of the vicinity, that the proprietor of "The Grove" was either a madman or a miser, or something in the criminal line. Such is invariably the penalty imposed upon all citizens who too strictly confine themselves to their own affairs. But that all these views were wholly unjustifiable, a glance inside of the study, this particular October night, would have readily demonstrated.

Two men were conversing in the room. In an easy-chair, near the fireplace, reclined Victor Russell himself—a clean-shaved, good-looking young fellow with a kindly eye, and open, regular features. Close by, with some papers in front of him, and leaning on the table occupying the centre of the apartment, sat Mr. Lawrence Musgrave, a man some years the other's senior, a rising solicitor by profession, and who, among Russell's limited circle of acquaintances, passed as his most intimate friend. Just now, as he drew his fingers through his well-trimmed black beard, and glanced curiously at his host, he conveyed an impression of latent capacity combined with a disposition towards severity, which pushed to extremity might imply utter mercilessness. His voice, though carefully modulated, contributed a certain ring of hardness, which without doubt presaged ill to any adversary who crossed his purposes.

"I've now got all the particulars necessary for drawing out your will, Russell," he said; "there now remains only the name of the fortunate legatee."

"Quite so," replied his host. "Please insert the name of Miss Helen Travers in that capacity. She will be my wife within the next three months, but in case anything should happen to me in the meantime, it's as well to be prepared. A codicil to meet her change of name, after the event, will obviate any necessity for a fresh document, I presume?"

"Miss Travers!" ejaculated Musgrave, with sudden and wholly unprofessional emphasis. Then realising the necessity for some explanation— "Pray pardon my apparent discourtesy. The fact is I expected the name of some male relative, and had no idea that you were a marrying man. Oh, yes, a codicil would answer all requirements; but what could happen to you before the happy event? Why not let this stand till it's over?"

"That is precisely what I want to talk to you about, old man," replied Russell, as he threw away his cigar, and bending forward, gazed seriously into his friend's eyes. "Some little time ago I received a letter from my mother's people in London, which greatly upset me. Both my parents, I may tell you, lived in Hampstead; and my father, as well as my mother, was buried in the local family vault, which since many years has been the property of my maternal ancestry. My father was a successful stockbroker, of ordinary lineage, but my mother's connections were quite of the 'blue'-blooded type and recognized my father only after he had risen in the world, and in their estimation had earned the privilege of participating in their family heirlooms and other paraphernalia of greatness. My mother died nine years ago—that is to say, five years before my father. Well, last year, it seems that, owing to certain alterations in Hampstead cemetery, it became necessary to shift the coffins in our family sepulchre. During this process it was discovered that she had turned in her coffin and had evidently been buried alive. A further investigation revealed that no less than nine out of the other fifteen corpses contained in the tomb had undergone similar transpositions! My father, however, to all appearances, must have escaped his companion's fearful fate, or else was too weak to turn. Now, as it is a law of heredity that the mother transmits her characteristics in the more active degree to her sons, and the father, his to his daughters, in families, I have grave fears that cataleptic predispositions must be contained in my system. Latterly I have noticed intermittent periods of languor stealing over me, without any accountable reason. Accordingly, I have taken precautions which should effectually prevent my falling victim to a similar horrible fate. And your help is necessary to the success of my arrangements."

"Mine! In what way, Russell?" inquired the astonished listener.

"In this way," answered the speaker. "My back wall, as you know, divides my property from the Rookwood Cemetery. Within a stone-throw outside of this boundary I have built a special vault. In its centre I have constructed a raised sarcophagus, with a movable stone covering containing two ventilators at the ends. In my will I have mentioned my wish to be buried in this tomb, but have abstained from any particulars. When I die, I want you to see that an open space is left over my face in the coffin, which you will have constructed specially for me, and when you place this casket in the sarcophagus, leave the lid off until unmistakable evidences of dissolution appear. I can't expect you to keep a permanent watch over me, but I'd like you to leave some stimulant and food close by, and to give me a look in every day until you are certain that I am actually dead. Will you promise to do this for me?"

"Of course," answered Musgrave. "But haven't you told anybody about your symptoms and fears, Russell? Why not consult a medical man? and should you not confide in Miss Travers, who will—?"

"No, old man," interposed Russell; "I would not like to alarm her; women are such peculiar creatures. I certainly do intend to see Dr. Macari, the eminent nerve-specialist, of Wynyard Square, about my case by and by. He was an old friend of my father's, but as I don't know him personally, I have somehow or other so far postponed my visit. I'll try to look him up next week, if he is in town, but he is so often away that it's a hard job to catch him with half-an-hour to spare."

"All right—I'll attend to your wishes, Russell," promised Musgrave, thoughtfully. "And now that our business is finished, and I've got a bit of a headache, I think I'll be going."

"Not without a parting glass, anyhow," said Russell, making for the sideboard. "You look awfully fagged to-night and—by the way—I've enclosed a cheque for your account to date, in the envelope, as I know the working horse must have his corn. You can send me a receipt when the will is ready for signature."

Musgrave muttered his thanks, but declined the proffered drink, and gathering up his papers, which he stuffed mechanically into his bag, he shortly afterwards withdrew.

"Poor old chap, he doesn't look very bright," soliloquized Russell, as he proceeded up-stairs after seeing his friend out and sank meditatively into his arm-chair once more.

Presently it occurred to him that Musgrave had seemed remarkably moved when he told him about his projected marriage. Was it so wrong for him to marry when he was a somniloquist or cataleptic? But then it was *before* and not after, he had told Musgrave about his dreaded affliction that this singularity had displayed itself. Was his case so serious though, after all? Mentally he reviewed the past history of his mother's family and tried to trace some analogies with his own constitution. Strange how his head throbbed with a sense of fulness, and how drowsy his eyes had become with looking into the fire! He glanced upwards at the portraits by the old masters which hung around the room. Surely that face, in the dark recess yonder, was not projecting itself forwards and approaching his own? A pulsating fire, heating him to an intolerable temperature, coursed through his veins, and he became aware of a gradual muffling of his intellectual faculties. His neck coil commenced to pain unreasonably, and his heart, which had now begun to flutter feebly, gave a sudden leap, only to react with proportionate violence, and then subside in nerveless pulsations. A frightful roaring burst in his ears, and the light became fainter and fainter, till it diminished into a mere glimmer. Suddenly there was an appalling explosion, which deafened him. His eyes scintillated like living globes, as they strained in their sockets—an intense and preternatural inrush of physical sensibility galvanized his quivering frame—then ebbed. Victor Russell knew that he was dead.

II. THE CATASTROPHE

Lawrence Musgrave had spent a racking and sleepless night, when he arose heavy-eyed on the morning following his conference with Russell. And no wonder. He was passionately enamoured of Helen Travers himself. With impotent rage he remembered that it was he who had introduced Russell to Miss Travers, and though they had known each other but a few months, while he had worshipped the girl since boyhood, his rival had established himself in her affections without his ever suspecting anything wrong. Musgrave lived with his widowed mother, in a small house at the far end of Rookwood; and Miss Travers dwelt with her two young brothers and mother, in a cottage close to Russell's abode. He (Musgrave) met Helen—as he had always called her—when they were both children going to the district State-school.

Being an unusually self-contained man, he did not contemplate speaking of love to his sweetheart till he considered himself in a position to marry, and this he had intended to do within the next few months—i.e., at Christmastime, when a small but sure regular income would be available, through the control of two estates and certain company retainerships, Russell's being one of these. In fact it was through his having mentioned to Russell that he would like to marry at the turn of the year, and the latter's generous offer to pay him twelve months' salary in advance, that he reckoned on being able to bring things to a head. Evidently while he had been absorbed in his night and day work, for the past interval, Russell had maintained unbroken communication with the Travers family.

It never struck Musgrave that no one is more reticent in alluding to visits of courtship than the bashful man, and forgetting his own lack of openness, he jumped to the conclusion that Russell had, grievously wronged him, and defrauded him of his rights. Without waiting for breakfast, he walked rapidly to the train and caught an early car for town.

Arrived at his office, he drew forth his books, with a view to ascertaining his precise financial position. Then emptying his bag, he pulled towards him the rough draft of Russell's will and was reminded of the envelope given him the previous evening, which thereupon met his gaze. He opened it. Inside was a cheque for £500, and a few lines telling him to credit that sum to the donor's account, as a token of gratitude for past services and expenses, and any balance might be considered as a small payment and contribution to his friend's domestic and business arrangements.

He smiled scornfully as he laid this missive on the table and cursed the day he first met its author. But after all, he asked himself, was not love a thing beneath the consideration of a practical and ambitious man like himself? Could he not still be Russell's—and Helen's—friend? Were not all men brothers so long as money aims were not antagonistic? His instincts revolted against such a theory, and he felt that he hated Russell malevolently, and the girl almost equally. Mental and moral precepts are valueless where the passions are concerned. Altruism, or spiritual love, is all very well, but where is the warm-blooded man who could sacrifice his idol for the benefit of another lover? Would he not rather sacrifice the whole world for her? People who asserted that the true basis of sex-attraction should be a spiritual rather than a physical one, could not realize what they were discussing. If sex-love were really spiritual it must be capable of existing apart from sex, but where was the lover who could survive the metamorphosis of his loved one's soul into a male transfiguration or into the body of a deformed or aged woman; and where was the spiritual but human lover who could with unaltered sentiments view his beloved one's sexual possession by another? It was absurd.

His sombre musings were interrupted by the entrance of his office-boy. "Here, Tom, go to the bank and lodge this cheque," he said, "and bring back my passbook; sharp!" Presently the lad returned and handed Musgrave a note from the manager which ran.

"Dear Sir—
Re Mr. Russell's cheque: we have placed this to your suspense account for the time being, but we fear that it will be impossible to credit you therewith, as, according to this morning's Herald, it seems that the drawer, Mr. V. Russell, died last night; and, as you are doubtless aware, the cheques of deceased persons are not recognized in banking procedure. Trusting that this will prove but a temporary inconvenience I am, etc., etc."

Russell dead! Good heavens, how sudden! Evidently their late conversation had been the means of bringing about the very catastrophe he dreaded. Mentally he reviewed all the circumstances of this singular case. Then there flashed through his brain a swiftly formed decision. He alone knew of Russell's peculiar physique. Let him die.

Later, another idea occurred to him. He would go and see Helen and ascertain for himself whether he had any chance as a suitor provided that his rival was out of the road. He seized his hat and stepped forth into the street.

Pondering over the pros and cons of the affair, he strolled up King Street, and proceeding absentmindedly, was about to turn the corner of Elizabeth Street, when Fate took up the running. Moving mechanically, he did not notice a steam-tram speeding in his direction; he vaguely felt that a cable-car was following behind in his track. Suddenly a hansom cabman, who was driving at a rapid pace, shouted his disconcerting warning, "Hi, there!" He stepped back startled. Next minute the tram struck him sideways, and amid a shout of horror from the busy pedestrians, he was dragged inextricably under its remorseless wheels. A medical man stepped forward and made a careful examination.

"Drive him to the hospital at once," he said, as he at length rose, and then noticing for the first time the victim's card, he exclaimed, "Stay, no; I will attend to this case myself;" and having by the aid of several bystanders lifted Musgrave into the same cab which had caused all the trouble, he directed the driver to bring them to Musgrave's address.

"Is it serious?" asked a lady.

"He has concussion of the brain," was the answer. "Lucky if he ever gets over it; but at the best he can't regain his faculties for a couple of months at the earliest. Drive on, cabby."

III. TO FACE WITH THE DEAD

Nearly three months later, when Christmas was at hand, Musgrave regained consciousness, and opened his eyes to find his mother leaning over his bedside. From her he learned that Helen had called several times with messages of sympathy and solicitous inquiry, and also that Russell had been buried, a woman caretaker having been placed in charge of "The Grove," till Musgrave returned to sensibility. As no will had been found, the Curator of Intestate Estates was holding the property in trust. The office-clerk having discovered certain instructions left by his employer upon the table, on the morning of the accident, had communicated their nature to the proper authorities. Mrs. Musgrave was proceeding to give further particulars when the doctor called and remonstrated with her for talking business at so early a stage of his patient's convalescence. Before leaving, however, he assured his charge that his recovery—with ordinary care—should occur within ten clays or a fortnight. Musgrave was sorry that he had not died. Was it possible that Helen could come to love him by and by? Had she any knowledge of the contents of the rough draft of the will, which that fool of a clerk had handed over to the Intestates office? He wondered shudderingly how Russell died in his living grave, and for the following week passed a brain-racking and restless time. Helen came to see him daily. Always sympathetic and lovely in his eyes—as she told him that he was the only friend she had left now—the dread of losing her stimulated him to a definite decision. If he could only be *sure* that Russell was really dead! He had read cases of Indian fakirs who had suspended animation for over a year. He astonished his mother by asking her what kind of a coffin Russell had been buried in. At last, he was able to get about again. Then his overpowering desire to see for himself how matters lay culminated in the execution of his decision.

It was a very dark night, and his mother had gone to bed. Donning a light overcoat, and taking a box of matches from the cupboard, he stole noiselessly from the house, and walked towards "The Grove." He knew that by proceeding along the stonework at the side of the grounds, till he reached the cemetery wall, he could scale the latter obstruction by prizing himself against the angle of their intersection. It was very dark, and stillness reigned around, as he effected this manoeuvre, and made for the vault, which was dimly visible with its white coping-stone. Descending the half-a-dozen stops leading down to the paved basement, he struck a match, and found himself in a chamber about ten by twelve feet wide, with the roof almost touching his head. In the centre, and at about three feet from the ground, stood the raised sarcophagus. Placing his candle and matches at its corner, he essayed to lift the lid. Though heavy, it gradually yielded to his efforts, and slid aside. Nervously, he looked into the receptacle for the coffin. There it lay sure enough. What would he find when he opened that also?

Much to his astonishment, there was no unpleasant odour discernible. The coffin was evidently an ordinary hermetically sealed casket. Still there ought to have been some evidence of decomposition, he argued. Could he open it without a chisel? Almost unconsciously he tapped the case. It gave back a strangely hollow sound. Would the lid give at all? He attempted to raise it. Then occurred the unforeseen.

Leaning over and drawing the top of the coffin towards him with both hands, it came off easily. Filled with superstitious dread, he looked downwards—fully prepared to behold a spectacle which would test his iron nerves to their fullest limit. Paralysed with horror, he let the lid drop with a loud crash and simultaneously the matches rolled to the floor and a gust of air blew down the stairway, extinguished the candle. The coffin was empty.

IV. A GHASTLY STRUGGLE

Probably nothing more contradictory and confusing to the human intellect can be discovered than the extraordinary tendencies of the human senses. For instance, the writer is acquainted with a deaf-and-dumb girl, who will sit for hours watching anyone playing the piano, when she will press her forehead and hands against the woodwork, and delightedly intimate that she can "feel" the music. Another most remarkable case is that of a deaf-and-dumb man, who was instructed by his father—a late composer—in the theory of music and harmony, as thoroughly as it could be imparted from books. This man never touches a piano but give him a book of new music and he will at once sit down and *read* it, just as the ordinary lover of romance reads fiction. In fact, his role enjoyment lies in *reading* musical scores. Again, the sense of taste primarily depends almost invariably on the sense of sight. Given a number of different substances to taste in rapid succession, with the eyes shut, and any person will be unable to discriminate between tobacco and turbot; but in none is the sense of touch and taste more highly developed than in the blind, who in the ordinary sense see not it all. Variations in powers of the senses in individuals are as wide as the poles asunder. Experience has shown that the hawk tribe, when at a height in the air which renders them invisible to the human eye, can discern a mouse on the earth. Accordingly, the apparently supernatural powers of sense possessed by a few uncommon people need not excite abnormal wonder. The blind, and even certain animals for example, have been known to see "spirits," which to the average person are imperceptible. And yet there is an absolutely logical explanation of these phenomena. To the blind man there gradually arrives a development of the sense of touch described as "facial perception" by some scientists. The skin of the face receives a sensation of the resistance or compression of the air on approaching close to a solid body and warns the observer of the obstacle in his path. To him the varying sound of his footsteps on the ground tells him when he nears a post, the presence and height of a side-wall, and whether it is of stone, brick, or wood; and the solid buildings and walls give back a distant echo, which instantly ceases at the openings and crossings. This echo is always more or less present, but sighted people notice it only on a dark still night, in a very quiet street.

To him the slightest disturbance in the air is perceptible, and the approach of visitants from another world is immediately recognizable, through "face perception," which is undoubtedly a sixth sense. The blind perhaps see best of all the human species, and feel with the greatest acuteness.

Let us return, however, to Lawrence Musgrave, whom we left standing in the dark, in his victim's tomb.

Midnight had just finished striking, as the chimes from the Post-Office clock died away. The soughing of the wind through the trees above him had a more disquieting effect than would a fusillade of pistol-shots. The matches—he was certain—must have rolled to the other side of the catafalque. Suddenly he felt that he was not alone. A faint rustle issued from the stairway. He slowly turned his head and looked. A pair of gleaming eyes glowered straight down into his from the top. His heart began to thump and twang like an overstrung harp-string. In the darkness his breath was suspended, even the flow of his blood ceased, and thereby assisted the frightful silence. Presently the eyes, like the lamps of a doomed vessel, swept downwards, and at the same time he heard a light, soft step—the sound as of bare feet upon the stairway, and then upon the floor! He was terrified beyond the power to cry or move; he was like a man of lead. Doctors say that patients who have watched an impending and inevitable accident are always harder to cure than those whose injuries have arrived without warning: the dread of death, and not death itself, is the real horror of human existence. Musgrave now realized this. At last the hateful eyes disappeared, and he was about to stretch forth his hand and grasp the matches, which he remembered he always carried in his overcoat ticket-pocket, straining his eyes meanwhile into the gloom, but without daring to shift his feet or body, as he listened intently. Who, or what, had disturbed him?

All at once the eyes gleamed forth again, and this time quite close to him, just across the sarcophagus table, and a horrible gurgling issued from that direction, as a hot and foetid breath swept across his face. With a shriek he thrust his hand into his pocket, drew forth a match, and struck a light. Before him, on the ledge of the bier, he saw a terrible head, the head of an enormous satyr-like fiend, with protruding tongue and distended jaws. Terror, in its excess, now robbed him of all reflective faculties. Breaking-strain had been reached. With an appalling yell he dropped the match and, as a madman incited to fury, struck wildly at the staring eyeballs, but the blow falling into unresisting space, he almost dislocated his shoulder.

Then a heavy body hurled itself upon him with a guttural and blood-curdling ejaculation, and almost knocked him to the around. In an ecstasy of fear, he strove desperately to rid himself of the dreadful thing, which was tearing with teeth and talons at his throat, while its eyeballs were almost touching his own.

Insensately he writhed and fought giving vent to scream after scream, as the nameless terror tightened its grip, and the mocking eyes burned fiercer and fiercer. Soon his struggles weakened, and his cries subsided into a faint moan. After a stifled sob, and a final shudder, he succumbed to the merciless tortures of his frightful antagonist.

V. A MEDICAL MIRACLE-WORKER

"Your nerves must be in a very dangerous condition, my dear boy," remarked Dr. Macari as he thoughtfully regarded his wild and haggard-featured patient—a young man to whom admittance had promptly been granted although it was eleven o'clock at night when he called and sent up his name. 'Your father, when last I saw him, had a splendid constitution, but I hardly expected to meet his son under the present peculiar circumstances."

The visitor, who was none other than Victor Russell *redivivus*, resumed with a wan smile—

"Yes, but I've been through enough to kill half-a-dozen strong men. After I burst through my flimsy coffin—and it was fortunate that it happened to be one of those ready-made, gaudy concerns—I carefully replaced the lid, as I was anxious to discover why my friend hadn't kept faith with me. All the previous three months, during which I was intermittently conscious and unconscious of my fearful condition, and when I lay helpless in total darkness, it is a marvel that I did not perish from the mere horror of my state. It was night-time when I emerged from my dreadful sepulchre, and slowly made my way to the wall at the back of my house. With difficulty, owing to my stiffness and the encumbrance of my grave cerements, I scaled it, and proceeded through the backgrounds, where my Great Dane hound was chained. He was so overjoyed at seeing me that I thought he would break his chain, but as I had trained him never to bark, he did not raise a hue-and-cry, which was the last thing in the world I fancied at that particular juncture.

Everything was in profound gloom at the back of the house, not a solitary light glimmered, though I fancied I had noticed a shimmer when surmounting the garden wall. The back door was bolted. Going round to the front, I found that everything was locked with praiseworthy but inconvenient fidelity. I was on the point of ringing the bell when it occurred to me that it would be best—if I wished to succeed in my project of discovering the true reason of my late incarceration—to proceed cautiously. Reflecting that in my graveclothes I might terrify people out of their wits, I resolved to try a certain kitchen window, which I remembered having observed to be without a fastener. To my delight, the aperture was unguarded, and I speedily hoisted myself into the premises. Although it was summer-time, and the night was warm, I felt cold. Having no boots to remove, I stole carefully upstairs to my room. No one seemed to be in the house. My room door was unlocked, and I found things untouched, but not a sign of a match could I find anywhere. At last, I came across a lucifer in an old pipe-case, and I held it up when struck to the wardrobe mirror. Heavens, what a sight I presented! My beard had grown almost to my stomach, and a ragged moustache gave me the air of a veritable brigand. The match fell from my trembling fingers, and no other was procurable. The gas, I discovered, was turned off at the meter. Then it occurred to me about you, doctor, and I felt that immediate medical attention was necessary. Hastily putting on an old suit of clothes and providing myself with a hat and a pair of boots, I crept down-stairs, and closed the kitchen window after me. I couldn't very well let the dog loose, as that would arouse suspicion, but this time he was oblivious of past instructions, and emitted a single but dismally eerie howl. Then I walked swiftly away, caught the last train, and here I am. Now what is the best thing to do, doctor?"

"Well, I can guarantee that you won't have to undergo a similar experience again, Victor," replied Dr. Macari, "but you must stop here with me for the next few days and submit yourself entirely to my orders and treatment. Take this opiate and go straight to bed, and to-morrow we will commence your cure."

After Russell had imbibed the draught tendered to him, he followed his conductor to a comfortable bed in all adjoining compartment, and soon afterwards sank into a deep slumber.

Dr. Macari threw himself into his arm-chair preparatory to retiring for the night.

"A splendid subject for the demonstration of my powers," he said to himself. "To-morrow I will submit the whole of his system to a searching investigation by the Röntgen rays. The fools, if they had only known, the proof of death is easily obtained from that analysis alone. Afterwards I will hypnotize him and make him catalepsy-proof by suggestion. Once I can assure him that he will never fall into a similar condition of coma, he will be trance-proof. As for medicine, the only physic he will need will be that which he administers upon himself from himself. Whenever the dread of a living death recurs, he will go to the mirror and mesmerize himself into confidence again, by looking straight into his own eyes and repeating the prescribed formula, 'You, Victor Russell, are cataleptic-proof; Dr. Macari says so!'

"Ha! how the world of science moves," he muttered. "The drunkard is hypnotized into sobriety; the sex-maniac grows to loathe his former impulses; the kleptomaniac becomes honest; the insomniac snores in his heavy sleep. I have cured them all, and someday I'll cure the disease of death itself."

Then taking up his candle, he too sought the solitude and relaxation of repose.

VI. THE TOMB MYSTERY SOLVED

"And, Victor," said Helen Travers, after the lovers had been discussing the wonderful escape of her *fiancé*, "now that you are cured and, thank Heaven, have regained your health and strength, there is another curious matter which I have yet to tell you about.

"To-morrow will be Christmas Day, and the holiday season has reminded me of it. Do you know—no, of course, how could you, seeing that for the past week you have been closely imprisoned by Doctor Macari—that Lawrence Musgrave is missing, and can't be found anywhere?"

"How extraordinary! What can have become of him, dear?" exclaimed Russell.

"Well, it appears that three mornings ago, his mother went up to his room to see him, as usual, and found that he wasn't there. Somewhat surprised, she assumed that he must have gone for a stroll, but when dinner-hour arrived, and still he had not returned, she concluded that he must have gone to his office, as he had seemed recently much agitated about his affairs. When night came, and no tidings were received she grew very anxious, and finally communicated with the police. That was the day before yesterday, but so far nothing has transpired. It was positively ascertained that he had not been to the office, and nobody apparently had seen him. But this morning, when the milkman came round with his cart, he told my brother that he was sure he had seen Mr. Musgrave the other night, getting over the fence which borders your grounds. What do you think of that, Victor?"

"Why, that must have been only a couple of nights after I escaped from my tomb!" ejaculated Russell. "Let us take a walk over to "The Grove," and see whether the caretaker can give us any information."

"All right, dear," replied Helen, "but wait a minute while I put on my hat."

Ten minutes later they left the house and were on the road.

It was a beautiful morning, but is they neared the sheltered approach to "The Grove," and presently reached the sombre entrance of the building itself, both realized an unaccountable feeling of disquietude.

"You must leave this place, Victor, when we are married!" exclaimed Helen. "Its mere exterior somehow always gives me the shivers. Ring, like a good boy, and Mrs. Daniels, the caretaker, may perhaps be able to tell us something worth hearing."

After a little delay, the front-door was opened, and a tall, elderly woman eyed them interrogatively.

Helen introduced herself as a friend of the proprietor and stated that her companion was interested in the whereabouts of a gentleman who was missing, but who, when last heard of, was reported as having been rear "The Grove." On being asked whether she had noticed any one recently about the place, Mrs. Daniels hesitated. Then she observed that she might as well confess that she *had* seen something unusual.

"The other night," said the woman, with a mysterious air, "I had gone to bed, and not feeling very well, I, after a while, got up to open the window from the bottom, and to put my light out. My bedroom is on the second floor back, you see, and I had no fear of burglars. Well, it was a bright moon-light night, and I looked out, and leaned a moment on the sill, to catch a breath of air. Just then I distinctly saw a figure in white come up the grounds from under the trees. It did not make the slightest sound as it stepped under the window. There is a ledge over the first floor, below which it disappeared, and I waited, expecting to see it come out into view again, but it did not. Instead, I heard a stealthy gliding sound down-stairs, and I rushed into bed, and covered up my head with the clothes. Presently, up it came, right past my door, where it stopped. Then I fainted." Victor and Helen here exchanged glances.

"And what next, Mrs. Daniels? You haven't seen anything since, have you? What do you think it was—the late owner's ghost, eh?"

"Indeed, my dear lady," returned Mrs. Daniels, as she lowered her voice almost to a whisper, "it *was* my firm opinion that it was poor Mr. Russell's ghost, and I sent at once across the park for my little girl to come and keep me company; but I *have* seen it since, and that for the last three nights! Punctually as the clock strikes a quarter-past eleven, a tall man, dressed in a black frock coat, with a light Chesterfield above, comes up here and grimaces so hideously that it makes one's flesh creep. My little girl peeped through the key-hole last night, and said his face was awful. The features were frightfully distorted, and all bloody. As she looked, he moaned and then vanished.

"Only that I'd have forfeited my wages, I'd have gone into town and given notice, but now I don't care a button, and I'll clear out this afternoon, money or no money. Then, for another thing, the way that dog in the yard has been carrying on this last day or two is something awful."

"What's Turk been doing?" inquired Victor.

"I didn't know his name, sir," replied Mrs. Daniels, glancing discontentedly towards her questioner, "but he's a horrid-looking brute, and he's that savage that he frightens me dreadfully. When he was on the chain I didn't mind, but the other morning, when I came down, he was lying across the doorstep, all covered with blood, and with part of his chain hanging to his collar. I thought he'd been at the meat in the pantry, but I found that that was all right, so when the baker called, I got him to tie him up again. Not that he's really fierce with anybody, it's his looks that scare me most."

"How so? What harm can he do when he's tied up, Mrs. Daniels?" asked Helen.

"Well, he got loose a second time yesterday, and this morning he's broken his chain again. The strange part of it is that lately he won't eat anything, and there's a look in his eyes as though he were going mad."

"Will you let me see him please?" asked Victor insinuatingly. "I know the dog very well, and perhaps can tell you what is the matter with him."

"Certainly, sir; come this way," said the woman.

When the trio reached the out-houses, which were divided from the house by the usual wooden trelliswork, the dog made an eager bound, and would have sprung with fond exhilaration upon Russell, but he peremptorily ordered him to lie down. Sure enough, he was smeared about the head with dark clots of something, which if not of blood, appeared remarkably like it; and Helen drew her dress aside aghast, as she noticed that where his paws had dropped, they left several ugly-looking red marks.

"He runs to the cemetery fence as soon as anyone tries to get hold of him to tie him up," said Mrs. Daniels, "and I can't think what makes him go there. I know I wouldn't for a fortune."

Something apparently struck Russell's attention. He looked up hurriedly and spoke in an earnest tone.

"Wait here a minute with Mrs. Daniels, will you, dear?" he said to Helen. "I'll just go to the end of the grounds and see what his game is."

Without awaiting her consent, he started forward. Turk bounded delightedly along with him. Casting his eyes downwards, Russell noticed that all along the path leading to the wall there were tracks of blood, fresh and old, and crossing each other backwards and forwards. He quickened his pace, and with nervous energy scaled the wall. The dog followed, and immediately ran ahead and made straight for the tomb. Then Russell's heart began to beat violently. Slowly he approached the top of the stone stairway, which descended into the cavity.

What he had dimly suspected was there!

Lying on the bottom step was the figure of a tall man, whose face and hands wore as though battered and torn by furies. Only by the clothes did he recognize that this horrible, gruesome thing was the body of his former friend. The expression of its eyes, which alone remained in position, was such as he will never to his dying day forget. Evidently Musgrave had been dead some days.

Turk sprang up and wagged his great tail.

"Back, you hellhound!" shrieked Russell, as with one hand he strove to wave off the terrible animal, and with the other covered his face to shut out the appalling spectacle. A ghastly giddiness numbed his senses and stayed his feeble gesticulations. With a gurgle in his throat, he swooned heavily across the sward at the mouth of the tomb.

WHAT THE RATS BROUGHT

Ernest Favenc

Ernest Favenc (1845-1908) was born on 21 October 1845 at Wal-worth, Surrey, England, son of Abraham George Favenc, merchant, and his wife Emma, née Jones. He came to Sydney in 1864 and subsequently worked on stations in North Queensland while writing the occasional piece for the *Queenslander*. In 1878 Favenc led an expedition to prove the feasibility of a transcontinental railway to Darwin. His reports in the *Queenslander*, which funded the expedition, won Favenc acclaim. Soon after completing the expedition he settled in Sydney where he married Elizabeth Jane Matthews in 1880. Further expeditions followed, and he continued to write. His *History of Australian Exploration 1788-1888* was published to great acclaim in 1888, and is still a useful reference. From about 1890 he began to publish adventure and mystery stories, which drew on his outback experiences, in magazines like the *The Bulletin* and the *Australian Town and Country Journal*. He also wrote half a dozen horror and mystery stories for *Phil May's Annual* between 1899-1903. "What the Rats Brought" appeared in the Winter 1903 edition, and "On the Island of Shadows" appeared in Winter 1900.

It was during the prolonged drought of 1919, just about Christmas time, that the steamer Niagara fell in with an apparently abandoned barquentine about fifty miles from Sydney.

It was calm, fine weather; so, failing to get any response to their hail, the chief officer boarded her.

He returned with the report that she was perfectly seaworthy and in good order, but no one cold he found on the ship, living or dead.

The captain went on board and, being so close to port, he was thinking of putting some hands on her to bring her into Port Jackson, when a perusal of the barquentine's log-book in the captain's cabin made him hesitate.

From the entries it appeared that the crew had sickened and died of some kind of malignant fever, the only survivors being three men—a pas-senger, one sailor and the cook.

The last entry, which was nearly three weeks old, stated that these three had provisioned a boat and intended leaving the vessel in order to make for Australia, as the only chance of saving their lives, as they felt sure that the vessel was infested with plague.

The value of the barquentine and cargo being considerable, and the weather settled, the captain determined to take her into port.

He put three volunteers on board to steer her, took her in tow, and brought her into Port Jackson, and anchored off the Quarantine Ground.

On reporting the matter to the medical officer, he was ordered to remain at anchor until it was decided what course to take.

The season was very hot and unhealthy, and when the story spread it occasioned a slight scare amongst the citizens.

Both vessels were quarantined, and the barquentine thoroughly examined.

When it was found from the log that the deserted craft had sailed from an Indian port where the plague that had so long devastated Southern Asia was then raging furiously, the consternation grew into a panic.

It was determined to take the vessel to sea and burn her, for nothing less would pacify the public.

The claim of the owners and the salvage claim for compensation were rated, and the *Niagara* towed the derelict out to sea, set fire to her, and then returned to undergo a term of quarantine.

Nothing further occurred, and in due course the *Niagara* was released, and the people forgot the fright they had entertained.

The drought reigned unbroken, and the heat continued to range higher than ever.

Then, when the winter had passed, and the dry spring betokened the coming of another summer of drought and heat, a mortal sickness made its appearance in some of the low-lying suburbs of Sydney.

When it had grown to an alarming extent, grim stories got to be bruited about, and a tale that one of the sailors of the *Niagara* had told was repeated.

He was on watch the night before the vessel was to be destroyed, the two ships lying anchored pretty close together.

It was about two o'clock when his attention was drawn to a peculiar noise on board the ship.

He listened intently, and recognised the squealing of rats, and a low pattering noise as though all the rats on the ship were gathering together.

And so they were.

By the light of the moon his quick eyes detected something moving on the cable

The rats were leaving the ship.

Down the cable they went in what seemed to be an endless procession, into the water, and straight ashore they swam.

They passed under the bow of the *Niagara*, and the sailor declared it seemed nearly half an hour before the last straggler swam past.

He lost sight of them in the shadow of the shore, but he heard the curious subdued murmur they made for some time.

The sailor little thought, as he watched this strange exodus from the doomed ship, that he had witnessed an invasion of Australia portending greater disaster than the entrance of a hostile fleet through the Heads.

The horror of the tale was augmented by the fact that the suburbs afflicted were now haunted by numberless rats.

People began to fly from the neighbourhood, and soon some of the most populous districts were empty and deserted.

This spread the evil, and before long was universal in the city, and the authorities and their medical advisers at their wits' end to cope with and check the scourge.

The following account is from the diary of one who passed unscathed through the affliction. Strange to say, none of the crew of the *Niagara* were attacked, nor was the boat with the three survivors ever heard of.

* * * *

The weather is still unchanged

It seems as though a cloud would never appear in the sky again.

Day after day the thermometer rises during the afternoon to 115 degrees in the shade, with unvarying regularity.

No wind comes, save puffs of hot air, which penetrate everywhere.

The Harbour is lifeless, and the water seems stagnant and rotting.

And now, dead bodies are floating in what were once the clear sparkling waters of Port Jackson.

Most of these are the corpses of unfortunates, stricken with plague-madness, who, in their delirium, plunge into the water, which has a fatal fascination for them.

They float untouched, for it is reported, and I believe with truth, that the very sharks have deserted these tainted shores.

The sanitary cordon once drawn around the city has long since been abandoned, for the plague now rages throughout the whole continent.

The very birds of the air seem to carry the infection far and wide.

All steamers have stopped running, for they dare not leave port, in case of being disabled at sea by their crews sickening and dying.

All the ports of the world are closed against Australian vessels.

Ghastly stories are told of ships floating around our coasts, drifting hither and thither, manned only by the dead.

Our sole communication with the outer world is by cable, and that even is uncertain, for some of the land operators have been found dead at the instruments.

* * * *

The dead are now beginning to lie about the streets, for the fatigue-parties are over-worked, and the cremation furnaces are not yet available.

Yesterday I was in George Street and saw three bodies lying in the Post Office Colonnade. Dogs were sniffing at them; and the horrible rats that now infest every place ran boldly about.

There is no traffic but the death-carts, and the silence of the once noisy street is awful.

The only places open for business are the bars; for many hold that alcohol is a safeguard against the plague, and drink to excess, only to die of heat-apoplexy.

People who meet look curiously at each other, to see if either bears the plague blotch on the face.

Religious mania is common.

The Salvation Army parade the streets praying and singing.

The other day I saw, when kneeling in a circle, that two of them never rose again. They remained kneeling, smitten to death by the plague.

The "captain" raised a cry or "Hallelujah! More souls for Jesus!" and then the whole crew, in their gaudy equipments, went marching down the echoing street, the big drum banging its loudest.

As the noise of their hysterical concert faded round a corner, a death-cart rumbled up, and the two victims were unceremoniously pitched into it, one of the men remarking, "They're fresh 'uns this time, better luck!"

Such was the requiem passed on departed spirits by those whose occupation had long since made them callous to suffering and death.

All the medical profession stuck nobly to their posts, though death was busy amongst their ranks; and volunteers amongst the nurses, male and female, were never wanting as places had to be filled.

But what could medical science do against a disease that recognised no conventional rules, and raged in the open country as it did in the crowded towns?

Experts from Europe and America came over and sacrificed their lives, and still no check could be found.

All agreed that the only chance was in an atmospheric disturbance that would break up the drought and dispel the stagnant atmosphere that brooded like a funeral pall over the continent.

But the meteorologists could give no hope.

All they could say was that a cycle of rainless years had set in, and that at some former time Australia had passed through the same experience.

A strange comet, too, of unprecedented size, had made its appearance in the Southern Hemisphere, and astronomers were a loss to account for the visitor.

So the fiery portent flamed in the midnight sky, further adding to the terrors of the superstitious.

It was during one night, walking late through the stricken city, I met with the following adventure.

My work at the hospitals had been hard, but I felt no fatigue. The despair brooding over everyone had shadowed me with its influence.

Think what it was to be shut up in a pest-city without a chance of escape, either by sea or by land!

I wandered through the streets, Campbell's lines running in my head, "And ships were drifting with the dead to shores where all was dumb."

Suddenly a door opened, and a young woman staggered out, and reeling, almost fell against me.

I supported her, and she seemed to somewhat recover from the frightful horror that had apparently seized her.

She stared at me, then said, "Oh! I can stand it no longer. The rats came first, and now hideous things have come through the window, and are watching his breath go out. Are you a doctor?"

"I am not a doctor," I answered, "but I'm one of those who attend to the dying. It is all we can do."

"Will you come with me? My husband is dying, and I dare not go back alone, and I dare not leave him to die alone. He has raved of fearful things."

The streetlamps were unlighted, but by the glare of the threatening comet that lit up the heavens I could see her face, and the mortal terror in it.

I was just reassuring her when someone approaching stopped close to us.

"Ha, ha!" laughed the stranger, who was frenzied with drink; "another soul going to be damned. Let me see him. I'll cheer him on his way," and he waved a bottle of whiskey.

I turned to remonstrate with the fellow, when I saw a change come over his face that transformed it from a frenzy of intoxication into comparative sobriety.

"Your name, woman; your husband's name?" he gasped.

As if compelled to answer, she replied,

"Sandover, Herbert Sandover."

"Can I come too?" said the man, addressing me in an altered tone. "I know Herbert, knew him of old; but his wife doesn't remember me."

"Keep quiet, and don't disturb the dying," I said; and giving my arm to the woman, went into the house.

We ascended the stairs and entered a bedroom; the rats scampered, squeaking, before us.

On the bed lay a man, plague-stricken, and raving in delirium.

No wonder.

On the rail at the head of the bed and on the rail at the foot sat two huge bats.

Not the harmless Australian variety that lives in the twilight limestone caves; nor the fruit-eating flying-fox; but a larger kind still, the hideous flesh-feeding vampire of New Guinea and Borneo.

For since Australia became a pest-house the flying carnivora of the Archipelago had invaded the continent.

There sat these demon-like creatures, with their vulpine heads and huge leathery wings, with which they were slowly fanning the air.

And the dying man lay and raved at them.

Disturbed by our entrance, the obscene things flapped slowly out of the open window, and the sick man turned to us with a hideous laugh, which was echoed by the strange man who had joined us.

"Herbert Sandover," he said, "you know me, Bill Kempton, the man you robbed and ruined. I'm just in time to see you die. I came to Australia after you to twist your thievish neck, but the plague has done it. Grin, man, grin—it's pleasant to meet an old friend."

I tried to stop him, but vainly; and from the look on the dying man's face, I could see that it was a case of recognition in reality.

The woman had sunk upon her knees and buried her head in her hands.

Kempton still continued his mad taunting. Taking a tumbler from the table he poured some whiskey into it and drank it.

"This is the stuff to keep the plague away," he shouted; "but you, Sandover, never drank. Oh no! too clever for that. Spoil your nerve for cheating. But I'll live, you cur, and see you tumbled into the death-cart."

So he raved at the dying man, and one of the great vampires came back and perched on the window-sill.

Raising himself in bed by a last effort, Sandover fixed his eyes on the thing, and screamed that it should not come for him before his time.

As if incensed by his gestures, the vampire suddenly sprang fiercely at him, uttering a snarl of rage.

Fixing its talons in him and burying its teeth in his neck, it commenced worrying the poor wretch and buffeting him with its wings.

Calling to Kempton, I rushed forward to try and beat it off, but its mate suddenly appeared. Quite powerless to aid, I picked up the woman, who had fainted, and carried her out of the room.

Kempton, now quite mad, continued fighting the vampires, but at last, torn and bleeding, he followed us into the street.

I was endeavouring to restore the woman, and he only stopped to assure me that the devils were eating Sandover, and then reeled off.

When the woman came to her senses I left her by her own request, to wait till the Death-Cart came round.

I called there the next morning, but never saw her again.

Amidst such sights and scenes as these the summer passed on, burning and relentless.

The cattle and sheep were dying in hundreds and thousands, and it looked as though Australia would soon be a lifeless waste, and ever to remain so.

* * * *

One morning it was pasted up that news had come from Eucla that the barometer there gave notice of an atmospheric disturbance approaching from the south-west.

That was all, and no more could be elicited.

The line-men at the next station started to ascertain the cause of the silence; and after a few days they wired to say that they had found the men on the station all dead.

But the self-registering instruments had continued their work, and the storm was daily expected from Cape Leuwin.

The days preceding our deliverance from the pest were some of the worst experienced; as though the approaching storm drove before it all the foul-brooding vapours that had so long oppressed us, and they had assembled to make a last stand on the East coast.

One morning I felt a change, a cool change in the air.

Going into the street, I saw, to my surprise, many people there, gathered together in groups, and gazing upwards at a strange sight.

The vampires were leaving the city.

Ceaseless columns of them were flying eastward, and men watched them with relieved faces, as though a dream of maddening horror was passing away.

Then came a sound such as must we been heard in the quaint old city of legendary lore when the pied piper sounded his magic flute.

The pest rats were flying.

Forth they came unheeding the people who stood about, and Eastward they commenced their march.

All that day it continued, and some reported that they plunged into the sea and disappeared.

At any rate, they vanished utterly, and with them other loathsome vermin that had been fattening on the dead and the living dead.

Everyone seemed to see new life ahead.

Men spoke cheerily to each other of adopting means of clearing and cleansing the city, but that work was taken out of their hands.

That night the cyclonic storm that had raged across the continent burst upon us. All the long-dormant forces of the air seemed to have met in conflict.

For three clays its fury was appalling. The violent rain and constant thunder and lightning added to the tumult.

No one stirred out during those three days of tempest and destruction.

Nature in her own mighty way had set to work to purge the country of the plague.

It was while this storm was at its fiercest that the Post Office tower and the Town Hall tower were shattered and hurled in ruins to the ground. No one, so far as I know, witnessed the catastrophe.

The morning of the fourth day broke calm, clear and beautiful.

At midnight the tempest had lulled; and when daylight came, the sun rose in a sky lightly flecked with roseate morning clouds.

Accompanied by a friend, I started out to see the ruined city, and those who were left alive in it.

The streets still ran with floodwater, but the higher levels had pretty well drained off; and once they were gained, our progress was easy.

Martin Place was choked with the ruins of the tower, and many other buildings that had succumbed, while not a single verandah was left standing in any street. We went to the Harbour.

The tide was receding, carrying with it the turbid waters that rushed into it from all points, carrying with it, too, wreckage and human bodies.

A strong current was setting seaward through the heads and bore out to the Pacific all the decaying remnants of the past visitation.

The deserted ships in the Harbour had been torn from their moorings and either sunk or blown ashore.

Wreck and desolation were visible everywhere, but the air was pure, cool, and grateful; and our hearts rose in spite of the difficulties that lay before us, for the looming horror of the plague had been lifted.

* * * *

Of what followed, your histories tell you.

How the overwhelming disaster knit the states together in a closer federation than legislators ever had forged.

How from that hour sprung forth a new, purged, and purified Australian race.

All this is the record of the Australian nation; mine are but some reminiscences of a time of horror unparalleled, which no man anticipated would have visited the Southern Continent.

ON THE ISLAND OF SHADOWS

Ernest Favenc

This is the story told by Eugene Tripot, convict from New Caledonia, of what happened to him during the boat voyage when he had succeeded in making his escape.

He died in the hospital at Hong-Kong, insane, having lost his reason through the suffering and privation he went through on that occasion.

He had lucid intervals, during which he repeatedly told this story, and insisted on its truth.

He was rescued from a sandy islet on the outer edge of the Great Barrier Reef, off the coast of Northern Queensland, by a China steamer taking the outside passage. He had been cast away there for some weeks, living on trepang and shellfish.

Nothing was seen to in any way bear out this story.

* * * *

"Three of us alone between sea and sky—three men with a wolf inside each, wolves that looked at each other out of our eyes. Gronard crouched in the bottom of the boat, gnawing at a piece of wood; Pelrine sat at the stern, with his sheath-knife in his hand, digging savagely at the thwart; I was sitting in the bow.

"The sail flapped idly at every little swing and roll of the boat, just as it had flapped during the last fortnight, never once bellying out.

"Beside us three there was the sun—the sun that hated us so. Hot and eager it rose in the morning—hot and eager to drink our blood. With anger that we should be still alive, it set in the evening. Gronard cursed the sun, Pelrine cursed the sun, and I cursed the sun.

"That was all we did from morning to night. It was all we had to do. It is bad for men to sit silent all day, only speaking to curse the sun, for then the wolf rages and breaks out.

"It broke forth in Pelrine, sitting digging his knife in the thwart, and suddenly he sprang upon Gronard. He would have sprung upon me, just the same, if I had happened to be next to him, for it was the wolf that sprung, not Pelrine, for Pelrine was always a good-hearted man.

"Gronard was taken at a disadvantage, but he was the strongest of us three, and grappled with Pelrine, and in the struggle the boat lurched, and both fell over the side. I saw them go down, down, in the clear water, turning and twisting, and all I thought was, 'They do not feel the sun down there.'

"They never rose, for I saw what looked like long flashes of white light dart at them, and I knew that the sharks that had kept us company so long had them for their sport at last.

"When I raised my head there was a ripple coming fast across the water. If Pelrine's wolf had not broken out just then both he and Gronard would be alive now. I went to the tiller and the sail filled, and the boat moved for the first time for two weeks.

"West was our course—anywhere west, to the great continent that reached for two thousand miles north and south. Merrily blew the wind, and in the evening there were clouds ahead, and a black thunderstorm flashed and muttered in the distance. All through the night there was the pleasant rip and gurgle of water.

"But the wolf gnawed still.

"Morning! and ahead of me I saw white water, but no land. It mattered little whether I died by the wolf or the wave, and I kept straight on. As I got closer to the breakers, I saw there was a low, sandy mound visible, with some low bushes growing on it, and to this I steered.

"The northern side looked to be the smoothest, and I endeavoured to make that side; for though there was no sea, the wind having been but light, the sweep and rush of the Pacific rollers was tremendous, and when they broke upon this submerged wall of coral and recoiled broken and shattered, the very air seemed to tremble.

"At the northernmost point of the islet the turmoil seemed less, though the rollers were as big; but the passage was deep enough to let them pass through and expend their fury in a sullen swirl over the flats beyond.

"As I approached, I was caught in one of the rollers and swept on with it, with great force and fury. We mounted on the crest of it, and then fell with a rush that made me feel sick. Next moment the boat was dashed on the beach, and I was flung unhurt beside it.

"Then the roller swept back and left us, the broken boat and myself, on the sand.

"It was a miserable little patch of dry land indeed, and when I had rested a little I commenced to examine it, first directing my steps to the low bushes on the highest part. I found it to be a ring of scrub surrounding a depression filled with water. I crashed through the bushes and stooped to drink, scarcely daring to hope that it would be fresh. It was, or at least fairly so, for the spray from the breakers drifted over into it.

"I drank, and the wolf was quiet for a bit, while I lay on the sand and looked around. A line of tossing white ran north and south—the line I had passed through—but to the west was a still sea, broken here and there in patches of shining foam, but mostly still, and of light, transparent green colour. The tide was falling, and by midday there were bare spots of coral showing.

"I went down and searched for shellfish, or anything left by the tide. I found what was better than all—plenty of the sea-slugs known as trepang. I soon had a quantity collected, and having the means of making a fire, I spent the rest of the day in cooking and eating; and again the wolf crouched for a time.

"That night I slept sound after the cramped space of the boat, and when the wolf clamoured at daylight I arose. It was a strange thing to be standing there alone on that patch of sand, with the wall of tireless breakers on one side, that looked far above me, as though when they fell they would overwhelm my refuge.

"I fed on trepang, and passed the day idly resting, for now I had tamed the wolf within me. I longed for my companions, but they were in the bellies of the sharks.

"When darkness came, I lay down and slept, but awoke in the middle of the night, dreaming that I heard strange sounds, I listened, and at first heard nothing but the boom and crash of the breakers; but presently I heard low voices and the crunching tread of feet on the coral sand. I leapt to my feet but could see nothing. I called, but got no answer; and still, distinctly, I heard the sound of voices and the tread of feet.

"I hastily traversed the island, but saw nothing, only at times I heard the voices talking, and though I called and called again, none answered me. Then there was silence, and plainly I heard the click and grind of steel meeting steel, the tramp, and quickened breathing of two combatants; and still I saw nothing.

"Suddenly the clashing came quicker and sharper, as though there was a hotly contested rally, and following it came a fall on the sand, and then a cry in a woman's voice, and a peal of musical laughter. There was low whispering, and the steps died away, heavy and slow, as though they carried a burden, and then there was no sound but the thunder of the tireless billows.

"I scarcely felt frightened—I had been living far too long hand in hand with death. I felt curious, and if terrified at all it was more at the idea that it had been a fancy of my brain—that it was my wits were failing me, for I knew well that loneliness serves some men thus.

"All was quiet for the remainder of the night, and in the morning, there were no signs nor tracks of any person but myself.

"Now, although I heard the voices, the tongue that they spoke in was strange to me, but I thought it was Spanish, from the way that I had heard old comrades of mine talk together who were Spaniards.

"Next night the ghosts were there again, and once more the duel, as I took it, was fought on that solitary speck of sand in the great ocean, to the music of the surf.

"That was a strange, unreal life—by day to pace the sandy shore and listen to the waves, and talk to myself, or gather and cook the trepang that supported me; by night to hear the crunch of the sand under unseen feet, and the quick clash of the blades. But stranger still was to come.

"I bethought me, from what information I had gathered, that this reef was the great reef that lay off the coast of Queensland, and that inside, between it and the mainland, ships and steamers were constantly passing up and down.

"My boat was too shattered to admit of my trusting myself in it to the ocean, but could I not patch it up sufficiently to carry me in the still-water channels of the reef? I would only have to keep due west to come out somewhere on the edge of the frequented passage.

"To this end I took to exploring the reef westward as far as I could go during low tide. The second day I came across a submerged object lying on the edge of a deep channel—the wreck of a ship. At low water it was partly uncovered, and the gaunt ribs showed above the surface for some height. It was an ancient hulk, encrusted with marine growth and barnacles. Only the heart of the timber remained; but that was as hard as flint.

"They built stout ships in the days when she left her bones there. She was firmly wedged on the ledge of a reef and must have been carried to where she lay in some tempest of extraordinary fury. How many years had she been there, and of what nation she was, I had no means of judging just then.

"But day after day I visited her, and in time found that out; I mustered courage to dive down and examine her below the water-mark of low tide. It was not the depth that required courage, but strange things had found their home amidst the waving growth around her. The banded yellow and black sea-snakes of those parts swam in and out, hideous shellfish with staring eyes and long feelers hid amongst the beams, and, for aught I knew, some loathsome octopus might be lurking in his lair there.

"I pushed on farther and farther by degrees, until I found many casks still preserving their shape and outline, having something within that was of great weight. I burst one open, and inside was tarnished metal so covered with growth and slime that it was impossible to say what it was. After many efforts I broke off a portion of it to examine at my leisure. It was a lump of silver dollars, welded together by marine growth, and discoloured by long submergence.

"I sat aghast at the thought of all those casks there being filled with coin—silver coin—ay, and why not some of them gold? I stood ankle deep in the salt water and looked around. A sea of light and shadow, calm and glassy, of ever-changing colour. Beyond, the restless tossing wall of white froth and foam.

"I had wealth—all I desired of it—in my grasp; and this was my domain.

"Was ever man so situated? When my turn came to die, should I join those ghosts on the isle, who must have been the men who sailed on this treasure-ship. There was blood on these coins, else why were they here, why was that nightly duel fought, what brought this ship so far south of her course?

"I returned to the island and cleaned the coins I held, scrubbed them with sand, and picked them apart with the knife that Pelrine had dropped when he went overboard. They were Spanish dollars, dated 1624 and a few years later.

"In successive journeys I examined some more of the casks and found that one smaller one was full of gold, and doubtless there were more. It was better they should remain where they were, safer in every way, until I found a way out of my present position. Such a terrible position in every way, with untold riches lying beneath a few feet of salt water of no more value than the leagues of coral north and south of me.

"And if I escaped and gained my fellowmen, of what avail would be my treasure to an escaped convict, who might at any moment be seized and returned to the living death I had fled from. My wealth alone would draw notice to me if I sought to enjoy it. At any rate, I determined to try and escape. I could decide afterwards about the treasure. Perhaps I should be able to purchase my freedom with some of it.

"I determined to wait till the moon was full (it being then half), as it would enable me to make use of the low tide at all hours, and it would also allow me time to patch up my boat, which I commenced to overhaul that day.

"I slept soundly the first part of the night and awoke as usual at the tread of the ghosts. The moon hung low in the west, and I saw—yes, saw that night the apparitions that haunted that tiny isle.

"The night was clear, save for some angry-looking clouds in the east, and the setting moon shone with spectral light over the still, shallow waters of the reef. The tide was low, and the passage I had passed through practicable for a well-manned boat with a skilful steersman.

"But was it the ghosts I saw? Half a mile out, or less, lay a ship with lights both in her rigging and streaming through her ports. A boat lay off the edge of the island, and I thought I heard another rowing in from the ship.

"I had no fear, and approached the group gathered on the sand. They were talking seriously, and, though the language was the same as I had always heard, I could now understand every word as though it was my own.

"They took no notice of me as I came near; I spoke to them but received no answer; I laid my hand on one's arm, and I did not feel him. My sense of touch was dead, my voice was inaudible, my presence invisible. For the time being we had changed places, and the ghosts were the substantial beings and I the impalpable shape.

"There were five of them, all richly dressed in the fashion of two hundred years ago. One was an elderly man of dignified appearance, and the other, who seemed his opponent, was a very handsome young gallant.

"'Before we meet, Don Herrera, and I send your soul to keep company with those of all the traitors since Judas hung himself,' said the elder man in a voice of deep hate, 'I would say something that these gentlemen may remember concerning you.

"'You, a trusted officer of his Majesty, have tampered with the marines of my ship. You tempted them to mutiny, but your vile plot was discovered, and your dupes hung on the yardarm, where you, too, would be hung, King's officer though you be, and noble to boot, but that I reserved you for my own hand.

"'You, who came on my ship as an honoured guest, honoured on account of your standing as my Master's officer, although I knew you for a ruined profligate.

"'You, in your greed for the gold and silver in yon ship, conspired against me, led weak men on to their death, and, above all, sought to dishonour me in a way that only death will wipe out. I would not slay you on my own deck, for death by my hand only would suffice, but I vowed that the first dry land we saw should witness the death of one of us. This spot will serve, and we need not wait for daylight.

"'I call upon you all to hear that this man is a perjured traitor, whom I greatly honour by descending to cross swords with him.'

"The young man answered not, only by an insolent smile, then tossed his hat down, and drew his sword.

"During the time the captain was speaking the other boat arrived at the beach, and two people left and came to us, a priest and a woman. They stopped close to where I was standing, and I saw the most exquisite face illumined by the level moon that I ever saw in my life.

"The priest was dressed in the soutane and broad-brimmed hat of his profession, and looked ill at ease, but his companion flashed a bold glance from her dark eyes at the younger combatant that at once told me the guilty secret, and why the captain had not hung him at the yardarm but brought him to this patch of sand to kill him himself.

"The fight commenced, warily and cautiously at first, but the two men soon warmed to their work, and then I saw the murderous trick of the young man. He was forcing the old man round, so that he should face the deceitful glare of the setting moon. Bit by bit he accomplished his object; then there was a quick, sharp interchange, and the captain fell, pierced through the body.

"'Bravo!' cried the woman standing by me, and she laughed merrily.

"I shuddered, and the priest darted from her side and knelt beside the dying man. He, too, had heard that devilish laugh, and lifted his head and gazed at his destroyer. He spoke, and his voice was clear and distinct.

"'Behold the judgment of the wicked is close at hand. The gold you plotted for shall never be yours; the beauty you lusted for shall be food for fishes. You shall not linger long behind me.'

"He fell back, as the edge of the ghostly yellow moon kissed the water's edge, its dying rays lighting up the scene of horror, the silent men, the recumbent figure, the dark-robed kneeling priest, holding on high the crucifix; the white sand gleaming out from that great waste of water.

"Suddenly a flash of lightning, accompanied by a peal of thunder, made everyone start. The clouds had banked up in masses to the east and were covering the face of the heavens. The party hurried off to the boats, taking the captain's body with them, the white breakers were already leaping high, and they quickly pushed off.

"I watched them as they pulled to the passage and saw the rollers rushing towards them. Then the darkness fell, but out of that darkness rung out cries of despair, and high above all a woman's shriek, the death-shriek of the woman who had laughed at her dying husband. Next instant the tempest burst and caught the doomed ship. I saw her lights coming closer; saw them, then lost them; then saw them again, and then I knew that she was in the breakers.

"They beat her with successive blows, and hurled her into the passage, a dismasted wreck; hurried her on with the rushing water as the tempest burst in the blackness and fury inconceivable, hiding all things from my view.

"I opened my eyes to a soft, balmy morning, and found myself lying in my usual place on the sand. No sign of the recent storm was visible, my clothes were dry, the sea calm, and the surf lower than usual. Bewildered, I looked around, scarcely believing my eyes. I looked again at the sea, noting how impossible it was for that to have gone down in an hour or two, and as I looked, I saw a steamer.

"Instantly the uncontrollable longing to see my fellow-men seized me.

"I made my fire up with a mad haste, piled on it planks torn from my boat, and branches torn hastily from the bushes. A straight column of smoke ascended, and I was seen at once. The steamer stood in, and a boat was lowered. I rushed into the water to meet it. Fear, such as I had never felt in silent, lonely nights, overcame me.

"'Take me from the ghosts!' I cried, as I scrambled in the boat, and fell insensible.

* * * *

"This is a hospital, and they think me mad, but the wreck of the Spanish ship is there."

THE ODIC TOUCH

Hume Nisbet

Hume Nisbet (1849-1923) was born in Stirling, Scotland. At the age of 16 he went to Melbourne, and later travelled around eastern Australia, New Zealand and the South Sea Islands. He started writing while living in London under financial hardship in the late 1880s and produced 46 novels. His fantasy novels, such as *The Jolly Roger* (1892), *Valdemar the Viking* (1893), *The Great Secret* (1895), and *The Empire Builders* (1900) are Haggard-inspired potboilers. His short story collections, *The Haunted Station* (1894) and *Stories Weird and Wonderful* (1900), contain supernatural and fantasy stories that are worth seeking out. The following tale of the occult is from the earlier collection.

I had been working hard, too hard, to keep up with the fierce competition of modern times, striving to advance in my art, do something better than my last effort, and keep at bay the many enemies which a man unconsciously makes who is climbing up the hill of life and I felt wearied with the struggle and almost inclined to sit down and let who liked reach the summit before me, when I received an invitation to spend Christmas with my old friend Dr. Grignor at his place in North Wales.

Dr. Grignor had, twenty years before, introduced himself to me in rather a peculiar fashion, and since then, although we had not met often, we had kept up a pretty constant communication in which, as far as the obligations of friendship are concerned, I was entirely his debtor; for as he began by serving, so he continued to help, advise and warn me whenever I required either of those services the most, without ever giving me an opportunity of repaying one of those favours, but this I did not mind, because ours was the kind of friendship which sometimes exists between the strong and the weak, and which is of too fraternal a character to count favours received as a burden, for it is only when we begin to consider equivalents that our affection has become a limited emotion.

It was in Auckland, New Zealand, that we first met. I had landed there some weeks before, almost penniless and without much of an aim in life, when one night as I was sitting on the wharf, looking broodingly upon the moonlit waves and wondering, for what purpose Fate had driven me here, suddenly I felt a light touch on my knee, and on looking to that side saw a grave-looking man of about thirty-five, who had placed himself close to me, with his hand resting lightly and as if accidentally on my knee.

In my morose state of mind, I might have resented this liberty from anyone else, only as the delicate hand touched me I seemed to have found the clue I had been so long and vainly in search of. Auckland disappeared with its troubles, and I was tracing a probable future out of the silver ripples that danced before me; I also seemed to see the folly of my past and present life, with the unreality of those friendships which had led me astray. It was as if my soul had woke up for the first time, and was looking out of windows which had hitherto been closely blinded.

A momentary panorama swept before me of the past, present, and future while that hand rested upon my knee, then it was withdrawn, while I came back to my normal condition with a purpose added to my experience and began to study my stranger companion with a sudden interest.

He was a thin, sallow-faced man, with black eyes, and clean-shaven, and when he spoke, his voice sounded gentle and soft.

"Yes, you have been wasting your time here, for although Nature is bountiful to all men it is only the workers who can enjoy her gifts; you must leave to-morrow."

"I don't know you, sir," I replied, thinking about the impossibility of me leaving New Zealand without a cent to pay my passage anywhere.

"My name is Grignor, Dr. Grignor, and your friend if you will permit me to be so, John Gray, or rather I am your friend already; go on board that vessel to-night, which is loaded and ready to sail for England; you are expected on board as a passenger.

"But I have no money and only the clothes I sit in, Dr. Grignor."

"You will find all that you require when you get on board; mention your name, and the steward will show you your cabin and trunks."

It was like page out of the 'Arabian Nights' to me, the homeless, penniless and almost starving outcast, to hear that my desires had been accomplished without an effort on my part, and in a dazed way I looked towards the ship which he pointed out, forgetting to utter a word of thanks or enquiry as to how he knew me and his reasons for helping me in this extremity.

It was a fine clipper, moored alongside of the wharf and a little way from me, and after taking in her proportions I turned once more to my new friend, to discover the place vacant; he had left me silently while my gaze had been concentrated on the vessel, and although the wharf was a long one and at this hour almost deserted, I was astonished that he could have disappeared so quickly, and rose with an eerie feeling as if I had been conversing with a spirit.

It was not without a tremor of doubt that I crossed the gangway and made my way toward the cabin, at the companion of which I saw a figure smoking a cigar. It seemed ridiculous for me to be there, and I paused to think how I would announce myself, when the smoker, who turned out to be the steward, saved me the trouble by addressing me instead.

"Are you our passenger, Mr. Gray, sir?"

"Yes," I replied, my doubts beginning to give way to amazement.

"The captain is expecting you to-night, as we start early in the morning; you will find him below."

"And my luggage?" I stammered.

"Is all in your berth," answered the steward.

"Thanks."

I found the captain enjoying a late supper with his mates and one or two friends who had come to wish him *bon voyage*; my seat had been kept empty for me and they welcomed me with respect for I was the only passenger he had on this homeward passage.

Seeing my name on a card by the side of my plate, I did not trouble myself with any uncomfortable surmises, but murmuring a private prayer of thanks to God and my unknown benefactor, I fell to, with the appetite of a starving young man who had not encountered such a supper for many days.

Upon retiring that night the steward handed to me a sealed packet which had been left for me by my beneficent friend, Dr. Grignor, which, when I opened, I found to contain a purse with fifty sovereigns and a bunch of keys (the keys of the three travelling trunks which were ranged out for my inspection), and the receipt for my passage to London; so that I had no further need to bother my head about the position I was to hold on board ship, or the first months after I landed.

Perhaps it would have been better had this friend not acted kind Providence quite so completely, better for my independence I mean, yet I had done so little with my past freedom, that the change was a decidedly pleasant one to what my former uncertainty had been.

We had a fairly good voyage, taken all in all, with the tempests, doldrums, and calms, and at last I found myself with three well-stocked trunks in the great city where men come to carve their fortunes, which holds everything that a man can desire, which seems everything to him at the distance, and which swallows and wipes out so many hopes and visions.

With the fifty pounds which I possessed I fancied that nothing was impossible to me, and therefore I plunged recklessly into the battle; recklessly and with as much wisdom as a child might possess who has been left on a doorstep by his unfeeling or desperate mother.

I was once more alone, or fancied that I was, and with my own fate in my hands; the fifty pounds did not last long, although I was wonderfully penurious over the spending of it, yet it melted away while I tried to open door after door without success, until I came once again to the position that I had been in in New Zealand, with the River Thames to sit and watch instead of Auckland Bay. I was a failure.

One day, I was in the National Gallery, trying to comfort myself with the glories of Turner in lieu of breakfast and dinner, when I felt once more the odic touch on my arm, and, on looking, round, I encountered the deep, earnest eyes of my friend, Dr. Grignor.

"You require me once more, John Gray, therefore I have come to you."

"What is the use of it, Dr. Grignor?" I replied. "I have tried and failed."

"Not so, my friend, you have only begun, you have mastered a little of life, but you do not know your own powers yet, but that knowledge will come in time."

As he spoke, the blinds were once more lifted from the windows behind which sat my soul, so that I saw where I had gone wrong; I had been frantically pushing and crushing behind a crowd, all eager as I was to get into a narrow space, as we may see any day on Westminster or Blackfriars Bridges, the mass striving to get a half-penny omnibus, forty people seeking to get into the place which can only hold ten, and not one with the wisdom to stand aside and wait his chance or walk on. It was my selfishness and imitation which had made my efforts failures.

"Yes, the best way over the bridge is the way you make for yourself, without crushing over your neighbour; it looks the longest and most laborious, yet it is your own; take that, and you will reach the other side in plenty of time."

That was nearly twenty years before the day of my invitation, but I tried to follow the track, which was then pointed out by my friend, and wait patiently, while I worked steadily in the profession that I had chosen.

I never knew Dr. Grignor more intimately than on our first and second interviews; he came to me without warning at some serious crises of my life, and set me right after I had tried my own methods without success; until at last I grew to expect the quiet presence, and perhaps owned his supremacy by praying or unconsciously wishing for him at the desperate moment. I had experienced his wonderful gifts and beneficent mind so often, that at last I grew to depend entirely upon his help at the critical pause and went forward with the boldness of a blind man under the guidance of one who sees ahead for him, without questioning why the guide is taking all this trouble for one so incapable.

Slowly, and through innumerable difficulties, I had made my way, hopelessly stumbling on, under the impression that I was doing nothing all these long and weary years, that the world knew me not, and only at occasional times, when my friend came to me and with his touch made me see, for a brief second, the real progress which I had made.

At last, my hour had come, and the world that did not know anything about these many years of gnawing disappointments and delays, said that John Gray had risen with startling rapidity. My work was recognised at last, while it needed no lifting of the blinds to see the future now. I was a lucky fellow, people remarked, and friends gathered round me in shoals with smiling lips and congratulating words, yet with eyes which looked watchfully and strangely upon me, and at this point my friend came to me once more.

"You have reached the most dangerous period of your life, John Gray; the time when you must take your choice either to sit down contented with your prison walls and shaded windows, or else sit on the ruins and see all round you. Which will you have, contented illusion or relentless vision?"

"Which is the best for me, my friend?"

"Reality is always the best, although it does not give content."

"Then let me have reality," I answered promptly.

Dr. Grignor was a man of vast learning, and occult power, and I could not but regard myself as entirely his creation; he had watched over me for long years, enveloping me with his influence, without attempting to bias me in any way, he left me free to follow my own bent and only pointed out a fresh direction after the path which I had pursued had become hopelessly blocked up.

Time appeared to be no object to him, as far as I was concerned, and he was always ready to congratulate me upon my failures. Indeed, he seemed to be better pleased with these results than with the evanescent successes which served to flatter my vanity and cloud my vision.

I had no knowledge of the amount of his fortune, or from whence he obtained his money; it was only when the lack of money meant annihilation to my hopes, that he came to my rescue, and he never gave me more than just enough to cross the gap which yawned before me, for all the rest I was left to my own exertions; also until this Christmas which I speak about, he had not told me where or how he lived.

He left me after this conversation, pleased, I think, at my resolve to grasp knowledge rather than slavish contentment, and I went on with my work, satisfied that when I was ready, he would fulfil his promise.

Men said I was lucky, and I felt myself to be so, not because I was beginning to be recognised but because I had one so powerful at my back; true my talents were my own, but it was the proud consciousness of this secret power and supporter that imparted to me the patience which was so needful to ultimate success.

It might have been the fruit of long experience or some strange force which passed from my friend to me, but as I moved about nothing escaped my observation, and my instinct was almost infallible when I trusted to it alone. At this stage I could read the envy of those watchful eyes, and the hatred of those smiling lips which greeted me at every turn; I had only to touch the arms of the ones who were protesting and they at once began to tell me their real intentions towards me, my rivals and enemies revealed their plots against me, and told me what misfortunes had overtaken them since they began to work me evil. I was now walking through a world where men and women were ranged about me with crystal bodies, through which I could read their motives at a glance.

I had this power as long as I remained inactive and uninterested towards them, but with my passionate inclinations I had also the power of making this crystal opaque, so that I could not penetrate past the surface of those I flung my friendship over, and as I could not live without affection I found myself continually trying to crush my instinct and glean comfort from the affections, also continually being betrayed and frustrated and misunderstood. I would not look at the man whom I had made up my mind to like, until I had drawn over him the cloak of my affection, and therefore when he betrayed me I was enraged, whereas I need not have been; but it felt so lonely to be always reading minds and recoiling from them, that I preferred the after agony for the hour or two of comfort.

It was at the hour of my deepest dejection, that this invitation came from my one friend, Dr. Grignor. I had been clinging long to one of these opaqued crystals, a man who had a winning manner and a truthful mask, but who every hour unconsciously bared his falseness for my inspection; all round me I saw his accomplices and tools, as transparent as I could have wished, and while counteracting their conspiracies, which originated from him, I persisted in my affection and trust for him, making all sorts of excuses and going out of my way to change the semblance of affection into reality.

In vain I tried, out of pity, when I had no longer trust, to warm up the ice of that opaque crystal, and when, at last, I had to abandon him to the curse of his malice, for I had drawn from him, by my contact, all his powers of hurting me, I felt overcome with the struggle and isolation. He was doomed, I knew as others had been before him who had pitted themselves against me with this supernatural influence which had been about me since that night in Auckland. I had only to abandon him to his fate, and disaster would overtake him, which neither of us could stop after the fiat had gone forth.

A profound sorrow for the fate of this doomed man crushed upon me, as I took my place in the train bound for Wales, something akin to the grief which burdened the days of the Wandering Jew, when he left his unwilling curse behind him, a gloom of desolation in my heart, which was in harmony with the wintry day outside.

Through a landscape, beautiful in summertime, but now veiled by the swirling snow-storm, we swept as fast as steam could drive us, with the carriage shaking and swaying as the wild blasts, flake-laden, dashed against the windows, and covered them up with that white density.

Two men and one woman occupied the same carriage, and as I looked at the shivering objects through that obscurity, their actual features disappeared and I could see their spirits sitting nude before me, while they told me all their intentions and past actions.

The woman was going home to comfort the hearts of her aged parents and dazzle their eyes with her rich costumes and ladylike appearance, gained at such a fearful sacrifice; she had left her native village a servant-girl and was going back decked like a duchess, with a pack of lies which would send them to their graves happy and proud that they had such a daughter. As I looked at this poor, wrecked soul, preparing itself for the ordeal of deceit, it appeared to grow luminous with the brightness of its motives, and to warm with its unselfish affection that chill atmosphere.

One of the men was young, and had appeared good-looking at the first glance at his features, but as they disappeared, I saw the spirit sitting within him, old and shrivelled; he also was bent on a mission of deceit to his home circle, but there was no brightness about him.

The other was a sailor coming home from a long voyage, his spirit was that of a child without a care. I bent my head before the woman, and turned from the young old man, to play with the soul of the sailor.

At the station my friend met me with a dogcart, and together we drove through a wild country with the tempest of snow-flakes dancing round like white elves. His house was a lonely one, perched half-way up the sides of a mountain with the windows all to the front, while the back portion had been excavated into the hill, it was a long house of one storey and stood alone in the midst of a forest of pine and birch trees, just the kind of site which I would suppose a man like Dr. Grignor would fix upon as a retreat.

We were received by an Indian when we arrived, and after my friend had seen to the horse's comfort, we sat down to supper, still waited upon by the same dark-hued servant, who appeared to be the only other inhabitant of this singular household.

I knew that my friend had brought me for a special purpose to this place and therefore I waited anxiously to learn what he would say and do, thinking little about my surroundings or of what we were partaking. As soon as I had finished eating, he said as he rose:

"Now come with me, my friend, to my study."

I followed him passively to a room at the back of the house, which was rounded like a cave, with no windows; over the doorway by which we entered fell a thick carpet of oriental stuff, while in the centre stood a brazier containing live charcoal.

"Sit there, my friend," said Dr. Grignor, pointing to a stone chair near the brazier.

I sat down as he desired me, while he stood in front of me, as the Indian who had followed us threw something into the brazier which flamed up with a rosy light and filled the room or cave with a strange perfume.

"I have given you the gift of seeing things as they are, my friend, also the power to influence the lives of those who come in contact with you, for good or evil; hitherto it has been good to those who have befriended you, and evil to those who have wronged you; this is the natural plane of humanity, but you have now come to a point, where you can control these destinies as you may desire at a sacrifice to yourself. Look at both sides of the picture, and decide for yourself which gift you shall take, the gift of power or the gift of sacrifice."

As the doctor spoke, the Indian threw some fresh powder on the fire, and as I watched the flames rising and the perfumed smoke curling round like a silver frame, I saw a picture of my false friend destitute and in rags, with his starving children around him, while I crowned with success and surrounded with wealth.

"That is power and revenge," whispered my friend, while a thrill of triumph shot through me at the pleasant prospect, tempered with a feeling of commiseration for my overthrown enemy.

The Indian flung another powder into the flames and another picture rose up inside the silver-smoke-frame, my false friend surrounded by luxury and myself in rags watching his exalted state from the outside.

"That is sacrifice and abnegation," whispered my guide as the picture vanished, "Take your choice, John Gray."

Was it his presence which saved me, with the touch of his hand as it clasped mine after a moment of hesitation on my part, while my passions surged up, and ambition, with anger, gripped at my heart like the talons of a vulture, or had my twenty years of struggle prepared me for this test moment? As I made my choice the features of Dr. Grignor grew luminous with a divine light ere he disappeared in that silver mist.

TOLD IN THE 'CORONA'S' CABIN ON THREE EVENINGS

J.A. Barry

John Arthur Barry (1850-1911) was born in Torquay in England and came to Australia in 1870 to join the goldrush. His first collection of short stories, *Steve Brown's Bunyip and Other Stories* (1893) drew largely on his experiences in the bush. Most of his later collections were of sea stories and include *The Great Deep* (1896), *Red Lion and Blue Star, With Other Stories* (1902), and a volume of mainly reprint stories, *Sea Yarns* (1910). "Told in the 'Corona's' Cabin" is from *Steve Brown's Bunyip and Other Stories.*

THE FIRST EVENING

In the south-east trades, and the big ship moving steadily through the water with every sail full. Not a quiver of the tightly strained canvas, not the rattle of a reef-point, broke the stillness aloft.

A glorious evening in the South Atlantic, with the sun setting, as is often his wont in those latitudes, in a bed of crimson, gold and amethyst. The passengers, who had been watching the many-hued passing of the day-king, went below as the cool night breeze began to whistle with a shriller note through the top-hamper and the water to swish more loudly along the sides, and fall back with a louder plop. Very comfortable, snug, and home-like the Corona's cabin looked. It was a cabin, remember, not a "saloon."

There was nothing of the modern curse of varnish and veneer about it. Everything was handsome, also substantial, from the dark mahogany casing of the mizzenmast to the highly polished, solid panelling of rosewood, relieved with only a narrow gold beading. The cabin might aptly have been termed a study in brown and gold, so predominant was this combination. Even the curtains in front of each berth door were of brown damask, with gold fringe. The general effect, if a little sombre, was good.

Especially good it seemed this evening to the passengers as they came trooping in with talk and laughter; especially snug and home-like, with its three big swinging moderator lamps, its long table covered with odds and ends of female work, books, papers, etc., etc., its piano, and its comfortable couches scattered here and there.

The Corona's great beam had been utilised to some purpose, and, thus, her cabin was not, like the saloons of so many sailing ships, a sort of stage drawing-room, all white paint, gilding, glass, spindle-shanked chairs, and turn-over-at-a-touch tables.

The company suited the cabin. There was only a dozen or so of them, mostly middle-aged married folk, who had left their grown-up families in Australia whilst they took a trip "Home," and were now returning to their adopted country. Amongst them, however, were two or three single ladies of uncertain ages, bound to the Land of the Golden Fleece in search of fortune, even if it should only come in the shape of a husband. There was, also, Miss Amy Hillier, an Australian heiress in her own right, returning to her native land with an uncle and an aunt. This is another man's story; so that I am not going to take up space by a description of Amy Hillier's charms; suffice it to say here that she was young and pretty, and as good as she was young and pretty.

Wonderful to relate, the company of passengers fitted each other. Each seemed to have discovered in another his or her affinity, and, up to this, there had been none of the usual back-bitings, heart-burnings, and malicious tittle-tattle usually so inseparable from a sea voyage in a sailing ship.

Miss Hillier had seated herself at the piano, and was playing something from *Lohengrin*, when a remarkable-looking man, entering the cabin, doffed his gold-banded cap, and made his way to her side.

Strongly, yet gracefully built, upright as the royal pole, active in all his movements, one would have taken him to be scarce arrived at middle-age, but for the fact that his thick, closely cropped hair shone a dead white under the lamplight. His features were regular and good, albeit they wore, in general, a rather serious expression. Altogether, it was a strong, pleasant face, full of energy confidence, and the power to command.

As he rested one hand on the corner of the instrument, it might be noticed that, from wrist to fingertips, it was covered by the white cicatrices of long-healed scars. Despite his grey hair and disfigured hands, Captain Marion, of the *Corona*, Australian liner, was called by many people a handsome man.

"Sing me my favourite, please," asked the captain presently.

"On condition," was the reply, "that you will tell us a story in return."

"It's a bargain," said the captain. "I'll relate the legend of Vanderdecken, the Flying Dutchman. Thoroughly appropriate it will be, too, as we are just entering his domains."

"We don't want to hear about the Flying Dutchman," answered the girl promptly.

"Well, then," continued the captain, "what do you say if I tell you how

I was cast away in '69, on the coast of—"

"No, no, Captain Marion," interrupted she, smiling shyly up at him, "we don't want that either."

"Ah, I see!" exclaimed the captain, after a pause, "a conspiracy! Well," he went on, after a still longer hesitation, "I don't care much about it. The telling, I mean, of how I got this" (touching his hair) "and these" (spreading out his hands), "for, of course, that is what you wish to hear. It reminds me of a time I would rather not recall."

"No, Miss Hillier"—for the girl had risen in dismay and almost tears at her thoughtlessness and was attempting to apologise incoherently enough— "it doesn't matter a bit. Besides, I somehow feel in the vein for story-telling this evening; and as well that as anything else. With some passengers, I find that I must put a stopper on their curiosity rather abruptly. But" (with a grave smile and a bow to the group) "it being a rare thing, indeed, to meet so well-assorted and pleasant a party as we are this trip, I'll spin you the yarn, such as it is. And now Miss Hillier, my song."

"What would you like—the same as usual, I suppose—'The Silent Land?'"

"Yes," answered the captain; "your rendering puts, a new interpretation on Salis' words for me, and I seem to bear with me more strongly than ever the promise, as I listen, that he

Who in life's battle firm doth stand
Shall bear Hope's tender blossoms
Into the Silent Land!"

* * * *

"It is," commenced Captain Marion, the song finished, and taking his accustomed seat, whilst the others gathered round him— "It is nearly fourteen years ago that the strange, and what many may deem improbable, adventure happened which I am about to relate. I was then about twenty-two years of age, an able-bodied seaman on board a ship called the *Bucephalus*, belonging to Liverpool. It was my first voyage before the mast for, although I had duly served my apprenticeship with the firm who owned her, and also passed my exam as second mate, there was no vacancy just then open. They, indeed, offered me a post as third; but, knowing that I should be none the worse for a month or two in the fok's'le, I preferred to ship as an A.B. The *Bucephalus* was an Eastern trader, and on this trip was bound for Singapore and China. All went well with us until we entered the Straits of Sunda. Then, one afternoon, the ship lying in a dead calm off one of the many lovely islands which abound in those narrow seas, the passengers, chiefly military officers with their families, asked the captain to let them have a boat and a run ashore.

"He was a good-natured man and consented. Luckily for me, as it afterwards proved, the gig, a very old boat, was full of lumber, fruit, fowls, etc., procured at Anjer, and so the lifeboat, a stanch, nearly new craft, was put into the water instead.

"At the last moment someone suggested that a cup of tea might be acceptable on the island. Not tea alone but provisions for an ample meal were at once handed in, together with a keg of fresh water. This also was, as you will discover presently, another lucky or—ought I not to say?—providential, chance for me.

"With myself, three more seamen, and eight or nine ladies and gentlemen, we pushed off towards the verdant, cone-shaped island. Landing without any difficulty on a shell-strewn beach which ran up between two lofty and abrupt headlands, all hands, except myself and an elderly seaman known as Tom, jumped ashore and went climbing and scampering about like so many schoolboys out for a holiday. For my part, I had been on scores of similar islands, or imagined I had, and felt no particular wish to explore this one. Neither, apparently, did my companion. So, hauling off a little from the shore, we threw the grapnel overboard and prepared to take things easy, each in his own fashion, he with a pipe, and I with a book lent me by one of the cabin passengers.

"We made a rough sort of awning with the boat's sail, and I lay in the stern-sheets, my companion between the midship thwarts, under its grateful shelter. It was a drowsy afternoon and a very hot one. To our ears the shouts and laughter of those ashore came at intervals, gradually growing fainter as they made their way towards the summit of the mountain, for such one might say the island was.

"Presently, looking up from my book, I saw that old Tom was fast asleep, his pipe still in his mouth. Very shortly afterwards I dozed, and heard the book drop from my hand on to the grating without making any effort to recover it. I fell asleep in the broad sunlit day, between ship and land, in the motionless boat, with the voices of my kind still in my ears, and awoke in thickest darkness, moving swiftly along in utter silence, save for, at times, an oily gurgle of water under the bows. Not that I realised even so much all at once. It took me some time. I thought I must be still dreaming and lay there staring into the blackness with unbelieving eyes. Then I pinched myself and struck my hands sharply against the thwarts. But it was of no use. I could not convince myself that I was not the victim of some ghastly nightmare. Then the idea came into my mind that, although awake, I had suddenly become blind; that Torn had gone ashore for a stroll, and that the boat, drifting, had been carried out to sea by some current. Under the influence of this notion, I leaped to my feet, only to be at once struck down again, as if by a hand of iron. Although not completely stunned, I was, for a few minutes, quite bewildered. I could feel, too, that my head was bleeding freely. Sitting cautiously up, I called "Tom!" I listened intently, but nothing was audible save the faint gurgling sound of the water. I called repeatedly, but there was no answer. Suddenly I recollected that in my pocket was a large metal box full of matches—long wax vestas.

"Striking one I held it aloft and gazed eagerly about me. I thanked God that I was not blind. But, so far as I could see, I was alone.

"On each side, and a foot or so above my head, barely visible in the feeble glimmer, were swiftly passing walls of dripping rock, covered, in many places, with high clusters of shiny weeds. So amazed was I at my perfectly inexplicable situation that I stared until the match burned my fingers and dropped into the water, whilst I fell back quite overcome by astonishment and fright.

"Then, after a bit, I struck more matches. But things were just the same. Always the rocky weed-grown sides, sometimes within touch, at others seeming to widen out; always the rocky, dripping roof, sometimes at my head, at others out of sight; always the darkness, the hurrying boat, and the water like liquid pitch.

"Unable to see thoroughly over the boat, I presently crawled for'ard, feeling, as I went, under the sail which had fallen over the thwarts. As I feared, I found no one.

"Groping about, I picked up Tom's pipe. And then I feared the worst for him.

"The darkness was horrible. It was so thick that one seemed to swallow mouthfuls of it. The atmosphere was close and muggy, with a smell reminding me strongly of a tannery. Although lightly clad, I was bathed in perspiration as I half sat, half crouched, at the boat's stern, straining my eyes ahead, and now and again lighting one of my matches. Time nor distance had any meaning for me, now; and I have no idea how long I had been voyaging in this unnatural fashion, when there fell on my ears the loud threatening roar of many waters. Commending my soul to God, I laid myself in the boat's bottom. The next minute she seemed to stand nearly upright and then shoot downward like a flash, whilst thick spray flew in showers over me, and the imprisoned waters roared and howled with deafening clamour down the narrow chasm, so narrow that more than once, in her headlong course, I heard splinters fly from the boat's timbers whilst masses of dank weeds detached by the blows fell upon me.

"I now," continued the captain, after a pause, during which he glanced from the "tell-tale" compass overhead to the attentive, wondering faces of his audience—"I now gave myself up for lost, or, at least, imagined that I did so. But the love of life is strong indeed within us; so that when after shooting this subterranean cataract, or whatever it might have been, I found my boat once more steadily gliding along, ever with the same dull gurgle of cleft water at her bows, a faint ray of hope took the place of despairing calm. I was young, remember; healthy, too, powerful and agile beyond the common, and I felt it would be hard indeed to die like a rat in that black hole. What accentuated the hope I speak of was the fact that the lessening roar of the torrent I had just passed sounded as if directly overhead. In vain I told myself that it was but a deceptive echo. Hope would have her say, and buoyed me up, though ever so little, with the idea, incredible as it seemed, that this horrible underground river had doubled back beneath itself and was making for the sea once more. It has well been said that drowning men will clutch at straws! This one, indeed, was soon to fail me; for presently, to my utter despair, the noise of tumultuous waters ahead gave warning of another cataract—another, or the same one, for, what with the din and the darkness, I became quite confused. The passage was a repetition of the last one, only, if anything, rougher; and, crushed in spirit, all courage flown, I sank back, listening to the rush of the falling water dying away overhead again. Was I, I wondered, descending to even lower depths of earth's bowels in this fashion, or merely driven to and fro at the caprice of some remorseless current in what was to prove my tomb! I believe that, for a time, under the stress of ideas like this, my mind wandered; for I have a vague remembrance of singing comic songs, of shouting defiance to fate, the darkness, and things generally; behaving, in fact, like the lunatic I must have become. Whether I descended any more rapids or not I cannot say. I have no recollection whatever of the last part of my strange journey. When, however, I came to my sober senses again I was at the end of it. The boat was motionless, and I was standing upright in her."

At this point in the captain's story, and while the interest of his bearers was at its height, the chief officer came quietly in, and, catching his superior's eye, as quietly made his way out again.

Now, four bells struck, and the captain exclaimed, "What, ten o'clock already! My yarn has somewhat spun itself out, and I'm afraid the rest must keep for another evening."

At this there was quite a chorus of remonstrance. "It was cruel to have excited their curiosity and leave it unsatisfied," was the general verdict.

"No sleep for me to-night," said Miss Hillier; "I shall be wandering through that horrid place in my thoughts and puzzling my brain to discover how you got out, unless I know the sequel."

"It grieves me to think of your disturbed rest," replied the captain, with a bow and a quizzical smile, "although honoured by the cause of it. I am afraid, however, I must refuse even you. I saw heavy weather just now in Mr Santley's eye; and the ship, you know, before all."

Then the sound of ropes thrown heavily on deck was heard, together with tramp of feet and shouting, the ship heeled over, and the captain went out, and was not again seen that night by his passengers.

THE SECOND EVENING

Close-reefed topsails, with a wild, high sea, met on 'rounding the corner,' did not prevent the Corona's passengers from appearing the next evening to hear the continuation of the captain's story.

"Well," he remarked, as he took his seat, "this yarn of mine seems to bring us luck, judging by the way we exchanged our trades last night for this rattling westerly breeze that is now taking us round the Cape so nicely. I think I left off my story," continued the captain, "as the boat came to a stop in her travels, through the darkness."

"I had recovered from my temporary fit of madness and was standing up. I was trembling violently, and my limbs felt cramped and stiff. I fancy I must have been a long time on the journey, for I was sick and faint, principally from want of food. The air, though still heavy and warm, was not so oppressive as it had been. But the former silence was broken by the most unearthly noises imaginable, sobbings, deep cavernous groans, and hoarse whistlings resounded on every side. For a long time, I did not stir. I just stood listening with all my ears and expecting every moment that something awful was going to take place.

"After a while, slightly reassured and feeling the boat's bows scraping some hard substance, I crept into them, and putting out my hand, and groping about alongside, felt a mass of smooth honeycombed stone. Striking a match, the possession of which, in my confused state of mind, I had almost forgotten, I got hold of the painter and took a couple of turns around a projecting ledge of rock.

"Then I scooped up a handful of water and tasted it. It was as bitter as gall, also quite lukewarm. Happily, that in the breaker was unspoiled. Rummaging about, I found the case of eatables also intact; and, sitting there in profound darkness, made a meal of cheese and white biscuits, listening between the mouthfuls to the mysterious noises, whose origin, however, I was now enabled pretty well to guess at.

"It was very warm, and the tannery smell more powerful than ever. A sensation of surrounding vastness and space, however, was with me as opposed to the confined cramped feeling of being in a narrow channel, such as I suppose myself to have emerged from. Now, I could stand upright and thrust an oar out and upwards without touching anything; and, shouting aloud, the sound went echoing and thundering away over the surface of the water with reverberations lasting for minutes.

"I can take you into that place," continued the captain impressively, "and tell you about it as far as my poor words will serve. But I cannot tell you my feelings. At times I almost imagined that I was in Hades, and that the ceaseless noises about me were the cries and groans of lost souls therein. At others, a wild, forlorn hope would seize me, that, it might all turn out to be only a horrible dream, and that I should presently awake to see God's dear sun shining brightly on the gallant ship and the green island once more. It had all happened with such startling rapidity, the transformation had been so utter and complete, that to this day I wonder I did not become a raving madman, and so perish miserably down there in the depths. But God in His infinite mercy took pity upon me, and brought me at the last out of such a prison as it is given to few men to see, much less escape from.

"Like the majority of seafarers, I, in those days, seldom troubled my head about what is vaguely called 'religion.'

"The careful and pious teachings of my childhood had been forgotten almost wholly. But, in that awesome place, in solitude and misery, bound with darkness of Scripture, "that might be felt," many things came back to me; and, kneeling down, I clasped my hands and prayed fervently that I might be saved out of the valley of the shadow of death which encompassed me. Feeling better and stronger, I took my sheath-knife, and with it cut away at one of the oars until I had quite a respectable pile of chips. Placing this on the rock alongside, I set it on fire, and soon had the satisfaction of seeing it blaze cheerfully up and, for a few yards, dispel the darkness. I kept adding fuel from the same source, with the addition of a couple of stretchers, until I had a good-sized fire. By its light I saw that I was on a flat rock some twenty feet in circumference. Round about were other islets, shaped most fantastically. One, close to, resembled a gigantic horseshoe; another towered up, the perfect similitude of a church spire, into the darkness. At their bases were holes, into and through which the water, flowing and ebbing, produced the sounds that at first had so alarmed me. Look as I might, I could not distinguish the way I had come in, although I thought I could hear the steady pouring of a volume of water not far away. Breaking off a lump of the stone on which I sat, I examined it closely, and felt certain that it was lava. I hid seen such before at Mauna Loa, in the Sandwich Islands.

"Was I then in the womb of a volcano, extinct just at present, doubtless; but, perhaps, even now, taking in water preparatory to generating steam and becoming active? Somewhere in my reading I had dropped across an article on seismology, and one of the theories put forward came to mind as above.

"The idea made my flesh creep!

"I seemed to feel the air, the water, and my lump of lava getting hotter and hotter.

"Hopeless as my case appeared, and almost resigned to face the end as I had become, even so, I did by no means relish a private view of the preliminaries to a volcanic eruption.

"Strangely inconsistent, you will say, but so it was. When face to face, even with the last scene of all, it seems there can yet be something of which one may be afraid.

"Meanwhile, my beacon blazed up brightly, and, peering around, I presently made out a pile of stuff apparently floating against the base of one of the nearest islets.

"Taking a flaring firestick, I got into the boat and sculled over to it. It was a heap of driftwood. Lowering my torch to examine the stuff more closely, I nearly pitched overboard, as, out of the reddish-black water within the ragged patch of light, a white, dead face gazed up at me with wide-open, staring eyes. I recognised it at once as that of my old shipmate. Tom, on awaking, had evidently been knocked out of the boat and drowned, as so nearly happened to me. The current had as evidently carried him here with me.

"I leaned over the gunwale as if fascinated. What would I not have given for his living companionship now!

"Lifting, at last, one of the stiff arms, I shook the unresponsive hand in silent farewell, and paddled back towards the flame that marked my islet, actually feeling envious of the quiet corpse. Misfortune makes us sadly selfish, and so little had my thoughts ran on the fate of my comrade that the shock of his appearance thus was a heavy one.

"I took it as a bad omen and what spirit I had nearly left me.

"After sitting motionless on my rock for a very long time, with my head bowed on my knees, and nearly letting my fire go out, I shook myself together a little, threw more chips on, and examined my stores.

"All told, with cheese, biscuits, several tins of potted meat and preserves, I reckoned there was enough, on meagre allowance, to last me for a week. Water about the same.

"More than once I felt tempted to throw the lot overboard and follow it.

"But youth and health and strength are indeed wondrous things, and a man possessed of them will do and dare much before giving up entirely, no matter how drear the outlook, how sharp the arrows of fate which transfix him!

"Feeling weary and fagged, I lay down in the boat and slept, I suppose, for hours very soundly.

"The awaking was bad—worse even than the first time

"One thing comforted me somewhat. I found that by the constant endeavour to use my eyes in the darkness I was becoming able to discern at least the dim outlines of objects.

"Renewing the fire with a lot of driftwood I picked up at the further side of my islet, I proceeded to carry out a plan I had formed. Taking the gratings out of the stern-sheets, I arranged them firmly in the bows. Then, breaking off projecting lumps and knobs of lava, I beat them smaller with an iron pin, which I fortunately found in the boat, and spread them thickly over the gratings, thus forming a sort of stage. Upon this I built a substantial fire. I was, you see, bound on a voyage of exploration.

"There might, possibly, be some avenue to freedom out of this subterranean sea other than the one I had entered it from, exit by which was, of course, hopeless.

"It was, I argued, useless to stay on the rock. I could not be much worse off, no matter where I got to.

"How I yearned and hungered for light no tongue could tell. It seemed so hard to wander in the gloom for a brief night of existence. And then, the end! Do you, any of you, wonder at my hair turning grey?

"As I scraped the last embers off the islet on to the tin dish used as a baler, in order to throw them on the new fire, the light fell full upon the corpse, which, to all appearance, had just floated alongside.

"My nerves were evidently getting unstrung by what I had gone through, for, letting the dish fall, I shouted with terror, and, jumping into the boat, pushed wildly away from the poor body. To my unutterable dismay it followed me, with one arm extended and raised slightly, as if in deprecation of my desertion of it.

"I have thought at times" remarked the captain parenthetically, "of what a picture the scene would make—the boat floating in a patch of crimson water, with the fire flaring into the blackness on her bows, myself standing up grasping an oar, and gazing intently at the nearly nude body as it came closer and closer, and everywhere around the thick darkness.

"I think that in another moment I should have leapt overboard, so great was my fright, but that I happened to catch sight of a piece of rope leading from the boat to the body.

"Getting hold of it, I pulled, and the corpse came also. Then I understood. On my leaving it the first time a portion of the sail halliards, which had been towing overhead, had got foul of the body, and, unperceived, I had brought it back to my islet with me.

"My presence of mind returned, and not caring to run the risk of more surprises of the sort, I again landed, and pulled the body on to the islet.

"There must have been some preserving agent in that water, for, despite the heat, there was no sign of decomposition, and the features were as fresh as in life.

"Sculling gently along, with my fire blazing bravely and comfortingly at the bow, I set off into the unknown.

"For a time, my attention was thoroughly taken up in trying to avoid the numerous lava islets, whose presence I could scarcely detect until right upon them. Indeed, once or twice we bumped heavily enough to send showers of hot ashes hissing into the water.

"At last, after a long spell of this kind of blind navigation, I seemed to get clearer of these provoking islets. The noises also, to which I was becoming quite accustomed, nearly ceased.

"As I sculled warily along, I listened with all my cars for some indication of a return current. It was my one hope, and it kept every sense on the alert.

"But the water within the radius of my so limited vision was quiet and still as in a covered reservoir—much more so, now, indeed, than at my old resting-place. This fact I accounted for by the emptying near there of the underground, possibly under-sea river, which had brought me into such an awful fix.

"Presently the boat bumped more violently than ever, and by the flame-light which shot up from the disturbed fire, I saw, rising far aloft, a solid wall of rock. No lava islet this, but the end of all—the boundary, in this direction, of my prison.

"To right and left stretched the same grim barrier, dropping sheer down into the still black water. With a sinking heart I turned the boat's head along the wall to my right hand, keeping a little distance out, moving very slowly, with just a turn or two of the oar, sufficient only to keep way on her.

"It may have been minutes, or it may have been hours, when, straight ahead, over the somewhat feeble light of my fire, which had proved, after all, more help by way of company than use, I imagined the darkness looked thinner. Inspired by the mere idea, I sculled vigorously along, at the risk of complete wreck from some sunken rock, and in a short time the boat shot into an oblong-shaped streak of light—light, that is, comparatively, for it was as dim as starlight; although, so acclimatised, if I may use the term, had my eyes become to the denser medium, that by its aid I could see clearly every article in the boat.

"I will not trouble you with a description of my feelings, nor of all the extravagancies I committed in the first flush of delighted hope that had visited me. I seemed to be once more in touch with the upper world through that column of dim greyness ascending through the darkness, and so weak as hardly to be able to conquer it."

Here the captain paused. He had told his story well, seldom at a loss for a word, and with now and again, but rarely, an appropriate gesture.

So successful had he been in gaining the attention of his listeners, that, when he ceased, they sat quite silent, gazing at him fixedly, and for some minutes no one spoke.

Then four bells, which struck on deck during a lull in the roar of the gale, came with such sudden distinctness to their ears, as to make some of the ladies start and utter timid little ejaculations.

The spell broken, a chorus of tongues clamoured out. Miss Hillier alone was silent. Then some dear foolish female affinity said, "Why, Amy, love, you've been crying!" This the girl, with flaming cheeks denied, only the next minute to affirm, quite inconsequently, that if she had wept (which she was certain she had not), was not such a tale enough to make one, with any heart at all, shed tears?

THE THIRD EVENING

East by S-½-South, under fore and main courses and upper and lower topsails, sped the *Corona* with the wind on her quarter. Aft, rose great water-hills darkly green, with white crests, seeming, as each followed each, to hang momentarily suspended over the stern and threaten to overwhelm everything; then, as the good ship rose just in the nick of time breaking with a long surge in sheets of milky foam away for'ard.

The sun was setting sullenly behind a dense cloudbank. An albatross or two flew screaming from one wave-crest to another right in the wake. It was a typical evening in the Southern Ocean, the long wash of whose seas reach from the foot of Cape Leuwin to the rugged cliffs of Fuego.

"Well," continued the captain, without any preface, as he took his seat facing the waiting and expectant little party.

"Well, stare as I might aloft, I could not discover to where this Jacob's ladder led. You see, at its best, it was only a column of dusky twilight, and the further end, from where I stood, was lost to view. As I gazed, it appeared to be gradually fading away. I rubbed my eyes; and when I again looked, all around was blacker than the blackest midnight, except where my fire still burned. For a while, I was puzzled to account for the disappearance of the light. Then the thought struck me that it might be caused by the fall of night in the upper world. Was I, I wondered, as I turned sadly to my fire, ever again to look upon the bright day, the sun, the moon, the stars, and all the wonders of that fair earth now grown so dear to me? Truly was I one of those unhappy men who, as the Psalmist says, 'sit in darkness and in the shadow of death, being bound in affliction and iron.'

"Close to the pillar of light, just on its outside edge, I had a long, slender, almost perpendicular pinnacle of lava towering upwards like the Spire of a church.

"At the base of this I securely moored my boat. Then, thinking that a cup of tea would cheer me up a little, I brewed one, and made a good meal. After this, lying down, I pondered many things, gazing always aloft.

"Once I imagined I saw a star; but it disappeared before I could make sure.

"The one question uppermost in my mind was whether the glimmer would reappear when the morning broke above, or had it been an illusion? One thing encouraged me to hope for the best. It was perceptibly cooler, a grateful change from the warm mugginess I had encountered everywhere else. I had, by this, contracted a habit of talking aloud, and I presently caught myself saying that I would climb the lava pinnacle in the morning and try to get a better look-out.

"'In the morning.'

"The utter vanity of the so familiar phrase as it fell on my ears struck me with all the force of some terrible shock, whilst the cold deadening thought seized upon me that, for me, in this world, there was to be no more morning. Through darkness was I to make the last journey towards that dread borne whence no traveller returns? The slow death in the darkness, drifting about on the bitter waters of that secret sea—that was the thought that my soul revolted from. And strange thoughts, horrible thoughts, a man thinks placed as I was. At times his reason leaves him, his whole soul rises in impious revolt, and the devil rages freely therein, as if already his victim's bed were made in hell.

"But, thanks be to God!" exclaimed the captain, fervently, "that the recollections of that hideous time—of the fits of doubt and despair and terror and madness, of which I have said but little to you—grow dimmer and weaker with the years, leaving only in enduring relief the memory of a great mercy!

"It pleased me, though, unproved as it was, that notion of being able to distinguish between night and daylight. The very fact, pure conjecture though it might be, of having the power to say, 'Night has come,' seemed to bring peace to my wearied eyes; so that I presently lay down and slept dreamlessly, and on awakening found again, to my intense joy, that mild, soft haze falling upon me.

"Scarcely giving myself time to snatch a mouthful of biscuit and a draught of cold tea, I jumped ashore and commenced the ascent of the tapering mass of rock. It was, as I have said, nearly perpendicular, and there was no lack of foot and hand-holds sharp as razors, formed by the drippings of the once molten lava. Thanks to my trained vision and the help afforded by the proximity of the light, I could see dimly. Higher up, the projecting spurs and knobs grew scarcer, and the surface more smooth and slippery. It was terrible work. At home I had had some practice as a cragsman, and this stood to me well now. As I climbed, sometimes vertically, at others spirally, wherever I could feel the firmest hold, the atmosphere grew palpably clearer, and this infused new strength into my aching limbs as I crawled upwards, now hanging by one bleeding hand over the abyss beneath me, now with both hands breathlessly embracing some sharp spur that cut into my flesh, whilst my feet groped convulsively for precarious support.

"When just about spent, I unexpectedly came to the top. I found only room enough there to sit down and pant. A wild hope had filled my breast that this rocky ladder would lead me to liberty—a hope growing stronger with every upward step. As I looked around, these hopes fell, and the old leaden weight of despair seemed to settle once more upon my soul. Slanting away from me on every side, stretched the rugged acclivities of a vast amphitheatre, converging again towards its summit, where the blue sky was distinctly visible. Picture to yourselves an hourglass with a long tunnel-like waist. Place a straw, the end of which rests on the bottom of the lower section of the glass and reaches up through the tunnel until just on a level with the sloping-upward portion of the top section but touching it nowhere. Now place a minute insect on the very tip of the straw, and you have my situation as nearly as I can explain it to you. And there I crouched on my lava straw, stretching out unavailing hands to those scarred cliffs of liberty, betwixt me and which spread that dark abyss, with the mournful waters of the bitter sea at its foot. The distance between where I sat on the top of the pinnacle and the sloping walls of the crater all round must have been about twenty-five feet. I think it was afterwards measured as that. A hundred plans darted swiftly into my mind for crossing this little space, which meant so much to me, only to be is quickly dismissed as impracticable.

"Although still very far from day, it was yet light enough to let me see that the sides of the crater, nearly equidistant around my perch, were cut and ploughed into deep furrows, and that, once there, I should have comparatively little trouble in reaching upper air.

"Would it be possible, I wondered, to splice what remained of the oars together, and thus make some kind of a bridge along which to creep? But the idea of again facing such a climb with such an unwieldy burden made me shudder. Also, I doubted much if there was length enough to reach across, supposing I ever got them to where I was. This one amongst many other plans. All at once, as I sat gazing alternately at the far, far away patch of blue overhead, and the dark rocks opposite, there flashed across my thoughts the recollection of the boat's grapnel. I had seen nothing of it. But it might still be hanging under her bows. Attached to the sternpost by a short length of chain shackled to a ring-bolt, it would have taken a heavy shock to shift it. If I could but get a line across and, by help of the grapnel, firmly secured to the opposite side, I felt I was saved. Tearing up the light dungaree jumper I was wearing, and which, with the remainder of my clothing, was little else but a rag, I bound pieces around my stiff and wounded hands and feet and commenced the descent. It was an awful journey, worse than the coming up. Then, my skin was whole, at the start, anyhow; now, the cuts and tears re-opened and bled and string more than ever. At one time, indeed, I felt that I must give up and let go. But the thought of the grapnel appeared to endue me with fresh strength, whilst, in my mind's eye, I kept steadfastly the memory of that dear glimpse of blue sky. At length, looking down and pausing for a moment, I saw a flicker of light. It was from the dying embers of my fire, and, in a few minutes, I was in the boat. Although nearly utterly exhausted, crawling for'ard, I felt for the chain. It was there; and pulling it rapidly in, what was my delight to find the little grapnel still at its end. Replenishing my fire, I made some tea, preparatory to having something to eat, for I knew I should want all my strength presently. In hauling at the chain my hands had got wet, and, to my surprise, the bleeding had ceased, and the pain almost departed. I immediately bathed my feet and felt wonderfully relieved thereby. Now, I had my tea, and then considered whether it might not be wiser to pass the night where I was and take a full day for my attempt. God knows how eager I was for the moment of trial to arrive! Still, I chose the prudent side, and sat and watched the hazy column turn first to a dull green, then to ashen grey, then go out suddenly, and so I knew, certainly now, that the day was over on the earth.

"As the darkness, thick and impenetrable, closed me in, I lay down thinking to sleep a little, but my rest was disturbed and broken. Always, as I dozed off, I was clambering painfully up that terrible rock, with bleeding hands and feet, staggering under huge, burdens of rope and iron. Once I dreamt that my shipmate's body had floated off the islet, and was, even now, with white clammy fingers, striving to lift itself into the boat, whilst the ghastly face peered at me over the side. This effectually awoke me; but so strong was the impression, that I seized a firestick, and, making it blaze up, searched sharply around. I had my trouble for my pains. But further attempt at sleep for me was out of the question.

"My dawn, such as it was, came at last. I had already detached the grapnel from its chain and unrove the halliards from the mast. These last I wound round and round my body, fully thirty feet of line, small 'Europe' rope, but tough and strong. The disposal of my precious grapnel, which, luckily, was one of the smallest of its kind, only used, as we had used it, for a temporary holdfast, bothered me a good deal.

"Finally, I placed my head between two of the flukes, one of which then rested on each shoulder, whilst the stock hung down my back, swinging loosely. To make sure of the flukes not slipping, I passed a piece of line from one to the other and knotted it securely.

"It was a most uncomfortable fixture altogether, a tight fit for my neck into the bargain, but I could think of no other way.

"I'm not going to inflict upon you a detailed description of how I reached the top—I believe it must have been fully five hundred feet—carrying that half-hundred weight of iron, to say nothing of the rope. Indeed,

I hardly know myself. However, get there I did; but, as you may guess, in a very evil plight.

"I recollect, when still some thirty feet from the top, unable to bear any longer the horrible chafing of the flukes, which had broken through the skin, and were grinding against the bone, that I rested, or, rather, balanced myself on a sharp ledge, whilst casting the grapnel adrift from my shoulders, and unwinding the rope from my body. Then, making one end of the line fast to the ring in the stock, I fastened the other round my waist, the grapnel all this time resting loosely on the rock.

"Leaving it there and paying out the fine cautiously into the void below me away I went again, bracing myself at every step to withstand the awful jerk should the grapnel slip off, and tighten the rope with the momentum of its fall. If such a thing had happened; and the chances were many, my fate was certain—a few scrambling clutches and annihilation. But where it went, I had made up my mind to go also.

"It was my only and last hope, that bit of crooked four-clawed iron! Death was in every step I took, and I believe that it was in those last few feet that my hair turned its colour, so terrible was the suspense and expectation.

"But God was very good to me, and I reached the summit with a couple of feet of line to spare. Dragging the grapnel up, I crouched down on the little flat, table-like top, and fairly sobbed with pain and exhaustion.

"To my alarm, I felt myself growing weaker instead of stronger from my rest. The fact was that, with the awful cutting about I had received, I had lost a good deal of blood. Many of the deeper cuts on my hands and arms were bleeding still. Evidently there was no time to lose. Standing up, feeling sick and dizzy, I coiled down my line for a fair throw, and, grasping it some three feet or so above the grapnel, swung it to and fro until I thought impetus enough was attained, then hove with all my remaining strength.

"I shut my eyes, expecting to hear every second the sound of iron clanging far beneath against the sides of the pinnacle. When I opened them again, the line was hanging in a slack bight across the chasm. The little anchor had fallen directly into one of the deep furrows, but perilously close to the edge. With trembling fingers, I hauled the line in. Tighter, tighter, tighter still, then with all the force I could command. Would it support the weight of my body, or would it come?

"Without staying to argue the question, I made it fast afresh to a round nob, the only one on the place. Then, saying a short prayer, and taking a last glance at the blue sky, I let myself slip gently off the rock, hanging with my hands on the thin, hempen line.

"It sagged terribly. I could plainly hear my heart knocking and thumping against my ribs. It sagged and 'gave' still more. Imagining that I heard the noise of the grapnel scraping and dragging, I looked upon myself as lost. But I still continued to drag myself across. It was a long, terrible agony, and, more than once, I thought I should have to let go. My hands almost refused to close upon the rope. But I still, almost as in a dream, worked myself along. Once I caught myself wondering if I should fall into or near the boat and whether the dead man would be there to receive me. Then a horrible fancy seized me that I was making no progress, but that my hands were glued to the rope with blood—ever in the same spot. Then suddenly, in my now mechanical motions, my head hit with great violence against rock. This effectually aroused me. I was at the threshold of liberty—the edge of the crater, where it sloped quickly away below.

"I hung there whilst one might count twenty, looking up. I was three feet beneath the rim. The rope had given that much.

"I don't remember in the least pulling myself up and over that overhanging ledge. When my senses returned, I was lying in the furrow alongside the grapnel, and a rush of cold water was sweeping under me. How long I had been there I have no notion. Certainly, a great many hours. The rain was pouring down in tropical torrents; thunder pealed above me, and the lightning flashed and darted in vain endeavour to pierce the lower abyss.

"After many fruitless attempts, I staggered to my feet. I felt so dreadfully weak and faint that I thought I was about to die. But a glance aloft gave me fresh heart. The dark clouds of the thunderstorm were passing over, and full upon my nearly naked body fell the warm rays of the glorious sun. I almost at that moment, pagan-like, worshipped him.

"Painfully, stumbling at every step, I crawled upwards, with many a rest and draught of the rainwater, caught in rocky hollows, until, after a weary time, and feeling as one risen from the tomb, I emerged into the full light of day once more.

"Naked, bleeding, bruised, but free, I stood on the topmost peak of that fateful island. At first everything swam before my vision. Trees, the ocean, the far horizon, reeled and shook, advanced, and receded to my dazzled eyes. The sun was low in the heavens. As things gradually assumed their natural appearance, I became conscious of a great ship lying at anchor, of a cluster of white tents not a hundred yards away from me.

"But of these things, for a space, I took no heed. Sun, air, water and sky held my regards in ecstasy. I drank the beauty and the newness of them in till my soul was saturated with the tender loveliness of that nature to which I had been for so long a stranger. Then, and not till then, I tottered towards the clump of tents lying just below me.

Men were there, carpenters apparently, hammering at a tall wooden structure. Other men—men-o'-war sea men by their rig—were arriving and departing with burdens.

"I was close upon them before they saw me. Some shrank back. One, I recollect, picked up a rifle and brought it to his shoulder. A man with a gold epaulette on his coat struck it up and spoke to the sailor in English.

"Presently I was taken into a tent, a doctor appeared from somewhere, and, whilst he dressed my wounds, they gave me a cordial, and I told my story with what seemed to me like the voice of a stranger. I don't remember much afterwards until I awoke, swinging in a hammock under a shady tree close to the tents.

"I was a mass of bandages, but sensible, though terribly weak.

"'You've had a narrow escape of brain fever, my lad,' said the doctor. 'But we've pulled you through all right. Lucky, we happened to be here, though, wasn't it? A nice time you must have had down there. We found your rope—but our men didn't care about venturing any further, as steam was beginning to come up.'

"'Four days,' replied the doctor, in answer to my question, 'it is since you appeared on the scene and scared the camp.

"'The *Bucephalus*? Yes, curiously enough, we met her just entering Singapore Harbour. That's ten days ago. She spoke to us and asked us to keep a look-out for her boat with two seamen. We have one of them, at all events. I suppose the other poor beggar will be thrown up presently.'

"I looked at him. 'Yes,' he continued, 'The old volcano is showing every indication of renewed activity. We came here to observe the transit of Venus but shall have probably to pack up and form another station if those symptoms don't subside. See there!'

"Looking in the direction of his outstretched finger, I saw several tall puffs of what seemed like white smoke issuing from the depths of the crater.

"The observers were loath to shift their quarters; but, when some red-hot cinders from below set one of the tents on fire, they accepted the hint.

"Still in my hammock I was presently carried down the mountain and on board H.M.S. *Hygeia*, where, with careful and skilled attention, I soon recovered."

The captain ceased speaking. For a time, nothing was heard except the steady blast of the 'Roaring Forties' overhead.

Asked a passenger presently—

"And did the volcano really explode after all?"

"It did, indeed," replied Captain Marion; "but not for a month afterwards, and then so fiercely as to scatter death and destruction throughout those narrow seas, grinding the island of Krakatoa itself into cosmic dust visible, according to scientists, nearly all over the world."

Here ends the story proper as compiled from the notes taken by one of the passengers and jotted down in his cabin of a night as the captain finished each section of his narrative.

Lower down on the last pages of these notes is gummed, however, a printed paragraph, cut from a Sydney daily newspaper, which runs as follows:

MARION-HILLIER.—On the the 29th ultimo, at St James's Church of England, Sydney, by the Rev. R. Garnsey, George Wreford Marion, master in the British Mercantile Marine, to Amy Margaret, daughter of the late John Hillier, Esq., of Pevensey, Miller's Point, Sydney, and Eurella and Whydah stations, Riverina, N. S. W.

THE HOUSE OF ILL OMEN

Rosa Praed

Rosa Cambell Praed (1851-1935) grew up on her father's properties in the Logan and Burnett districts, at Cleveland and in Brisbane, and
moved to England in 1876 with her husband. She wrote over 45 books,
about half of them with Australian content. Praed developed an early interest in spiritualism, and several of her novels incorporate occult themes,
most notably *The Brother of the Shadow: A Mystery of Today* (1886), *The
Soul of Countess Adrian: A Romance* (1891), and *The Insane Root: A
Romance of a Strange Country* (1902). These themes also appear in her
short fiction; the following story is from her rare collection of linked short
stories, *Stubble Before the Wind* (1908).

We were all having tea in the hall at Castle Strange. Aunt Felicia sat in her
high-backed oak chair looking like an old picture, with a black mantilla
draped over her prematurely white hair which was dressed *Marquise* fashion and only made her look younger and more attractive from the contrast
with her brilliant brown eyes and dark pencilled brows and lashes. She
was in one of her quiet moods, and her gaze would wander often to Uncle
Gaston who had been troubled lately by a sort of sore throat which the local
doctor had ordered him to nurse indoors. So he had given up hunting these
last few weeks and was horribly bored in consequence. He only brightened
up a little now that Aunt Felicia, after telegraphing round the county and
up to London, had got together a small house-party which she hoped would
amuse him. There were two or three men—a soldier from India, the hero of
a frontier fight; a Europeanised Virginian-dilettante artist and a distant connection of Aunt Felicia; Sir Thomas Hathaway, a kindred soul with Uncle
Gaston in the matter of short-horns, and Lady Hathaway who cared for
nothing but hunting and cards, and who played piquet-bridge had not then
arrived—when she was not in the saddle, or visualising runs and picking
her places in imagination from the seat of an armchair.

Uncle Gaston did not seem in the humour however for short-horns, and
to hear about runs made him cross. He was in an aesthetic mood to-day and
had got out his photographic camera to make pictures of a pretty London
woman—a young widow who, with her half-Oriental father, Bastian Pacha,

had come down just before luncheon. There were only two other guests to arrive, a Colonel and Mrs Bray. Uncle Gaston had been making whimsical complaints that the features of Mrs Maunde, the pretty widow, were of that faultlessly regular type which lends itself to Madonna effects and will not produce an artistic surprise.

"Ah, if you want artistic surprises, my dear Gaston," said Aunt Felicia, "you must study Beatrix Bray when she comes this evening."

"Thanks for the opportunity," he returned. "All this time I have not been permitted to make the enchantress's acquaintance. My wife has a way of preparing artistic surprises for me," he added, turning to Bastian Pacha, "and this is one of them."

"Beatrix Bray? Ah, to be sure! The lady is—" He stopped.

"Mrs Bray is the wife of Colonel Bray, who was in the Maroons, and the most charming creature in the world," put in Aunt Felicia. "I met them at Cannes last winter and as he was sick of golf and dying, he said, to follow hounds again in England, I recommended him to take a house in Elchester. They have been looking at one or two, were to hunt today and come on here after the run."

"Colonel Bray used to come to our house some years ago," said Bastian Pacha. "I believe that he was in love with Elinor!" The old man glanced over at his daughter upon whose interesting *spirituelle* face there came a quick blush, and she made a little gesture of repulsion.

"Oh, yes, I know," proceeded the Pacha. "He was too material in his tastes to please Elinor. And now I hear that he has married the exact opposite of himself—a Galbraith!"

"A Galbraith! Ah, that accounts," began Aunt Felicia, and checked her speech.

"For a morbid twist in her, you were going to say? Is she also—?" And Uncle Gaston touched his forehead significantly.

"No, no," hastily answered Aunt Felicia. "There never was a brighter creature than Beatrix."

"So was poor Rose Galbralth, her mother," observed Bastian Pacha, "until—" and he too paused.

The eyes of several of us turned towards him expectantly.

"Homicidal mania which developed after the birth of her second daughter," he explained. "The poor Galbraiths had a narrow escape from a bad tragedy. I wonder if Bray knew what he was undertaking. It's a double inheritance unfortunately. Galbralth married his cousin. Do you happen to know what became of poor Mrs Galbraith?" Bastian Pacha added. "I heard that she had been put in confinement."

"Poor lady, she is dead," said Aunt Felicia, gently. "I think we should forget that sad episode—I saw nothing in Mrs Bray that could have suggested such an association."

There was a short silence. Sir Thomas Hathaway broke it. "I remember hunting with Bray in Leicestershire," he observed; "a bit of a brute, but a straight goer. So he's settling in Elchester. I wonder what house they'll take."

"Felicia," broke in Uncle Gaston, "I suppose you know that the House of Ill Omen, as you call it, has been done up again for letting. You'd better warn the Brays not to be caught by its picturesqueness, and in inveigled into taking it."

Everybody exclaimed at the name—everybody, except Lady Hathaway and the Virginian gentleman who were absorbed in their piquet. All were anxious to be told the reason for so christening the place. Mrs Maunde, who looked as if she herself might have psychic experiences, was specially pressing in her inquiries.

"But why—why the House of Ill Omen?" she asked.

"Because of all the dreadful things which have happened in it," returned Uncle Gaston. "Don't you know that there are two houses in Elchester which have a very evil reputation. One belongs to an old lady called Miss Crosson, who is said to deal in familiar spirits, and the other is Kingdon Lodge—the House of Ill Omen"

"Is it haunted?" asked Mrs Maunde.

"By invisible and inaudible ghosts who prompt to murder and suicide," he replied. "Don't you ever go near the place, or you'll be tempted to kill yourself or the Pacha."

Mrs Maunde laughed uneasily, as she twisted a long chain which she wore, of gold links and valuable uncut stones. She had much beautiful jewellery.

"If Father Canalis were only anywhere near, I should beg him to go and exorcise the evil spirits," said Aunt Felicia, gravely. "I feel sure that he would be able to do it. But, alas, he is at Cannes, so ill that his doctor will not allow him to come back to England."

"Tell me about the dreadful things that have happened there?" pleaded Mrs Maunde

"Nobody ever sees anything, or hears anything," Aunt Felicia began, "but everyone who lives in the house seems to become infected by some horrible influence, which first showed itself, they say, about fifteen years ago—after the sudden death of its owner. I remember well the talk at the time, about the old gentleman and a manservant who was always in close attendance upon him. At first there was not any suspicion of foul play on the part of the servant, for he had appeared devoted to his master—so much so that the old gentleman's nephew, who came into possession of the property, kept him on in his service. It was noticed, however, that the man fell into great depression after the death of the old gentleman, and a year later he was found dead in his bedroom. He had hanged himself and left a written confession that he had murdered his master. The whole affair was most odd," proceeded Aunt Felicia. "That servant must undoubtedly have been insane, for in his confession he told that for years he had been haunted by the desire to kill. He was evidently psychic in a peculiar way. He believed that the spirit of some old black magician talked to him, and put homicidal ideas into his head; and apparently, he was fairly well educated. He had a passionate love of reading, being particularly fond of out-of-the-way literature. I remember he described having got hold of some queer blackletter books on magic, and practising, from the directions in them, devilish incantations and unholy rites with wax images, and the sacrifice of cats and dogs, in order to bring about the old gentleman's end by sorcery. That accounted for the disappearance of a number of pets which had greatly puzzled the neighbours. Then, not succeeding by these means, the servant related how he had at last yielded to the temptation now become irresistible and had deliberately done away with his master by a course of slow poisoning."

Mrs Maunde shuddered, and Bastian Pacha asked whether any further crime had followed the murder.

"The place was shut up for a time," replied Aunt Felicia, "for the owner's wife was so upset by what had happened, that she made her husband take her and their children abroad for a few years. After a while, they came back to inhabit the house, and things went on in an ordinary fashion. There were two schoolboy sons who came home every Saturday to Monday from Westminster where they were being educated, and it was in the summer vacation that the second tragedy took place. One of these boys was delicate and of a morbid turn. He had got into trouble at school, and this so preyed upon his mind that he killed himself with a dose of cyanide of potassium. He went in for photography, and that was how he came into possession of the poison. After this, the owner gave up the place, and by and by it was taken by an Elchester solicitor with a large family. I used to see these people occasionally, and never did there appear a healthier or happier set of human beings, with the exception perhaps of the youngest—a boy of about ten, who looked a sickly creature, with big, melancholy eyes and a nervous, shrinking way with him. Well, he was the next victim. His death was looked upon as an accident, but afterwards, people used to say what an odd coincidence it was that for some time before the boy's death he was always harping upon the thought. He would play games with his sister's dolls, in which he would pretend to kill them in different ways, and he continually asked questions about the boy who had lived in the house before him and who had committed suicide there. Finally, he was one day amusing himself attitudinising before a mirror with a toy pistol, which, unknown to everyone was loaded. Suddenly, he exclaimed: 'Now, let us see how people look when they are going to shoot themselves,' put the pistol to his head and pulled the trigger. The tiny bullet killed the poor child. He just lived long enough to say: 'I didn't want to do it, but something came and made me.'"

At that moment, the butler entered with a yellow envelope on a salver, and Aunt Felicia, as she took it, observed, with a rather shaky laugh—

"What is this, I wonder? In the country, after second post, nothing happens except a miracle!"

"The Brays are not coming, and I am to be cheated out of my artistic surprise," growled Uncle Gaston. "Is that your miracle?"

"No," said Aunt Felicia, putting down the telegram—"though you are partly right. This is from Beatrix Bray saying that her husband has to remain on business at Elchester, but that she is taking the liberty of bringing her sister, Eve Galbraith, instead of him. So my dear Gaston, it is possible that you may have *two* artistic surprises instead of one."

The prospect proved fallacious, however. Miss Galbraith was a disappointment—frightfully shy, with pale yellow hair, pale blue eyes, an immature figure, and shrinking carriage. She seemed, in fact, little more than a raw schoolgirl, and looked to Mrs Bray for her cue in everything.

But Mrs Bray was artistic and brilliant enough to atone for every shortcoming in her sister, and before many minutes it became clear that Uncle Gaston was enchanted with her. She had a lively, almost volatile and easy manner, so much so that one might have imagined all the men present were her intimate friends. Perhaps they were—I don't know. When we sat down to dinner, the Virginian—Mr Vignolles—had already arranged to make an impressionist portrait of her, and Uncle Gaston was studying her exhaustively, with a view to a photographic sitting on the morrow. She appeared to take all the admiration with a delightful naturalness, as if it were a mere matter of lightly discounting her own attractions.

"Oh, I know I'm not pretty, but I think I'm effective," she said with a little audacious laugh.

"Nowadays that's about the highest compliment you can pay a woman," said Bastian Pacha, turning to her with a gallant bow.

And certainly, as she trailed past me into the drawing-room after dinner, I thought her extraordinarily effective—an immensely tall and ethereally slender being, with an irregular-featured face perched upon a long, thin throat, a face all expression and colouring, illumined by a pair of startlingly bright and restless grey eyes and framed by a mass of crinkly hair, in tint the veritable Venetian gold. Her dress was no less effective than her eyes, her hair and her vivacious smile. In the early eighties, it would have been called aesthetic—long, clinging draperies of soft silk and rose velvet edged with brown fur and gathered at the waist by a golden girdle. Bastian Pacha, coming into the drawing-room, as in one of her restless movements she pulled out her voluminous skirt with the tips of her dainty fingers, made an admiring comment, at which she curtsied gaily.

"You put me in mind," he said, "of Nietzsche's 'Flame.'"

She was delighted at his appreciation of her costume.

"I made my dress myself, every bit of it!" she said. "Why, Mrs Strange, it was not difficult—only to run together yards and yards of Liberty silk and send it to be accordion-pleated; then to fasten two strips of red velvet on each of my shoulders and to twist a girdle round me—and here I am!"

She tossed her head like a child, and one of the loose coils of hair fell down her back.

"Mrs. Bray has promised me an artist's privilege," announced Mr Vignolles. "I am going to see her hair in its natural state, unconfined."

"You'll be fearfully disappointed," returned she. "It has nothing but its colour to recommend it. My hair is dreadfully short, though it looks a great deal because it is fluffy!"

Uncle Gaston ventured gently to remove the hairpins. Mrs Bray's red-gold tresses now stood out round her fascinating face, the strands separating as though each hair were electrified. She ran her fingers through the mass.

"I'm like a cat. I give out sparks. My life is in my hair," she said.

Mr Vignolles cast envious eyes at Uncle Gaston who ventured gently to lift one shining lock. "Cousin Oscar, I too claim an artist's privilege," he cried. "Mrs Bray allows us both to admire."

"Oh, I don't mind," said Mrs Bray. "How funny you all are! I was never asked before to put down my hair at a dinner-party. If I had only known, I would have made Louise wash it before I came. That brings the colour out and makes it look thicker."

Somebody commented upon the harmonious toning of red-gold hair, flame-coloured silk, and the deep red velvet upon her gown.

"Talk of Rossetti!" exclaimed Mr Vignolles, enthusiastically. "There's a Rossetti before you—a blessed Damozel. A living picture. The dress, the eyes, the tinting of the face—it is a perfect whole. We reverently adore."

"Gaston," said Aunt Felicia, "tonight you should study for a pose and tomorrow morning you must have a plate suitably and carefully prepared and photograph her, against the window—eh?—the head a little thrown back and the light shining through the wonderful hair."

"And I will get my sketching-block and paints and dash off an impression now, tonight," said Oscar Vignolles.

Mrs Bray smiled on them all whimsically. Bastian Pacha surveyed her somewhat in the manner of an Eastern potentate, between his half-closed eyes. Mr Vignolles went for his painting things. Uncle Gaston posed the model and then he too produced a sketching-block. The Hathaways, Mrs Maunde, and the Indian man settled to whist. Aunt Felicia called for music, and I sat down to the piano and played Grieg.

Bastian Pacha still surveyed the model. The two artists worked diligently.

"What an exquisite harmony!"—from one. "How it composes with that background of tapestry!"—from another.

Mr Vignolles would get up at intervals to arrange a fold of the drapery, to adjust a tress of hair.

"Oscar is improving," mocked Bastian Pacha. "Gaston's old port has made him bold." And then he whispered to Aunt Felicia: "Should we have had the hair down if the husband had been here?"

"The modern husband likes to show off his possessions," said she.

"You remind me of my Lorelei picture," murmured Uncle Gaston to his model.

"I thought I had a little more on," derisively returned Mrs Bray. "Good gracious!" she cried, "what does your butler think of me? Isn't he scandalised?"—as Aunt Felicia's sedate servant brought in the tray with spirit decanters and sodawater, and discreetly retired, carrying off sleepy dachshund which yapped in his arms.

"Oh, he's used to this sort of thing. He's always being dressed up in hunting costume for me to experiment upon," said Oscar Vignolles, "when I'm doing illustrations for the American papers of English country life."

"Model, may I get you a lemon-squash? Poor Model! It shall be looked after; it shall take a rest. Does it like plenty of sugar in its squash?"

"Have I become 'It'?" cried Mrs Bray, tragically. She left her seat and now posed herself before the fire, spreading out her flame-like draperies.

"Don't I make a good screen? What will you pay me for being an ornamental fire-screen?"

"A stuffed flamingo with outspread wings!" remarked Lady Hathaway, getting up from the whist-table.

"No—no, an Ophelia, a Saga Woman; a swan-eyed Daughter of the Bards; a Circe. Can't one think of some Homeric definition?" exclaimed the Virginian.

It was trivial chatter, losing its sparkle in repetition, but I let it stand, for looking back upon that evening and the interest centring round this gay, attractive creature, the sinister sense of contrast becomes, to me, dramatically sharpened.

Mrs Bray laughed and caught up the ball of talk. Then presently noticing Miss Galbraith's drooping appearance she made a movement to retire.

"We ought to go to bed," she said. "I am sure that I have kept Mrs Strange up later than usual and Lady Hathaway has said goodnight. As for poor Eve, she's only a baby and can scarcely keep her eyes open. Besides, we've got a very fatiguing business before us tomorrow—looking over our new house. Did you know," she added, addressing Aunt Felicia, "that we have really signed the lease of a delightful house in Elchester? The quaintest place, with a dear old-world, walled garden. You must come and photograph me there, Mr Strange."

"What is the name of your house?" Uncle Gaston asked quietly.

"Kingdon Lodge. Is it not like a suburban villa? I shall change the name. I should like to steal for it Henley's idea of 'the Castle of the Drowsy Doom.'"

"That is what my niece Ruth sometimes calls this old house," said Aunt Felicia. "But my dear Mrs Bray"—she looked very grave—"do you mean to tell me that your husband has really signed the lease of Kingdon Lodge?"

"Most certainly. There's no getting out of it now—even if I wanted to—which I don't. Isn't it a nice house for us to take? Why do you look as if we had done something dreadful?"

"The house has some unfortunate associations," said Aunt Felicia, "but we won't talk of them now. Gaston, Lady Hathaway would like some lemonade," and she made a diversion towards the other end of the room.

Eve Galbralth and Mrs Bray took their candles and we watched them as they went upstairs. Mrs Bray turned halfway and pulled a petulant face.

"I'm so sorry to miss the run tomorrow," she said.

"It's too bad of you to be going away," said Uncle Gaston.

"I must."

"Oh, get out!" exclaimed Sir Thomas Hathaway, in his rough fashion.

"I *am* getting out," said she, mocking.

"No, no, keep in... Why must you go?"

"Because my husband has made appointments with sanitary engineers and electricians and furniture people and gardeners, and heaven knows who besides. He has set his heart upon our being settled in *my* Castle of the Drowsy Doom before a fortnight is over."

A sudden chill seemed to fall upon the company below. We looked at each other, the same meaning in the eyes of all of us. But Mrs Bray had followed Eve Galbraith's drooped head and shadowy form which disappeared first in the darkness of the corridor and then the flame figure was swallowed up likewise.

"Felicia, can't you stop them from going into that place?" said Uncle Gaston, anxiously.

"I shall try," replied Aunt Felicia.

But Aunt Felicia's efforts met with no success. Poor little Eve Galbraith whitened at the tale, while Beatrix Bray became slightly hysterical over the horrors recounted, and left rather earlier than she had intended, on the plea that she must immediately consult with her husband and persuade him to give up the House of Ill Omen if there were any loophole for escape. Aunt Felicia did not gainsay her departure. Mrs Maunde looked doubtful and apprehensive.

"I'm afraid that Henry Bray is not a man to be persuaded out of anything upon which he has set his heart," she said, "and least of all for any superstitious reason."

The result proved that she was right. In less than a fortnight, the Brays were established at Kingdon Lodge.

I did not see Mrs Bray or her sister again during this particular visit to Castle Strange. Aunt Felicia wrote to me, however, that Colonel Bray had merely scoffed at his wife's entreaties, declaring that since he had taken at her desire a charming house which suited him exactly, he did not intend to sacrifice his money or his convenience because she was frightened at there having been two or three deaths in it. It was silly nonsense, he maintained, to say that the place had an evil influence about it. For his part he did not believe in influences or ghosts or anything of the kind, and nothing should induce him to pay heed to such twaddle. Thus had he delivered himself to Uncle Gaston, Aunt Felicia told me one day when the Brays drove over to luncheon at Castle Strange after their installation in the ill-omened house. At that time Mrs Bray was without her sister's companionship, Eve Galbraith having gone back to the aunt who had brought up both the motherless girls.

Then later, I heard that Mrs Bray had been very ill. She had caught some kind of fever and had lost all her beautiful hair, which was a terrible grief to her. I remembered what she had said about her life being in her hair and thought of the adoring way in which Oscar Vignolles and Uncle Gaston had gazed at the redgold masses of it that evening when she had worn her flame-coloured dress and had sat to them as a model while I played Grieg.

* * * *

In late summer of the following year, I went on my customary holiday visit to Castle Strange. It was the time of garden-parties, and Aunt Felicia was very full of engagements in the near neighbourhood, so that I did not at first go to Elchester, which was a longish drive. Mrs Bray was not to be seen at any of the garden-parties, but at one of them I made the acquaintance of Colonel Henry Bray. I found him a fine animal-handsome, fresh-coloured, devoted to out-of-door pursuits, strong-willed and stupid. Indeed, it was no surprise to me that fragile, intellectual Mrs Maunde had disdained his suit.

He answered rather irritably when I inquired after his wife.

"Oh, she's all right again as far as health goes, but I can't get her out. She's full of whimsies; it's always one thing or the other with my wife," he went on. "When we first settled here, she wasn't happy unless she was in the saddle. Everything had to give way to hunting—she was worse than Lady Hathaway. Then she tired of it before the runs were nearly over and was all agog for balls, theatricals, skating—the Lord knows what, and I don't, except for the fact that she couldn't be still for a minute. I never saw any body so restless as Beatrix until she fell ill at the end of the winter. Now she's well again, she has gone to the other extreme. She won't stir and I can't shake her out of the dumps. So she stops at home, and I come and play at tennis tournaments."

I hazarded the remark that perhaps Mrs Bray found Kingdon Lodge depressing. A contemptuous yet angry look came over his florid face.

"I know what you're thinking of—that ghastly rot about the house being haunted. All I can say is that it would be a brave ghost who tackled *me*. Of course, there ain't any ghosts—how could there be? *I've* never seen anything, and nobody else has ever seen anything; and it's a first-rate house and suits me down to the ground. I'm not going to budge, until I take my trip to Algiers in the autumn."

"Is Mrs Bray going to Algiers with you?" I asked.

"No, I'm going on business. I've got an interest in a vineyard up in the Kabyle country where it's rather rough and not fit for a lady. I'm hoping to get some shooting, though I don't suppose there's any chance now of bagging a lion. I shouldn't wonder if I made a dash into the desert."

"But you wouldn't leave Mrs Bray alone at Kingdon Lodge?" I asked.

"Why not? No harm could come to her. She's got the servants and plenty of friends to visit her. You'll be one of them—and Mrs Strange?"

"Of course I will, if I stay so long, but I think she ought to have somebody in the house with her," I urged.

"Well, she can have Eve—her sister. Not but what Eve would be a bit depressing herself. She's been having an unlucky sort of love-affair—the man broke off the engagement and wouldn't tell her why. If he hadn't gone straight out of the country, I'd have given him a good horse-whipping!"

I took no particular interest in the love-affairs of Eve Galbraith, who had seemed to me a very colourless young woman, but I could not help thinking that the Galbraith family history, if revealed to an aspirant for Eve's hand, might well give the suitor pause. Equally, it occurred to my mind that if Colonel Bray had been fully informed upon the subject, he would have spoken a little less jauntily. However, this was none of my business. I did not wait for Aunt Felicia to find a spare afternoon but drove into Elchester on my own account and called on Mrs Bray. I found her alone and, as I had expected, very much changed. She looked pinched and haggard, the vivacious smile and pretty, whimsical faces were gone, the grey eyes had a frightened, furtive expression; the irregular-featured, once brilliant face, retained but little of its former odd attractiveness. I attributed the alteration in a certain measure to the loss of her beautiful hair, which had seemed to impart to her its own peculiar vitality. Certainly, her face was still framed by a coiffure of so-called Venetian golden hue, the achievement of an expert hair-worker. But the crisp, artificial waves looked entirely different from the old natural undulations, and all the sheen of life was wanting. The whole effect was unmistakably meretricious, and I felt very sorry for the poor woman shorn of her crowning glory.

She put her hands to her head, exclaiming plaintively—

"Oh, yes, I know! It's perfectly horrid. I hate to look at myself. And do you remember that night at Castle Strange—how they gloated over my hair?"

"But it will grow again," I said reassuringly.

"No, I don't think so. Anyhow, it could never be the same… You know," she added, "I had a queer fancy about my hair—I've had it always—that so long as my hair kept thick and healthy no real harm would come to me. I had the idea that it was a kind of protection. And now," she concluded piteously, "it's gone—it's gone."

The pathos of her voice touched me deeply.

"My dear friend, what do you mean by saying it was a kind of protection? A protection against what?"

"Don't ask me!" she shuddered and turned away her face. "I can't tell you anything definite. I—I can't bear to think of it—" Her manner grew extremely agitated, and she cast round that scared, apprehensive glance I had previously noticed. After a few moments, however, she seemed to recover herself somewhat and spoke, though with evident effort, in a conventional tone. "Tell me, do you like this house? Do you not think it quaint and comfortable?"

I agreed that it was certainly quaint and to all appearance comfortable. One could not have formed any other opinion. The room in which I sat and those I had passed through were very homelike and picturesque. The general effect was most agreeable—artistic furnishings, some fine pieces of Chippendale, old prints, a valuable collection of china, and, through the long Georgian casements at the back, glimpses of a delightful walled garden.

"The house is charming," I said.

"Henry likes it," she volunteered. "The stables are excellent, and of course, the position is very central for hunting. Nothing would induce him to give it up... Oh I liked it too very much at first," she added, in reply to a vague question of mine.

"And don't you like it now?"

Again, she gave that nervous backward glance, and her voice lowered as she asked a counter question.

"Do you believe there's any truth in the things they say about the place?"

I inquired evasively: "What things?"

"Why, that it is haunted by an evil spirit which puts dreadful thoughts into the minds of people who live here?"

"I've never stayed in the house," I answered. "How can I tell?"

"It's the general idea," she went on, "that all those murders and suicides which have happened here were due to the promptings of that wicked spirit. Yet there was no real ghost. You couldn't say the house was haunted. I've asked people—servants, guests, tradesmen—everyone—and nobody has ever seen anything: nobody ever heard anything. So how is it possible for the house to be haunted?"

I tried to get her off the subject and began to talk county gossip, but she would hark back to the house and its evil influence.

"I haven't felt like myself since I came into it," she said. "That is why I should like to leave the place if only Henry would consent to give it up"

I could not, however, get from her any definite particulars as to the form her sufferings took.

"There is nothing definite—*yet*."

The way in which she pronounced that word 'yet' alarmed me, but she only gave vague answers to my questions.

"I was so abominably restless after we came here, more so than ever in my life. I had to be out and about all day. The hunting was splendid for that: it took me out of myself. But I got frightened. I had one or two falls. I was always being driven to take impossible places. So I gave up hunting. But when I stayed at home it was worse. I couldn't occupy my thoughts quietly because strange, dreadful thoughts would come into my mind. It was as if they were in the air around me—as if I took them in with my breath. I had to find some excitement outside in order to escape from them."

"But your husband told me that now he cannot persuade you to go out," I said.

"Oh, *now* it is different. *Now*, I don't want to go out. Because you see"—her voice lowered—"it wouldn't be of any use to try and fight against the things. I'm like Samson with my locks shorn. The strength has gone out of me."

She laughed wildly. In vain I begged her to describe the special 'things' which distressed her head. She shook her head. "I can't tell you. I *mustn't*. Besides, you'd think as Henry does, that I'm hysterical!" And no more would she say upon the matter. We did our best, Aunt Felicia and I, to draw the poor thing out of her unwholesome seclusion. But Mrs Bray refused all invitations, and several times when we took the long drive to Elchester hoping to see her, we were denied admittance. Colonel Bray had not yet started for Algiers, and therefore we did not agitate ourselves about her so much as we might otherwise have done, seeing that he was there to take care of his wife.

One day a little while later, I had driven over by myself and having been told at Kingdon Lodge that Mrs Bray had gone out, that Colonel Bray had left but that Miss Galbraith had arrived a few days before his departure, I went with a somewhat relieved heart to take a stroll in the town while the coachman baited the horses. Passing the cathedral, which was open, I turned in and found the church empty, save for one woman who was kneeling in a side pew, her head buried in her hands, her body bent and shaking in the abandonment of devotion. At once I recognised Mrs Bray and stole softly into the seat behind her. She was praying in an audible whisper broken by long-drawn sobs, and I caught some of the words of her petition, repeated over and over in a wild fashion.

"O God, send him away…O God, don't let me do it. O God, do make him go away."

I waited until the paroxysm of emotion had passed. Then, gently attracting her attention, I made her come with me into the cloisters and there implored her to tell me what was the matter.

Her manner became odd and secretive and she seemed to resent my interference.

"Nothing is the matter. I was only saying my prayers. My husband has gone abroad. I was praying for his safe return."

"It sounded as though you were praying for somebody to be sent away," I answered.

She retorted angrily.

"You were listening—spying on me. I do not care for that sort of thing. You're like Eve who won't let me alone for a minute. I had to run down a side street just to come in here and say my prayers. There she is now. I wish she wouldn't always come worrying after me."

As Mrs Bray spoke, Miss Galbraith, looking anxious and upset, turned into the Cloisters.

I saw that she too had changed since last year and was certainly less crude and schoolgirlish. I could tell that the girl had passed through some painful experience which had matured and strengthened her and remembered what her brother-inlaw had told me about her unhappy love-affair.

She upbraided her sister for having left her, and afterwards said explanatorily to me—

"Henry gave me charge of Beatrix when he went away, and I don't like her leaving me."

In Eve's presence Mrs Bray appeared more like her normal self, and we chatted upon indifferent topics as the three of us walked back to Kingdon Lodge for tea. But every now and then, there would come a queer furtive gleam into Mrs Bray's eyes which disturbed me. Going out to the carriage I had the chance of a few words apart with Eve Galbraith about the condition of her sister.

"Don't you think," I said, "that it would be a good thing to take her up to London for a short change and, while she is there, get her to see a nerve specialist?" For Mrs Bray had positively refused to consult any of the Elchester doctors.

"That is what we are going to do," Eve replied, "though it is only this morning that Beatrix consented to go. I am not easy at all about her; she is so odd and nervous, and I feel that she ought to see a doctor," the girl went on. "She is so restless at nights, and, when I go to her room to see if she is sleeping, I find her walking about and muttering to herself in the strangest way as if she were frightened at something. But she has promised that to-night I may have a bed in her room, and I am hoping that I may be able to soothe her to sleep."

* * * *

It is impossible to tell what really happened that night. The servants slept in another part of the building and heard nothing. When a maid took up hot water in the morning, she found the bedroom door locked and the silence of death seemed to reign within. From beneath the door there crept a thin sluggish and horrible stream of dark red, and on breaking the lock one glance showed that another tragedy, more terrible than any which had preceded it, had occurred in the House of Ill Omen.

A THING OF WAX

Morley Roberts

Morley Roberts (1857-1942) was born in London and came to Australia at the age of nineteen. He travelled extensively in New South Wales and Victoria, working on sheep stations, and contributing to *The Bulletin* and other publications. He returned to England in 1879 and became a prolific author, writing over eighty books. "A Thing of Wax" is from *Midsummer Madness* (1909), which also includes the horror stories, "The Fog" and "The Blood Fetish." His best-known tale is probably "The Anticipator", about an author who finds his stories are always written by another first.

"So you are immortal, if not of the Forty," said Jules Lepin, laughing.

The immortal one smiled. They called him 'The madman,' in Paris. There was something in his laugh which suggested tears. His smile was transitory, full of melancholy.

"Wax!" he said.

"Le Musée Grèvin adorns itself with Monsieur Jacques Landerer, politician, poet, revolutionary," said Lepin. "I shall go and see you!"

"So shall I," said Landerer. His smile had gone. There was an uneasy wrinkle between his eyes.

"After all, it's a compliment—"

"A compliment! The pigs—"

"Well, you are indeed someone when you reach wax! Marble is always there at so many francs! So is paint. There are the two Salons! But wax—*mon cher, vous être vraiment illustre!*"

Paris roared about them. They stood in the shadow of the Louvre. A dozen passers-by said—

"There is Jacques Landerer!"

"Illustrious, am I? Well, adieu," said Landerer. He went away with his head down. Wax, in wax! These waxworks were horrible things. "They're—they're so devilishly like," said Landerer. "Art—"

Yes, art was art, and though it might sting, it was, after all, art. But wax was a copy, a dreadful copy.

"I wonder if they've got my clothes, too," said Landerer. "I don't like it. The idea—"

Yes, the idea of man, of life, of reality, and of nothingness!

"I don't think I ever liked a looking-glass," said Jacques. And yet he was a handsome man, some said. "One's eyes are not one's own in a glass. By God! what is one, after all?"

Why, one was clay, perhaps, and now one was coloured wax with clothes on, sitting or standing, never moving, staring without a wink. Well, some day one wouldn't move, wouldn't wink, wouldn't live, or love, or fight, or speak.

"I'll not see it," said Landerer.

He meant it as he spoke. But all day long, friends said—

"So you are immortalized in wax. You should see it! Very good, my dear fellow; oh, excellent! You to the life I wanted to shake hands. You smiled like an enigma and wouldn't know me. I was outraged by your indifference, and almost agreed with a miserable bourgeois who abused you. Go and see it."

He had been in the Musée Grèvin years ago. It had disturbed him. The dead who yet lived were dreadful, but the living who were dead in wax and glass and cloth were more dreadful still. How could the living endure to see themselves? It put them in the grave, even as it tore up the great dead from their tombs. But only now did Landerer understand his boyish uneasiness before those wax masks. He understood death better, and he understood it less! It was the same with life, with living, with being, with enduring and fighting, with all the anodynes that make us forget stark death in the smiling, enigmatic mask which stands at the doorway of each man's warm house.

"I get confused," said Landerer the illustrious.

All Paris knew him, the very *cochers* smiled at him. He was popular even with his enemies, who laughed at him and enjoyed him. Now people passed him with a strange smile, so he thought.

"They've seen Me at the Musée," he said.

"Me! What is Me?"

* * * *

That night, when the outer Boulevards hummed, and the world was in the streets, with a clear, warm sky of stars overhead, he marched towards the Museum. But no one recognized him in an unusual dress. He wore a slouch hat, pulled over his eyes; he had curled his moustaches differently. They now stood up in waxed spikes instead of drooping towards his shoulders. He looked strange; he had rouged his pale face and browned it.

"No one will know me," he said. Truly it appeared that no one did. As he stood by the entrance, he heard a man say—

"Landerer is the only new one. It is marvellously Landerer."

Others said, "Landerer;" he caught a woman saying he was handsome. One man said to another, "That poor fool Landerer." His skin twitched in a sudden shiver, and he entered the building.

In the Théâtre Grèvin the orchestra was playing during an entr'acte; he heard the music and frowned. Somehow it hurt him. What should anyone be playing for in this devilish Morgue? He stared at a ghastly representation of a scene in the outworks of some fort in Port Arthur. The sun rose and blood ebbed. The ghastly horizon burned while lives went out. A sentry stood and stared at him—at him, a spy! And the live music danced all the while at this perpetuated agony of stained wax. It was hideous, bestial! For it was not triumphant, this music, not the wild music of war, but a trivial patter of indifferent, callous song. He looked at the dying man.

"He'll be dying for years," said Landerer. "This is worse than the doctors, who prolong things."

The white mask agonized before him. The sentry stared.

"Where am I?" asked Landerer.

He saw in wax many men he knew. Rodin, for instance—clumsy, wonderful Rodin, tyrant over marble and bronze, a brutal but great god of matter into which he flung a soul. There was Napoleon in his dead men's company and his dear dead women's; little Napoleon, little, trivial, magnificent Napoleon, Emperor, corporal, tyrant, martyr, the instrument of the awful gods, who made earth their Musée Grèvin, and played trivial, terrible music near at hand.

Then he saw Himself.

At first there was no shock in seeing Himself—or he thought so. He was sitting down, musing, musing quietly as he did sometimes. It was impossible to see His eyes. They looked on the ground.

"It can't be like," said Landerer. But he knew it was like. He averted his eyes and walked on with his heart beating.

"Why should I mind, why should it disturb me?"

It did disturb him. He sat down a little way off and watched. People passed; many stopped. They talked of him; said it was very like, or not so like, or exactly like. "I thought it was the man himself. I knew him well," said one man. He lied, for Landerer, who never forgot, did not know him.

"Here's the madman," said another.

"When will he make his next revolution in a teaspoon?" asked one, yawning. He's nothing; nothing but wax!"

Landerer said this man was right. How could he, a little living foolish figure, do anything, as the gods and the earth lay before him? The little people drifted back to the theatre. He heard laughter and applause. Someone was imitating something again. All things were wax. By God! Rodin himself was wax! The worshipped gods were wax. Who was the sneering

Maker of wax? Who owned the earth and let in devils to see the wax play?

It had been a shock to see Himself, after all.

"It's so like me," said Landerer, writhing. It got more and more like him. "It—it breathed," said Landerer, as he choked. It seemed to move a little. He rubbed his eyes and rose and went closer.

Yet outside Paris flowered, loved, laughed and grew: Paris the fair, the wicked, the wonderful, the logical! And he was of Paris now. Part of the life of La Ville Lumière, part of its ambitions, its laughter, its foolish hopes, its admirable ridicule which still could not kill him.

Inside there was no Paris. There were wax things and music afar off, and futile applause of things unseen by him. He was quite alone.

"I don't know—" he said. Then he paused. There were tears in his eyes. He wiped them away.

"I—I don't know—" he said again, as he stared at Himself: the calm, inscrutable, quiet Landerer, musing on the world. I don't know which is which!"

For one awful moment this was true—absolutely true; so true that he stiffened to a dull white mask beneath his rouge. If He had got up from the bench and walked away, Landerer would have sat down!

"By God! I must be mad," he said, as he came back to himself; "I must be mad. Perhaps I shall be like that when I'm—dead?"

He would sit on a bench—in hell, perhaps—and muse on life, on vanity, on emptiness, on success; on Sisyphus, on revolutions which changed nothing, on progress, on the churches, on God, on wax and human clay. A very quiet bench in some calm place of nothingness!

"I'd like to smash it," said Landerer threateningly. But perhaps if he struck it, he himself would bleed! So mad a thought appalled him. He dragged himself away. And he believed that the wax Landerer looked after him. He seemed to hear a thin voice say something. What did it say? He came out into the living stream of men without knowing, and Paris laid hold of him as a stream lays hold of a leaf. He came back to himself before he slept. Or so he said.

But he dreamed of the Museum, and saw the Figures walk, and heard them speak. But it was only the really dead ones who moved and spoke. The figures of live men, such as Himself, remained as they were, motionless, staring, or musing and thoughtful. This seemed strange at first to him, but after a little while it was not strange at all, for a reason he could not quite explain. And yet it seemed to him that some of the silent, motionless figures were more alive than others. Of all men it was Napoleon who explained this to a newcomer.

"They are nearer our life when they are asleep," said the Emperor. That seemed very reasonable to the dreamer. He now saw that His eyes were not fixed on the ground. They smiled inscrutably but were strangely hostile.

"I hate myself, and myself hates me," said the dreamer. He saw the Emperor speak to the Russian sentry. The sentry saluted, gave up his rifle and lay down, and the Emperor took his place outside Port Arthur. The other generals drank coffee with the ladies. Ah, they were charming, but very sad, it seemed!

Then there was a big gun fired! Someone knocked at the dreamer's door. It was morning in Paris.

He went again to the Museum. And again, and always in disguise at night. At this hour his life was empty of its old excitements. Paris was at rest. France was like a theatre during an entr'acte; or like one between two tragedies, those wonderful tragedies of laughter and woe in which she shows herself ridiculous, impassioned, devout and cynical. Landerer was out of political work: he sank into himself. Not now was he the madman some adored. But he was the less sane. He began to live in the darkness of the mind: in the shadows; and considered during long hours those things which darken even the sanest souls for dreadful moments. What was he, what was life, what the flesh, what God, what death? All these things were—wax! He laughed. Truly he was not so sane as when they called him the politician of delirium. He went to see Himself, to ask himself questions.

He began to get answers. Wax answers in time. So does the face in a mirror, always, always. So does clay. Ask, and it shall be given you! Try, questioner.

The wax Self became a vice, a monstrous vice, one he loved and hated, and took a foul pleasure in that was hideous because it was hideously close to religion and philosophy and was neither. The Figure ate up love and divorced him from his weeping mistress: it ate up faith and religion (once he had both), and the enthusiasm that one time burned within him worthily. His Cecile became a figure of wax, a puppet: she strained him to her heart in vain. He shivered horribly at her touch, and she grew pallid. He thrust her away.

"You look like—wax!" he said.

Men who knew him wondered at him. They said he changed, and he quailed, knowing it to be true. He said so to Himself at the Museum.

"I become wax; you become—what?"

The sombre Figure smiled. The face looked like flesh, many said. The little god who had made it said it was his masterpiece.

Perhaps it was.

"It grows better every day," said the little god.

Perhaps it did.

Once, and once only, Landerer found himself compelled to face Himself as himself in the company of friends: of Lepin, of Morier, of Alfonse

Fée, and Ligonnier. They met him near the Museum and dragged him in, laughing.

"You haven't seen yourself; come in and be introduced," said Lepin: fat little jovial Lepin, who should have been Lapin, a skipping rabbit of the warrens of journalistic Paris. Big Morier roared with laughter at the notion. Fée smiled and watched Landerer. Fée wrote horrible tales: some of them wonderful, and he understood the underneath of things. Ligonnier was a sculptor of the outside only, and very successful.

"Let us enter," said Ligonnier. "All work is interesting, and I want to see Landerer in wax."

"Faith, he's waxy to look at now," thought Fée.

Lepin chuckled, laughed, chattered. Old Morier (he was a philosopher of the cafés) shrugged his fat shoulders as they went in.

"Be cheerful, Landerer," he said. We will see you and He don't quarrel. It is an ordeal, I know, but be polite."

The people at the entrance smiled at the party and at Landerer, whom they now knew so well. The manager went before them proudly.

"I hoped to have seen you before, monsieur," he said to Landerer. "This figure is a triumph. The artist proclaims it. He says 'Behold, it is the man Himself.' *Sapristi*, he's right. It is good, artistic, a *chef-d'oeuvre!*"

He came to the Figure.

"Behold," he said.

"Allow me, Monsieur Fait-de-cire, to introduce to you Monsieur Jacques Landerer," said Lepin, taking off his hat with a bow.

"It's wonderful," said Fée. "Horrible!"

Landerer smiled faintly.

"What do you think of it, Jacques?" asked Morier. "It gives me the shivers. I hate waxworks."

"It's all right, I suppose," said Landerer.

"Of course it's not art," began Ligonnier.

"What is art?" asked Lepin.

"What Ligonnier does," said Fée, "and what those do who get less than he for their work."

"Beside Fée what is Anatole France, then?" asked Ligonnier, who could also bite.

"Peace," said Lepin. "Quarrel not in the face of our quiet, strange friend Landerer, Marquis de Cire! How strange. Can the world, can Paris, support two of him? Landerer, you overpower me."

"Sit down by the side of it," said Ligonnier. "Let me pose you as it is posed."

Landerer was wax in his hands.

"Marvellous, wonderful," said the manager. "Oh, that our little artist was here now. He would weep tears of joy."

"Well, that's enough. I think it horrible," said old Morier. "Let's have daylight, and a bock, and a game of dominoes. I prefer Père-la-Chaise to this."

He turned about and back again, and saying, "Come, Jacques," laid his hand on the figure of wax. Landerer smiled. He rose, and they went out, and had their bocks, and Lepin played dominoes with Morier.

"I hate all things," said Landerer, musing. He fell into the attitude of the wax Figure. Fée saw it and so did the sculptor, and when Landerer looked up he knew what they thought. After that he avoided them all. His mind melted, perhaps, or perhaps it was his brain.

He thought of nothing but the Figure, who sucked his blood. He knew the stories of magic, of magic tortures, of wasting figures of wax before fires to torture an enemy.

"Perhaps I can't die while it lives," said Landerer. Decidedly he was not sane. But he knew that very well. Like Fée, he knew the underneath of things. But he hadn't Fée's strength.

He dreamed again of the Figures and saw them move and heard them talk. But this time he did not see Himself. This was strange, because he knew it was a dream. It was stranger still that, do what he would, he couldn't see the bench on which He sat. This puzzled him. He said so aloud, and it appeared that the Emperor, who was with Marshal Lannes, heard him. The great Emperor was in his best mood and very kind. He took a great interest in everything and was pleased to speak with Landerer.

"You appear to be troubled, *mon ami*," said the Emperor.

It seemed rude to Landerer to call the poor Emperor "sire." One sees the unhappy politician spelt it with a *c*, as was natural. But he got the word out, and the Emperor turned to Lannes.

"Explain to Monsieur Landerer," he said. Of course, Napoleon knew every one's name. So, Lannes explained that Landerer was probably dead, as they said in the world outside, and that He was now wax.

"I see," said Landerer. He had been sitting all the time, in spite of the Emperor's presence.

"It appears, then, that I can walk?" asked Landerer of the Marshal.

"You might try," said Lannes. "Let me help you."

And Landerer in wax rose to his feet.

"I feel stiff," said Landerer apologetically.

"We all do at first," said Lannes; "but it wears off little by little. Even the Emperor"

"I was very stiff," said the Emperor, smiling.

It appeared that, there were so many figures of the Emperor that even his big soul could hardly go round. The explanation was perfectly satisfactory to Landerer. He strolled about the Museum very happily until he tripped up.

He found himself lying on his bed with all his clothes on. The clocks of Paris said it was two o'clock, and he crept into bed and shivered till dawn.

"I'll destroy it," said Landerer.

Every now and again he said he was mad, but on growing madder he saw how sane a proceeding the proposed act was. This damnable thing was killing him. He saw that he grew paler: his eyes were dark-circled, his wan cheeks sunken.

"Life's being sucked out of me," said Landerer indignantly.

He cared nothing about politics. The Republic was no longer an enemy. He loved the Orleanists as much as the Bonapartists. He refused to speak: refused an undoubted opportunity for causing trouble in Paris, and even avoided the most obvious chance of a duel.

"He's extinct," said his enemies.

"But the Enemy in the Museum was not extinct," said Landerer. He dreamed he was himself every night and in the morning was horribly exhausted.

"I must act," said the waking man. For when he dreamed as the thing of wax he scorned the sleeper of wax, which had so little life.

"I—I must act quick," said Landerer, shivering. "I must act quick, or when the summer comes in hot I shall—melt!"

Yes, that was it, he was becoming wax: he knew it: saw it. He had to be very careful of himself, most exceedingly careful. One sees how necessary it was. If one is wax, made of wax, the least carelessness, and, pouff! one is done for! One runs into a pool. You see, my friend, the need of care. One must avoid fires, hot sunlight, hot soups. A careful man of wax will live on ices and iced wines, and if he dares to take a bath it will be a very cold one. Landerer was a careful man of wax, a very careful one. The other Landerer was becoming flesh, of course.

"But I can stop it," said Landerer. "I will."

He knew every hole and corner of the Museum by now and laid his plans carefully.

"They will be surprised," said Landerer.

When He slept that night and dreamed, He was aware that He stood in danger. The Figure of Wax, as it moved jerkily among the other figures, was apprehensive: yes, very much afraid. The others, on learning His fears, did their best to calm Him. His friend Lannes offered to stand by Him: he offered Him, moreover, the especial protection of the Emperor.

"We must stand by each other," said the Marshal.

"Fear nothing," said Napoleon gloomily.

So he cheered up. And when the sleeper woke, it was he who feared.

He touched his skin delicately.

"I'll do it tonight," said Landerer.

He went into the Museum late, this time without any disguise. As it chanced, no one noticed him. The man at the Caisse was sleepy. Landerer heard sounds from the theatre, and knew the play was coming to an end.

"All plays come to an end," said Landerer threateningly, as he passed Himself. He felt very cold and feeble. But that was better than feeling hot, of course. He saw his friends of the night and hated them. It was so dreadful to think they lived in the fashion he knew so well. He saw the Emperor —

But this was the corner he had selected. No one would find him. Presently the theatre would empty, and the lights would be extinguished. Then he would kill the Figure and break out and go home, and sleep without dreaming, and become flesh again. To-morrow he might be able to have a warmer bath; perhaps a little soup, not too hot, but still not cold. He tried his corner, and it seemed too small.

"If anyone goes round, he'll see me," said Landerer. He stared about him. And then he smiled joyfully.

"The beast shall go there," said Landerer. He ran to the Figure, lifted it up, carried it to the corner, thrust it in, and then went and sat upon the bench whence he had taken it. A nail that had kept the Figure firm caught his coat. He took its very attitude, exactly as the sculptor had posed him. He waited.

The last act of the farce was a long one. He heard the people laugh, heard them applaud. The Museum seemed warmer, he thought. That made him uneasy. Then he heard footsteps. A man and a woman came round, looking at the Figures. The man pointed out some of them by name. He came at last to his bench.

"That's Jacques Landerer," said the man.

"I don't think it's like him," replied the woman.

"I saw him last year."

"Oh, it's like enough," said the man. "After all, it's wax, my dear."

"I think they're all horrible," said the woman. "Let's go home."

Then there was a roar of applause from the theatre.

"The farce is over," said Landerer.

A few of the audience came round his way. Some noticed him. A boy nearly touched him, but his mother pulled him back.

"He's alive," said the little boy.

"You are foolish, child," said the mother.

"I'm sure of it," said the boy.

"It's only wax, *mon petit chou*," said his father. They moved on. No one else came till the theatre was emptied. Then a man walked round hurriedly. The lights went out. The door was locked. Landerer said he was alone. He felt colder, more feeble. His heart beat so that it shook him. He raised his head and, in the storm, saw the figures standing. They seemed to whisper. He struck a match and lighted a candle. Then he dragged Himself out of the corner and trod upon its face viciously.

"You're dead," said Landerer. "You're dead."

He thrust the bundle of stuff into the corner again and kicked at it. He wiped his feet as if he wiped blood from them.

"I feel cold," he murmured, "very cold."

He sat down upon the bench again in his posed attitude, but with the candle in his hand. He breathed with great difficulty. The Figures whispered again. He sighed.

"What am I?" asked Landerer. He felt his cold cheeks.

"I'm still wax," he whispered: "wax, wax!"

He thought he screamed. He was mistaken. No one would have heard that scream ten yards away. He dropped the candle on the floor. It lay there still alight for fully a minute. Then the light went out. Landerer said so to himself.

"My heart's wax," he said. "I've been too late."

He stiffened into the attitude of the Figure and could not move. He heard the Emperor speak to Lannes quite plainly. He was sure of it. There was a ghostly light in the Museum! The Figures moved!

But Landerer did not move.

THE PROPHETIC HORROR OF THE GREAT EXPERIMENT

James Edmund

James Edmund (1859-1933) was born in Glasgow, Scotland, migrated to New Zealand in 1878 and to Australia in 1884. He joined the *The Bulletin* in 1886 and was editor from 1903-1914. Through his editorials in *The Bulletin* he had some influence in shaping the Australian constitution and Australian politics. The following two stories are from his collection, *A Journalist and Two Bears* (1913), with illustrations by Norman Lindsay. George Locke, in the 3rd volume of *A Spectrum of Fantasy* (2002), writes "[t]he fantasies are imaginative and a cut above the average; they would have fitted well into *Weird Tales*, and Edmond would have made an excellent addition to the Lovecraft Circle had it existed then."

I—HOW IT BEGAN

This is the tale of the most wonderful experiment ever made in the world, and of how it ended.

My hair is snow-white now, for the experiment bleached it in a few hours. One of my partners is dead, and it was the experiment that killed him. Another is a maniac in an asylum He lost his senses the day our wonderful scheme fell through, and now he howls in old dead languages about the big halls and corridors of Yarra Bend in Melbourne and makes night hideous with strange specimens of Sanskrit. And ancient Syriac and Hebrew. He has quite forgotten his mother-tongue; he lost it on the last day of the experiment, and never recovered the slightest shred or vestige of it from that day to this. A fourth member of the party is still living in this city. He is a strangely wrinkled and aged young man; that is to say, he was young when we all went down together to watch the results of our project, and he was old—very old and shattered—when we came up again a few hours later. It was the project that made him old—that project of ours which still haunts us and refuses to be forgotten. As for the last member of the party, he has gone away somewhere—gone away to travel and forget what we found out that day, if he can forget. But then I know that he never will. Ten thousand years would not be long enough to wipe out the recollection.

No one ever tried harder to forget anything than we have to lose the memory of our discovery—the most wondrous discovery that any human being ever made, or ever will make until the Last Man is left alone on the dying earth. But none of us can succeed, barring the man who died in the very hour when the problem was solved, and so escaped it. I would like to die too and lose the great revelation in Nirvana. But then, just because of the revelation, I dare not die. I dare not! So, I eat opium instead. That means temporary oblivion. Then I come back to earth again and remember it all once more.

There is a deserted shaft in a lonely spot on a certain worked-out Australian silver field. Nobody has found it, I believe, since the day it was abandoned. I see it now and then in my dreams; and the great ferns have grown over it, and the trees are springing up around it, and a solitude like that of a dead world is everywhere. Someday, however, it will be found, and the finder will probably fail to notice any difference between it and any other abandoned mine among the thousands which are scattered over the mineral fields of Australia. Then, probably, he will try to sound the depths of that cavity and will be surprised at its immensity. You might drop a whole cliff down there and not hear an echo of its fall in the void beneath. It is the deepest mine on earth; the deepest that ever will be on earth, for if anyone sinks deeper, he will strike something which will put an end to the earth altogether. Even the Deluge was nothing compared to what would have been if we had gone just a little deeper. It goes down—far, far down—into the old ribs and pillars of the world, and in my visions, I can still see the fire-blasted, smoke-blackened rocks below, where the sun perhaps used to shine some thousand million years ago, or which stared up into the ebon skies when the sun was still unkindled and the stars unlighted, and there was nothing anywhere save blackness and air. There are lakes and pools in these abysses, where the waters are like a glassy surface of unspeakable Night, and never a sound arises amid all the miles of solid murkiness, and probably the first shadows ever seen down there were those which we made when we went down on our way to the Discovery.

Nothing in particular ever came out of that excavation—neither gold nor silver nor lead, nor anything else that is useful. Nothing at all, in short, except bare and hungry rock, and the strangest information with which any mortal was ever cursed since Creation.

* * * *

Twenty years ago we struck the great idea of exploring the underground world. We were all enthusiasts in matters of geology, and we had an unknown world underneath our feet to experiment upon. Other men had harassed themselves about the frozen Poles, and the mystic lands of Central

Asia, and the deserts of Africa; we wanted to explore a land only a little distance away—underground. There were 7000 miles of it which had never been penetrated within historic times, and we had it all to ourselves.

As for our plan, it was simplicity itself. It was simply to start a shaft, and keep on sinking into the unknown, until death compelled us to leave the work to another generation, or till floods or volcanic fire or some other irresistible force brought our scheme to an abrupt conclusion. And if nothing did stop us, the shaft was to go down and down into the very middle of the globe.

We were looking for the unknown—for the hidden mysteries of life, and the story of the buried past. We were seeking for the original home of gold and precious stones—the great deposits whose merest fringes have been found by the seekers after treasure; and for the fires which are supposed to burn for ever in the earth's centre. We wanted to investigate the ancient myths about an interior world in the hollow globe, where subsidiary planets revolve in a toy firmament, and strange races of humanity, or races that are apart from humanity, have their being. We guarded the idea jealously—so jealously that no one, until to-day, has revealed even a hint of the mystery and how it ended.

It was not an easy secret to keep, but we kept it none the less. Our shaft was situated in a region where, at that time, travellers were few, and those who did come got no information, and, for various reasons, could get none. Our workmen were all Asiatics, and the one qualification on which we insisted was their ignorance of the English language. Daniels, the most enthusiastic member of our company, superintended, his two qualifications being a good knowledge of mining and a better knowledge of Hindustani; and for lieutenant, factotum, and assistant he had Tanjia Topi, an energetic and desperately profane man from somewhere among the Five Rivers. Daniels is the individual who died on the day of the Discovery, and we ran over Tanjia Topi and broke his back in one of the subterranean galleries, in our haste to get away when we made our final exit. No doubt he also died down there and went over the bridge of Al-Sirat to be with Allah in Paradise. Poor, forgotten, abandoned Moslem—he was a square and honourable Mohammedan, but not for all Paradise would we have gone back to pick him up.

The rest of us subscribed the money and the balance of the enthusiasm. Venables, professor of dead languages at Melbourne, was, curiously enough, the most useful man of the lot. Dead languages are seldom of much use in mining, but in this case, they did service. Also, Venables has found them come in handy ever since, for he shouts them among the lunatics of Yarra Bend and asks for his dinner in old Sanskrit roots and broken Hebrew. Raymond was a voting and immensely rich Englishman with no knowledge worth speaking of, and he went into the great scheme from pure love of novelty. It failed to answer his expectations for some weary years, and then in one wild hour he got all the novelty for which his soul had craved, and so long as he lives, he will want no more. For my own part, I was the originator of the scheme, and my motive was an insatiable hunger after knowledge. I have got the knowledge now, and I would give up all I possess to buy ignorance in its stead. So would Franz Heller, the remaining member of the company. We meet at times, and eat opium together, and swap visions and dreams, and drink to the memory of Tanjia Topi, lying dead with his broken back in the bowels of the earth, where no one will ever find him till the Resurrection.

As for our gang of Asiatic workmen, we left them in the depths, and never heard of any of them anymore. How they died there I cannot tell. Possibly the thing that we discovered came out (it was halfway out when we saw it) and took them, but this is mere conjecture. None of them knew any dead languages, and, in consequence, they failed to understand the Hebrew warning which enabled us to escape just in time.

This was how the Experiment commenced.

II—HOW IT PROGRESSED

For years the mine produced no results. All through that period Daniels pushed on the work with feverish energy, and no shaft ever went down so fast before. We got through the stratified rocks, and struck granite below, and then for a long while we bored ceaselessly downward and found nothing at all save rock. There was no serious increase of heat as we went down; there were no caverns, nor traces of primeval man; there was nothing at all, in fact, for 6000 feet and more save solid building material of the most ordinary description. So far it was the baldest, dreariest, most commonplace tale in all history.

Then the solid rock ended, and we struck a new region, where there were vast caverns, and natural galleries, and black lakes and murky rivers flowing between banks of solid Night. And among them we found a stupendous funnel-like opening—a species of ready-made shaft some thousands of feet deep—and at the bottom of it the air was thick and hot and vaporous, like the breath of a volcano. Evidently the investigation was going to lead to something at last, and we all hurried to the scene of action to watch progress.

In another gallery at the bottom of this natural shaft Daniels had fixed a powerful boring apparatus, and day by day it kept going down through soft, friable rock. And day by day Daniels watched it, and waited for results, and perspired profusely in the burning atmosphere. And Tanjia Topi hurried about looking like a sweltering demon among the shadows. And the rest of us roamed through the rifts and chasms and speculated on the prospects of the future.

I have crowded the history of all these years into a few lines for a sufficient reason. The tale of the great experiment is really only the tale of one day, and that day was the last one of our enterprise. What we discovered—apart from the final discovery of all—is of small account and hardly worth mentioning.

III—HOW IT ENDED

I had been dreaming that night.

It was a strange dream, too. I imagined that our shaft was the mouth of Gehenna, and that Tanjia Topi was at the bottom I was fishing for him with a shark hook and twenty-five miles of line, and a Koran for bait; but, though Tanjia bit several times, and I once hauled him halfway up with a steam crane, I could never get him to the surface. I was depressed at this failure, and was complaining in cuneiform inscriptions, like those on the old ruins of Western Asia, when I was wakened by Daniels shaking me by the arm.

"Come down, old fellow," he shouted. "Look sharp! We're all going! There's something about to happen. I don't know what it is, but whatever it may be, it's mighty near. I believe there's going to be the biggest circus in that old mine that you ever saw."

I scrambled out of bed faster than I ever scrambled before, and while I was dressing Daniels threw himself all over the room in galvanic jerks and pervaded the house generally.

"What have you found?" I asked impatiently, while I bounded around in search of my boots and other sundries.

"It isn't what we found—it's what we've heard. There's the father of all rows going on down the borehole; nobody ever heard anything like it."

"What! Going to be a volcanic eruption? We'll be frizzled up down there."

"Volcanic eruption! Not much. It sounds like a whole nation walloping its wife. It's like all the furniture in the universe being smashed right inside the earth. Great Scott! I don't know what it's like. A billion fellows breaking crockery is the nearest to it, only the crockery's ten miles away, you know, and the sounds seem to come through a funnel, you know; and there's guns going off, and a racket like a parrot the size of a mountain, and shrieks; and then you can hear somebody hitting somebody else with a club as big as a tree—or that's what it sounds like, anyhow. And—"

"Daniels, you must be drunk!"

"Drunk—no, of course I'm not drunk. I'll have a drink, though, before I face that place again. You'd better, too. Where's the brandy?"

We had two drinks, and I rushed about madly in search of my clothes. My bedroom was in a wooden shanty about 200 yards from the mine, and the sunshine of the bright spring morning was streaming through the window. The breeze that came in through the casement was laden with sweet scents from the bush on the mountain sides; there were birds singing, whistling, and twittering on the trees, and the wind came down from the hills with a musical murmur like the babble of far-off streams. And inside the building there was one man, attired in a shirt and one boot, rushing in aimless excitement all over the apartment, and another—muddy, haggard, and in a state bordering on frenzy—rushing round also.

Venables, Raymond and Franz Heller were waiting for us when we burst out of the doorway and ran for the shaft. It was not a dignified exit that we made. I was half-dressed and being incapable of getting coherently into any more of my clothes, Daniels had simply seized me and galloped for the mine. He left his hat behind him, and when we got jammed in the doorway through both trying to burst out simultaneously, I heard one of his braces snap with the unexpected strain. Venables was also in a disorganised condition and hatless, and Raymond had been shaving when the summons reached him and had come away covered with lather. As for Heller, he was in full dress, with a clean collar and a shiny hat, and his spectacles astride his nose, and looked as calm as if he was in church. Heller was the sort of man who would put on a clean collar on Judgment Day and brush his hat for the occasion.

As we started down in the cage the telegraph, by which signals were conveyed from the bottom of the mine to the upper air and vice versa, began to ring like a telegraph possessed. Evidently Tanjia Topi was in a tight place down below and was hanging on to the instrument like a Mohammedan in fits.

"Go like thunder!" shrieked Daniels, as the machine started.

We went like—well, just like the thing Daniels had mentioned. The black walls of the mine seemed to rise around us in one infinitesimal fraction of a second and shut out the sun and air. The black atmosphere of the mine sprung up in a bound and seized upon us, and the whole earth seemed to be falling away beneath our feet, so rapidly did we descend. Every 500 feet or so there was a short gallery opening off the shaft, and in each of these an electric light was burning, and a telegraphic signal was fixed. I could gauge our speed by the way we shot past these illuminations, and I could also gauge the size of Tanjia Topi's excitement by the riot that was bellowing forth from each signal. Plainly the Moslem down below meant to die at the handle before he gave out.

"I say, what do you think's the matter?" Raymond yelled in my ear. I couldn't see him, and all voices sounded alike in that confined atmosphere;

but I knew it was him, for when he had done speaking my ear was filled with lather.

"I don't know," I yelled back. "I think it's everything. Only I wish Tanjia would let go that bell. It sounds as if Gehenna had broken loose."

But when we reached the bottom of the first shaft Tanjia Topi had evidently let go the bell, for there was a dead silence everywhere. Also, there was nobody in sight. We were in a long, natural gallery—so long that we had never explored it to the end; and fully 800 yards along this gallery was the great funnel-like cavity which served as a second shaft and opened a way further into the bowels of the earth. There was another cage and winding apparatus here, and the subterranean road between was illuminated by electric lights, fixed at short intervals. Very long and silent and shadowy and ghost-like looked that underground highway, and not a trace of a human being could we see in all its length. And yet we had fully expected to find the most frantic of all Asiatics tearing around in this same gallery and waiting for us to come to his assistance.

"Are they all dead?" said Venables, in a whisper, as we hurried along.

"What on earth would they be dead for?" Daniels retorted, wiping the perspiration of heat or sheer terror off his forehead. "How could twenty-eight men be all dead, and yet no signs of anything wrong? You're an ass!"

"Vell, who rung dot pell?" suggested Heller.

"I don't know. Can't you wait till we find out?"

We reached the other shaft and found out absolutely nothing. There were three Asiatics in charge of the cage, and though Daniels addressed them in a whole torrent of language that sounded like cats on a wall, the results were nil. They had heard nothing and seen nobody. They had rung no bell, and nobody else had rung any bell, and no single event had happened it all. They were examined and cross-examined, and turned inside out, all to no purpose, and then we gave it up and entered the cage. Only we entered it very slowly and reluctantly this time, and our enthusiasm had evaporated like a fog in a summer sun. The only remark made came from Heller. In a blank, sepulchral tone he addressed himself to the empty air, and asked again: "Who rung dot pell?"

Nobody answered him.

* * * *

Down in the lowest gallery we found Tanjia Topi sitting like a gaunt bird of prey on guard and peering with his sombre black eye into the borehole. His report was discouraging.

In the first place he had not rung the alarm, and nobody else had rung it. The weird noises which Daniels had reported had altogether ceased, and our great mine seemed to be exactly like anybody else's mine, so far as any new developments were concerned. Tanjia announced that he had got all the men down in case of need but had sent them to work at the further end of the gallery, lest they should be scared by any new and unexpected proceedings; and then he had sat down, with his shifty black eye and his capacious brown ear both on the alert and had not moved either of them from the spot during Daniels' absence. Moreover, he knew nothing of the amazing noises which we had heard, or thought we had heard, and altogether he was the most unsatisfactory Mohammedan in all the regions of Islam. I took Heller aside at this stage of the proceedings, and communicated my firm belief that Daniels was very, very mad. But the German only shook his head, and said sadly:

"Who rung dot pell?"

Just then there was a most amazing sound from the borehole—a long, weary sigh, followed by a wail of anguish and grief. I fell back eighteen feet.

"Below, there!" yelled Daniels into the hole.

"Below-ow-ow! Who's there?"

Something came up in response. It sounded like "Yow-yow-wow-wow-wow!" And close behind it there arose a puff of yellow smoke, and a strange odor. Then there was a long pause, and after that I heard one sharp syllable, and if that syllable was not "D-n!" I knew nothing of the English language either then or thereafter. Raymond fled from the hole and concussed heavily against me in the gloom.

"This i-i-is aw-w-w-w-ful," he gasped. "It's the m-m-most surprising th-thing I ever heard in all my life."

"Berhaps it is the berson who rung dot pell," said Heller.

There was an unearthly smashing sound just then, and it came right up from the depths of the earth. Daniels and Venables fled on the instant, and Tanjia Topi turned a sudden somersault and ran away on his hands and feet.

The noise seemed to be the noise of voices, and yet they were not human voices by any means. There was a strange metallic note as if a thousand throats of brass were screaming in chorus. Then it slowly died away, and again there arose those faint wreaths of smoke, accompanied by the same wail as before. As he heard it Venables scrambled suddenly to his feet and addressed us (he had been sitting speechless in a pool of foul water for half a minute or so):

"Bless my soul," he cried. "That's a voice speaking in Hebrew!"

Daniels sat up in his pool of water and looked at him in scorn.

"Hebrew! Just 11,000 feet or so below the surface! And Hebrew, above all things!"

There was another yell from below, and Venables hopped around like a madman.

"That's Sanskrit!" he yelled. "I'll swear to it! I don't care if it's 5,000,000 feet below the surface! And that," he added, as another bark and bow-wow ascended from the depths, "that's an old Coptic root—it is, as sure as fate."

We sat down and looked at each other in a paralytic manner, and Tanjia Topi crawled back from some dark recess and joined us. After that there was an interval of dead silence save for an occasional scratching sound. It was the very loudest scratching I ever heard. If a rhinoceros, forty times bigger than any other rhinoceros, had been scratching himself by steam power with a harrow it would have about explained the situation. The air was growing remarkably hot, too.

At last Daniels roused himself.

"Look here," he commenced dogmatically, "the only thing we can do is to bore that hole a bit deeper and see what is the meaning of all this trouble. We must do it cautiously, for there may be gas, or some incandescent matter, down there, but that's all we've got to be afraid of. If we've struck a deposit of Hebrew, or a lot of Coptic roots," he added with withering scorn, "that doesn't matter. It's nothing alive, anyhow."

"Perhaps," said Venables in a terrified sort of tone, "perhaps it's something dead—or else something that can't die. Suppose we've struck Perdition."

"Dot might aggount for dot pell, now," mused Heller, but nobody else took any notice.

Daniels had the boring apparatus refixed in a wonderfully short time. Then the machine went round with a clanking noise, and we sat in the gloom and waited.

It was uncomfortable work. The minutes dragged slowly along, and we had nothing to do but loaf among the mud and the shadows and listen. Daniels and his indefatigable lieutenant, Tanjia Topi, flitted around attending to the machinery, with two silent, spectral-looking Hindoos to assist them. Heller began to smoke, and looked on with a dull, ox-like expression on his round face. Raymond sat in a pool of water and never moved, but his teeth chattered tremendously. So did mine. Presently Venables began to chatter, too, and we made a chorus of it; in fact, he chattered so much that we left off and let him have the field all to himself. He was, without exception, the most terrified professor of dead languages who ever went underground. Finally, he crawled over to me on his hands and knees and whispered.

"Don't you know what we've found?" he said in my ear. "That's Sheol down there. There isn't a shadow of doubt about it. That language I heard has been a dead language for 2000 years, and they've been speaking it in that place ever since. We've struck the department of ancient lost souls— that's what we've done. Daniels is prodding up the old kings of Egypt with that accursed drill, and next thing he'll strike a deposit of old Israelites—the ones that died in the wilderness, very likely. Can't you make him come away? I daren't go by myself."

I shook him violently in my sudden excitement.

"Look here, you lunatic," I cried, "there aren't any dead languages in that hole. It's all your diseased imagination. We've struck a geyser or something—the Lord only knows what. And if it is the department of ancient lost souls, what then? You seemed quite happy about it when you heard your blessed Coptic root. What's gone wrong with you?"

"I didn't know what it meant then. I know now. For the Lord's sake let's get out of—"

Something happened to the drill just at that second, and Daniels was sent flying into the darkness, while Tanjia Topi landed right against the two assistants, and drove them madly against Venables, and the whole lot concussed heavily into Raymond, and fell—a struggling mass of capsized humanity. But Daniels and the Mohammedan were on their feet again in a moment. Also, there was yet another howl from the borehole; but we had heard so many of them by this time that we stood our ground.

"We've holed through into some place," said Daniels. "Now then, haul up, and we'll find out the meaning of it all. Go ahead."

We gathered round in absolute fascination and waited. There was a look of expectancy on every face, and the light overhead shone down on five ashen visages, and one—that belonging to Tanjia Topi—of greyish blue. And as we stood there the drill was drawn out and attached to it was a freshly severed tail!

It was covered with a horny incrustation, as if it had been japanned, and at the end of it was a spike. The drill had severed it just at the root, and brought it away impaled on the point. Daniels made a snatch at it, but the same instant he dropped it with imprecations. It was worse than red-hot.

And as we listened, petrified and spellbound, I heard a deep bass voice howling in a strange, uncouth language, apparently halfway up the borehole. The words were foreign to me, but if the owner of the voice wasn't using the most embittered profanity ever heard on earth or elsewhere, I will never trust the evidence of my ears again.

"That's Syriac,'" said Venables, briefly, and then with a shriek of terror he galloped for the shaft.

We waited for the tenth part of an instant, and saw a head and face, which might have been human only for the indelible traces left by ages of fire and sin, come up out of the hole. And then, as the creature, who seemed partly man and partly boa-constrictor, got his hindquarters hitched somehow in the narrow orifice, and hung there, wriggling insanely to get out and shaking his black front claws at our heads, we fled for our lives.

Tanjia Topi got away first in the race, but we overtook him and ran over him, and crippled him with our feet in our excessive haste. We found Venables ringing the bell like ten thousand lunatics, and two other Asiatics just leaping into the cage; but as there wasn't sufficient room for us all we threw them out. When we reached the next gallery our cries and our stampede for the other shaft alarmed the Hindoos on duty, and they also bolted madly for liberty. But again there was no room in the cage, and we threw them out. And then we tore at the bell till the telegraph apparatus was dragged into eight pieces and the machinery was set in motion, and we went up to the air and the blessed sunlight and left the mine for ever.

We never even sent down the cage for the heathens below. If we had, that Object might have come up, along with more of the same sort, and we dared not face the risk. There might be any number of them, and we had seen one, and that was enough.

The two engineers on top were a difficulty, but I within an hour of our exit we contrived to fill them with drugged liquor, and before they fully recovered, we had got them away. By hard lying and lavish payment we drove them on board a tramp steamer bound for Valparaiso. Also, those of us who had some senses left blew up the engine-house and made all the surface works a wreck.

Then we left behind us the ruins of the Great Experiment.

THE PRECIPITOUS DETAILS OF THE HIGH MOUNTAIN AND THE THREE SKELETONS

James Edmund

I.

Up on in inaccessible shelf of rock in the New Zealand Alps may be seen a gathering of skeletons. At least they might be seen there if it were possible for anything unfurnished with wings to gain so much as a bird's eye glance at that crag that hangs midway between earth and heaven. But the precipitous wall bulges out above and obscures the view from overhead, even supposing there was any place overhead where a man or a goat could hang on for a second and consider things; and the same precipice swells out again beneath and blocks the view from the pass below. The pass itself is narrow, and no one ever climbs the mountain on the other side of it, partly because no one ever comes that way; partly because there is nothing to be gained by climbing, for the whole peak would not, sell for a cent in the open market, being merely good road-making material; partly because, if anyone should scale that pinnacle, it would only lead him to a razor-backed ridge, and the ridge itself leads nowhere; and chiefly because even the Prince of Darkness himself, hanging on with horns and claws and tail and all his other appurtenances and utensils, would find no footing there, and must needs let go and come down among the rocks and boulders underneath. Consequently, the one spot which commands a view of the ledge and the skeletons is a spot which no one will ever reach, and even if it could be reached no one would ever come back again from it to tell what he saw.

And the skeletons rest up there peaceful and untroubled, and the years drift by, and the seasons come and go. In rain and shine and thunder and wintry storm they sit and look out on the vast monotony of the Alps, and ponder on the silent, changeless majesty of the great unchangeable mountains. They look as if they themselves were wondering how they had reached their amazing elevation, for neither in front nor behind is there any possible pathway, and above and below there is nothing but bare, slippery, overhanging rock. They are wrecked among the clouds, and until Gabriel climbs up to look for their remains on the day of the general resurrection, they will probably remain in their niche undisturbed.

They are planted in single file, for the shelf is long enough to accommodate them, but not wide enough to admit them comfortably two abreast. The man in front—or the dry and creaking wreckage of what was once a man—still sits on a tattered and rusted saddle. The next man in the line is lying on his back and the rain has drifted in at his jaws and his disused eyeholes, making a sort of hightide within his fleshless skull. When there is a spell of dry weather he evaporates, and in wet seasons, on the other hand, he is in a state of perpetual overflow. It is evident this process has been going on for a good many years, for his head is nearly half-full of an alluvial deposit left by many succeeding storms. Otherwise, there is nothing remarkable about him. The third member of the party is practically undistinguishable. All that call be seen of him is not even enough to found a reasonable tale upon. He was futile while he lived. He is hazy now that he lives no longer.

There are a few other properties almost too small to be worth mentioning. A rusted billy-can, the fragments of a gun, and a half-mast rag that might once have been a blanket are about all.

For the rest, there is silence above and silence underneath. There is little light and much weird shadow in the narrow pass, and the sunlight only creeps in with difficulty, and the moon plays fantastic tricks thereabouts. And when there is neither sun nor moon, and the only light is the gleam of the icy stars, a new life and expression seem to awake in one at least of the three dead men, but it is only the radiance shining through the empty eyehole of the individual whose head is half-full of water and silt, and reflected back at an acute angle through his half-open jaws. It gives a sort of semi-humorous cast to his countenance, but humour is wasted in a place where even a goat could not climb up to join in the mirth. Considering how little amusement there is in the earth it seems a wasted emotion that the dead man should laugh his unchanging laugh on the mountain with never an audience to bear him company.

II.

There were three of us, and we had gone forth into the waste places of the Southern Alps to look for gold. We prospected among the rocks and cliffs, and on the bars of many a casual stream and up many an untrodden gorge, and everywhere we met ill-luck.

Jack Hamilton was the leader and guide and general support of the party. He was a weather-beaten, dusky individual of 40 or thereabouts, and his qualifications, apart from his experience as a miner, were a wide, far-reaching, complicated humour, and a power of misquoting Scripture which was never equalled before or since. Where he came from, or why he came from there, I never knew.

Percy, the next member of the company, was also remarkable, inasmuch as his other Christian name was Adolphus. He was a long, pale, silent youth, and a conspicuous failure in every way that one man could fail without hiring outside assistance. He had been exported by his uncle, who was alleged to be a nobleman, and almost the only remark which he ever made by his own volition—except when he was roused to a sort of mild anger—was that he intended to write for money to take him home. Owing to the circumstances hereinafter mentioned, however, he never did write.

The third member of the party—myself—was noted for nothing at all except the conspicuous foolishness which led him to clamber with a pick-axe over a damp hillside on such an errand, and in such company, and hope to grow rich out of the venture.

And so when the summer began to wane, and the first breath of the chilling autumn was felt in the breezes that swept down from the Alps, we gathered up our camp and started for some newer and wilder regions than any we had yet visited.

III.

"Boys," said Hamilton emphatically, "it's all very good for you to laugh, but I told you we'd find that mountain yet, and by the immortal there it is."

The mountain alluded to was Jack Hamilton's pet craze. He was filled with a tale concerning a certain wondrous peak which he had seen years before, and somehow lost again past all recovery. There was a deposit of gold there—great masses of gold—and for some elaborate reason he had brought none of it away with him on the memorable occasion when Providence threw the treasure at his head, in a manner of speaking, and he had neglected to pick it up. His story varied a good deal, and the mountain grew higher each time we heard of it, and the gold more abundant; but as far as I could make out the original circumstances were something like these. Jack Hamilton was a newly imported stranger at one time—an unsophisticated lamb digging promiscuously in the most unlikely places, and vainly plunging around with a space and a pickaxe upon the face of Nature. He found nothing in particular at this period of his life, not even himself sometimes, for being fresh and new and harmless he was often unable to turn a corner and find his way home again afterwards. And in consequence of this failing, he lost himself badly on one occasion, and wandered away among the boundless ranges, and there led a precarious existence upon substances never clearly specified. By the most vigorous and ceaseless walking, and by rushing over every obstacle that came in his way, assisted by the fact that he bad taken the wrong direction at first, and had succeeded—though steering by the sun—in keeping wrong ever afterwards, he contrived at last to be discovered, delirious and almost dead, in quite a new part of the country. The Samaritans who picked him up conveyed him many miles to an hospital and left him there without stating where they had met him. And in consequence of all this, when Hamilton woke up at last, and remembered about the mountain and the gold which he had seen or dreamt of in his wanderings, there was no geographical information to go upon.

He had grown middle-aged since then and had made and lost small fortunes in the gold industry, but he had never found the lost peak and the lost millions. When our prospecting expedition began to grow weary and unprofitable, he let Percy and me into the great secret, and we also grew enthusiastic for a while, but we had seen not a trace of the place either. Yet, according to Jack's description, it was the sort of mountain that nobody could pass unnoticed. It was square and vertical, and on three sides inaccessible, while the top seemed to be sawn off as if someone had removed the original summit. And, most surprising thing of all, there was on the fourth side a gently-sloping road—it had probably been a precipitous path in the first place, but it had been improving in Jack's brain for years, until he was almost prepared to swear that there was an iron gate with a knocker, and a hotel with choice refreshments, and that ham and eggs grew wild on the mountain side, while the ice-cream blossomed on the trees. And about halfway up this track was Jack's gold mine—a species of cave with all Golconda lying about loose inside.

We had long since lost faith in the mine—Percy and me. We believed in it at first, when Hamilton laid it before us one day as a bald, unvarnished statement; but the next day he wandered into details about the riches it contained, and we grew dubious; and the day after that he threw in so many surprising facts about the scenery that we became sceptical. A little later he told us in a solemn tone about the road, and gravely propounded the theory that his mine was the original mine of Solomon, and that the way which led up to it was the work of some Israelitish engineer, and then we set him down as a bad description of lunatic, and prayed that we might escape him, and get back safely to civilisation. But unluckily we were lost among the mountains, and the experienced maniac was our sole hope and reliance if we were to find our way back.

And now, when we were weary of the whole enterprise, and would gladly have shunted our guide into an asylum and sold our share of all the prospective millions for a song, the mountain of gold was looming up before us. A moment before we would as soon have expected to see the Himalayas in front of us, or the peaks of Lebanon. Then the mist opened, and straight ahead was a great square mass of rock, with the summit sawn off as if the upper peak had been cut away and thrown into the depths beneath.

We were toiling along through an enormous cleft in the hills, when this vision burst upon us, and on each side of us the cliffs rose like walls and blotted out the sunlight. There was a little stream, or rather a little noisy river, meandering through this pass, and we scrambled painfully amid the shingle which lined it on either side. When we came to a patch of comparatively easy travelling we mounted our packhorses, for there was now so exceedingly little to carry that they were packhorses only in name; and when the track was difficult—which was usually the case—we dragged the animals after us. As it chanced, we were all three in our saddles when Jack's great discovery rose on the horizon, and instinctively we pulled up and sat glaring into futurity.

Then Hamilton gave a shout that made the rocks ring and re-echo, and kicking his bony black horse into a furious scramble, he tore away and left us.

Then I said nothing, for I was too full of bewilderment for words, but I pounded furiously on the ribs of my dejected steed like a man who flogs a nightmare in a dream and rushed after him.

And finally, Percy gathered up his scattered faculties and followed us, and as he followed he threw out an exclamation into the air.

"By Jove!"

IV.

Yes, the legendary mountain was there in all reality. And, more wondrous still, the road was there too, winding in a curious zig-zag fashion away up in the misty atmosphere. And as to the gold, we never doubted it now—not even for a moment.

It wasn't much of a road after all, but it was enough for our purpose. It was cut in the face of the cliff and it afforded abundant room for one horseman, but very little for two. It had once been smooth and exceedingly regular, but rain and frost and lightning had dented it, and rotted away the edges, and filled it with cracks and slippery places, and here and there it seemed to have been repaired very long ago by some rough and ready artist in masonry, and his handiwork was now falling into pieces. But it was a road, and Jack Hamilton's dream was coming true after all.

"I knew it," he yelled. "I knew I would find it. It's all there—thousands—millions—hundreds of millions—it's been waiting for us all these years, and now we're the richest men on earth. We are—we—"

"Yah—ha—aha—yaha!"

It was a long-drawn, musical cry that came from some great way overhead, and apparently a dozen pairs of human lungs were combined in the chorus. And it was so sudden and wild and unexpected that Percy turned his horse's head there and then and fled for a quarter of a mile down the pass.

"What in all the universe is that?"

Then we both sat and listened, and as we did so the same cry rose again and swelled and rolled with a solemn reverberation through the air, and awoke long echoes among the gnarled old Alps.

"Yah—ha—aha—yaha."

"By the Immortal, we're too late! Our claim's jumped!"

All the joy and energy went out of us in an instant. Hamilton turned an ashy grey and wiped great beads of perspiration off his forehead. I climbed slowly out of my saddle and sat down helplessly on a boulder. It seemed as if I had actually owned uncounted gold only a moment ago, and now it had dissolved and fled away into absolute nothingness, and all that remained of that wealth was an old, battered, grey horse, some ancient blankets, certain provisions, and a billy-can.

"Let's go on anyhow," suggested Hamilton. "We may as well see what's happened. But if there's anybody up there, they must have found the claim long ago. Nobody but a corpse could miss it, and a pretty cold corpse at that. O Lord, the gold's just staring you in the face—heaps of it—piles of it. Well, we may as well look at it anyhow, even if we don't get a cent. But, after all," and here he brightened up visibly, "there may be only three or four fellows altogether, and if that's so we'll get a share or there'll be a row—such a row there will be. Come on; we'll thin out these pioneers a bit if we've any luck."

"We haven't any luck, Jack," I answered. "That's just where it is."

Then we started up the hill in a dejected procession. Percy came back cautiously, and tailed on to the rear of the caravan, but he was obviously scared and uneasy, and his ears seemed to stand up more conspicuously than usual on each side of his head as he listened. Furthermore, he sniffed the air in all directions. But there was no repetition of that wild, pathetic wail that had come apparently from he clouds, and stranger still, there was not a footprint to be seen anywhere, nor a single thread of smoke against the sky, nor was there the echo of a pick stroke to be heard. The old stillness of the Alps had settled down once more on all our surroundings. The ancient highway seemed to be crumbling to pieces beneath our horses' hoofs, and even when we came at last to a yawning gap which we crossed with difficulty and considerable danger, there were no signs of any recent attempt at repair or improvement. When Hamilton saw this, he drew a sigh of relief.

"Boys," he said solemnly, "I believe it's all right after all. If anyone was working the claim, he must have left some signs, and there hasn't been a foot or a hoof on this road for years. And as to these voices it doesn't matter where they are so long as they aren't here. Well, I'm d—d, some more!"

Right above our heads came a long, shrill blast like a conch or a tuneless horn—a blast so shrill and so long-sustained that I thought any human lungs must have burst under the effort.

"There's one man about anyhow," I said; "but where is he? He must be a mile up in the air from the sound he makes."

"He isn't a white man—that I'll swear," said Hamilton. "Did you ever hear such a note as that?"

"He isn't a Maori, either. There aren't any about these parts."

"Well, I don't care. We're going straight on. We haven't got so far as this to be scared by any fool with a brass trumpet. Inside an hour we'll reach the mine, and then we'll find out the meaning of this circus. Mind where you're going now," he added, for a piece of the rock suddenly crumbled away in front of us and went thundering down the mountain side, leaving another awkward chasm to be leaped over.

"The mine's just about half-way up," said Hamilton thoughtfully, after another long pause. "Now this festive orchestra seems to be holding its performance right on the top, and that's what I can't understand, for, so far as I know, the road ends just beyond the cave. All that's left after that is a dead wall like the side of a house, and there's no place where a goat could get any further. And I don't believe there's another track up the hill anywhere—I'm dead sure there isn't—I'd bet my life on it. Well, then, how did that party get up there with his trombone, if he is up there, and if he isn't there—where is he?"

"You didn't hear anything when you went here before, I suppose?" asked Percy nervously.

"Great Scott! Do you suppose somebody's been up there for fifteen years playing his music and camping out for the fun of the thing?"

"No—o, I don't mean that. But how would it be if they can't get down."

"Then how on earth did they get up?" I asked. "And supposing they did get up and yet can't get down again by the same track, how do you think anybody lives up there? Do you suppose they plant potatoes and grow oats and rear families up among the clouds?"

"Perhaps they've been up there always."

"Always! Been born up there you mean, and never came down, and can't find a way out of it. Percy, I've known a good many fools, but for a plain unmitigated ass you beat any ass I ever heard of."

I stopped then, for there was a roaring, clattering sound, and a perfect avalanche of stones came down over our heads. They flew past us so closely that I could feel a rush of cold air on my face, and one immense boulder struck a projecting knob above us and broke into a thousand splinters like a bombshell when it bursts.

"I say, for God's sake let's get out of this!" shrieked Percy as he turned a ghastly white.

"Lie down, you idiot," yelled Hamilton. And suiting the action to the word he dismounted and doubled himself into an amazingly small compass and squeezed himself flat against the cliff: "Lie down and hold on!"

We were down in the smallest fraction of a second. Above us there was a rending, humming noise, as if some stupendous object was tearing its way through a mass of vegetation. Then there was a concussion that made the ancient rocks shake and quiver, and an immense tree flew out almost horizontally above our heads and disappeared into the great empty depths below.

And behind it came—

It was a man, spinning through the air. He was brown-skinned and naked, and his long hair flew out behind and all around him. He came and passed like a flash, but I saw him turn over and over as he went—now doubled up—now spread out as if grasping at space for some support, and then he landed right in the centre of the little brawling river that foamed along underneath our feet and was seen no more. But doubtless the river clutched the unrecognisable fragments of him with its arms of foam, and rolled them over and over, and cast them up, and sucked them in again, and churned them round and round in its angry whirlpools and tore them against stones and snags and jagged rocks. And at last when it was tired of this play it bore away the scattered remains of the wild man of the mountains, and swept them out into the far Pacific, where the long, black locks of his hair rose and fell like seaweed with the ceaseless rhythm of the unrestful waters, and the shrimps and the prawns came to see him, and the crabs and the lobsters wrestled for the debris of the feast, and the patient barnacles walked over his battered bones as they lay on the floor of the great ocean.

And then far, far above our heads came that same mournful chorus.

"Yah—ha—aha—yaha!"

V.

When the naked visitant from the upper air had passed and vanished, I deliberately lay down on the pathway and clutched the rock with both hands to keep myself steady, for earth and sky and mountains seemed to be all dancing a frenzied jig around me. Percy lay behind me, almost insensible from terror. And as for Hamilton, he craned his neck outwards and upwards to see if any new dangers were threatening and seeing none he finally sat up and laughed hysterically with chattering teeth and passed his hands through his hair.

"I think we must have disturbed a whole city-full of niggers," he said. "There's the rest of the menagerie raising the same old hymn. What a chorus!"

He spoke in a strange, jerky fashion, and seemed to grope for each word before he uttered it, as if he were looking for it in the pages of a dictionary and was uncertain about the pronunciation even when he found it.

"Th—th—that was—shave," I gasped; "— close shave—I mean. I suppose that—tree was meant—for—for us, wasn't it?"

"I should think it was. And the bricks, and the rest of the furniture as well."

"For heaven's sake, let's make a run for it, then, and get out of this," implored Percy, huskily. "It's certain death to stay here."

"We can't go back in daylight, my boy, if that's what you mean. We couldn't get to the bottom again in less than an hour, and that gang of alien dynamiters'll shoot trees at us all the way. We'll run for the cave and lie there till dark, and then we must bolt and—and leave all the gold behind us," he added regretfully. "No, I'll see that tribe hanged twenty thousand times over before I'll do that. I'll come back and blast every one of them off his perch with nitro-glycerine first. I'll float a company, and we'll turn the whole mountain upside-down and shake them off the top of it into the river. There's another rock coming down I expect—come on—we've got to run for it, and no mistake."

And we ran. The horses had stampeded long ago, but we travelled faster than any horse could have carried us over such ground. It was about 200 yards, and we covered it in a few seconds, though it seemed to take whole ages. There were awkward turns and angles in the road, and as we shot round each one I expected to find a crowd of strange-looking aborigines rushing at us, but no single human being appeared in sight. The wailing chorus had died away; there were no more missiles booming down the mountain side; there was nothing, in fact, but a profound stillness—the Sabbath calm of long, long centuries. Yet above our heads somewhere a heathen tribe was pervading the mountain top, and getting ready some new project for our destruction. Then suddenly we came on a strange sight—a solitary tree growing out of this world of stone, and a tiny stream of fresh water that trickled out of the rock, and beside them was the cave where the glory of Pactolus lay hidden waiting to make us rich past all comprehension.

It was a little depression in the rock—only that and nothing more. Its walls were bare and hungry stone. There was no sign of gold—there had never been any—there never would be any. It was all emptiness and fraud and hollow delusion and ruin unutterable. I could have made as good a gold-mine any day in the middle of a pavement. I could have made a better one in an old dry well. It was the only part of Hamilton's dream that had no foundation—the mountain and all the other surroundings were there, but the gold was a delusion and a delirium. And just as we gained the scanty shelter of the cave the air was filled with an ear-splitting yell of malice, and a huge mass—ten tons or more of solid rock—came down the mountain side.

It was the first really good shot they had made. Ten yards behind us it struck the crumbling pathway, and the rock split and rent asunder as if it had been a wall of earth built up against the hillside. And when it was gone, we were wrecked up in the air—stranded among the clouds, with nothing— absolutely nothing—remaining but the ledge on which we stood, and the wall of rock behind us, and the abyss in front and on either side.

VI.

It was nine o'clock in the morning when we caught our first glimpse of the golden mountain, and by noon the gold had vanished and the great vision faded, and everything was over.

The night came and found us still sitting there and indulging in dreary speculations.

"It was hundreds of years, I suppose, since this road was made—or thousands perhaps," said Hamilton. "The upper part of it must have fallen in somehow, and that tribe of fiends has been wrecked at the top and lived there ever since. Just think of it. Likely enough their ancestors were there when St. Paul was on the earth. Perhaps they were there in Abraham's time, or before the Deluge. There may be some of the patriarchs among them, or some of the giants that were left over from Noah's day. And I suppose they've lived and married and grown old and died on the top of this accursed mountain, and they've raised vegetables up there, and caught birds, and lived on in just the same savagery as their fathers did at the beginning of the world."

He was in the first stages of fever. His hands were burning and his eyes glassy and his cheeks flushed, and he talked on with a wild, incessant volubility that was maddening to listen to.

"And all this time perhaps they've been picking and gnawing the mountain away, for the only way to get down is to cut away the rock under their feet. And when they've grubbed the entire peak to pieces, and worked down to the level ground, they'll come out into the world—their remote descendants will, that is—and what a world it'll be for them. I suppose this was the highest peak in New Zealand once, and they've torn it up bit by bit with their hands till they've worked down—down—"

"Jack," I said, "for goodness' sake be rational. How are we to get out of this? Never mind about all the rest."

"I suppose we're the first strangers they've seen for ages, and it's the nature of the animal, when he sees a stranger, to throw something at him.

And that cheerful old father that came through the air so suddenly, all scattered and spread out, and with his hair flying behind him—he must have been lifting for all he was worth to start the tree over on our heads, and he was too near the edge, I expect, and when the thing went a little faster than he expected, he went after it. What a surprised-looking person he was as he went past," and Jack laughed at the recollection. "I wonder who he was? Some of these old prophets in the Bible seemed as if they never would die. Perhaps he was one of them. I suppose a patriarch would last a long time in a healthy atmosphere like that? Maybe he was Genesis."

"Jack, stop that talk, for heaven's sake. We must find a way out of this."

"Out of this? Why, there isn't any way. We can jump down, of course—the same track that the naked father took this morning. There isn't any other road now. What a smash that rock made. If they'd blasted the path away with dynamite, they couldn't have done it better. I wonder if we could get up, seeing we can't get down, and then we might join the naked clan on the top, and marry some plain native female apiece—ha, ha—and bring up families and—oh, what a joke, ha, ha—ha, ha!"

He gave a yell of laughter and crawled out along the ledge though we had inspected it a dozen times already. But in a second or two he turned back again.

"There's nothing there but the beginning of universal emptiness—only fresh air and a cliff that a fly couldn't climb. No, this is the finish—the whole game ends right here—a wall of rock above us, and below us, and on each side of us, and here we are sitting on our shelf with our feet hanging over, and there's no gold after all—I must have dreamt it, I suppose, or—"

"Jack, there's always a chance that someone may pass along away down there—a prospector or something of that sort. If we were to call for help somebody might hear us, and—"

"Nobody'll come this way till next century now. And what difference would it make, anyhow? It would take half-a-mile of ladder to do us any good, or else a balloon. They couldn't shoot meat at us with a gun, or fire jugs of water at us, you know, or anything like that. It's all up, I tell you—oh, I wish the duke there would stop groaning! He makes me ill."

Percy was lying at the furthest extremity of the ledge, a mere huddled-up mass of clothes and misery and blank, despairing wretchedness. Poor Percy. One of these days, when his lordly uncle has dropped gently into the family mausoleum and left the mortgages and the pedigree and the hereditary spoons behind him, somebody will go looking for the heir to all these properties, and no one will dream that he is lost among the kites and crows away up in the Southern Alps.

By-and-by the moon rose and made curious shadows among the gaunt crags and peaks, and we tailed off into dejected silence, and sat looking out solemnly on the magnificence of the great snow-topped mountains. And then, after awhile, I somehow fell into a horrible sleep and dreamed.

I woke again with a start—

* * * *

Extract from the *Inangahua Times*, 4th January,1891:

"A man, name unknown, was brought up at the police-court yesterday, charged with being a lunatic at large. He made an incoherent statement to the effect that he had taken to vagrancy owing to his skeleton, and the remains of two other men, being on the top of an inaccessible mountain, and not able to get down, and he asked the court if it had a ladder half-a-mile long. The arresting constable reported that he had searched the prisoner, and found in his pockets two buttons, a piece of rock weighing three pounds, and an almost illegible manuscript in an unfinished condition. The case was remanded for a week."

THE STRANGE CASE OF ALAN HERIOT

Lionel Sparrow

Lionel Sparrow (1867-1936) spent most of his life in the small Victorian town of Linton where he was proprietor of the local newspaper, the *Grenville Standard*. Between 1887 and 1908 he published a couple of dozen horror and adventure stories in the *Australian Journal*. "The Strange Case of Alan Heriot" is the last story by Sparrow I have been able to locate and was published in July 1908. His last few stories are notable for the strong influence of Eastern mysticism.

[The remarkable lapse of memory which afflicted my friend, Alan Heriot on his return from a long absence in Japan and other Eastern countries, and which culminated in a very dangerous attack of brain fever, presented some features so extraordinary that I induced him, after much persuasion, to relate the story of this part of his life. It will be seen that the phrase "loss of memory" is far from correct, if what he has act down be true; but whether his narrative is to be taken as a record of actual facts, or as the weird adventures of a sick brain in the shadowland of dreams, the reader must judge for himself. I append Mr. Heriot's MS. without further comment.]

It was in a Japanese coastal village that the long-sought "Word of Power" was revealed to me. The old bonze, Atzu Sumangala, whom I had journeyed so far to see, would, however, tell me nothing, except that I was not deceived in my conviction regarding the potency of certain of the ancient mantras or spells. He refused to teach me the least of them, and I wanted the greatest.

For many years psychic research and other occult studies had been my ruling passion. Latterly, it is true, the beautiful Miss Alison Grant had drawn a good deal of any attention away from scientific and pseudo-scientific pursuits, for which she had but scant sympathy. The rupture between us, however, was not caused by my studies; it was the work of a very cunning and unscrupulous enemy—a rival in fame and love—Gregory Hawke, the well-known Orientalist. This man, who, I must admit, loved the lady with all the strength of his nature, had, by a most adroit presentment of half-truths, against which it was impossible to fight, succeeded in poisoning her mind to my injury—an injury so serious that it seemed irreparable along ordinary lines. It would he painful to both of us for me to go into details on this matter; so I must leave the bald statement as it stands.

Now, this Gregory Hawke was an old colleague of mine. We were engaged in the same great search. It was the quest for a certain formula of words, or rather sounds, of a class known in the East as "mantras"—sentences so constructed that they possess peculiar powers. At first, we had both laughed at the claims made for such things, treating them as mere superstition. Determined investigation, extending over many years, had, however, made one fact very clear to us—viz., that all so-called superstitions, or nearly all, are the fragmentary or corrupted traditions of what in far-distant ages were great truths. A study of ethnology reveals the fact that all races have their infancy, their maturity, and their decay. When a nation declines it loses the mental power of its prime.

In the East, this rise and fall is explained by the theory of reincarnation. The decline of a race means that the more advanced egos, or souls seeking re-birth, no longer find in that race the necessary environment for their further evolution, and so it becomes the training school for lower and lower grades of egos, until, reaching its nadir, it is either absorbed by conquering nations, or dies out. However this may be, the fact remains that decaying races no longer preserve their ideals, nor cherish their best traditions; yet these ideals and traditions are never wholly lost. Here and there a great soul is compelled by its "karma" to reincarnate in the dying race; and the sacred truths, debased by the multitude, are preserved by the few who can see their inner meaning. Much, of course, is lost; yet not a rattle survives. A conviction of this fact led Hawke and myself to form a theory that behind many of the seemingly absurd superstition of the East there may lurk not only much valuable knowledge, but even some great and portentous secrets of nature—the discoveries of long-forgotten sages, not yet recovered by orthodox science. Further research tended to the conviction that amongst the more erudite and exclusive of the Brahmins and Buddhists there yet lingered men of extraordinary wisdom and profound knowledge—men who, knowing well the folly of casting their pearls before swine, or throwing that which is holy to the dogs, preserved an unbroken silence to the outside world.

Urged by such conclusions as these, and passionately desiring knowledge not yet vouchsafed to our own race, we embarked upon an enterprise not less difficult than extraordinary. It was our purpose to wrest from those who guarded it a "Word of Power"—which had the virtue, when chanted in a certain prescribed way, of enabling him who used it to pass out of bodily consciousness and to function mentally in that mysterious division of the great realm of nature which lies next above the physical. The vista which this possibility opened before us was alluring beyond expression, yet the love of a woman came between us, and our search for forbidden knowledge was interrupted by mutual jealousy and ended finally in death and disaster. But this is anticipating.

After my quarrel with Gregory Hawke over his treacherous conduct, I pursued the search on my own account. I threw myself into it with all the more determination, now that my hopes of winning Alison were wrecked. I did not follow Hawke's movements; my jealous fancy pictured him relinquishing the great search in order to win a dearer prize; though something seemed to tell me that Alison would never surrender her life to his keeping.

So, I wandered over the East in search of the "Word of Power." The quest of the Holy Grail was, apparently, not more hopeless, but this was not less fascinating. From a Hindu kajayogi I at last learned that a certain Buddhist bonze, Atzu Sumangala, of the Tendai sect, in Japan, might by a bare possibility give me a hint. This yogi saw, or pretended to see, that my "karma" was bound up with that of Atzu, who, he said, owed me a debt contracted in some bygone life.

But Atzu smiled pityingly when I spoke of this.

"If the yogi has attained samadhi, he might know this thing," he said; "and the mere fact that you are here shows that your karma is mixed with mine. But what of that? Our Dharma says we should do no ill, and surely it is ill done to reveal the secrets of the wise to the vain and foolish."

I thanked him rather ironically, though I could not help liking and respecting the old fellow—he was so obviously a man of high development, intellectual and spiritual. I urged that I was perhaps not foolish above other men, that I did not want the mantra for any selfish purpose—but here I stopped, for his eyes seemed to be looking straight through me.

"Not till one has conquered Trishna," he said, solemnly, "can wisdom be imparted; and you have scarcely attained Vivella; in your inmost heart Vairagya is only a name"—meaning that I could not yet discriminate between reality and illusion sufficiently to have a clear grasp of the former. Though a Buddhist, Atzu used Sanskrit terminology in preference to the Pali but this, I believe, was because he had studied the former in his old age, and liked to display his knowledge, many Buddhist priests being ignorant of both tongues.

Returning to my quaint little lodging, who should I meet but Gregory. Hawke! Well for him that I was unarmed. The great Orientalist, however, greeted me as coolly as if we had never parted in anger.

"No hard words, Heriot," he said. "Let this be a business interview. I've got what you are looking for!"

"You—you've—"

"Found the mantra—yes. Got it from a hoary old Chikku of the Malwatta Vihare at Kandy!"

Though I feared he was lying, my heart beat wildly.

"And—and what is it?"

He laughed.

"What should you say, Heriot, if I told you that it was simply the well-known so-called Thibetan prayer—'Aum! Mani Padme Hum!'"

I made a despairing gesture.

"You've come all this way to laugh at me!"

"Not likely. I'm not that kind of humorist. It's as I say. As with all extant mantras, everything depends on the correct intonation and the rate of repetition. Once you produce the requisite soundwaves the effect follows."

"I know—I know. Vibration is the whole secret. And—you've seen it tried?"

"Without doubt. The old rascal of a Chikku chanted it seven times, and then—the separation was effected, palpably. Not content with that, I tried it myself. I very nearly followed the Chikku—only just stopped in time."

"Why did you stop?"

"Caution, Heriot—or fear. It's a deuce of a thing to tamper with. One mightn't get back, you know. Besides I've other plans now."

"And you are willing to teach it me? On certain conditions, I suppose?"

"One only, which I ace you guess—that you give me a free hand with respect to a lady I need not name."

I repressed my anger and reflected. I had lost all hope of winning sweet Alison Grant by any effort exerted on the physical plane. On the other hand, I had little fear that Hawke would gain the prize. I knew the proud girl too well; she was the wrong sort to encourage with the suit of a slanderer.

"I will not interfere with you down here," I said, emphasizing the last two words significantly. "You have my word."

"That's enough for me," he replied. "And for any other sort of interference you may attempt, I care not; she is no sensitive."

"Very well; that's settled. Now for the mantra."

* * * *

Gregory Hawke had not deceived me. The longsought mantra was mine at last! To the commonality of the East, "Aum! (or Om!) Mani Padme Hum!" ("Oh, the pearl on the lotus!") is a prayer to Buddha—the pearl representing the illustrious teacher, and the lotus his heavenly abode. But to the more enlightened it becomes an invocation to the inmost spirit—"O Thou! the God within me!"—and is used by the religious devotee in his effort to raise his worshipping soul to as great a height of spiritual exaltation as it may be capable of attaining. Chanted in a peculiar way, known to very few, it has the extraordinary—it will be said the incredible—power of so affecting the purely mental part of the human constitution as to cause a separation, similar to that which takes place at death, except that the body, instead of disintegrating, remains in a kind of trance. My friends, who look upon me as having suffered a "loss of memory," will smile sceptically, I fear, at these statements, and the still more remarkable ones to come; but the thing is as much a scientific fact, and as susceptible of scientific analysis, as is "wireless telegraphy," the germ theory of disease, or any other now accepted hypothesis. This, at all events, I know—that as the Word from the darkness spoke the universe into being, so is it possible, given the secret formula, to command the spirit, the real man, to leave his tenement of flesh and range at will over the phenomenal world.

Before I left, something prompted me to go and inform the old bonze of my success. He was deeply perturbed. Raising his withered arms, he uttered a solemn warning against the use of the mantra. It was a sacrilege for which I would surely suffer. Nameless perils would beset me. I was not fitted—not sufficiently advanced upon the "Way"—to use such awful powers with impunity. He quoted a Buddhist adage, the equivalent of our own proverb—"fools rush in," &c. He spoke of the "Gunas," the three qualities. I was not beyond the second, "Rajas"—the quality of activity, passion, desire; whilst the human love of life—physical sensation—"Trishna," would drag me down and destroy me. But I heeded not his jeremiad, though I was struck with the gentle old ascetic's evident anxiety, and I had an uneasy feeling that much of what he said was true.

In a month I was back in Melbourne. Anticipating experiences unheard-of among my countrymen, I made elaborate preparations for my physical safety. I need not describe these, since they proved futile. During this time I had more than once, by cautious experiments carried to a certain point, proved the mantra's power; and now I was ready for the full trial.

When the time came my heart almost failed me. The old bonze's solemn warning, added to my own theoretical knowledge of that condition of existence bordering on the physical—known in India as "Pretaloka," or "Ghostland"—was not encouraging. But, relying upon my trained mental forces—above all, upon a will power developed along unusual lines—I determined not to recede from my momentous enterprise.

It was necessary that I should chant the mantra in that "bitter hour before the dawn," when physical vitality is at its lowest ebb, and the principles of man's being are most readily separable. At length I conquered the shuddering body, the quivering nerves; and, having attained to a state of complete mental and physical tranquillity, I began that weird chant. Seven times I repeated the fatal syllables, and then—the awful separation of soul and body was consummated!

There was no loss of consciousness, though my form sank down upon the couch prepared for it. I was still in the room, but all was changed. I saw with rising apprehension that, without having moved more than a few feet, I was in a strange world, to the conditions of which I should have to grow accustomed, much as a new-born child has to accustom its senses to their proper use. What bewildered me most was that all objects seemed to be pulsing with life, and to have lost their appearance of solidity. Moreover, I could see all their sides at once, as if they were spread out flat before me, while yet retaining their natural shapes. It was some time before I realized that this was merely the result of the enlarged perception belonging to my new condition; I was in a realm of more dimensions than the familiar three known to physical eyes. The vibration of everything, too, meant that my new sight was more than microscopic, so that I could see plainly the atomic life with which even the densest or heaviest matter is permeated.

As I was trying to accustom myself to these strange conditions, I suddenly became aware that I was held in the room by some force which I could not overcome. This seemed the more remarkable because my prevailing sensation was that of lightness. I felt that I could will myself anywhere with the speed of thought—that I *was* thought, in a vehicle of desire—if only I could tear myself away from the spot. Then I knew that my body was the point of attraction, and with that thought came an almost unconquerable impulse to return to the fleshly tabernacle. Would that I had obeyed it! But my will prevailed. After an indescribable struggle, which lasted I know not how long, I found myself free, and gliding, much as I had often done in dreams, over the surface of the sleeping earth.

A description of the sights and scenery of Pretaloka—could it be rendered intelligible to the physical intellect—would make a bulky treatise. Someday I may attempt the task, but here I must confine myself to my personal history. My chief motive in thus daring to tamper with the mysteries of life and death had been the quest of knowledge. Of this I had assured my friend the bonze—to say nothing of the yogis, swamis, bhikkus, shamans, &c., whom I had vainly besought to help me. Evading the toll usually paid, I had slipped through the gates of death; I had pushed into the beyond—an alien adventurer without a passport. A spiritual lawbreaker—such I was, and a bitter penalty I paid. But I had reasoned that my purposes were not entirely selfish, even though the desire for knowledge was now mingled with another motive less pure. That motive concerned my love for Alison Grant, who had, as I have said, been turned against me by the half-truths of a cunning slanderer. Although the passion for knowledge would alone have impelled me to dare the perils of the unknown world, a novel and entrancing motive was added in the singular chance offered me to regain Alison's esteem, if not her affection. Denied physical access to her, I would seek her presence on another plane, and endeavour to influence her mind—to undo the evil work of my enemy. This, surely, was but just to herself, for I felt—nay I knew—that she loved me.

It would be interesting, but apart from my main purpose, to detail the experiences I went through in my efforts to accustom myself to this new state of existence, and to the very bewildering and sometimes terrifying sights of Pretaloka. The millions of shadowy beings like myself, and others of a higher and a lower order; the vast expanses of what I must call scenery for want of a fitting term, but which far transcended the scenery of earth in glory, and in many other qualities which are quite incommunicable in words; the light that was not light; the sounds that were not sounds—how can they be described? Only by constructing a system of metaphors and symbols could even an approach be made to anything like an intelligible account of the wonders of Pretaloka. And yet this realm is coextensive with the world we live in, and is separated from us merely by the limitations of our consciousness.

As soon, then, as I had accustomed myself, in a degree, to my new condition, I "thought" or "willed" myself into the presence of Alison Grant. It was morning. She was in a garden, gathering flowers. I saw her in the luminous cloud that surrounded her—the many-coloured envelope of etheric mist which psychics call the "aura." It was an object far more beautiful even than her bodily self—as well it might be, for it was her "robe of glory," the true vehicle of her spirit. It projected from her figure several feet; its size and purity of opalescent colour were eloquent of her lofty development of heart and mind. My own smaller and comparatively turbid vehicle rebounded as I sought to mingle it with hers. Yet I succeeded in impressing her, for I saw her start, grow pale, and fall into deep thought Then she turned, and plucked a scarlet carnation—my favourite flower—and gazed upon it intently. I saw that I was remembered, but that was all—unless a sudden flush of rose-pink in her "aura" might indicate that love mingled with her memories. A passion of desire surged through me as I beheld it, and I hurled myself against that protecting wall of luminous ether, invisible to mortal eyes, but impervious as granite to the intrusion of unwelcome or alien influences.

Then a strange and solemn thing happened. She drew herself up to her full height, dropping the flower; her eyes hardened and flashed; her hands were clenched; and faded from my sight! Thus it seemed; but it was I who departed. She had willed me away!

It was clear, then, that such high-souled purity was proof against the influence of a desire-nature so ill-controlled as mine. With the expanded intuition of my present state, I grasped the position instantly. To regain her confidence, to teach her the mantra, to have her for companion and helper in my occult investigations—above all, to show her, more plainly than by any physical means, the essential honour that underlay all the natural dross of my being, and the manly as well as the manlike quality of my love for her—such was the framework of the fabric I had raised, and it had fallen like a house of cards.

I was aimlessly drifting about in the etheric currents, wrapped in gloomy thoughts, when suddenly I felt that my physical form was in danger. I flew to it with the speed of thought. Too late! My body—mine no longer—was seated on the floor of the room, with a large scientific work on its lap, the pages of which it was turning with quick, jerky motions, now and then tearing out a coloured plate. I felt the vibrations of babbling laughter, of baby glee; and despair seized me as I saw that some ego waiting for reincarnation had drifted into my soul-deserted body. I tried frantically to drive out the intruder, but in the newly incarnated "Trishna" is strong and I only succeeded in frightening the child-soul, which thereupon used its physical vehicle to set up a prolonged and lugubrious howl.

I fled in horror. I knew that only by the aid of beings usually called "supernatural" could I regain my physical tenement; and who was there to help me? I was doomed. It was exactly as if I had "died." I should have to wander in Pretaloka for centuries, perhaps—until my "vehicle of desire" aged and fell away, leaving me another of still finer texture, which would respond to the rarer vibrations of a higher state of existence. The only gleam of hope left to me was that, in course of time, Alison must also "die," and that she would voluntarily descend from her own loftier sphere to cheer my purgatory. But the immediate prospect was too appalling to admit of any comfort in such attenuated hopes.

Losing the mental balance so essential to the dweller in that realm of spectres, I abandoned myself to the agonies of despair. This left me a helpless prey to all the horrors of Pretaloka. I was instantly surrounded by a host of grinning demons—foul and loathsome shapes, such as not even the diseased imagination of a mediaeval hermit could have conjured up. In my normal state I could easily have willed away such base creatures, who are the mere refuse or scum of the lower levels—souls of debased savages and of criminals, degenerates, &c.; but now, given over to terror, I fled—a disembodied Tam o' Shanter—before the horde of my goblin persecutors. Through sulphurous clouds, down flaming cataracts, into more than volcanic gulfs of living fire, I was harried—fearful hells, the illusive but all too realistic thought-forms created by my own senseless terror and their hateful exultation—hells such as Dante saw in his immortal vision, and such as only he could have described. I fled in vain. Horrible eyes glared into mine; great mouths, with red vampire lips, hovered hungrily about me; I shrank from beastlike fangs and talons, from hands armed with gigantic weapons.

Forgetting that no injury could be inflicted upon me save that of terror, I became a fitting object for the mocking sport of these degraded beings.

How long this persecution lasted I cannot tell. But suddenly the fiendish myriads left me, and with them the scene so easily shaped from the plastic matter of Pretaloka by artist-egos, whose ruling passion dies not with the bodily form; and my old friend, the Japanese bonze, was beside me, soothing my still agitated being. He it was who had rescued me from my hellish tormentors before I had, as I might have done, sunk to their level through a kind of dreadful perverted sympathy, the effect of my terror. I thus owed him more than life itself.

As is customary in Pretaloka with those who have not long quitted earth, we "thought" ourselves into the semblance of our bodily forms, and, stretching ourselves upon the grass of that lovely, though illusive place, we conversed in the telepathic language of the plane, which I translate.

"You are here?" I said.

"Yes. My body fell away at last... My poor friend, you heeded not my warning, and now—what suffering!"

"Yes, you were right, Atzu. But what you have saved me from is not all. I cannot return—my fleshly vehicle—"

"I know. But do not despair... The ways of Karma are strange. I am here to help you. I must dwell in this dense and gloomy medium till you are free."

"What do you mean? This is not, then, your place?"

The old man smiled sadly, yet with a certain gentle pride.

"My place is in Devachan (heaven)," he said. "There might you so dwell but for Trishna. Ah, how strong is Trishna! This terrible craze for physical life—how enduring it is! I have seen the Blessed Ones, the Devas (angels)—and they, even they who possess all knowledge, gaze with awe and wonder at the myriads of souls madly pressing downwards into incarnation, content with misery, pain, sin, and all forms of earthly suffering, so that it be but physical life! Oh, mystery of mysteries!"

"Old man," I cried, passionately, "for a year—ay, for one day—of earth-life with my beloved I would accept annihilation, could such be!"

"I know," he said, sadly. "Many, many lives must you endure before you will even begin to tear Trishna from your heart. Karma is just—she gives unto each his desire; but the nature of the desire may be moulded by the reason; and thus, in some degree, man is the master of his fate, and every man must and will work out his own emancipation. Thus have we heard," he added, with true Buddhist humility.

"But, Atzu," I said, for I was in no mood for philosophy, "what will happen to my unhappy vehicle?"

"I know not yet. A soul has been permitted to enter it. That soul remembers not its former life on earth; thus it is an infant on the physical plane, and must acquire knowledge like any other. But this kind of incarnation is quite abnormal—though not unique—and there are ways... Well, my poor friend, we can only watch and wait. In the meantime, if you choose, I will be your instructor in the lore of the superphysical planes."

I had to submit. Intensely interesting was his instruction—strange beyond credence were the secrets he revealed; but Trishna held me constantly in her thrall, and the passionate longing to re-enter physical life never left me. Here there was a vast freedom of motion and of intellection; the ills that flesh is heir to, and the clogs that thought, working through a physical brain, must contend with, did not exist; knowledge, within limits, came by intuition. But the feeling that I was shut out from all that I had been accustomed to regard as solid realities made me desire to get back at any cost—even if it were in the form of a cripple, a dwarf, a savage—so wildly did I desire to quit this world of shadows. The bonze told me that this feeling would wear off in time, and that if I brought it under control I should get rid of it in the course of two or three centuries—a cheering prospect.

"Give yourself up to knowledge, my son," he urged. "Knowledge will conduct you to Devachan, where there is bliss; and in the ages to come, when you have conquered Trishna, knowledge will bring you even unto Nirvana, where there is supreme peace."

Of course, it was chiefly my love for Alison Grant that drew my thoughts constantly back to earth. Lacking this powerful magnet, it is possible that in time my Buddhist friend and helper would have won me over to his benevolent plans; and that, under his direction, I should have taken the first steps upon that long and difficult path which leads the neophyte to higher and higher states of consciousness. But this is "taking the kingdom of heaven by storm," and I shrank appalled at the magnitude of the task, preferring, like the majority of men, to progress towards perfection in the normal way.

Be sure that I lost nothing of what took place in respect to my fleshly form, so strangely lost. The baby soul that inhabited it soon played such havoc that he had to be restrained; and I had the mortification of witnessing the wonder and grief of my friends, not to speak of the somewhat contemptuous pity of certain acquaintances who "had always doubted Heriot's sanity," and who were "not at all surprised!" Alan Heriot's "strange loss of memory" made quite a sensation in scientific circles; and the papers "wrote it up" rather more fully than the real Alan Heriot, whose memory was only too distinct, relished. It was thought that the "famous scientist," as they were good enough to style me, had dropped back into infancy, as far as the mind was concerned; and many noted brain specialists were much interested. I succeeded in impressing the mind of one of these men with a vague idea of the true facts; but the only result was that he became alarmed, and fancied himself suffering from brain-fag, the result of overwork, and he gave himself a long holiday.

My mortification was strangely added to by the self-sacrifice of Alison Grant. As soon as she heard of my supposed condition, she undertook the task of nursing me, and lavished a world of womanly care and tenderness upon a perfect stranger—a baby-ego who came from, heaven alone knows where. It was a peculiar situation—a painful one for her, poor girl. She naturally thought my psychic studies had cost me my reason. This was bad enough for her but the fact that she could never arouse the slightest gleam of recognition or memory in her helpless charge, try how she would, was a terrible affliction.

How I strove to gain access to her mind; how at times I almost succeeded; how she once or twice trembled on the very verge of comprehension; my despairing struggles to lead her on to the right train of thought—these things must remain untold. And there was no respite for my sufferings, for sleep comes not in Pretaloka. The bonze would not help me in these attempts, but besought me to desist from them, pointing out that the mental strain that Alison was enduring was sufficiently great without making further demands upon her. But for the soothing and strengthening influence of this truly great and highly-evolved being, I must surely have sunk into a condition which would have left me a prey once more to the rabble souls—if souls they can be called—of Pretaloka, to whom the sport of harrying and torturing some weak-willed or affrighted spirit of a better class than themselves is a kind of frantic happiness—not without its counterpart on earth, by the way.

The bonze could not always be with me. His life was as full of work as it had been when he was in the body; in fact, he was far more constantly occupied, as there is no sense of fatigue in Pretaloka, and thus no need for rest or recuperation. Probably the help and sympathy he so ungrudgingly gave to me formed the lowest or basest kind of all his occupations. I gathered, also, that he was receiving spiritual instruction from certain very exalted beings who were helping him upward, even as he, in his degree, was helping others. I found that the higher the stage of spiritual evolution attained, the greater is the responsibility of assisting those on the lower rungs of the great ladder; that sacrifice becomes more and more the life principle of these lofty spirits, and that the greatest of them exist for nothing else.

How well I remember my last interview with Atzu Sumangala! We stood in the midst of a sylvan scene surpassingly beautiful; it was wrought by the thought-power of one of the masters of landscape-painting, who, since his "death," used the plastic matter of the spirit-world instead of earth's dull pigments, and realised his grandest art dreams unhampered by the difficulties and obstacles inseparable from physical resources. Pretaloka is indeed a "land where our dreams come true," but, alas! our dreams are what we make them, and many that I saw were far different from this. I saw the dreams of the vain and foolish, the narrow and the bigoted, as well as those of the earnest and sincere, the kindly and the single-hearted.

We stood and gazed, he with the calm, sad eye that recognises illusion but does not despise it; I with that yearning joy which seizes one in presence of supernal beauty. But my thoughts could not long stray from my personal concerns.

"Atzu," I said, wearily, "is there no way? With your great powers, surely you could drive away that baby-soul that is keeping me out of my body."

"That could easily be done," he said, calmly.

I felt my being vibrate wildly.

"Then why, if you desire to help me—"

"My poor friend, a great danger menaces you. You have an enemy on the physical plane—one Gregory Hawke."

"It is true. He it was who discovered that accursed mantra and taught it me."

"I know. And he uses it, too. He, like you, is waiting, waiting for that infant soul to be driven out. And his will is stronger than your own. He has trained it more assiduously, and on a better plan. His object is to abandon his own body and to steal yours. Thus, he will win the lady that loves you, for she will imagine that it is you, and that your memory has been restored... Gently, friend Alan, gently; you attract the pretas, the Shûtas, and all evil beings by these swirling passions. Alas, poor friend! why hunger so for the things of earth? Let them go; give yourself to me—to wisdom—and I will teach you how to will your desires away, how to kill this Trishna that drags you down. And I shall take you with me to the higher realms, and you shall be initiated into the knowledge of the Buddhi—the Pure Reason— knowledge too glorious, too divine, even to be approached in the language of the physical intellect, which you must use on earth. And this knowledge, this divine wisdom, will make you a guide and helper of the humanity that you already love, when, in the course of time, you return to earth in a new incarnation."

But I could not listen to his gentle entreaties... So, Hawke had outwitted me after all. I had thought he lacked the daring to cast off his physical form and enter Pretaloka. Yet he had done so, and even designed this double robbery, impelled by his passion.

I calmed myself.

"How will he proceed?" I asked.

"He will find a way to cause your body to fall into a sickness—brain fever. Then, awaiting his opportunity, he will take possession."

"I will fight him for it," I cried passionately.

"He is the stronger," said Atzu, "but the more evil, and therein lies your advantage in the fight. Yes, you must battle with him for the physical existence that you value so much... And now, friend Alan, we must part. It is not my karma—alas!—to help you further. Not until you have trampled Trishna under foot may we meet again. Peace be with you. Farewell!"

Overcome with sorrow at the parting, I found no words in which to reply. He faded from my sight, withdrawing himself into some higher state of consciousness whither I was powerless to follow him. I saw him no more.

Soon after this, as Atzu had predicted, my body fell sick. I expected to see the etheric vehicle of Gregory Hawke in its vicinity, but he did not appear. The idea struck me to will myself to him and see how he was occupied. I found myself in a secluded house in the great city of San Francisco. Very soon I discovered that Hawke had prepared a safe place for his body, even as I had done. At this moment he was alone, idling away the time with some magazines. I did not stay long. There was something abnormal in the etheric currents of this place which I could not understand, though I had a vague feeling that it boded ill. I returned and watched unceasingly beside my unhappy body.

The fever advanced rapidly. In my savage resentment against my unknown supplanter, I at first rejoiced to see him suffer; but very soon that feeling gave way to pity. I felt that neither of the two beings I most revered—Alison and the bonze—would admire me for such a hateful sentiment. Besides, the poor creature's agonies would have disarmed an anger even greater than my own. Alison's hospital training made her an invaluable nurse; but she needed all her fortitude and wore than once the strain was almost too much for her. Indeed, my desire was that she should break down and be taken away, for I dreaded the effect that her sufferings would have upon me. In Pretaloka the joys and sorrows, the pleasure and pain of those we love on earth have a powerful effect upon the fine and sensitive matter of the mind's vehicle; and I would need all my thought-power in the conflict with my desperate and determined enemy. I drew some solace from the reflection that he also, in his reckless passion for her, would suffer with her even as I; yet I knew him to be made of sterner stuff than I could boast. He showed his wisdom, too, in keeping away. For many days I saw nothing of him, and even began to hope that, after all, he had not the hardihood for such an unheard-of adventure.

But at last, I saw a spirit-vehicle hovering near—larger than my own, and of a portentous and sinister luminosity. It was the ethereal counterpart of Gregory Hawke. I felt that his will was indeed more powerful than mine, but, happily for me, also more evil. He passed continually through and through my prostrate body, except when Alison bent over it; but the infant soul held strongly to its new-found home and would not be ejected. Sometimes, in the delirium of the fever, it left the body and hovered near—a pallid, almost shapeless cloud—but at the approach of either of us it regained its position. I saw, however, that, as the fever advanced, its hold would be weaker, and that a strong-willed spirit might easily drive it out. Then would come our strange contest. Hawke would have the advantage, being the stronger; but then, after all, the body was mine, and perhaps would more readily accept my return. This thought was suggested by despair rather than knowledge, and it gave me but little comfort. I learned then, as I had learned in my flight from the "bhûtas," as Atzu called them, that suffering does not belong to flesh alone—the vibrations of the spirit-vehicle, set up by mental perturbation, may cause the most terrific torture; but what I endured cannot be told. In these moments I often thought of my friend the bonze, and almost wished I had yielded to his entreaties and joined him in the calm pursuit of wisdom and knowledge, leaving to unevolved humanity its unquiet passions and distracting desires.

The fever raged more and more fiercely, and I saw that the time was near when the baby-soul, too weak for a man's agonies, could no longer cling to a body that caused it such excessive torture. In what I may truly call an agony of spirit I waited for the crisis, watching the delicate vehicle of the child-spirit, and the passionate crimson and black cloud that embodied the soul of my enemy.

Suddenly the vehicle of Hawke vanished! A few seconds later the agonised baby-soul fled, and I leapt into my fever-racked body, glad of the pain, glad beyond expression of the weakness, the parched throat, the burning beat that possessed my limbs; glad to suffer any tortures, only to know that I was once more a denizen of earth, our mother—so cruel, yet so well beloved!

"The delirium has ceased," I heard a gentle voice say. "There is a change!"

"Thank heaven for that," was spoken in still sweeter tones—those of Alison Grant. "And look! his eyes—he knows me! Oh, God! he knows me at last!"

I was too weak to utter a word—too weak to return the pressure of her hand, or her fervent kiss. They led her away, weeping hysterically, and I was left in a half delirium of joy as well as of fever.

* * * *

How was it that Gregory Hawke had fled just at the moment when he must have been anticipating a speedy victory? For many days, during my convalescence, I pondered over this question. But when I was strong enough, Alison told me of the death of my younger brother, whom I had not seen for many years; he had been killed in the San Francisco earthquake. I was grieved; but almost instantly my thoughts flew to that secluded house in the doomed city where had last seen Gregory Hawke. I knew then that disaster had overtaken his physical form, and that the sudden danger had drawn him irresistibly to it; the "Trishna" instinct had betrayed him and saved me. Subsequently, the fact that Hawke really perished in the calamity, together with a careful comparison of dates and times, confirmed this theory. Further, Hawke had willed his whole fortune to his "friend and colleague, Alan Heriot," expecting, of course, to enjoy it himself when he should have exchanged his physical vehicle for my own. I relinquished the money to his next of kin.

Wonderful indeed was my enforced sojourn in the strange realm of the Pretas; vast is the knowledge, too, that may be gathered there. But I have done with mantras, and not for all the wisdom of the ages would I chant that spell again.

THE BLANKET FIEND

Beatrice Grimshaw

Beatrice Grimshaw (1870-1953) was born in Cloona, County Ant-
rim, Ireland on February 3, 1870. Tutored privately, she went to school at
Caen in France, and later attended Bedford College, University of London (1887), and Queen's College, Belfast (1890-91). She did not take a
degree and never married, seeing herself as a liberated 'New Woman'.
She travelled extensively while working for various shipping companies,
and in 1907 travelled to Papua in the employ of *The Times*, London, and
the *Sydney Morning Herald*. She ended up living there for twenty seven
years, writing mostly adventure and romance fiction set in the Pacific.
Her stories were published in the popular magazines of the day, including
the *Blue Book*, *Red Book*, and the *Premier Magazine*. She wrote several
horror and supernatural tales that, like her other tales, perfectly capture
the atmosphere of the Pacific. She retired to Bathurst, New South Wales
and died there on 30 June 1953. "The Blanket Fiend" is from *The Beach
of Terror and other Stories* (1931).

There is secret bread in the wilderness and on the edges of the world. That
thunderous green evening I was eating mine; it may have looked like camp
biscuit, but it was far other and more precious. For it, I had paid down
love, youth, strength, home and friends. Worth all this? I do not know. Ask
the opium-eater if his little ball of dreams is worth all that it has cost him.
Whatever the answer may be, he will hold to the ball and the magic in it.

So I ate my biscuits and looked down, in the last light of day, upon the
tangle of valleys, like the spreading fingers of a hand, that I had reached
that afternoon. And the secret bread was very sweet in my mouth, because,
once again, I had conquered the unknown. No white man before me had
seen these valleys, or climbed the enormous, nightmare slopes that led to
them; slopes on which my carriers and I had endlessly laboured, enchanted
to one spot, like ants that climb and slip upon a marble wall. But at long
last we had conquered; the days were over, and the weeks that went before
them, and we saw what no man save the wild head-hunters of the ranges
had seen—the deadly river talked of away down the coasts; whispered
about of nights round the smudge fires of camp, when mosquitoes whined
and the murder-bird cried in the bush; laughed at in merry daylight, but

cringingly believed in under night—the river that was called in a score of dialects, a dozen different languages, "Wicked."

Between tribes who killed each other at sight, over places all but unclimbable, through the air it seemed, or on the wings of the streaming south-east trade, the stories about that river passed, somehow. On the "Cape of Good Hope" that is the nose of Northern New Guinea, in the great prison Bay of Humboldt, on upper mysterious reaches of the warlike Sepik, they told you about Wicked River. Not men lived in that valley, but devils. No such devils were ever seen or heard of elsewhere. They caught you in a dusky fog, and the fog turned to living wings and bore you down to hell. They made horrible noises, and when you heard the noise, your bones melted away inside your skin, and you sank down, poured out like water, and so ended...

There were white traders on the coasts who had heard these tales; their story coincided with those that I had gleaned among the natives, but they believed none of it. It was "nigger nonsense," "yarns invented by travellers to make themselves look big," and, as a last, damning comment, it was "koi-koi," the untranslatable native term which includes every kind of hoax or lie.

So, when I went off the deep end, with a handful of carriers and very few stores (but that was all I could afford), I said I was going to look for gold. Otherwise, I think, they would have kept and bound me, as one mad.

But I knew what I knew. I had paid enough for knowing. And one piece of knowledge was, that there is never quite nothing in a native tale. What about the devil pig of Mount Victoria? What about blue "sorcerer-lights" that danced where oil has now been found? What about the Papuan tree-climbing alligator, in which no one believed until someone, recently, found dragons on the Malayan isle of Komodo? I could go on till you were tired...

It had been told me, and I believed, that the Wicked Valley and River were found over the top of an "unclimbable" mountain, which, if you did succeed in climbing it, gave you a view of five rivers like the fingers of a hand, all running into one. There were the fivefold rivers, there was the valley; and the sun, that night, was going down upon a view of fine meadows, chines and slopes and coppices, meant by Nature for the growing of banana, sugar-cane, great sweet potatoes, giant taro... But in the valley, along the whole of one side, and that the richest by far there had not been a tree cleared away: no burn-off, no digging or preparing soil. The other side was rocky cliff, unusable.

If I had doubts before, they vanished at that spectacle. For in the distance, touched by one fingertip of sinking sun, I could see the little brown shapes of a mountain village, like fungus clinging to rock. That the folk of the village should leave such a valley untouched, argued for the truth of all

I had been told.

I had an interpreter with me, a man who knew English and something of two or three hill languages. I was minded to march upon the village next day, make friends with the people, if that might be, before they had the chance to attack us, and afterwards, sure of my ground, investigate the valley. Now that I had arrived, I was mad to get into it, but I knew that I should be mad in another sense if I did not first make sure of the people. They roll rocks on your head in the inland mountains, and they do it very well from their point of view, which, naturally, is not yours.

Quite sure that I should find myself alone, I turned out early next morning from my tent, and stepped across the few feet that separated me from the carriers' fly. I was scarce round the other side when I saw a procession of from sixty to eighty men winding across the nearest slope, dim as ghosts in the dawn. The valley was full of mist; as I watched, light, boiling up from the lands below, frothed over into the far end of the valley and showed, for a moment, a deep, dark pool in the river.

Then I perceived the warriors on the other side of the valley ranging themselves above that point and coming to a halt. They were a long way off, but the concerted shout they raised rang so clearly as to wake my carriers out of sleep and set them fumbling nervously for the loaded rifles that were always within reach.

"Hold on," I ordered, "don't fire." For I wanted, above all things, to be friends with these people.

The sun was up a bit now, and I could see the mountaineers plainly, standing on the extreme verge of the precipice. They seemed, with their fluttering crests of cockatoo feathers, their bristling spears, and the unstable, poised look of their bodies, like a covey of strange birds just about to take flight. I should not have been surprised if they had spread wings and planed away across the valley.

Instead of that, they parted right and left, there on the edge of the cliff, and two men, stepping from behind, swung out across the cliff, like children playing "honey-pots," something big, brown-pinkish and screaming...

I felt as I felt once in the War when an army mule lunged out and kicked me in the chest. That was for a moment. In the next moment I saw that the screaming creature had four legs. They swung it solemnly several times and then let go. It went down, into the mist, turning over and over. I heard it scream again as it struck bottom, and then there was silence.

For some few minutes the file of Papuans stood motionless, save for the wimpling of their head feathers in the breeze; and I will swear that every man of them had his toes right over the edge. It made me giddy to look at them.

Then the white fog below them changed swiftly to red, and the sun came up sliding behind a hill, very quickly, like the pushed-up sun in a theatre. The warriors melted. In another moment they were running hell-for-leather up a height of one in three, heading for my camp. They had the air of men who say, "Business is done, now for pleasure." And they shook their seven-foot bows and leaped a bit, whoo-whooping loud, like hounds. Exactly like... for exactly the same reasons.

Now I wish I had time to tell, and you had time to listen about my making friends with these wild things, as I had done in similar tight places more than once, as I shall do, please the Red Gods, another time or two before that day arrives when the gamble with life goes the wrong way, and my stake, so often hazarded, is lost. But you are not of the wilderness; you have no patience. So you must know just this—that by night-time, I and my carriers were sitting among the men of Wicked River, fed with tit-bits by their hands, caressed, adorned, almost cried over.

They were splendid creatures, with naked chests like barrels, and legs sheer bunches of muscle; their shoulders would have wedged tight in any ship's cabin door, and their black, deep-buried eyes scintillated when they spoke with fires unknown to civilized men. I found myself hoping that civilization might never find these magnificent, untouched creatures. What could it give better than that they had?

They took me for a god from heaven, as untouched mountain people generally do. But there was something in their way of receiving me that puzzled me a little. For they were not surprised by my white skin quite as other tribes had been. They seemed, in their own odd way, to know some-thing about me. The interpreter was little use, and my own scraps of coast language did not carry me far; still, I judged that the finest of the men, a village headman, was pleased that I had come, and thought I might do him some service.

He took me by both hands again and again, chattering loudly and re-peating his words, so that I might wake up to understanding—just as John Bull is wont to do on a holiday trip to Boulogne. I have his picture clearly in my mind as we sat all together on the ground in that high camp, with the sun going down again, and the remains of a handsome feast of pig and potato, white baked yam and crayfish, scattered about for the women to pick up by and by when we were gone. The air was golden glass, and the hill peaks had a bloom on them like purple damsons ripe to fall; but farther off, they climbed up, chalcedony blue; and no man owned or knew them. The headman's face was like a coin against it all, profile of copper, nobly traced. I saw in it the sudden liking that blooms in these tropic hearts, liking for me, and trust—he who had been eager for my dangling head an hour or so before. And with it all a sort of terror.

"He is afraid of something," I thought. "He wants me to deliver him from his fear." I realized how strong and immortal I must seem to him; how powerful to aid, as our gods seem to us. "If he thinks well to grant it...!" was in the headman's burning, bison eyes, fixed anxiously on me. He was taking bracelets from his arm now; the twice coiled tusk of a great pig; twists of red seeds with little black eyes in them. He was offering these...

It is strange how you may catch yourself suddenly in another's eyes. One does not think of one's appearance, till one sees it, mirrored there. I had forgotten I was six feet three, blue eyes, with yellowy hair, long untrimmed. I remembered it then, because I saw the headman was thinking of my looks, judging me by them. In another minute I saw the reason.

A girl, very slowly, but not, I thought, timidly, came out from behind the mass of warriors and stood beside the headman, not far from the carriers and from me. And when I saw her, it was my turn to be surprised. She was naked, native, savage, but she was part white.

I don't say she was not well-looking. Her nose and lips had escaped flatness; her hair was Papuan hair, an immense, teased, floating bush, but it was brown, not black, and it had lights in it that made it look like the expanded feathers of a bird. As for her figure, she being a native girl and young, it was naturally perfect. Her colour, fully displayed by the mountain "dress"—which is a piece of decorated string, no more—was a not unpleasing deep amber.

Of course, I tried her in pidgin English, but she merely shook her head. I saw by her ornaments and her uncut hair that she was unwedded. And it became plain, in another minute or two, that the headman (whom I had mentally nicknamed "Georgy," because he looked jolly and capable, and just a bit sly—like a certain statesman we all know) had something very important to say about her.

I cursed my luck and the stupidity of my interpreter, who didn't know more than three or four dialects, little more than I knew myself, and hadn't hit it off with anyone. What could "Georgy" be up to? Offering me the girl as a bride? That might be, since they seemed to have some inexplicable strain of white in the tribe and, what was more, to value it, which was by no means usual. But even if he were offering her, that was not all. There was something of more importance afoot than the mere disposal of a girl.

Bagi-Bagi, the interpreter, only increased my perplexity by the stray words caught here and there. He translated haltingly, almost weeping over his inability to understand more.

"He say—he say—he say—Bad. Very bad. He, say—he say—he say— he say—Sky. Good."

"Oh," I shouted of a sudden, "he's saying things are bad up here, and it's well there are angels from heaven come along... Go to it, Bagi-Bagi; you're beginning to catch on."

There followed an interlude of rattling speech that sounded as if it had been shot from a machine-gun. Bagi-Bagi gave up in despair. But it was I who was catching on now; I captured a significant word or two, many times repeated as if for emphasis. "Georgy," it seemed, was telling me that if I could handle a certain job that nobody else could tackle, nothing would be too good for me. Bracelets. Yams. Pigs. Potatoes. Girls. (In the plural, the elaborate multi-plural, if my knowledge of dialect was not running away with me.) And something that seemed to mean times of year, seasons, stars—I could not make that out at all.

But I nodded my head a great many times, told "Georgy," gravely, in English, that he was a fine old fighting cock, and that I would do my best to oblige him, whatever it might be. I think he gathered my meaning. He turned off the tap of his eloquence, said something brief and commanding to the girl, and, with his followers, settled down for a happy evening.

The girl melted away, and I didn't think any more about her till she came back, with twenty or thirty others and a number of young men carrying mantles of bark cloth.

"This is going to be a dance," I said to Bagi-Bagi somewhat wearily, for I had seen a hundred and half a hundred more, in years gone by, and was by no means anxious to sit through another.

"By Scott, sir, it is," he answered readily. (Bagi-Bagi was nothing if not idiomatic.) "I very bucked, I think they dance all the (embroidered) night." But they did not; whereby both of us were disappointed, and only one disagreeably. The dance was very significant, very wonderful and astonishingly short.

After some of the usual preliminary caperings, the men and the girls formed into two opposite ranks. The former, holding high their bark cloth mantles, and dancing tiptoe with amazing lightness, approached the girls, who fled, dancing all the time, but acting terror effectively. Along the verge of the cliff, in the light of the torches and the fires, they danced, towards a space of reed-grass, eight or ten feet high. Here there was semi-darkness; the lights of the flames just showed the last and most astounding figure of the dance, wherein each man flung his enormous mantle over a girl, fought with her for a moment, and then—just as I was anticipating the usual, commonplace, love-struggle—danced back, completely alone. The girls had vanished under the mantles, as a conjuror's rabbit vanishes under his handkerchief. The mantles, after a moment, were picked up by their owners, flaccid and empty.

By and by the girls reappeared from behind us, mysteriously, danced a little more and departed. I saw the amber girl was crying, but I was too much obsessed by the dance to notice her particularly. Of course, the high, dusky reed-grass had helped in the disappearing trick, but it was all immensely effective, and I clapped with vigour. Then I began to wonder—what did it all mean? Native dances are never meaningless. Was it possible that this was a representation of the mystery I had come to solve?...

The girls passed by. The amber girl had stopped crying; she stared at me as she passed, her eyes big with feeling. I nodded to her and went on thinking.

It was then that I felt, as the solitary explorer does at times feel most bitterly, the want of a white man to talk to. There's much to be said for journeying alone, and much against. On the latter side, the impossibility of discussing plans is perhaps the heaviest count.

I was bursting with the thought that had come to me; and yet I could not say for certain whether I was a fool to entertain it or no. When you are infinitely wiser than anyone within sight; when you are being obeyed as a father, honoured as a god, it is hard sometimes to keep your balance, and remember that you are, after all, only a very ordinary sort of ass.

I think that BagiBagi, who was used to the ways of white men, guessed something of this. When the dance was over and the headman, with much back-slapping and grinning, and many incomprehensible signs as to what we were all going to do on the morrow, had disappeared, Bagi-Bagi, on soundless bare feet, came up to where I sat alone. I was smiling as I thought. That is a trick, and a good one, that I learned from books—never let your followers see you down-hearted.

Perhaps he guessed. "Sir," he suggested, "more better you talkem along me. More better you spittem out everyfing all same beach-de-mar."

I remembered the look of a bêche-de-mer in sea shallows, turning itself hideously inside out because somebody had looked at it, and I burst out laughing.

"Well, Bagi-Bagi," I said, "I think I know what's the matter here, but I can't believe it."

"E!"

"You see, Bagi-Bagi—you know what a Chinaman is?"

"Me savvy Sinaman all right. Plenty stop salt walter."

"Well, in the Chinaman's country, ever so long ago, a big white chief travelling found a valley like this and there was a bad devil in a river. It was in a place a long way from anywhere, that they called Lu Tzu Chiang. The white chief was in a great hurry to get home and talk about where he had been, so he didn't try to look up the devil, he just heard what they had to tell him, and said it wasn't true, and went away. But I think he must have believed some of it, for he put it in a book. And then everybody died or grew old, and nobody went there anymore, and all the world forgot about the devil. But I have the book and I've read it, and I'm damned, Bagi-Bagi, if the same devil hasn't turned up here."

Bagi-Bagi, squatting like a monkey at my feet and solemnly chewing betel-nut, turned the quid in his cheek before he answered.

"I think, sir," he said presently, with a lick at his lime spatula, "I think you-me go see."

* * * *

The valley, in morning light, was even more beautiful than I had thought. From the summit of the cliffs, one could see its opulent green slopes and the furry tops of its thickets; but it was only on near approach that fern-trees like parasols of finest lace; pawpaw, that lovely little palm with golden fruit and ivory flowers; bamboo; begonia; flowers the shape and colour of orange candles, set out on ropes of green; flowers like amethyst goblets, growing bare on the ground, became clearly visible. A mountain paradise, yet silent and lonesome, somewhat strange, for all its sweetness of flower and of fruit, not friendly...

Bagi-Bagi and I had climbed all the way down from the top alone; the carriers would not go within a bowshot of the brink, and our mountain friends had not yet appeared. That was all to the good, so far as I was concerned. I wanted to investigate, unhampered.

Bagi-Bagi was not the man to stop me; curiosity was at once his virtue and his vice. But I thought he liked the unfriendliness of the valley no more than I did; understood it better, perhaps. It was he who nailed it down with a name.

"Sir," he remarked, standing up very straight, with his feet dark brown among the fallen yellow pawpaw fruits, and his coppery thin body outlined against a bush of jasmine, "Sir, this place be too blanky quiet; he no talk."

It was true. Down here in the belly of the hills, there was no wind to ruffle the rich grasses, no stir among the fern-trees and bamboo, that are the greatest whisperers of all the mountain woods. The river, fed by its five thin streams, was oddly silent. Its width may have been about fifty yards on an average, save where it opened out into a longish shallow or pool, and there it was somewhat wider. In the midst of the shallow there was not quite a ripple, but a stir, a breathing of the black water.

"That's where the ford will be," I thought. "These mountain men are poor swimmers; that is the place where they would naturally cross to get at the garden land on the other side. If they ever did cross. I see no gardens, but there's certainly something like a track. On one side only... Queer."

The sunshine, thick as honey, filled the place. You could almost hear the exultant singing of the light sky. Red dragonflies, like shards of living coral, planed above the candle flowers. "They do not care whether one lives or dies," I found myself thinking. "*It* does not care." Long I had known that nameless power that walks in the wilderness, godless, incurious, magnificently apart. Was not my secret bread the very shewbread of its altar? There are some who will understand.

With an effort I shook myself free of dreams, walked forward, Bagi-Bagi following cautiously some distance behind. Yes, there was a track that led towards the shallow; towards it, not all the way. It stopped short, oddly, some feet clear of the riverbank.

I paused here and thought hard. I remembered the wild tale of the Victorian traveller, Baber; the fiend that inhabited the river ford in unknown China. Could it be true that such a thing existed? Or was the coincidence of two similar tales due only to the presence of a few stray Chinamen upon the coast, who had brought with them some of their native legends?

But there are strange creatures in the world's dark places; survivals, it may be, of an earlier day. Who knows but a living dinosaur may yet be found? Who has pierced to its depths the mystery of the Australian bunyip?

These things were in my mind as I stood, motionless, in the hot still valley, with the last few feet of the track untraversed before me, and just beyond the end of the track, below a fringe of reed-grass and tree ferns, the ford that was talked of from main range to coastline, from wild head-hunter tribes to poaching, sly Chinese. Lies, all lies, the white traders had said... and yet—

Under ordinary circumstances, that ford should have been trampled like a cattle-yard, on both sides of the river. It was the only way from the rocky side where I stood, to those rich agricultural lands just opposite, the natural food gardens of the village behind me—and, let me tell you, the inland Papuan does not value good garden lands lightly. They are his bank, his gold-mine.

Yet the village had never touched, would never touch that land. All its food was obtained from the inferior gardens, miles away, that I had glimpsed in the distance, coming up. No wonder "Georgy," that good-humoured savage with the sly, clever eyes, had promised me girls and potatoes and pig-tusk bracelets by the score if I, the strange chief descended from the skies, proved powerful and kind enough to deliver the place from its terror. No wonder he had done his little best, throwing precious live pigs and other things from the crown of the precipice, to placate the monster...

Other things? I found myself dwelling upon the words. What had put that in my head? I had seen a pig thrown, no more.

Old days, near twenty years ago, came back in a rush. The Papuan side, before the coasts were civilized. The Western rivers, stately processions up and down the Bamu, Turama, Purari, that I had seen and marvelled over; bands of fighting men, armed and plumed, singing loud brassy songs, as they ferried along a decorated canoe with sometimes a dead pig upon it, sometimes a dead man. The secret talk among cannibal tribes, in which pig and man were words almost interchangeable; a certain tendency to look upon the two as coins of different value, meet for transactions with the spiritual world.

Why was the half-white girl crying last night after the dance? Why did she fix those strange grey-amber eyes of hers on you so anxiously? Fool—you thought it was because she admired your height and your yellow tousled head! It was nothing of the kind. She knew what was waiting for her and feared it. She saw that you were strong and hoped...

"Bagi-Bagi," I said, turning round to speak to the interpreter, "what do they think of white people here? How did that girl get her colour? Down on the coast they usually kill half-castes."

"True, sir. True they kill them. This feofle another kind. He don't know white man." (Oh, bitter, unconscious sarcasm!) "I telling you, sir, you-me we seen everything, not like these dam cannibals. You-me we know about airaflanes. Sir, bee-fore Englisman take this place, one time Siamani [German] man come along in airyflane, flied over. One village he stop, one night. Beehind, he go. This girl's mother, she have her piccaninny, she die. Piccaninny half white. Belong one great devil-devil, this feofle say, devil living in the sky. Sir, they think a dam lot of this girl, thass what for they pay you with her, if you taking away the devil along river."

"Yes, yes, but what will they do with her if I can't manage the job?"

"Then, sir, they frow her all same they frow that fig. Fig no good, try another thing, try devil-devil girl."

I had known it. I had known—seen!—worse things than that. Yet the golden valley seemed to turn grey as I heard; the river, creeping among the flowers and ferns like a long black leech in a swamp, became suddenly horrible to me.

"Bagi-Bagi," I said, and I heard myself grinding my teeth as I spoke, "if I wait here a year, this thing, whatever it is, dies, or else I do."

"Me," declared Bagi-Bagi scornfully—yet I saw that he was edging away from the river, "me, I don' believe nothing stop."

We were both standing with our backs to the black river and our faces to the little mushroom houses high on the cliff. I think I was looking for the girl; I don't know what he was looking for. But while we stood there, something occurred behind us that made me swing round in my tracks as if worked by a machine. As for Bagi-Bagi, he yelled and ran.

It was merely a sound—but what a sound! If one had ripped out, in one piece, the deck of a sizeable cutter, and flung it violently upon the surface of the sea, the noise might have been something like what I heard.

I was just too late to see what had caused it. But the whole surface of the ford, that had been smooth and shining as black onyx, was ruffled into tiny cross waves, pitching and foaming like the breakers in an ocean storm, and the reeds by the margin swayed as if an invisible hand was shaking them.

Nothing more happened, though I waited so long that Bagi-Bagi had time to scramble half-way up the cliff, think better of it and slowly, uncertainly, come back. The valley relapsed into silence, so heavy that we could hear the hum of the red dragonflies and the faint, papery rustle of some small, creeping thing that moved among the reeds. Slowly, the exultation that had held me so long, the curious, malicious joy at being out of reach, right over the edge of the world, died away. And in its place, I knew the nightmare despair that is the other side of that glittering shield. I felt myself dead and done for, wandering in a world of shades...

If it is not good for man to be alone in an ordinary world of passing people; it is, still less, good for him to encounter the blinding solitudes, the aloneness, so cold that it burns while it freezes, of the world's far edge. Yet one will pay that, and pay again, for the sake of the strange joys and the bread that has enchantment in it.

I suppose all these things were in my mind as I climbed the side of the steep gorge, half mechanically. I suppose I was thinking, too, of the horrible, mysterious thing I had heard, but not seen, planning what my next move must be. But I do not remember anything about that, because of what happened when I reached the top of the cliff.

There was a patch of timber there, some tall fir trees, shaped like trees in an old-fashioned "farmyard" box of toys, a cedar or so, a clump of shiny things like laurustinus. The trunks of the firs and cedars and the low bushiness of the smaller trees hid the top of the cliff from the village. I had just set my foot upon the level, when something darted out at me from among the brushwood and seized me by the legs.

With the monster of the ford haunting my brain, I had almost fired off the revolver which all New Guinea explorers keep in their belts. It was lucky that I did not, for the next moment showed me that the thing which clung about me and held me fast was no wild beast. It was the amber girl.

She had been newly decorated after a fashion familiar to me, and significant. Shell beads, white dogs' teeth, feathers, scarlet and black seeds, had been tied into her hair and wreathed about her neck and arms. Her cheeks and her bosom were rouged with the red paint found in the pods of a mountain bean. In fine, she was decked for marriage.

But—even a native girl, I knew, to whom marriage brings no romance, does not meet her change in life with the sobs and cries that were now being uttered by the amber maid. She crouched at my feet, rebellious, terrified, defying the tradition of her people in a manner that would have seemed nothing short of blasphemous to the village women had they seen her. It did not astonish me; I and Bagi-Bagi knew that—the supposed supernatural love which had given her birth, had in truth moulded her very differently from the meek, black, bare creatures who were her ordinary mates.

Nevertheless, I was taken aback. Because it seemed as if the very idea of being given to me was producing this frantic terror and dismay.

Now you may be as far as possible from wanting to marry, permanently or temporarily, a young thing with the shape of an Oread, a skin like golden bronze and no clothes at all, but if you are human, you will not be flattered to discover that she shares your point of view. I was inclined to call the girl a silly little idiot. But she wouldn't have understood me anyhow. So I acted in the best classical tradition, raised her off her knees and set her upright, loosened her clutching hands (they were pretty, but a mass of wet red paint) and said something or other in a soothing tone.

It had no effect at all. She pointed to the valley, far below, with the black snake of the river slipping through, clapped her palms together sharply, and shook her head with violence.

Bagi-Bagi, who had waited at the top for me, and was now squatting unconcernedly on his hams, licking his eternal betel-nut spatula, remarked:

"Sir, I think she very dam disappoint you no kill that thing."

"Wait till I see it," was my answer. A plan had suddenly arisen in my mind; perhaps the sight of clutching, painted hands, half-white, of grey-amber eyes dropping tears, had given my straining mind the one last impetus it needed.

"What's she worrying over besides that?" I asked. "You needn't tell me that's all." The girl, silent for a moment, had broken forth again. Her weeping was terrible to see.

"Sir, lass night the night before full moon, thass why."

"Well, what in the name of—"

"Sir, full moon proper time for try something. Lass night close up full, them feofle they frow one fig. Tonight, suppose you can't do nothing, sir, they frow girl. They no wait. Girl she tellem me, she makem talk with her hand."

The amber girl had managed then to communicate clearly with Bagi-Bagi, by means of sign language, in which the savage woman is always more proficient than the man.

"I don't see," I objected, "why they make such a fuss about the thing anyhow. Can't they keep out of its way?"

"All-a-time," said Bagi-Bagi succinctly, "him live along big water, sometime him live along small water. Sometime woman she go get water, debil-debil catchem woman. All garden belong feofle he no good now, want this good garden, can't get him. By and by very hungerry-hungerry."

Yes, they had reason enough, this little isolated tribe, whose food gardens were almost used up, whose women were taken and devoured (but

I added a grain of salt to that)—reason full and plenty, according to their standards, for sacrificing the amber girl, daughter of gods, and possession most precious. She knew it. She looked at me with the eyes of a hunted wallaby, than which there is nothing more piteous, and pawed me with her little painted hands.

She had reason to, more than she knew or could have understood had I talked an hour. For I was suffering at that moment the greatest temptation of my life, and she was concerned in it.

No, not what you think. Something much less commonplace, less easily dealt with. You must remember I was an explorer, and one from whom, hitherto, the laurels of success had been withheld. Not, I may say, because I had done nothing to deserve them—I had won medals and fellowships a dozen times, so far as good and original work goes, which isn't very far, after all. But I had done nothing spectacular; I hadn't got lost and been rescued, or lost and found somebody else; I hadn't been captured by cannibals, I hadn't discovered purple cows or yellow dragons anywhere...

Now, I thought, there was the most brilliant chance that had ever befallen man, waiting for me down in that valley, if my conjectures were right, and if I could only do as I wished and not, perhaps, as I ought.

The fiend of the ford could—in my judgment—be one of three things only. It might be a legend, an obsession of terror, that had no actual base in fact. That was what most folk would have thought. Baber and his contemporaries waved away the Chinese fiend in just that fashion, and I have not heard that anyone has ever tried to prove or disprove their verdict.

Or—it might be a previously unknown variety of stingray, such as are common in the seas about New Guinea, a giant freshwater-ray, with the ray habit of flinging itself into the air and driving down whatever happens to be in the way. Good enough for a certain amount of glory if I discovered, and proved, that.

Or—but I hardly allowed myself to think of the third possibility. It was just as exciting, should it prove true, as the Piltdown skull, and the Java tailed man, and might prove or disprove just as much—if...

I had dynamite with me; I could use it, and it would certainly be successful. One could not miss with dynamite. I had also some thin iron bars, meant for trading, that could be hammered into big shark-hooks, strong enough, with a line of lawyer-cane, to hold the Great Sea-Serpent himself. I inclined very much to the hook and line business, because I knew that if the devil proved to be a ray, one was as good as another, but if it was what I hardly dared to hope, the use of dynamite would be fatal to my chance.

So—I had to choose between the eighty percent chance of the hook and line, and the hundred per cent chance of the dynamite—which last would, incidentally, beggar me of the finest opportunity man ever... I said that before, I beg your pardon. The very memory of it excites me beyond all—

To get back. I told Bagi-Bagi to go and fetch the iron bars and a good length of cane. Also, a couple of stones for hammer and anvil; to bring them down to the riverside where I would wait. And I began climbing down again... As I went, I shouted, on an afterthought, "Bring the dynamite."

The amber girl came with me. It was Rupert Brooke, I think, who said, *"There's wisdom in women, of more than they have known."* He was right. That girl was a savage, except for the little trace she may have kept of half-white heredity; yet she guessed instantly at what was in my mind, understood me, as a dog understands, without the necessity of translating thought into words. She knew that the balance of safety, of certainty rather, was falling in the wrong direction, and she would not leave me, any more than a dog will leave you if he suspects you of intent to desert him.

She stayed with me as I climbed down to the river flat again, followed after a long interval by Bagi-Bagi, who had brought with him the iron bars, a file, a length of cane, the stones and a firestick; also the plug of dynamite and a fuse...

She sat on her heels like a little wooden image of the kind the northern Papuans perch on house-tops, watching. Her tears had ceased; she was saving them until she knew whether they were going to be needed or not.

It took Bagi-Bagi and myself a long time to heat the iron and hammer it into shape with our primitive tools. She never moved. The sun sank down towards the ranges and struck fire into the dusky pool. Once, when I went to look at it, I thought I saw the whole under-surface stirring, as if the water had suddenly come alive.

The girl watched me and said nothing.

"Gad," I thought, "the white blood in you tells. You've pluck, and you can hold your tongue." She looked at me with those strange grey-amber eyes of hers, and I swear you could see the white soul of her coming up and unfolding, as a lily rises and opens in a lake.

I went back and hammered at my iron. I did not know—yet—whether I was going to use it or not.

It was done, and I grasped in my hand a hook and line that would be powerful enough to hold anything on earth or under water. Only remained to find a bird or some small animal, secure it, living, to the hook, and make one's trial.

In the other hand I held the plug of dynamite with the fuse cut short and inserted. And which of the two I was going to use I could not for the life of me decide.

The dynamite would assuredly make all things safe; so safe that there would be no evidence left for me to carry back. The hook might, probably would, catch the monster and, in any circumstances, leave me enough to swear by. But it was not a certainty. One might miss—and then?

If there had been plenty of time...but that was just what there was not. Our rough amateur blacksmithing had taken too long. I could not try both plans, fish for an hour or two and then, if unsuccessful, use the dynamite. I had thought of that, earlier. Now, with the afternoon beginning to darken, with, swift sunset very near and the night of the full moon almost upon me, I knew that I must decide quickly. Which was it to be? The chance of fame, that through my life had eluded me, or immediate and certain sacrifice of it all?

I don't pretend to be more high-minded than my neighbours. I do not know what I should have done, though I think I can guess, if the deciding factor had not suddenly appeared in the shape of a wallaby.

The creature, brown and furry, a kangaroo in all but size, came bounding down the scarps of the cliff, as if pursued by some enemy. I heard the villagers coming and guessed that it was flying from them. It took no account of Bagi-Bagi or the girl or myself. It went past us in a series of amazing leaps, making for what must long have been the wild things' sanctuary—the land beyond the river. From the low bank it leapt off, in a tremendous bound that should have carried it across, but did not, because, at the critical moment, a booming shout came down from the top of the cliff, terrifying the already terrified creature and making it swerve.

It fell with a splash right into the middle of the pool. And as it fell there rose, out of the water, something enormous, black, blanket-shaped, of indeterminate outline, a thing more like some maniac's half-formed idea of a fish flung out of the world of thought before it had time fully to materialize than anything else one could conceive. It was not natural, therein lay the horror.

The wallaby screamed, a cry like the cry of a child, suddenly stifled. For the huge thing, wrapping itself in an instant about the frantic creature, simply abolished its existence. The first white ray of full moon looking over the top of the ridge, fell on the monster as it quietly and without disturbance, sank.

Then the amber girl opened her mouth and screamed as the little wallaby had screamed when falling. And I gave myself no more time to think, for the knowledge that was on me now tempted, scorched like fire. I cut the fuse an inch shorter, lit it, and flung the plug into the pool. It exploded with a dull crash, and the cliffs echoed back the sound.

A black bubble the size of a bell-tent shot up, weltered for a moment in the mingling rays of sunset and full moon, and then dissolved. The pool was filled with floating bits like blots of ink. I was half mad with the thought of what I had done; I flung myself half over the edge and reached for some of the pieces. They came up, masses of dark jelly that slid through my fingers.

BEATRICE GRIMSHAW | 169

"I might have kept parts—I could have waited—photographed," I thought. "But it's gone!"

Behind me the shout broke forth again, much nearer. The warriors were coming down the cliff. They had seen.

"Georgy" was at their head. It is frightful to remember how he hugged and embraced me. I understood him to say that not only the amber girl but all the girls in the place were mine, if I chose, and that as for pigs, I had only to name my fancy. I was almost too sick to answer him. Virtue, I was beginning to discover, is by no means its own reward.

* * * *

A month after, in Humboldt's Bay, that region "at the back of all God-speed," I was talking, in the Chinese store, with a travelling Dutch doctor, a man of considerable scientific attainments. I don't know what induced me to tell him my story, I never expected he would believe it. I do not think he did, but he was extremely polite about it.

"Your description," he said, "suggests a form of life from which all animal life is supposed to have sprung; the amoeba, the blind, formless, embracing mass that eventually differentiated into a thousand higher beings. Minute in size, it persists in certain waters. Its discovery of the size you mention would be an epoch,"

"It would have made me, wouldn't it?"

His cold eye sparkled. "It would have made and unmade a score of men and a hundred theories. But..." He was too polite to finish. He changed the subject. "And the remarkable girl," he asked, "what became of her?"

"Oh," I said, staring out to the limitless sea, so seldom ruffled by the keel of any ship, "I was up against it in various ways, and sick of things, so I thought I might as well commit suicide as not."

"Commit—suicide?"

"There are various ways of doing it. I took a way that's not unpleasant... I married her."

The Chinaman, as I went out, leaned over his counter to touch my arm. His wrinkled, ancient face was alight with strange feelings.

"Dutchman not light, all long," he whispered. "Me savvy."

I shall never leave the Bay. I have called the girl Amber; she is a good wife. Sometimes I have wondered if she was worth it all. Science is a sacred thing... The old Chinaman knows.

THE PHANTOM SHIP OF DIRK VAN TROMP

James Francis Dwyer

James Francis Dwyer (1874-1952) was born on 22 April 1874 at Camden Park, New South Wales, fifth son of Michael Dwyer, farm labourer, and his wife Margaret, née Mahoney, both from Cork, Ireland. He moved to Sydney when he was 14 and worked first as a publisher's clerk and then as a postal assistant. He married Cassandra Stewart in 1893 and they had one son. In 1899 he was convicted of forgery and uttering with two associates and spent three years of a seven-year sentence in Goulburn gaol. While in gaol he sent a poem to J.F. Archibald, editor of the *Bulletin*, who published it. On his release he published several stories and poems and became a journalist. In 1906 he moved to London, believing 'the Australian writer has no real chance in his own land'. There followed a lucrative and prolific career as a writer of mostly adventure and mystery stories, many of them set in the exotic locations where he travelled. In December 1919 he divorced his wife, and on 30 December married his agent, Catherine Welch. Impetuous, ill-tempered and obstinate, his time in gaol developed in him a determination to succeed. The following story is from his collection of stories detailing the adventures of the German naturalist, Hochdorf, *Breath of the Jungle* (1915).

The tropic sun, looking like a flaming truck-wheel, lurched behind the blue smear of jungle that marked the horizon, and the heat-smitten trees waved their tops languidly, as if congratulating each other on the fact that the blazing afternoon had come to an end. A soft purring note came from the underbrush where the panting birds felt the first breath of cool air from the ocean. The purple haze of the dusk filmed the landscape, softening the outline of the distant hills that the rays of the westering sun had made wonderfully distinct.

Ford, the tall American, lifted himself upon one elbow and looked across the clearing. He called Hochdorf, the naturalist, by name, and receiving no answer, sprang from the hammock and ran to the end of the veranda that extended the full length of the lonely bungalow. Here he stopped with a grunt of astonishment and gazed toward a clump of mohor trees to the right of the little dwelling. Hochdorf was kneeling in front of the clump, his rifle pointed at the shadows beneath the great trunks, and Ford watched him intently. Three times the German naturalist removed the rifle from his shoulder, and three times whipped it sharply back into place. The American was puzzled. He could see nothing, and he muttered to himself as he watched the kneeling marksman.

"It must be a wild boar," he breathed. "There's nothing—Gee! did you get it Hochdorf?"

Ford had sprung from the veranda as the German fired, and the curiosity with which he had viewed the actions of the naturalist was increased a thousand times as he raced across the clearing. Hochdorf had dropped the rifle on the grass the moment he had fired, and when the American reached his side, he was mopping the perspiration from his forehead with a large bandanna. He was pale and sick looking, and his deep-sunken blue eyes were fixed on the spot he had fired at.

"What is it?" cried Ford. "What did you shoot at?"

The German pointed at the underbrush with a shaking forefinger. "See, did I—I get him?" he cried. "Do not show him to me! I cannot look at such a thing!"

Wondering much, Ford approached the bushes, kicked them aside with the point of his shoe and disclosed a huge black rat, vainly attempting to drag its mutilated carcass to safety.

"Why, it's a rat!" he cried. "A rat as big as a prairie dog!"

"Ja, I know!" gasped the German. "Do not bring it out! *Himmel!* no! I cannot look at a rat without being sick. I am sick as the devil now!"

Ford dispatched the injured rodent and followed the big naturalist to the veranda of the bungalow. Hochdorf called for a glass of gin, and when the Dyak boy had brought a stiff nobbler, he drained it hastily and sank back in the big desk chair as if exhausted by the happening. For a few minutes he did not speak, then he turned to the wondering American.

"A rat is the only living thing that I cannot handle," he said slowly. "I would sooner handle a king cobra or one of those little poisonous kraits that can put you in Charon's ferryboat inside three hours. I have been made sick by that rat. Ach! yes! Did I ever tell you of the Phantom Ship of Dirk Van Tromp? *Nein?* Well, it is hot indoors, and if you like I will tell it to you now. There is a countryman of yours in that story, and it might interest you."

Ford pulled his chair closer, and the German continued.

"He was a fine fellow was that American. His name was Delnard, and I owe him my life. He thinks I have paid him back, but I am not sure.

"Delnard and I were going from Trengganu to Pathia, and we had a passage on the Lost Peri, a schooner owned by a Singapore pearl buyer. The mate of that schooner was as much like me as one mangosteen is like another, and that was unlucky. It was mighty unlucky. The Malay boatswain had a grudge against the mate, and one evening when I was looking over the rail something fell on the back of my head, and before my knees had time to sag I was lifted up and tipped overboard. Before I lost my senses, I had come to the conclusion that it was the mast that had fallen on my head. I did so!

"When I got my wits back, I found that the schooner had waddled off into the night, leaving me and the man who had rescued me to look after ourselves. And I knew that it was Delnard, the American, who had rescued me. Fill up your glass and we will drink to him. By the bones of St. Philip of Neri, he was a brave man!

"After a while, we struck a fringe of mangrove trees, and Delnard hauled me ashore.

"'How are you?' he asked.

"'My head aches,' I said. 'Did the mast fall on me?'

"Delnard laughed when I asked that question. 'That Malay boatswain thought that you were the mate,' he said. 'He walloped you on the head with a jackblock and hoisted you overboard.'

"I started to thank Delnard, but he clapped his hand over my mouth, and I was quiet. I was mighty quiet.

"'There is someone talking on the other side of this clump of trees,' he whispered. 'Don't make a noise till we see who it is.'

"That American started to climb through the slimy trunks of the mangrove trees, and I followed him. For about ten yards we crawled on our hands and knees, then we peered out through the branches. The moon was full and immediately in front of us was a patch of white sand that glittered like diamond dust.

"It was then that we saw the Green-eyed Woman and the monk. I shall always call her the Green-eyed Woman, *Ja*. I will! As we peered through the bushes her face was turned toward us, and her eyes shone like the two emeralds in the face of the cat-eyed goddess, Pasht, that they worshiped at Bubastis thousands of years ago. *Himmel!* they were wonderful eyes! When I saw them shining like that I thought of the stories that the Shans tell of the Queen of the Leopards who takes the shape of a beautiful woman so that she can torture the men who hunt the leopard folk. For that woman was beautiful. She looked like a naiad taking a rest on that strip of white sand, and Delnard and I stared with all our eyes.

"She wore the most wondrous sarong that we had ever seen. It was the most wonderful sarong that ever was made. It was purple—the peculiar, wicked purple that they can make at Srinager and Saharanpur, and it suited that woman. She was wicked looking. She was so. She was lithe and tigerish, and those green eyes and that mane of gold that fell down over her breasts, made her look unreal. Many a day have I wondered how she came by those green eyes and that golden hair. I have seen nearly every breed of woman between Blair Harbor and Okhotsk, but I have never seen one like her. Never!

"'Look at the man,' whispered Delnard. 'Look at him!'

"I tore my eyes away from the woman and looked at her companion. He was a monk, a long, lean, bare-polled monk, wrapped in a yellow robe, and he stood in the center of that sand patch with one arm stuck out like the statue of Friedrich Wilhelm in the Konigstrasse. And he was talking. It was his voice that we heard when we were on the other side of the mangrove clump, but we could not hear him speaking when we were looking at the Green-eyed Woman. Her beauty had made us deaf to noises. It had so.

"But when we had wrenched our eyes away from the purple sarong and the curtain of golden hair, our ears got a chance to listen to what the monk was saying. He had some leaves of the talipot palm in his hand, and he was reading that woman a story. He was reading her a story, my friend, a story that was more wonderful than any that Scherezade told to the sultan. He would read a little and then he would explain it to her, and we listened to that story with every fiber of our beings. We could follow him in what he said, and we listened like two hill tigers waiting for the deer to come down to the watering place.

"Have you ever heard anything of the Phantom Ship? Ja, you have heard a little; I know. You have heard the stories that the old maids tell on the veranda of the Minto Mansions Hotel at Rangoon. I heard those stories when I first came to the East. They will tell you of the phantom ship that beats up and down the China Sea from Pulo Tiuman to Koh Pennan, but that bare-polled monk knew more than those old women. He knew why that ship was kept in the South China Sea. Ay, he did so. He knew the history of the whole business, and he was telling it to the Green-eyed Woman when Delnard and I found them on the sand patch. My friend, there are things happening in the Orient today that are just as wonderful as the things that took place in the reigns of Omar and Osman and the gay old Haroun.

"That was a wonderful story that we heard. Dirk Van Tromp, a big-nosed Dutchman from Amsterdam, rocked round the Cape of Good Hope in his old high-pooped ship and came up to the China Sea with his nose sniffing the south wind to get the scent of gold. That was a few days ago. It was before Buxar, and before Plassey. The Dutch were great rovers in those days, and Dirk Van Tromp and his bunch were the toughest that ever crept out of the fogs of the Zuyder Zee.

"That Dutchman had a nose for gold that was sharper than the snout of a Colombo Chetty. He could smell a piece of treasure a hundred leagues away, and once he got a whiff of the yellow metal, he would circle round like a vulture swinging over carrion till he got his big hands on the stuff.

"Van Tromp heard that there was much treasure in an old grey monastery that was tucked away in the hills above Tahkeehi, and he swore an oath on his big flat blade that the treasure would be his in a mighty short time. He was a determined gentleman was Mynheer Van Tromp. Delnard and I lay in the shadow of those mangrove trees, and we listened to the bare-polled monk telling the Green-eyed Woman how the Dutchman went backward and forward in his old high-pooped ship trying to think out a plan to get at that hoard. And the monks in that monastery knew that the big-nosed pirate was waiting to get a chance at the gold and jewels in the vaults. You bet they did. They looked out from their towers and saw that Dutch ship go up and down like a big white-winged bird of prey, and they didn't say any prayers for Mynheer Van Tromp. Not any prayers that would do him good.

"Now the keeper of the keys of the treasure vault was a young monk who had never seen a woman. Never! Mind you, this is the story that the bare-polled monk read from the leaves of the talipot palm. He told her that the treasure keeper had been found in a paddy-field by the monks of the monastery when he was a little baby, and they had reared him inside the walls till he grew up and became one of them. He had never seen a woman at a distance even. That place was quite some distance from a village, and that youngster was not allowed to stray. But the monks liked him, and when he grew up, they gave him the keys of the vault and made him the guardian of all the wealth that was stored there from the time of Tamerlane.

"For three months that thieving Dutchman rolled up and down the coast, and the monks stayed inside their walls and waited. The head priest gave an order that the big gate should not be opened while Van Tromp was on the coast, and, to make matters more secure, he asked that young monk to stay in his cell and keep the keys with him. They were afraid of the Dutchman, and they had good reason to be. He was a fiend. He waited for an idea to get into his big, round head, and at the end of three months that idea came. And it was a devil of an idea. Ja, it was.

"Can you guess what that Dutchman did? He went down to Sebah, and he got a temple dancing girl who was as beautiful as the singing houris in the seventh heaven. She was more beautiful than Mura, whose loveliness killed the seven Nubians who dared to look upon her. She had eyes that she stole from Helen of Troy, and hair that was of the bronze tint that you see on the wing of the bird of paradise. That was what the monk told the Green-eyed Woman. Her little feet were so small that the children's slippers in the bazaar fell from them, and her hands were like the petals of a flower.

"When the bare-polled monk was telling of her hands and feet, the woman with the green eyes stopped him and put a question.

"'Was she more lovely than I?' she asked.

"'I am only reading what is written on the palm leaves,' said the monk.

"'But was she?' persisted the woman. 'Tell me at once.'

"'No,' stammered the monk, 'she was lovely, but not as lovely as you!'

"When he said that to the woman, she laughed in a way that chilled my blood. She gave Delnard a chill too. It was a devil of a laugh. It was a laugh of scorn, a laugh of contempt. If a man laughed in the same way you would have killed him with the nearest thing you could get your hands on. Ach! I have never heard anyone laugh in the way that woman laughed.

"The monk went on with his story, and Delnard and I listened in the shadows. Dirk Van Tromp and his crew took that girl up to the monastery one night when the moon was at the full, and I choked with temper as I listened. The window of the cell in which the young guardian of the treasure slept looked out over the wall, and when that young monk got up from his prayers on that night he looked out on the moonlit hillside. *Gott in Himmel!* It was a dirty trick to play on that youngster. When he looked through the bars of his cell window he saw that temple dancing girl pirouetting in the middle of that grassy patch, and she looked like a silvered houri!

"That Dutchman was a cunning devil, was he not? He was hiding with his men in the bushes, and that girl was dancing the Dance of the Seven Delights before the eyes of that monk who had never seen a woman till that moment. He pressed his lean face against the bars and watched with eyes of astonishment. She was the first woman that he had ever seen, and she was one of the loveliest of her kind. It was not a fair trick, my friend. It was not!

"That girl danced and danced. That bare-polled monk described that dance to the Green-eyed Woman, and he described it so well that I could picture everything. I saw that moonlit hillside, and I saw the girl dancing that intoxicating dance to the poor devil in the cell, and I saw Dirk Van Tromp and his crew waiting in the shadows for the climax of that little performance. I never felt like smashing the bones of a dead man as I did on that night when we listened to that yarn.

"And the climax came to that affair. The dancing girl stopped dancing after she had driven that young monk half crazy, and she beckoned to him to come out to her. Beckoned to that poor devil who was wondering if she was a spirit from another world. He forgot all the orders of the head priest when she did that. He forgot everything. He only knew that someone more beautiful than the white orchids of the valley was waiting for him outside the walls, and he rushed madly into the corridor.

"It was then that the Lord Buddha took pity on that poor fool. He performed a miracle by stretching a silver wire across the corridor as the treasure guardian was hurrying along. A silver wire, my friend. But that monk was not in a fit state to see a miracle when it was performed right under his nose. His brain and his blood were aflame with the sight of the vision that he had seen in the moonlight, and he hacked that wire through with his knife. That is how the monk read it from the palm leaves to that witch-woman lying on the sand.

"The treasure guardian dropped his knife in his hurry, and he did not wait to pick it up. He ran on like a madman. But it was clean love that was drawing him to that girl, my friend. Ay, it was! And just because his love was good and sweet, Buddha performed another miracle. The Great One stretched a gold wire that blazed like a flaming thread across that corridor. The treasure guardian had no knife, but he had his two hands. He gripped that thread of gold and snapped it. Then he rushed down the dark passage.

"The blood pounded through my head as I listened to that part of the story. I believed that yarn! If you had heard that bare-polled monk read it to the woman you would have believed it, too. It was one of those stories where the truth shines through the little places between the words.

"The treasure guardian ran across the courtyard toward the big gates that the high priest had ordered to be closed while Dirk Van Tromp was on the coast, and as he raced across the yard, Buddha made another attempt to save him. The Holy One flung a rope in front of that youngster, a rope whose ends went up into the clouds, but that monk could not be stopped by anything just then. *Nein!* He had no knife, and he could not break that rope with his hands, so what do you think he did? He gnawed that rope through with his teeth, then he opened the big gates and rushed out to the dancing girl who was standing like a silver statue of Aphrodite in the moonlight!

"In the morning the monks of the monastery found the treasure guardian trussed up like a capon, and they also found that the treasure chamber was empty. Dirk Van Tromp and his crew of cutthroats did not leave an ounce of gold behind them, and you can just guess what sort of a temper the head priest was in. The treasure guardian told him of the dancing girl in the moonlight, and the old ancient went crazy with temper. He sentenced that young monk to be buried up to the neck in the sand at the point where the girl stood, and when that was done, they left him there, bareheaded, and the sun licked at him like the hot tongue of a dragon.

"Every morning for six mornings the monks paraded past that poor devil who was buried in the sand. His tongue and his lips were black and swollen, but they could see that he was praying for forgiveness. They could see that. He was sorry for what he had done, but he blamed himself. He did not blame the girl that had lured him outside so that the Dutch pirates could pounce on him.

"On the morning of the seventh day the head priest and the rest of the monks got a surprise. Ay, a big surprise. When they went out to, look at that poor wretch they found the temple dancing girl lying on the sand close to the spot where he was buried, and she was dead. Dead and cold. She had become sorry for what she had done in bringing him to his ruin and death.

She knew that it was love and not lust that had brought him out to her, and she had come back to tell him that she was sorry. But it was too late to tell him that. She found him dying in the sand, and when he would not let her dig him out of that pit she killed herself beside him.

"The young monk was still alive, and as he looked as if he wished to say something they put water on his swollen tongue so that he was able to speak a little. Then he told them something that made their flesh creep. He said that Buddha had appeared to him in the night, and that the Great One had told him that Dirk Van Tromp would never take the treasure out of the China Sea. Never! He said that it was written that the Dutchman's ship would beat up and down between Pulo Tiuman and Koh Pennan for all time. At every full moon it would rock past the monastery, and if there was a monk in that place who was brave enough to swim out to the ship and recover the treasure, the souls of the treasure guardian and the temple dancing girl would find peace. When the young monk told them that he uttered a little prayer to Buddha and died.

"That was a strange story to listen to in the moonlight, was it not? The bare-polled monk looked at the Green-eyed Woman when he had read all that was on the palm leaves, and the woman looked at the big moon that was swinging over the hills. Delnard and I watched her green eyes flash, and we thought things. All the wonder of the East was in those eyes. They were as cold as the icicle eye of a crocodile at times, and then they would soften suddenly so that one felt that he was being dragged toward that witch on the sand.

"'And you believe that the Dutchman's ship goes up and down the coast to this day?' asked the woman.

"'It is written here,' said the monk, tapping the palm leaves. 'They say that it goes by on the night of the full moon. The monks of the monastery looked out many times after that happening, and they saw that ship go rocking by, the moonlight flashing on her gilt figurehead.'

"'And now?' she questioned.

"'I have waited for eight nights,' answered the monk, 'and I am certain that she will go by tonight.'

"'And you will swim out?' queried the witch-woman.

"'If you go with me,' muttered the monk. 'My heart would turn to water if you were not near me.'

"She laughed again, that cursed sneering laugh that made one wish she was a man so that one could strike her dead, and just as she laughed, I did something that caused a sensation. A mighty big sensation. There were some wild capsicum bushes under those mangrove trees, and those bushes made me sneeze. Ja! I sneezed loud enough to wake the dead, and before I had stopped sneezing, Delnard was out in the clearing explaining to the woman and the monk how we came to be there.

"That American had a smooth tongue. You bet he had. The monk looked right mad, but the Green-eyed Woman was not disturbed one bit. She listened to Delnard's story with a smile on her face, and when he finished, she started to question him.

"'So, you heard the story that he read to me?' she said, pointing to the monk as she spoke.

"'Yes, I heard,' said Delnard. 'It was a mighty good story, too.'

"'Do you think the ship will come?' she asked.

"'I do not know,' said Delnard, grinning at her, 'but if it does come along, I'd like to go out with you when you board it.'

"She smiled when he said that, but I cursed him for a fool. That was not our business at all, and there was something in the night that I did not like. I had that sort of gooseflesh feeling that makes people say that someone has jumped over their grave. 'You can come with us,' said the woman. 'Sit down and wait.'

"Delnard and I sat down on the white sand, and I kept thinking of that story as I watched the woman with the emerald eyes. I was afraid of her. I was so. She had the appearance of a sphinx, a sphinx that had just come to life, and who would laugh as she crushed one beneath her feet.

"'Why do you want to stay here?' I asked Delnard. 'It is foolishness.'

"'We will stay for the fun of the thing,' he said, and he laughed because he saw that I was nervous of the woman. 'We will have to stay till dawn to find our way from this place, so we might as well stay close to a mystery.'

"'You are a fool,' I said. 'That woman's eyes remind me of the eyes of the hamadryad.'

"The night was a silent night, one of those nights when you feel that the *lieber Gott* has slowed up the wheels of the planet before doing something that will make you sit up and take notice. The silence came around us like a cloak, and the longer we waited the more annoyed I was with Delnard. I did not believe in phantom ships, but I thought as I sat there on the sand that it was the kind of night that you would expect ghostly things of that class to go wandering around.

"A wispy fog came creeping in from the Gulf of Siam, a creeping, low-lying fog that was wet and cold like the hand of a corpse. It swept over us, touching our faces as if it had a million invisible fingers, and it surged up the estuary. I was shivering then with cold and suspense, and I cursed under my breath.

"'This is foolishness,' I said to Delnard. 'It is nonsense to wait here any longer.'

"That woman with the emerald eyes turned her head as if to listen to what I said, and then she gave a little suppressed scream that made my blood run cold. It was not a scream of fear. *Nein!* It was a scream of amazement and wonder.

"'Look!' she cried. 'Look!'

"She was pointing up the estuary, and we looked. Ja, we looked. We stared with our eyes popping out. That fog was thin and broken, and through a break in that curtain we saw something that startled us. The monk and Delnard, the Green-eyed Woman and I saw, my friend. Now you can laugh when I tell you what we saw, but I did not laugh that night. Waddling down through that rent in the fog, her broken masts thrust up like black fingers, and her high poop tilted up like the tail of a Muscovy drake, was a ship that was out of fashion a hundred years before!

"*Himmel,* didn't we stare! I rubbed my eyes and I looked and looked, thinking that it was a mirage, but it was no mirage. It was an old Dutch ship that was of the same type that Van Edels and Pelsart and Dampier and Van Diemen used when they first stirred the foam of the Eastern seas with bull-snouted craft that were built at Antwerp!

"'*Aie! Aie!*' gurgled the monk, as he climbed to his feet and stared at the old ship that was heading for the open sea. 'It is she! It is she!' he cried.

"That monk was a mighty scared man at that minute. It was all right to read about the phantom ship, but it was a different business to watch that black hulk breaking through the wispy fog. You bet it was. That bare-polled storyteller looked as if he was inclined to sneak away into the mangrove trees, but the Green-eyed Woman looked him up and down, and he seemed to stiffen under her eyes.

"'Shades of Caesar!' cried Delnard. 'Did you ever see the like of that?'

"'I did not,' I snapped, and my lips were dry as I spoke to him.

"That woman was the only one of us who did not lose their wits. While we were staring at the apparition that was drifting down toward the point where we were standing, she was calculating the distance and thinking which would be the best place to intercept that ship. That woman had nerves of steel. She was like that jade who was married to Menelaus of Sparta; she could stand by and see battle and bloody murder without turning a hair. She could do anything.

"'We'll swim out from here,' she said, pointing to the water. 'Get ready or we will miss her.'

"Delnard looked at me, and I glared back at him. I was mighty mad with him at that moment.

"'What will we do?' he asked.

"'Do?' I snapped. 'We will do nothing! What has this fool business to do with us?'

"That woman was standing in front of me when I said that. She was twisting that purple sarong around her hips, and she heard what I said. Ja, she heard. She took three steps into the water, and then she turned her head and laughed at Delnard and me. Laughed that cursed sneering laugh that she had turned on the monk when he was telling the story. Holy St. Catherine! I have never heard a laugh in all my life like that! It was like a whip of scorn. It would drive men to their death quicker than anything I know of. She called us curs with that laugh! Do you understand? It was a lash that made us feel like worms, and the next moment we were in the water, swimming beside her and the bare-polled monk.

"We were swimming in a line, the four of us. I guess we were mad, my friend. It is foolish to sit out on the sand on moonlight nights and listen to stories of the kind that we had listened to that night. There is witchery in the air of this Orient, and one does foolish things under its influence.

"The fog closed in on us and blotted out the black shape of the ship, and I stopped swimming. I had what you call cold feet just then, but that laugh was ringing in my ears. I was tired of that business, and my head was aching from the blow that the Malay boatswain of the Lost Peri had given me. I could not see Delnard just then, and I shouted out to him.

"'Where are you, Delnard?' I cried.

"'Here,' he answered, speaking out of the fog, and just as he spoke, that thick curtain was split apart, and I saw the black hulk of the old Dutch ship rolling down on us. Ach! I can see her now as I saw her that night. There was a little smother of foam at her forefoot, and she had a coating of barnacles that the Kiel shipyards could not peel off in a week. Then the fog closed in again, and I heard the voice of the Green-eyed Woman calling from above me. That witch-woman had got a grip on the side of that craft and she was calling the three of us to her.

"I made a clutch at the rotten timbers as the ship lurched past me, but my fingers slipped on the slime. I made another grab at her, and this time I caught the rotten timbers of a porthole, and I clawed myself up out of the water. That woman was calling out to us, and I knew by the shouts that came from the fog that Delnard and the monk had got a footing on the old hulk as she slewed by. Driving my toes into those barnacles and scratching with my fingers at the rotten wood I climbed higher, and presently that woman's fingers gripped my shoulder and dragged me over the side. Delnard and the monk were close behind me, and when we hauled them aboard, we stood a moment to get our breath.

"It was just as we stood there near the rotten bulwarks that the old boat drove out of the bank of fog. She lurched out of it suddenly, and the moon washed us in a bath of silver. That was when the monk gave the yell. He gave a yell that you could hear down at Sebah where the temple dancing girl came from, and he pointed to the deck in front of us. For a moment we did not see what he pointed at, then our throats went dry like as if we had been swallowing lime. That deck was alive! It was alive with rats!

"That is the reason why that rat turned me sick a few minutes ago. I think of those rats on the Dutch ship every time I see one. And those rats on that hulk were the biggest rats I have ever seen. The Paris sewer rats, the grey rats of the Orinoco, and the big black rats you see on the canals at Bangkok were small things compared to those devils on the rotten deck of that old craft. They were huge brutes, and there were thousands of them. Thousands! They were crawling up from the hold in armies that moved across the deck so that we could not see an inch of the rotten boards!

"'Look out!' I cried. 'They are attacking us!'

I made a movement to drop over the side of the ship, but that woman was too quick for me. She was too quick for me. *Nein,* she did not block me with her hands. She laughed at me. I tried to fight against the feeling that came over me, but I could not. I would not have been a man if I ran when she laughed as she did. It would take a mighty good coward to run away when that sneer came from her red lips. You bet it would. Delnard had turned to the rail when I turned, but she stopped both of us. I do not know how the piece of wood got into my hands, but I guess she gave it to me. She was the only one who could think and act. She thrust that stick into my hands, and then I struck at the army that was circling toward us.

"Have you ever seen rats attack men? Once before I had seen it, but I had never seen anything like the charge I saw on that deck. Those rats were mad with hunger. That old boat had been stranded up that estuary for a century, and she had become a castle for those big rats. I do not know how the tide had shifted her, perhaps she had broken loose from the trunks of the mangrove trees, but that rat army had come with her, and when we boarded her, they were hungry. They were mighty hungry. There were thousands of them there, and they were eating each other when that witch-woman brought three fools aboard, *Gott!* The sight of that brute brought it all back this afternoon, and I am sick yet. I will be sick for a week. I know I will.

"'Fight them!' cried the woman. 'Fight them!'

"It was our only hope, my friend. We had to fight like demons to hold those squeaking things off. The deck was covered with them, yet they were still crawling up through the rotten planks from below. It was a nightmare, and a terror struck into my bones. As I swung that stick, I thought that the whole business was some devilish plan to get us on board that hulk, and I fought like a madman. So did Delnard. So did the monk, and the Green-eyed Woman. As I watched her for a few seconds I knew that I was wrong in thinking that it was a plot against Delnard and myself. She was a crazy woman. She had become possessed with the idea that the old hulk was really the ship that Dirk Van Tromp had sailed in, and that monk was of the same opinion.

"'Fight them back!' screamed the woman. 'The treasure will be on the lower deck.'

"'We are insane,' I cried to Delnard, but he did not hear me. That laugh had made him lose control of himself, and he was slaughtering rats with a plank that it would take a Samson to lift.

"The rats broke before us, and the woman led us on. Led us on across the rotten deck where the cross beams had crumbled beneath the three-inch planks of oak. You can hardly believe it, can you? I was sweating with fear, but I could not turn and run as I wanted to. There was a squeaking in the bowels of the ship that made me feel sure that anyone that ventured down there would go to his death, yet every time that woman gave one of her steely laughs, I swung that lump of wood harder than ever. She was a witch; I am sure she was.

"'Take a rest!' she cried, and we stopped for a moment to get our breath.

"But those rats were waiting for us to take that rest. They swept over the deck in one thick mass, and we were at it again. I stuck my foot in a hole and fell down, but Delnard lifted me to my feet again. Lifted me to my feet after three score of those things had rushed over me. And she laughed and rushed us forward against the swarms that were pouring out of the holes in the planks.

"It was then that the Almighty heard the prayer that I was making. *Ja*, he heard me then. As I picked my club from the deck after I slipped, my hand clutched some oakum, and when I stumbled on after that mad jade, I got an idea. I got an idea that meant salvation to Delnard and me. You cannot guess what that idea was? I stuffed that oakum in my ears, my friend. I stuffed it in with one hand while I fought with the other. *Ja! Ja!* I knew that I could not turn back while that jade was laughing her laugh of scorn, so I made myself so that I could not hear her laugh. I fixed myself in just the same way that old Ulysses fixed his sailors a few thousand years before. I plugged my ears so that I could not hear the squeaking of the rats or her laugh, and then I dropped my stick and rushed at Delnard. I ran him to the side of the ship, and when he fought with me I hit him a crack on the jaw and toppled him overboard as the Malay boatswain had toppled me some hours before.

"I had luck then. I sprang over and found him in the shadow of the hulk, and, grabbing him by the hair of the head I struck out for shore. Once I looked back, and I saw that old black ship moving towards the open sea and I swam faster. Fear was in my marrow just then. My teeth were chattering together, and I could hardly speak when I pulled Delnard ashore.

"'Where is she?' he asked.

"'She has gone to sea with the rats and the mad monk,' I said.

"'Glory be to God!' he said and then he broke down and cried. And my nerves were that bad that I cried with him. I have been in a thousand tight places, but I was never in one that made me feel so queer as I felt on that night.

"We fell asleep on the sand, and we slept there till the sun climbed out of the sea and pricked our faces and hands. There was not a sign of a hulk. We stared at the sea for ten minutes or more, then Delnard got to his feet and shook himself.

"'We had better strike toward the south,' he said, and I went with him without making any protest.

"We walked about two miles without speaking, and then we found her. The Green-eyed Woman. Ja! We found her on the beach, her mane of gold covering her face as if the sea had tried to hide the staring eyes. In her left hand she had a tiny statue of Siva that had a Mogok ruby in its breast, and I wanted badly to get that little statue. But Delnard would not let me take it from her hand. He would not. We made a grave on the beach, and we buried her there."

THE DEVIL'S BALL

Dulcie Deamer

Dulcie Deamer (1890-1972) is an undeservedly neglected Australian writer of supernatural and fantasy fiction. The "Queen of Bohemia,"
a long-term resident of Sydney's cosmopolitan King's Cross district,
sprang to literary attention as a teenager when she won a lucrative short
story contest run by the literary journal, *The Lone Hand* for a story set
in prehistoric times. The following witch story, similar in style to her
werewolf tale, "Hallowe-en," was lifted from her novel, *The Devil's Saint*
(T. Fisher Unwin, 1924) and published in *Vision: A Literary Quarterly*
in November 1923, with illustrations by the great Australian artist and
writer, Norman Lindsay.

It was midnight of Hallowe'en.

Sidonia, the witch's daughter, blew out the sickly flame of the lantern,
and the loft was in darkness, save for the faint, pink phosphorescence of
the hearth and a greenish rumour of moonlight struggling through the thick
glass lozenges of one small leaded window.

Quickly the girl stripped herself to the skin. Wan as a ghost she stood
before the hearth between the embers and the moon. She shuddered, and
the quailing sensation of gooseflesh came over her. But she was determined
to fly, and equally convinced that she was about to do so.

With her forefinger she began, gingerly, to rub upon her body a little of
a foetid-smelling salve. Over and over she repeated the names of the four
aerial demons, adding, "Help me to fly! Help me to fly!" Her whispering
voice was insistent, though her teeth chattered. Her faith was absolute.

The dim figure of the naked girl, that had stood for a number of seconds
rigid as a figure of wood or a person hypnotised, gave at the knees and fell
suddenly to the floor, lying crumpled before the chilling hearth. The yellow
cat disturbed by the thump of the fall, started awake, stood up, stretched,
and settled down again. The black cat slept on. The strengthless, diffused
ray of livid moonlight was the only thing that moved in the loft.

* * * *

"Up! Up! Look, little sister!"

Sidonia opened her eyes which she seemed only to have closed for a minute.

Oh!

Moonlight, wide, feathered pinions, height, hurtling speed—and company. The shock was as though a pail of cold water had been flung over her. She nearly lost her balance on the back of the winged sable horse whose sides her thighs gripped, and she caught at the mane to steady herself.

"Don't fall, little sister! If you fall, and are afraid, you will instantly return."

"Where—where?"—Sidonia did not know who it was that had spoken to her, nor why she questioned. Her mind whirled: it was like a swarm of gyrating silver sparks.

A wonderful wild laugh answered her. It was inhuman, beautiful, terrible. There was the whoop of the wind in it, the chime of water, the scarlet of fire, the sonorousness of earth.

Her body, borne dizzily upward, seemed itself light as a wing—she could race on the air, she could run with the winds! Her hair streamed about her like a mermaid's in the swirl of the tide.

Moonlight, beating pinions, faces and swift shapes. Faces that had in them something of the eaglewide golden eyes that were soulless; arched brows and noses. Hair like tongues of fire, limbs flaked with golden scales or feathers. There were four—two upon either hand. Straight-standing in the air, they bore her steadfast company as the black horse rose. Oh, but the others! They darted like swallows, they circled, they poised, they drifted— they were uncountable. Black imp-things, wickedly grinning, that whizzed and somersaulted; translucent maiden-shapes, linked hand to hand and dancing wreath-wise in the void; bird-like creatures, sapphire-blue, white, rosy or sable—men's thoughts, plumaged in accordance with the emotion that had shaped and speeded them; the naked selves of men, women and children, sleep-released, drifting like vapour, dreaming, half-conscious; wandering flames, bat-thoughts, ghosts. Overhead the full moon, an inexhaustible, round lake of blinding silver, drenched everything in light.

Sidonia looked down. The town was a patch of darkness from which the needle points of a couple of moon-touched spires rose. She had no giddiness, just as she had no sensation of cold. But she wanted to descend—to sweep above the roofs that had witnessed her sad, trudging fatigues. Like a bolt from a crossbow aimed at the zenith the black horse with his mighty raven-feathered wings still hurtled upward.

"You shall fly down, little sister. Speak to the horse which your desire has shaped for you."

It was one of the four beautiful demons who spoke.

"Down, down!" breathed Sidonia, leaning forward and again twisting her hands in the lavish blue-black mane. The mad upward rush instanta-neously ceased. The horse hung for a second on pulseless wings, and then plunged earthward down the dizzy lapis lazuli precipice of the night.

It was heart-stopping—a swoop of utter horror if a grain of fear re-mained. But Sidonia shrieked with the pure joy of it.

Oh, the wind of the cloven air!

Now the shingled roofs rushed up to meet them, and the church spires were like cross-tipped javelins thrown at them from the earth. Now swept with a train of attendant sylphs, spectres and globular, will-o-the-wisplike flames over the gables and the winding clefts of the streets. Weathercocks crowed shrilly at them. Gargoyles yelped like dogs. A stone griffin clasping a stone coat of arms between its claws hissed out fire and lashed its forked tail, unable to join the flight. Cats clinging to thatch or shingles glowered with flattened ears. But one—a black wer-cat—leapt into the air with a cry of joy and followed the fleeing rout. The figures of saints enshrined in niches along the front of the Cathedral glowed with a soft, bluish light. The wer-cat sheered widely away from them, its fur bristling, its swollen tail as stiff as a ramrod. But Sidonia felt only the innocent interest of a kitten in church. She was elemental, and therefore in perfect accord with the aerial demons, who might harry the soul that feared them in sheer sport, but were the strong playmates of their own kind, and would fawn like gentle and puzzled hounds at the passage of an angel or a discarnate saint.

A nude, red-haired young woman astride of a bearded he-goat, whose horns she gripped, came hurtling over the roofs. She waved to Sidonia, and in a moment was flying with her. Her green eyes were elfish and had an irresistible sidelong shine. Her mouth, wide and laughing, was of a ripe, animal fullness.

"You're new!" said she. "I often fly, but I haven't seen you before. Do you live in this town?"

"Yes," said Sidonia, "near the Street of the Martyrs."

"How funny! My father is the head of the Goldsmiths' Guild, and we have a house that faces the Church of St. Saviour. Yet you and I are really good friends because we do the same thing."

They smiled unreservedly at each other.

"How did you learn to fly?" asked Sidonia.

"Oh, I heard a wandering friar preach a sermon in the marketplace against witchcraft. He described the devils, the broomstick rides, and the wild times they had at the witches' Sabbath. It all sounded so exciting, and I was feeling so dull, that I thought I'd try to do what they did—just for fun! So, I stripped naked at midnight and called on all the devils I could think of...and now it's easy."

There was something infectious in the sidelong twinkle of her eye. She was bubbling with life-joy, and utterly candid. But several of the creatures that followed her were unpalatable. There was a hog, a leering faun with furry cars, and a thick-lipped, hermaphrodite thing with woman's breasts and the hindquarters of a dog.

"Up! Up! Let's see the world, and then dance with the others at the Devil's Ball!" cried the red-haired daughter of the godly master goldsmith.

"Let's see the world!" echoed Sidonia. She was wild with the excitement of speed and freedom.

The winged horse and the he-goat, with their clinging riders, shot upward. The unhindered moon drenched them with its arctic silver. Forests unrolled below them like the undulations of a sable cloak, rivers resembled shimmering girdles, mountains lifted their snowfields, like peaked canopies of blue-white satin, and the blue shadows of the fliers flitted across the printless snow. Continually they were joined by others—solitary beldames with thinly streaming white hair, whizzing on broomsticks, young girls riding sows or goats, and a sprinkling of renegade monks, and of students of the forbidden sciences, mounted on hay forks, staves, or black dogs. One man—an aged wizard—rode a dragon with peacock-coloured scales.

The company was mixed, indeed, and Sidonia was so interested that she wanted to look two ways at once. The red-haired girl cried shrilly to this or that one, with whom it seemed that she was acquainted.

Now the moonlit sea glittered beneath them. Huge sable shapes towered and weltered, spasmodically shutting out the moon—cloud-giants. A hurricane wind arose; thunder bellowed, lighting glared, and to the right and left of them the thunderous torches of volcanoes painted the rolling vapours with auburn light.

"The Earth wakes, little sister! The Earth is alive as we are!" cried the demons of the air, and they darted hither and thither like summer swallows through the chaos of storm and speed.

"Yes!" shrieked Sidonia.

Everything lived, everything was in motion. How could one be afraid of that of which one was a part?

Higher and higher rose the blast of the hurricane. The moon was gone, Sidonia, clinging to her horse's mane, was whirled like a grain of dust, through a roaring blackness that had swallowed witches, wizards, neophytes, wer-cats, and all the strung-out train of following devils created by gross, lascivious, malicious or hateful thoughts.... Then sudden silence. Stillness that was dizzying.... A gradual greenish light, grateful and limpid. Sidonia saw that she was astride of a smooth tree trunk, sunk in grass, and that as she lay forward upon it, it was two tufts of grass that her hands clutched.

She sat up straight. Great trees surrounded her. Water fell in crystal sheets from cool cavern mouths. Everywhere there was movement—goat-legged fauns peeped; a young female centaur trotted close, her mare's body cream-white. Here were playfellows! But the light was dimming, the tree shapes became obscure. An intense red flame shot up and pulsated, nearly blinding her. Red! She had always loved it. It was, after all, a better colour than green. It was excitement.

Oh! what a blare of sound!—mewing, yelping, howling, screaming, laughing, grunting neighing, whooping. Sheets of fierce fire beat upwards, breathless conflagration, and against the scarlet, dark shapes pranced, mingled, or were swept pell-mell by veering currents of the maddest confusion.

Someone caught her arm. By the fiery light Sidonia saw that it was the daughter of the master goldsmith.

"The Devil's Ball! Dance with us at the Devil's Ball!" she screamed, her voice barely audible above the babel.

Hogs capered upon their hind legs. There were horned and beaked things, sealed things, bloated things smooth as slugs, obscene things with the shrivelled breasts of a hog, things with the heads of skulls, cocks, baboons, or dogs. Stripped girls danced with man-shaped devils. Shaven-headed monks—glimpsed for a moment between the red-lit eddies of the dance-parodied the sacred rites of Christendom with the assistance of grotesque acolytes, long-tailed and cloven-hoofed. Flutes made of dead men's bones were being played upon, with bagpipes and drums. Soft mouths were nuzzled by the loathly snouts they had desired. White arms embraced the metallically glistening bodies of tall demon-husbands. The whistling flames that streamed up like broad banners illumined a cauldron of chaos.

Sidonia was amazed. The noise deafened her, the glare dazzled her. She was horrified yet attracted. Something urged her to plunge into the fantastic debauch and mix herself with it—her starving hunger for excitement, perhaps.... Shrinkingly, like a bather stepping into water, she made a slight forward movement.... Oh! they were all round her—they surged and jostled. Feelers touched her, whiskers tickled, sleek fur rubbed. She had no feeling of kinship with these monstrosities, these obscenities. She shuddered, with arms crossed over her bosom.

"Dance! Take a partner!" came the high-pitched, laughing voice of the red-haired girl. She herself had been grappled by a shaggy satyr, and they reeled together, breast to breast.

"You shall dance with me, Sidonia."

Whose voice was that?

The tangle of creatures parted, and a tall man was before her. He was masked. He was all in black. Red-lit, the height and the proportions of him seemed of a strange splendour.

"Are you afraid, Sidonia?"

"No!" she said.

He caught her to him. Together they moved through the seethe of Hell. Premonitions of abandonment thrilled through the girl's body. They seemed be descending. The furnace-glare was above them. Below was a sullen flame the colour of dragon's blood. Thick tentacles reached and appeared to beckon. But Sidonia, with closed eyes, embraced the Master.

"Mine! Mine!"

His... Yes... But she was suffocating! Strangling smoke enveloped them. Her flesh encountered the touch of tentacles, slimy as snails. The quick grunt of hogs came from every side—surely a herd surrounded them! An unhuman leathery hand was laid on her.

"Give me air! Let me go!"

"Never, Sidonia." And he laughed.

* * * *

In the loft where the livid moonlight moved imperceptibly the yellow tom cat, disturbed a minute or two before by the collapse of a girl's stripped body, had just begun to doze comfortably with his front paws tucked in beneath his chest. The girl, lying upon her back, twitched, shuddered, moaned. Then there was the sound of a long relaxing sigh, and her breathing became gentle and regular. The mother of the girl, patch-work-shrouded, drowsed upon the three-legged stool. A pallid pumpkin hung from the rafters. The pot containing the noisome unguent had rolled into a corner. It was about ten minutes past the hour of midnight.

THE PLEDGE

Helen Simpson

Helen de Guerry Simpson (1897-1940) is a celebrated Australian novelist who died prematurely. She is best-known for her Australian sagas, *Boomerang* (1932) and *Under Capricorn* (1937), the latter of which was filmed by Alfred Hitchcock. Simpson was born in Sydney to an upper middle class family; her father was a solicitor, and her mother daughter of the French Marquis de Guerry de Lauret. Her father sent her as a boarder to the Convent of the Sacred Heart, Rose Bay (1910-11, 1913) and to Abbotsleigh (1911-12). She went to England in 1914 and read French at Oxford. Later she studied music there, intending to become a composer, but she developed an interest in the theatre and founded the Oxford Women's Dramatic Society. She was sent down from Oxford without completing her degree in 1921 for breaking strict rules prohibiting males and females acting together. In 1927 she married Denis John Browne, a nephew of the Australian author 'Rolf Boldrewood,' and they had one daughter. She died of cancer on 14 October 1940 at Overbury, near Evesham, Worcestershire, and was buried in the village churchyard. *The Baseless Fabric* (1925), from which the following story is taken, is a series of complex psychological tales, several of which have supernatural content.

In the old town was a most unexpected street, which, neglecting the opportunity offered by the level land to the north, turned away southwards to go shouldering up the hill in whose lee the town had been built, and under whose sheltering trees it lay like a ship at anchor. The street was like a street of ships and had been built by seafarers. The houses were ribbed with oak, their upper stories leant forward so that to a person standing in the street they seemed like wooden hulls curving to earth instead of water; their flanks showed round windows here and there, portholes against which on storm nights the rain flung itself with a sound as spray. The street was like that. People had heard of it and came in cars and buses to ascend it on foot, for the incline baffled all mechanism; these outlanders could be seen any day, staring right and left with the wistful look of those who have been told what to admire, but are uncertain as to details. Their conversation as a rule was fragmentary, owing to the climb. They said,

"This'll soon get that fat off you, Annie."

"Charming, of course, but almost too artificial."

"I should think they must get a lot of painters coming here in the summer."

"My, if my husband could see this street, he'd want to buy it right up."

"I wouldn't live in one of them, not if you was to pay me. I do like a nice bright room. Where we live, we got a great big window where you can 'ave a nice pot of ferns"

But the inhabitants of the crooked leaning houses were used to it; and the street, oddly enough, did not break out into little teashops with orange curtains, or little antique shops with brass candlesticks writhing in the window. A certain tenacity and unfriendliness came to the aid of the inhabitants. They refused to resign their houses, and the visitors had to retire to the far end of the town where in a charming but adroitly aged hotel they might consume the cakes and purchase the Staffordshire figures which the barbarians of the street denied them.

The barbarians, despite their houses, had ceased to think of the sea. They had forgotten it since it no longer occupied their immediate horizon. It had gone, leaving the marsh behind it, rich land where sheep were pastured; and so gradually did the meadows slope to a shingle and the shingle to water, that although it was only two miles distant the sea was not visible save on bright days as a thin silvery line. They built no ships now, and no houses save in ignoble rows with disciplined roofs. They were no longer adventurers and free men of the sea; the land held them fast. Only the strangers remembered.

Miss Alquist lived in one of the narrow houses halfway up the street of the ships. She was a newcomer. She had arrived one day from the outer world, unheralded, and at once, by artifice or simply by strength of character, had contrived to secure a foothold among the shipdwellers. She lodged with a family of them, renting one room at first, and gradually, as the elder children married, extending her domain till she possessed the whole ground floor with a lien upon the kitchen. As time went on she proceeded, to the dismay of her hosts, to oust their furniture and replace it with odds and ends of her own, which came sewn up in sacking from some place abroad whose name the Frants could never succeed in reading. They found themselves crowded in the remaining rooms, compelled to uncomfortable proximity, and obsessed by the rejected furniture which advanced upon them like a tide with their lodger's every acquisition.

Miss Alquist never considered the inconvenience and had never been heard to apologize. She was shabby and haughty and quite without consideration for the Frants, who, though appalled by her assurance, lacked the courage to send her packing. It is possible that had they tried to do so she might not have consented to go, and before that only too probable situation the stern over-night resolutions of the Frants would pale to morning civility. Her advantage was a moral one, and her strength lay in this, that for some reason unknown she loved the street of the ships. This passion, unsuspected by the rightful heirs, would have astounded them. They found sufficient matter for astonishment in the account of her possessions and the manner of the arrangement; for whereas they had iron beds with speckled knobs of brass, tables made of bamboo, and gilded vases, Miss Alquist kept her rooms bare, uncarpeted and vaguely redolent of salt and spices. She slept in a little narrow bed which had no wire mattress but was corded with rope; a bright coloured blanket covered it. Under the window of the back room stood a big dark chest with brass corners from which the smell of spices seemed to come; but in all the years of her residence the Frants had never once found it unlocked. That, with a small folding chair and hanging curtains in two corners, was all the furnishing of the bedroom.

The sitting-room, with bow windows looking on to the street, was almost equally bare. There was a wooden chair with a cushion tied to the seat, comfortable enough, though foreign looking; a table covered with a shiny cloth; a brass lamp; above the fireplace the photograph of a man. Near the window was a wooden stool, and the floor, like that of the bedroom, had no carpet or rug on the clean boards. There were five or six books huddled against each other on the windowsill, into which the Frants had never looked. They were not curious in such ways. But one most unaccountable fact they had observed that three or four times in the year other belongings would make their appearance, from the depths of the chest as it was supposed. They would follow each other in order, obedient to the canons of some private and unguessable ritual which went forward within their owner's mind.

First, towards the end of a strip of silk, claret-coloured, and embroidered in gold, with flowers of yellow and faded blue, would one day be laid across the table; it was not wide enough to cover the whole surface, but being rather long, hung down richly at either end with flowers and golden scrolls crowding together to fulfil their pattern. There for about twelve hours it would lie without explanation, and at the end of that time be engulfed, to reappear no more until another year summoned it.

Next, about five or six weeks later, on the dull black of Miss Alquist's everyday blouse would be displayed an ornament like a large round brooch, of a marvellous blue, with patterns and whorls of silver, and in the centre a bird with an orange breast. It looked soft, as though the bird and the circling pattern had been worked in silk; but Miss Alquist had once vouchsafed the information that it was made of feathers.

After this, no splendours would be set forth for nearly six months, when beneath the photograph, blurred with enlargement beyond its capacity, a little jar would be placed, coloured a clear brilliant green fading to white;

in this jar flowers grew in what seemed to be red soil, but which was in fact composed of tiny grains of powdered coral, the flowers themselves were of coral, pink and white, with carved spiky leaves of greenish-brown tortoise-shell. They looked so real, though fantastic, that it was almost shocking to hear them faintly rattling when someone trod heavily in the room overhead.

These were the only treasures on which the public eye might rest. They were sufficiently provocative, and each year as the ritual proceeded there was speculation in the Frants' kitchen. Miss Alquist disregarded hints and questions. She could be intimidating for all her shabbiness; her very sniff and the lean foreign look of her was enough to disquiet the ordinary questioner, and by degrees her hosts became accustomed to her apparition of the silk, the brooch, and the cold flowers, and accepted them as the years passed almost without comment. They had ceased to hope for any explanation.

All day long, save for a short foraging expedition in the morning, Miss Alquist sat in the wooden chair by the window making ugly little pictures in wool on a coarse stretched canvas. Nearly all these pictures represented ships, not sailing ships, but steamers, and one dirty little steamer in particular with two crooked funnels belching thick smoke, cutting stolidly forward through a grey woollen sea. No picturesque aspects for Miss Alquist. Even on canvas she permitted herself no illusions. The things had movement, though; the clumsy lurch of the broad-beamed tramp, the lift of the stern as she sank in the trough of a wave, the smoke streaming away in a cross wind, it was all recorded and set down in stitches. What became of these pictures when they were finished could never be discovered? Perhaps they descended into the oblivion of the brass-bound chest. Perhaps they were despatched as gifts to distant relatives whose existence was not otherwise recognised; if so, they were not acknowledged, so far as the Frants knew. In the thirteen years of her residence in the street only five letters had come to Miss Alquist, and these were type-written, and presumably to do with money; for she had an account, piteously small, at the local bank, on which she drew, every four weeks, an unvarying sum, and paid at once in cash for every need of her life—house-rent, food, and at rare intervals clothing.

That was her day. But in the evening, earlier or later according to season, she would fold up her work, or replace one of her uninteresting looking books, and go out. Slowly she would climb the street—the Frants' house was at the northern end, near the High Street—looking about her, seeing for the thousandth time the detail of a door, the colour of a roof in sunlight above another in shadow. And towards the top of the street where the port-hole windows were more frequent, she would draw long breaths and sniff noisily. Passers-by, or watchers in doorways who observed her, always thought that the steep ascent had distressed her; but they were wrong. Her thin body was healthy, though she took no exercise save this. She breathed deeply, expanding her narrow chest, because at this point, among the jutting house fronts, the round sea-windows, and with the flying buttresses of the church rigged against the sky, she felt at home.

Treading freely, casting looks of disdain at the tranquilly smoking householders who watched her daily progress, she would climb to the summit of the hill, which below the churchyard became a cliff, falling sheer to the green flats which stretched away to their shadowy junction with sea and sky. There she came every evening to the same angle of the churchyard fence; and every evening, watching the marsh darken, she would forget its lush earthy green, seeing instead the green of shoal water breaking to white against the cliff. That was how it had been; no grass nor sheep; no smoke, no crawling river with banks of yellow mud; no land to tame men's bodies, but the clean water shifting, flowing, offering and claiming life. Something in her, some legacy from unknown seafaring ancestors, hungered for this to be as it had been. Each day, coming to this place, she felt the passion in her, alive, incommunicable, that recognised and answered the passion of the sea. Motion, colour; fear and defiance; all craving and all fulfilment was there. She was stirred by the sight of that calm, distant water to a great longing for new perils and adventures of the soul, and these she might command, in imagination building the tumbling waters to storm, or subduing them at will. Standing there in the last light of the sun, a small, unconvincing figure, hands resting loosely on the wooden rail, she had experienced all the terrors and revulsions of one who has submitted himself to the powerful sea. She thought how danger might rise in the tropics. Out of a breathless sky would come a single gust of hot wind; it died down, and she could hear again the thud of the engines and the water whispering as it slid along the side. A feeling in the air of expectation, vigilance. Another gust, suddenly pushing against the ship like a hot hand; and now the reflected lights began to dance and to heave themselves into twinkling ominous patterns, and the severed water no longer whispered evenly, but came slapping sharply against the plates.

She knew how a steamer might lie waiting for the dawn outside the harbour of an Eastern port; the pale green of the water, reflecting untroubled the lines of the masts and ropes; the fishing boats with their top-heavy triangular sails veering by on the wind that blows before sunrise. She knew the grey-blue of the early sky. She saw the coolies running and yelling, with little baskets of coal no bigger than so many flower-pots, running, sweating, getting the bunkers filled somehow amid singing and sudden unreasoning quarrels. She watched the sky go green and the coast darken as night came; the stars were tremendous and their colours distinct, yet a swift wind might extinguish them in half an hour and set the water leaping and playing, pale with phosphorus, against the hull. She knew the unfathomable blue of mid-ocean, opaque, the colour of lapis-lazuli. She heard the hours go clanging by and the hurry of feet and voices in the night when the watch was changed. She knew monotony, the endless horizons of the sea, the eternal similarity of distant coasts, the throb of the screw.

She learned to long for the shore life, and to hate it. She watched the streets of the world; Australian streets with sporting placards at every corner, and sellers of lottery tickets offering their wares to hurrying men with wrinkled eyes; streets of Japan, with vertical shop-signs, and paper fish floating above the houses; South African streets where huge negroes wearing buffalo horns and kirtles of feathers stood in the shafts of the rickshaws.

This was Miss Alquist's life. These were the voyages on which she set out every evening during thirteen years, or longer, who knows? They were the voyages of which he had spoken, from which he had brought back the gifts which looked so exotic in her bare rooms, and which she followed in her heart; but the best of all was that which should have been the last. In it she stood on the bridge of a vessel steaming up Channel and saw the sequence of lights winking out the course. A heavy sea came clouding over the bows and sank in little whiffs and rattles of spray against the decks, against her cheeks. Lights of France to starboard; La Vache booming out her warning, fog off the coast. Voices below on the fore-deck, and a laugh, one of the hands playing the fool, all the rest thinking of home, and the drawn red blinds of stuffy little parlours, or bars with the strong lights glittering in gilt-framed mirrors. Quiet lights those, not the restless warning lights of the sea; a firm road to tread; stillness, welcome, safety; and their ship driving back to it all through the spray.

Strange that she should so love the sea, which had robbed her of her lover. At first she could not look at it. She remembered how once, just before the news came, she had gone down to bathe in a little sandy cove; suddenly she had become afraid, angry, and standing waist-deep in the water had struck down at it with her clenched hands, hating it because it yielded and slipped away, not resisting her strength. She had not known then, and the little scene remained in her mind unexplained. Since, she had come to think of the sea as a loved thing that had blundered cruelly. She could not forgive the townspeople their apathy about it. They had been glad when the sea, that had made them, departed. They lived within sight of it, oblivious, tilling the reluctant land, ignoring the treasure withdrawn from them. Their town was dead; better if it had gone down in flames, never to rise, when the French raiders sacked it long ago, in the first years of the fifteenth century. Going home down the tall street early darkened by its own shadows, seeing as she passed candles burning without fear of wind, seeing the people eating, secure and warm, Miss Alquist felt a kind of despair.

It was on an autumn night, an October night still and misty, that it happened. Mrs. Frant remembered very well how the mist began to roll in from the sea, like the ghost of a tide, at about half past five in the afternoon, when the sun was dropping, and Miss Alquist had set out on her pilgrimage. They heard her return and could follow the sound of her footsteps from room to room and could distinguish the tinkle of china as she prepared her supper. They did not consciously reckon up these sounds, to which they were so accustomed that they must rather have noticed their cessation than their sequence. The Frants finished eating, and Mrs. Frant piled up the greasy plates on a tray to take them down to the scullery. It will be remembered that Miss Alquist rented the ground floor. Mrs. Frant came downstairs carefully, the tray held out before her so that she might see where she was treading and had reached the kitchen before she raised her eyes. Then she saw that Miss Alquist was standing quite motionless by the door which led to her bedroom, apparently listening. The attitude was not strained or unnatural; that is to say, it would not have seemed so had the tense figure relaxed after a moment. Mrs. Frant said afterwards that they seemed to stand there for half an hour, the one stiffly with closed eyes, all senses save one forced to quiescence, the other with her tray held before her, staring, and wondering what sound could ever come up Ship Street that was worth listening for like that. Just as the immobility had lasted long enough to frighten the watcher, Miss Alquist turned away abruptly and went into her bedroom. Mrs. Frant advanced towards the sink with her crockery, mentally calculating whether they could afford to give up their lodger if she should turn queer. Her back towards the bedroom, she filled the sink with boiling water, shook in some soda from a tin, and began to scrape the fragments of cheese and bacon fat from the plates. Then she heard a step, and looked quickly round, apprehensively. Through the door she could see Miss Alquist standing with her hat on, and her hands fumbling at her bosom; then the figure moved and there came the sound of steps on the boards, the opening of the street door, its gentle closing. Miss Alquist had gone out. Mrs. Frant was so much astonished that she tumbled the plates into the hot water and left them to soak while she went upstairs to consult with her husband. He, too, was astonished, and went at once to the window; the mist was impenetrable, but they could hear plainly the short quick steps going up the hill towards the church.

"Looks like she don't know what time 'tis," said Frant, "did she go out for her usual?"

Mrs. Frant did not answer. They had both watched her go out, just after five.

"Thick night, too," said Frant, closing the window. "Well. None o' our look-out."

"Not our look-out," Mrs. Frant echoed angrily, "'T'll be our look-out if she comes over funny and tries to kill us all in our beds one night."

She had been frightened down there in the kitchen. Frant, who had not seen the still figure, grunted, and took up his paper again, comfortably saying,

"You don't want to go thinking of such things."

Mrs. Frant looked up and was about to speak; but realising how foolish the thing must sound told in her words, sighed, and went, not without qualms, back to the sink and the crockery. From time to time, she stopped her washing-up to listen, holding her hands still in the water. Ship Street was silent. The old walls cut off the sounds from neighbouring houses; no one passed on the cobbles. She dried the plates and hung up the cloth on the line that was stretched across the kitchen from window to fireplace; then slowly climbed again to the upper room where her husband sat. His pipe filled it with rich smoke; the new wick of the lamp gave a good light. Mrs. Frant took her chair by the fire and gradually forgot, in that atmosphere of familiar warmth, that half an hour ago she had been frightened by the sight of a woman listening.

Listening, astounded, to the thud and rustle of surf, breaking, so Miss Alquist thought, not a hundred yards away. At first, she did not heed it; a trick of the blood, perhaps, rushing in her ears. But it would not be denied. It was real. When she understood that, she was filled with a mad hope that the sea had come back to claim the town, advancing without cause, as it had retreated. The sound persisted, and she made her decision, to go up at once to the cliff by the church. From there she could watch it come crawling over the fields, lapping towards the town. In some haste she put on her shoes and hat, but delayed, strangely enough, over another matter which puzzled the Frants afterwards; then she set out, walking quickly through the mist to the churchyard. She was happy, until as she went it occurred to her that perhaps owing to the mist the sea might not be visible; but when she came to that part of the cliff from which she was accustomed to look across the marsh, she clasped her hands, pressing them in a kind of ecstasy against her breast. For the night was clear, with a half-moon rising, and not a quarter of a mile away she could see a line of white that sometimes drew back hissing, and then launched itself forward, at every such attack gaining a little ground. It seemed to her a battle of two surfaces; one dead, motionless, blindly resisting, the other vivid, alive, wrinkled into a million tiny strengths which at last must overwhelm the single strength of the land. It had reached the outlying dwellings. She saw it close round a cottage, coming creeping and fawning to the threshold, mounting in little waves and surges towards the windows, higher, higher. The glass burst inwards under the impact of a larger mass of water, which poured through, foaming over the jagged edges noiselessly. She observed this silence, and accepted it, though it had been the sound which had summoned her; now she watched while the drama played itself out and found it natural that it should be presented without sound. Every moment the liquid glittering surface increased, and the dull squares of grass yielded to it, dwindling one by one. The track of the moon grew longer, and was broken into shifting ripples of light, multiplied as the sea advanced stealthily, but more swiftly than before. At this rate, she thought, another five minutes must bring it to the foot of the cliff, and she strained towards it, gripping the wooden railing, thinking rather confusedly of those cities in the Old Testament, overwhelmed that the power of God might be made manifest. She thought of the limitless strength of the sea; of its hills and shadowy valleys, hidden too deep for light to discover them; of the strange jewels of the sea, living creatures, and pearls crusted together in obscurity. There were mysteries there of which the land could know nothing, wonders consummated in the utter darkness, shapes moving above in their own radiance, broken ships like leaves drifting down. She would not open her eyes, she resolved, until she heard the first beat of the waves against the foot of the cliff, for when the water had attained its goal there would be sound again. She began to count the seconds, blindly waiting; sixty rather slowly, and sixty again; and again. Now surely the victory must have been achieved, the walls of water must be piling up in withdrawal to fling themselves in a last assault upon the rocks that withstood them. Another minute went slowly by. She opened her eyes, looked, and felt the blood run to her heart.

There, across the brilliant pathway of the moon, a shadow was passing on the water. She could see and recognise the sturdy hull, the twin funnels streaming smoke, coming as she had seen it so often in thought, northwards, up-channel, home.

In an agony of joy she sprang forward, stretching out her arms; heard a cry, the sound of rending wood; and fell.

They did not find her till morning. The Frants, after a little vague speculation, retired to bed and slept heavily as was their custom. Miss Alquist had her key, and there was no need to worry. But Mrs. Frant, as she came last into their bedroom, secretly locked the door. She said nothing to her husband; she was taking no risks. At six o'clock next morning they heard a frantic knocking, which at first, they ignored, thinking Miss Alquist must answer it; but it was repeated past bearing, and finally Frant, grumbling, went down to the door. Tom Eldridge, a young farm labourer, cousin to Mrs. Frant, stood there. He was very white, and would say nothing but,

"You got to come with me, Ted."

"What you want? Coming making a row like the end of the world. Can't you say what it is?"

"She's dead."

"Who's dead?"

Tom Eldridge would not answer, except to repeat,

"You got to come."

The two men went together into Harbour Street and woke the constable. While they waited for him to come down Frant asked again for details. The boy shook his head. He did not want to talk about it. When the constable was ready, he led them down the steps, cut in the rock, which led to the foot of the cliff. She was there, on the grass. The constable knelt by her, felt her heart, then looked attentively at her face, and up at the height from which she had fallen. From below they could see the gap in the railing, and beside her, but a little away, lay a fragment of rotten wood.

"Not marked," said the constable.

He laid her back on the grass, and suddenly put a hand to his sleeve, twisting the cloth as though to wring water from it. The other men saw his fingers come away glistening with moisture.

"Dew," said Frant, "or the mist."

"Ground's dry," Eldridge answered, breaking silence.

The constable felt the grass. It was dewy, but not soaking. Her skirt and jacket were heavy and stiff with water. He looked again at the dead face, and rose to his feet, wiping his right hand across the front of his coat. He said, without relevance as it seemed,

"I seen two men that died o' drowning"

He stopped and screwing up his eyes peered towards the quiet sea as though measuring the distance; then with a quick movement he put the wet palm of his left hand to his mouth, and held it so for an instant, tasting, the big red hand spread out over his face. They watched, with a growing discomfort. Abruptly the hand was dropped; young Eldridge knew that the palm had tasted salt.

Fearfully, with hunched shoulders, they stared down at the little dark figure, lying so easily; it was only then that Frant saw pinned on her breast the brooch, the blue brooch made of feathers.

THE WATCH

Vernon Knowles

Vernon Knowles was born in Adelaide and worked on the Adelaide *Reporter* before going to England to pursue his literary ambitions. Amongst many works of verse and prose he published a semi-autobiographical novel, *Eternity in an Hour* (1932), describing his experiences growing up in Adelaide, and several collections of short stories with fantastic elements, including *The Street of Queer Houses and Other Stories* (1924), *The Street of Queer Houses and Other Tales* (1925), *Here and Otherwhere* (1926), and *Two and Two Make Five* (1935). "The Watch" is from *The Street of Queer Houses and Other Stories*, published in New York in 1924 by Boullion-Biggs. The following year a refurbished collection was published in London under the title, *The Street of Queer Houses and Other Tales*, from which "The House that Took Revenge" is taken. Apart from the title-story, the two volumes have only three stories in common.

Henry Wardly sat down to his dinner wearily.

He had had a heavy day's work at his office, and the hour's train journey home had been cold. He was glad to sit down calmly, eat what he knew would be a good dinner, and after, have a quiet evening with a book by the fire.

The maid set the soup before him, and with it, a small package.

"Just come by express, sir," she said.

Wardley disposed of the soup before his curiosity mastered him and caused him to break the string. Unfolding the paper, he came upon a cardboard box, and lifting the lid, beheld a neat gold watch.

Well, well!" he exclaimed admiringly, and with something of surprise; and then looked in vain for a card or note bearing the sender's name.

"What a nice present!" He noticed that the watch was going and was set at the correct time.

The word 'present' struck a chord of memory in his mind.

"Why," he said. "The third of February: it's my birthday to-day. Now, could I have received a thing more wanted than this?"

Two days previously, his pocket had been picked expertly in Piccadilly; and it was only when he arrived home the same evening, that he discovered his watch was missing and recollected a hasty young gentleman colliding with him outside the Ritz Hotel and departing apologetically.

"An anonymous donor, too;" he mused. "Well, thanks to him or her—whoever it may be. I will probably learn who has sent it, later."

And he put the watch into his pocket and went on with his dinner.

According to his custom, on going to bed, he placed the watch on a small table beside his pillow.

He always slept soundly, and it was exceptional for him to dream.

To-night he did the exceptional thing.

He dreamed.

He was in a long, dimly lit hall. On either side of him the walls were hidden by black curtains, hanging in many folds heavily; and on the floor was a thick black carpet.

And he was afraid.

Of what—he knew not.

He expected anything to happen, and his nerves were on edge with the suspense. So he felt a certain relief, when of a sudden, the heavy curtains about him were agitated, and four tall, bearded men surrounded him, and gripped him. They said nothing but drew apart a fold of the curtain on one side, disclosing a vault-like room. Its floor was stone-flagged, and its ceiling was low and had yellow blotches of damp on its surface.

In the centre of the room was a truckle-bed, innocent of any covering, and beside it, a table bearing a clock.

Almost without looking at it, Wardley knew that the clock was an infernal machine…

His four captors proceeded to stretch him on the bed and strap him in such wise that he could not move.

He tried to cry out but could not. His body felt cold all over and clammy with sudden perspiration. He could not move; he could not cry out…One of the four dark men addressed him with the information that the machine was set for five o'clock. At that hour—

He made a suggestive movement with his hands.

Wardley groaned inwardly.

His captors moved away through the heavy folds of the black curtains.

He was alone, alone with the machine. And he could do nothing.

He writhed but could in no way free himself nor even loosen his bonds a little.

In a while he grew calm and resigned himself to his end.

The clock was ticking rapidly.

Tick…Tick…Tick.

Death…Death…Death.

Wardley felt faint: his senses swam…

The ticking grew louder and louder. It sounded like a blacksmith's blows with a sledgehammer on his anvil...Now it came like thunder-cracks...

He could see the hands of the clock pointed to one minute to five.

With a supreme effort, he strained frenziedly at his bonds.

They rent—they burst.

He strained with all his might...And then suddenly the tumultuous ticking ceased. All was still...

He was saved!

He sat up

He had dreamed it all!

With great relief he switched on the light, and sitting up, looked at his watch.

At once, he recoiled with horror, his eyes stared wildly, and his face became grey...

The watch had stopped at precisely one minute to five o'clock...

For a moment terror held him statue-like. Then he recovered himself a little and became a creature of action.

He rose carefully, quietly, and compelled himself to take the watch in hand. Carefully, quietly, he went down the stairs and into the darkness that yet seemed to hold no promise of dawn.

Down a narrow path he made his way. It led to a little lake at the bottom of the garden...There, into the water, with a quick gesture he threw the watch and shivered as he heard it drop...

The stars were hidden by clouds, and there was no light. The easterly wind moaned in the bare trees, and it sounded to Wardley like the voice of the tall, bearded man who had spoken to him in his dream.

With many a glance around, he hurried back fearfully to the house.

THE HOUSE THAT TOOK REVENGE

Vernon Knowles

All the morning I had rambled along the cliffs, and as lunch time approached came to a realization that I was lost. I was beginning to wonder which way I should turn, when I heard the whirr of a lawnmower close at hand, and, making towards it, found facing me a double gate with "Highlands" painted on it; and a broad drive sweeping away beyond. I entered and came upon a gardener at work on a wide lawn.

"Good-day," I said. "Can you tell me how to get to Dilrenton?"

As I spoke, I glanced beyond him, and received a shock. The broad drive continued for another fifty yards or so, to end, if you please, at the cliffs' edge: it didn't lead to any house... There wasn't any house for it to lead to...

"Well, sir, I'm going that way myself: was just going to stop this very minute. If you like, we'll go together, then it'll be easier."

"Er—isn't there a house here," I asked, puzzled, called 'Highlands'?"

"Not now, sir. But there used to be."

He swung on his coat and started to lead the way.

"Used to be?" I echoed. "How odd! A house without a garden is a common enough thing, but a garden without a house—!"

And as we walked along to Dilrenton, he told me how it had come about.

Mr Rayner was wealthy and proud. So wealthy that he had not only a town and a country house, but also a villa in Nice. So proud that when his only son married against his will, he cut him off directly—declared that he no longer had a son, and refused to see him.

If the father could be so proud, the son was not far behind him with the same characteristic, and rather than ask help of his parent was ready to starve to death. And, sure enough, starve he did: both he and his wife; and when the old man learnt of their death, he crumpled up all of a sudden: stricken with remorse. For a while he declared that instead of food, they were giving him money to eat; and he would touch nothing. Consequently, he became very ill, but recovered slowly. His doctor advised him to go over to Nice for a long rest, but he refused. He also refused to go down to his country house, "Highlands."

"No! I hate the place," he cried, and would not budge.

Then, suddenly, one day he changed his mind and moved down to "Highlands." Of late years he had come to loathe the house, and would have sold it some time ago, but for his son, who loved it. And now that his son was dead, the old man decided to live there: as an act of penance: a kind of mortification business.

In those days the house was about two hundred yards from the cliffs' edge: lonely and quiet.

The old man used to storm about the place: curse its every brick and stone: calling it a tomb...

He had few friends. The oldest was his lawyer: who used to visit him some two or three times a year.

"Well; why do you stay down here, then?" the lawyer asked him curiously once. But it was no use. The old man wouldn't say anything but, "Here I stay, and here I'll die."

On one of his visits the lawyer remarked: "The cliffs must be falling down a great deal: you're much nearer the sea than you used to be, you know..."

The old man got up and cursed the house with his usual batch of curses and looked out of the window.

"Nonsense!" he cried...

But as the months passed, it became very plain...

And all the time the old man was gradually losing his sight and hearing, losing his strength. Finally, he took to his bed...

There could be no doubt about it. An astonishing thing—the cliffs were not falling down at all; it was the house. The house with the garden was slowly moving towards the edge.

When they told the old man, and urged him to leave, he raved at them.

"Stuff! A cock-and-bull tale! I'm not in my dotage yet, to have such a yarn thrust down my neck."

And he cursed them, and cursed the fine old house bitterly...

One afternoon he crawled from his bed, and dressed, and went tottering outside. He looked, but his sight was just about gone; he felt with his stick—and so close now was the house to the cliffs' edge that he nearly went over. His man just reached him in time. He went back to bed in a sweat.

"Don't care. Let it go; damn the place! Let it fall, let it..."

He only stopped cursing to sink asleep...

And that night the house took the final step. About midnight it crashed over the edge, holus-bolus, into the sea a couple of hundred feet below. There was only the old man in it at the time. The servants rushed out at the first alarm, feeling it shaking: thinking they were experiencing an earthquake. On their way they tried to take their master with them, but he sneered at them, and cleared them out...

They say that when the house toppled over every brick and stone and stick of wood in it laughed in a triumphant chorus...

The will provided that the gardener should continue to attend the grounds daily: his wages to be paid out of the Estate until he died.

And that happened seventeen years ago—the garden hadn't moved an inch since...

THE UNDYING ONE

Roger Dard

Roger Dard (1920-1996) was a science fiction and fantasy fan and collector who lived most of his life in Perth, Western Australia. His parents were Noor Dard, born in Pakistan, and Mary Dard, born in Dunedin, New Zealand. Dard was active in the burgeoning science fiction fandom scene in the 1950s and wrote regularly for the ephemeral fanzines of the time. He is best known for his ongoing run-in with the Customs authorities in Perth, who confiscated various books and magazines that he imported from the United States. In fact, the Department of Customs and Excise kept a file on Dard, which is now in the National Archives of Australia. He had a particular interest in the *Weird Tales* circle and owned an almost complete run of the magazine, as well as most Arkham House titles. The following story, in the *Weird Tales* tradition, appeared in the December 1950 edition of *Operation Fantast*, an influential fanzine edited by Ken Slater.

In all the great cities of the world there are dark places of mystery and terror, unseen by the bustling millions rushing to and fro on their prosaic errands, like so many ants around a hill. I think, though, that of all the cities which sprawl like festering sores upon this green planet that which contains the greatest possibilities of danger, mystery, and terror is London. For it is in London that one finds—Limehouse.

An avid reader of Sax Rohmer and Thomas Burke, it had long been my wont to wander the fog-wreathed streets of this strange quarter in search of the unusual, and that which was not to be found in the brighter Neon civilization of the Metropolis. Yet, until the singular occurrence of which I am about to relate, nothing worse than the muttered curse of a lurching drunk had befallen me.

Mystery was in the air on this night, and the smell of danger everywhere, as I groped down the foggy, ill-smelling streets on my way to the teashop of Tai-Long, an amiable Chinese with whom, in the course of my nocturnal wanderings, I had struck up some form of an acquaintance. A block before reaching Tai-Long's establishment I came across a small, dark side street, one which I had often passed before but had never ventured into. Strangely, on this night, I felt my legs—almost of their own volition—

stop, and the uncanniest feeling, a feeling almost of *compulsion*, came over me. I lighted a cigarette with hands that shook a little and, gripping my walking-cane harder in my hand, plunged into the gloomy street, for I had decided not to deny this strange feeling which had, for the moment at least, taken possession of me.

As I plunged further into the gloom, I mentally cursed myself, and with visions of thugs lying in every doorway to set upon me I would have retraced my steps, and indeed was about to—when suddenly I paused.

Across the street, in a strange, crazy house, like something out of a surrealist's nightmare, I saw a strange light flicker into being. As I stared, I began to mechanically walk toward the light, despite my every effort to resist. It was as if I were being attracted to the light, as a moth is to flame!

As I drew near, somewhere in that crazy house a dark slit of a door opened and a cadaverous-looking creature bowed low.

"The mistress awaits you, John Parker," he intoned.

I started with mingled surprise and dread. This eldritch creature knew my name! Knowing that I should flee that accursed place, yet did I enter the yawning portals.

The darkness of the interior made the gloom of the street I had just quitted seem almost light. Yet, strangely, as the creaking door closed behind me, I knew not horror or panic but rather a soothing peace. It was as if a cool voice had whispered in my mind, "Fear not, no harm shall befall you."

The eldritch creature conducted me into a dimly lighted, barbarously furnished room. The smell of incense was strong as I seated myself upon a pile of silken cushions, and the eldritch creature bowed himself from the room.

As if that were a signal, somewhere within the dim recesses of that monstrous house a cymbal clashed. And with it a strange, reedy, weird music began to throb forth from some hidden orchestra. A drum throbbed with a wild, barbaric rhythm, and soon the music was filling the room nay, it was filling my very blood with its wild intoxication!

Then—*she* came. Curtains parted with a sibilant rustle, and this elfin creature glided into the room. She was olive skinned, of what race I know not, perhaps Egyptian or Persian, and possessed of a beauty so overwhelming my brain reeled. As she weaved before me slave bangles jangled a refrain upon her arms and legs. She was clad in a single gauze-like garment, which revealed, rather than concealed, her exotic beauty. Around her waist she wore a slim dagger of strange design. It was a weird, mad dance that she danced, such as I had never seen before. It was Eve tempting Adam, it was the Siren of the Nile, Cleopatra, it was Helen of Troy, Madame du Barry— but most of all it was—*woman*. As the music rose to wild cacophony the dance grew wilder, and the single garment fell from her, as she plucked at it with scarlet-tipped fingernails. She postured before me, her small, perfectly formed breasts rising and falling with the rhythm of her body. Suddenly, with a last clash of cymbal and boom of drum, the music stopped, and this wondrous creature collapsed at my feet. Dark, smouldering eyes fixed upon mine, she extended her arms in a supplicating gesture.

When she spoke, her voice was like the tinkling of bells in the desert night. "John, John, beloved, come to me, who have waited these eons for you."

I took her soft body in my arms and covered her exquisite mouth with kisses. "Who—who are you?" I begged.

Her kisses burned like hot coals upon my mouth, and for a long time she did not answer. Then— "Look into my eyes," she softly commanded.

I looked—and suddenly it was as if I were looking into the very pits of Hell itself! I plunged into blackness, there was a roaring in my eats. The blackness lessened, became a yellow fog, swirling about me like the tentacles of some vile entity. I groped through the fog and found myself standing upon a vast desert. *She* stood beside me, and together we watched a toiling gang of slaves staggering under the great blocks which I knew were to build a great pyramid. She was a Princess of the Royal blood, I knew that instinctively. Perhaps I was a Prince, I knew not, for I had eyes only for her. As I stood with her, her lips, sensuous and cruel, smiled at me, her lover, so that I showed not horror when the whip she carried lashed the backs of the groaning slaves. Then the yellow fog was upon me again, and when once more it cleared, we stood together again, but this time in a rough, horse-drawn cart. There was a wild yelling, and as I looked, I saw the slavering faces of a mob, shouting obscenities, shaking fists, dancing with merriment. *She* stood proud, arm in mine, driving the mob to fury with her cold disdain and contempt. Dimly I perceived we were French aristocrats, on our way to the guillotine... Again, the yellow fog wreathed its vile fingers around me, and this time, when it reluctantly retreated, we were in old Salem. A figure, lean, ascetic, garbed in sombre black, stood with finger levelled at us, screaming "Witch! Demon! Thou servants of Satan..." As I saw the crazed faces pressing round us I knew in this life we, too, were doomed. More scenes faded and glowed before me, scenes of incredible horror and obscenities, as life after life, existence after existence, passed in review before me...

I woke, crying in horror, my hands pressed before my shuddering face, as if to blot out sights which once seen could never be forgotten. But fear ebbed, like tide from a beach, as I felt her silken body against mine, felt her burning lips against mine, felt her naked arms entwine my neck... "Now, do you know, John, my beloved?" she murmured.

"Pre-existence," I murmured, "but how? When?—"

"It began in that land the Barbarians of this age now call Egypt," she chanted. Her eyes burned into mine. "You were a Prince, and I a Princess of the Blood Royal. But, in addition, I was a Sorceress, the greatest in the land. In my studies I had long looked for some means of perpetuating my youth and beauty, and yours, too, my royal lover. All the land feared me, the Princess Sadi, the Sorceress of the Nile." She smiled, as if remembering.

"The eldritch creature who admitted you came to me. He was a powerful Sorcerer who had been banished from a far Kingdom. In return for my protection, he showed me the secret only he knew. The secret of how to transfer the living flame—that which some call soul—from one body to another. We drank, together, of the magic potion. And so, ever since, right down the ages, the flame has quitted our dying body to find refuge in another." Her sensuous lips smiled. "Now we go to fulfil our destiny, a destiny only I and yon Sorcerer know of."

A sudden chilling thought struck me. "But—I—" I gasped.

Her eyes glowed like hot coals. The sensuous, carmine mouth seemed amused. "I know, my beloved," she murmured, "there is one who would stand in our way. Take this," she handed me the bizarre dagger, "use it well, that me may be together again, for all eternity."

With a cry I took her into my arms and covered her perfumed body with my burning kisses. Then she was gone, and as I cried out in my anguish, her words floated back to me, "...use well the dagger."

The rest you know. How the police burst into my apartment, to find me standing over the murdered body of my wife, clutching a bizarre, bloodstained dagger. How I fought wildly, screaming strange names, among them one which sounded to their barbarous ears like "Princess Sadi." And now I sit in the death cell and wait for the grim-faced men to come and take me away. As the time draws near a little prickle of fear and doubt runs up my spine. Was that wondrous creature who danced the exotic dance for me really a Princess of Egypt, a Sorceress of the Nile? Or was she some evil adventuress who hypnotised me into murder—for some hellish sport of her own? Am I merely a prosaic 20th Century Englishman or am I, indeed, a Prince of Ancient Egypt? When my body plunges through the trap, will it be into eternal blackness or will it be into a new life—where Sadi, the wondrous creature of the Nile, will be awaiting me? I wonder...